Dying for a Fix

G.K. Parks

Copyright © 2015 G.K. Parks

A Modus Operandi imprint

All rights reserved.

ISBN: 0989195899
ISBN-13: 978-0-9891958-9-8

For grandma

ONE

Picking up the black leather case, I flipped it open to reveal the shiny metal and photo ID. I'd looked at it a hundred times in the last few days, but I still couldn't determine how I felt. Closing my federal agent credentials, I shoved them inside my top desk drawer, hoping the old adage out of sight, out of mind would be proven true.

Forcing myself to focus on the stack of files on my desk, I let out a sigh. My private sector days were coming to a close, and before that happened, I needed to finalize a couple of corporate gigs and an investigation I was conducting. The work was already completed, but I had to mail my reports, evidence, and invoices to the relevant parties.

Supervisory Special Agent Mark Jablonsky, my mentor, opened the door to my office. He looked around, making sure I was alone, before flipping the sign to closed and locking the door. He took a seat in my client chair and snatched the top folder off the stack.

"Ready to leave this behind, Alex?" he asked. I gave him a bittersweet smile and continued writing out the envelope. "You were never meant for this. I'm glad you're coming home. The Office of International Operations hasn't been the same for the last two years, despite the numerous occasions you've graced us with your presence."

"But strangely enough, I'm going to miss this." I stuffed a few documents in the envelope and sealed it. "Not the corporate crap with security consultations or acting like the scarlet letter brigade, but some of it did matter."

"Like Marty?" Mark asked.

James Martin was my first client after I resigned from the OIO and entered the private sector. I cut my teeth working personal security for him and then corporate security for his company, Martin Technologies, but that was before our relationship took off. Now we were just pleasure, no business. In my mind, the two didn't mix, even if he offered to rehire me on a regular basis, almost as often as he attempted to get me to move in with him.

"Yeah, I guess we can say he counts for something. But I will miss the guys at the precinct. Consulting for the police department and helping out the major crimes division gave my life some perspective."

Mark snorted. "For god's sakes, Parker, you act like you're moving to Antarctica or something. You'll still see your cop buddies, and you'll remember just how aggravating and cumbersome it is to deal with other law enforcement agencies, particularly the PD." He laughed. "You're coming back to work. You wanted this. It's time." He pressed his lips together, worried what my reaction would be. "You decided a couple of months ago to try to get reinstated." He swallowed. "You've finally dealt with the real reason you left, so it's time."

"Who are you kidding, Jablonsky? The only reason I got my badge back is because of the security breach. Thirty-seven active ops were compromised, and every undercover agent had to be recalled. You were running low on manpower and resources, so you had to scrape the bottom of the barrel."

"That's not completely accurate, and you know it."

"Did Director Kendall tell you what's going to happen after I complete this assignment? Maybe I shouldn't be throwing in the towel on my private sector work just yet."

"Let's take things one day at a time. The official briefing

is in two days, but I can tell you now it's a long-term undercover assignment. It'll take some time to get your background planted in order to ensure your cover doesn't seem rushed or questionable. This will be slow going."

"Great," I muttered sarcastically. Undercover work was never my favorite, but it was part of the job. And I loved the job, or at least there was a time when I did. Then I spent a long time hating the job and myself. At the moment, I still wasn't sure where I would land on any of this. "Do you know how long this might last?"

"A few months at least." He shook his head. "They'll tell you more at the briefing. But no one can know you've been reinstated. After the security breach, everything at the office is hush-hush."

"I do remember how this works."

"Unless you file the proper forms and move things through the official channels, you can't tell Marty either. It's for his safety and yours."

"Which is precisely why I didn't bother with the forms."

After discussing the possible ramifications in-depth with Mark, it seemed keeping my personal life separate from my work life was the best course of action. The point of the secrecy was to safeguard undercover operatives and their loved ones by creating an information black hole. The less everyone knew, the better.

Mark stood, giving the stack of paperwork a final glance and dropping the file he skimmed back on top. "For official reasons, I'm not saying this, but if you want to continue your P.I. work, just make sure it stays under the radar. Moonlighting is frowned upon by the federal government, even though we all do it occasionally. But if it'll make you feel better to continue helping the downtrodden, I won't take that away from you."

"Right, because I'm gonna have tons of spare time, especially if I get stuck pretending to be someone else 24/7."

"This assignment shouldn't be like that. We'll see, but from what I've been told, your cover won't require anything that extensive." He went to the door. "But just in case, I'd suggest you enjoy the rest of today and tomorrow."

"Thanks. I'll try."

A couple of hours later, I finished the paperwork. Giving my office a final look, I collected my belongings, made sure the mini-fridge was empty, grabbed my credentials out of the top drawer, and locked up. There was no telling when I'd be back. Was another chapter of my life closing? Or was this a book I would reread after my assignment at the OIO concluded? Only time would tell.

After dropping the stack of mail into the box, I drove to Martin's. Two days wasn't a lot of time, but I wanted to spend it with him. Of course, he would be spending most of it at work since multinational corporations didn't run themselves.

To kill time, I decided to put in a few hours on the equipment in his home gym. I work out often, but it was important to be back in fighting shape. Undercover assignments typically mean minimal support, so a girl needs to be able to take care of herself. Maybe when Martin gets home, I could convince his bodyguard, Jones, a.k.a. Bruiser, to spar with me. Bruiser had extensive military training, and he and Martin sparred on occasion. Perhaps he wouldn't mind mixing it up with his predecessor.

After a hundred push-ups, I dropped to the floor. My arms and back were the least toned because of my previously mending ribs. Thankfully, they finished healing just in time. It had only been a few days since my reinstatement, but this was the most aggressive workout I'd undertaken in a while. So there wasn't a doubt in my mind I'd be sore tomorrow. Still, that was a much better price to pay than to be easily overpowered by some goon. Granted, I was only a hundred and ten pounds, but those hundred and ten pounds had kicked the asses of men twice my size. Unfortunately, in a physical fight, size does matter. So it was best to avoid a brawl whenever possible. However, when push came to shove, I needed to be able to hold my own.

I was in the process of stretching when the garage door opened. A few seconds later, Martin appeared with his driver and bodyguard in tow. He smiled, arching an eyebrow at my pose.

"I thought you hated yoga," he commented.

"It's not yoga," I insisted, straightening up. "I was stretching." I shifted my focus to the two other men and gave them each a friendly nod.

"Well, whatever you call it," Martin smirked, deciding to keep the cruder commentary to himself, "it looks like it's working." His eyes twinkled, and I knew it was working for him.

"Shut up."

"I was just about to send Marcal to pick up dinner. Do you want anything special?" I shook my head, and his driver disappeared back the way he came. "Are you staying tonight?"

"And tomorrow, if that's okay."

"It's more than okay." He remembered Bruiser was standing awkwardly behind him. "Jones, you can take off, and don't worry about meeting me tomorrow at the office. I'll be working from home."

"Okay," Bruiser said, moving toward the door.

"Hang on," I called. "Can I persuade you to go a couple of rounds before you call it a night? It's been a while since I've stepped into the ring, and I'm itching for a sparring partner."

Bruiser stopped dead in his tracks and spun to face me, an amused grin on his face. This would be fun.

Martin pointed an accusatory finger at me. "Don't hurt my bodyguard." He headed for the stairs. "I have a couple of calls to make, but I'll make this quick if you do the same."

"Absolutely."

He brushed past, kissing my cheek and lingering just long enough to let out an appreciative little growl. "Bruiser, you don't have to agree to this," he said, disappearing up the steps.

While Bruiser changed and limbered up, I stepped into the boxing ring Martin had set up in the middle of his first floor. After shoulder surgery, Martin decided to take up boxing to rebuild muscle mass. So he purchased a ring and more boxing equipment than any normal person could ever need, particularly when his interests tended to change as often as the weather. But he had the money, and it seemed like added incentive for me to visit.

"So what gives?" Bruiser asked, stepping into the ring. "You've never made a request like this before. Why the sudden interest?"

"Well, I can't exactly go mano a mano with the boss man. He'd pull his punches, and I'd probably break his jaw," I joked. "Basically, I just want to make sure I still got it."

"All right," he shrugged, "what did you have in mind?"

"Grappling, basic self-defense, nothing too violent."

"Just to be clear, you're not gonna break my jaw either, right?" He grinned.

"As long as you don't break mine. And the nose is off limits too."

We spent the next forty-five minutes working on different holds, breaking out of them, and alternating between a mix of jujitsu and Krav Maga maneuvers. By the end, I was on top of Bruiser with my arms around his neck and my legs scissored around his torso. He slapped his palm against the mat, and I released him.

"I don't think you've lost it," Bruiser complimented, running a hand against the back of his neck. "But I'm gonna call it quits before I lose something besides my dignity."

"Thanks. I appreciate it."

"Anytime." He grabbed his bag and clothing from earlier and disappeared just as Marcal came in with dinner.

"Perfect timing," Martin said, appearing out of nowhere and reaching for the takeout bag. He handed Marcal something. "You and your wife enjoy the play tonight." Marcal wished us a good evening and disappeared after Bruiser. "It looks like it's just the two of us."

"Let me guess, I'm playing bodyguard for the next forty-eight hours." It was a joke of sorts. But since his staff had been dismissed and he pulled some strings to stay home, technically, my nine millimeter and I were the only line of defense, not that he had personal security guarding the perimeter under normal circumstances.

"I'm hoping that won't be necessary." He waited for me

to meet him on the stairs. "But some privacy might be."

"Well, this impromptu bodyguarding requires payment. A massage might be in order," I added, heading toward the guest bathroom that somehow ended up being stocked with the same products I used on a regular basis.

"That can be arranged." He began unpacking dinner. "But only if you teach me that last hold you performed."

"You were watching?" I turned on the water and stripped out of my sweaty clothes.

"Well, someone needed to make sure Jones was protected."

"And what about me?"

"If he hurt you, I'd kill him. The only question would be if I fired him before or after he was dead."

Rolling my eyes, I stepped under the hot water. Two days and then everything would change. If I disappeared for months at a time, what would Martin think? What would he do? And it's not like I could tell him what was going on in any real detail. A lot had changed between us, and I wasn't sure how we'd fare in the face of my reinstatement.

When we first met, James Martin was a womanizing playboy. But at some point, that came to an end. And when we started dating over a year ago, I made it very clear that monogamy was important. We'd been through more life and death situations than seemed statistically probable, and there wasn't a doubt in my mind that he loved me and would, in fact, try to kill someone who was intent on hurting me, Bruiser aside. So how could I hurt him like this? Suddenly, going back to the OIO didn't seem like a good decision, but it was too late now.

After showering, I returned to the kitchen. Dinner was on the table, but before I sat down, the phone rang. Martin looked at it and then at me.

"Go ahead." I jerked my chin toward the ringing. "I'm not going anywhere." Yet.

TWO

"Good morning, beautiful," Martin cooed in my ear, brushing his lips against mine. His fingers ran through my hair, and I opened my eyes. It better be a decent hour, or I would hurt him. "I'm going downstairs to get some work done."

"Okay," I mumbled, wondering why he felt the need to share unimportant details like that. "I'll be here."

His brow furrowed with an obvious question he wanted to ask. "Alex, I love it when you're here. I wish you'd stay all the time, but why are you here?"

"What?" Blinking, I struggled to process through the question.

"It hasn't even been a week since you kicked me out of your apartment." He exhaled. After my last case, he abruptly cut a business trip short and practically moved in because of a recent string of close calls. "But here you are. And you accuse me of being the clingy one. Shall I call you Reynolds or Saran?"

"I'm not cling wrap. But I have another job starting soon, and I don't know what the hours will be like. There might be some traveling involved. We might not get a chance to see each other much for the next few months."

"You've mentioned it," his eyes narrowed, "but you didn't say what it was."

"Nothing I haven't done before. It's a lot of paperwork. Some analysis. Y'know, the usual." Well, the usual for a federal agent.

He nodded. "Go back to sleep." He leaned down and kissed my forehead. "I'll come back to bed when I finish work, and we can have a repeat of last night."

"You still owe me a massage," I murmured, rolling over and snuggling under the blankets.

*   *   *

"You seem different," Martin said. He had spent the last few hours sneaking glances while he reviewed the paperwork for dissolving the short-lived merger he made with Hover Designs.

I looked up from working my way through a book of Sudoku puzzles and arched my eyebrows. "How so?"

He tucked the paperwork into his briefcase and closed the lid. "I can't seem to put my finger on it."

"Well, let's make this easier. No, I didn't get a haircut. And this isn't a new outfit. Maybe you're just not used to seeing me this often."

"Or maybe it's the lack of bandages," he quipped. "I greatly prefer you in one piece without the assistance of Ace or Band-Aid." He continued the uncomfortable scrutiny. "But it's not that either."

I put the book down, no longer needing to find something to do. "What can I say? It's a mystery."

He went to the fridge and opened the door, grabbing the steaks that were marinating.

"Do you want help?" I asked.

"Not with dinner." He pulled out the red potatoes, a handful of spices, and a couple of pans. "But maybe you can help me figure out what's different."

Nothing was different. The only thing different in my life was my return to my old job. Was he on to me? Did he overhear one of my conversations with Mark and was trying to goad me into admitting what my new job really was? Or was I just a paranoid lunatic? It was probably the latter, which meant nothing had jeopardized the status quo.

"Everything's the same. I start a new job tomorrow, and you'll go back to the office. The only thing different is the way you've been acting since that incident at my apartment. The old Martin would never take off work or cut trips short because I was spending the night."

"Well, he was an idiot." He diced the potatoes. "If a man in my position can't work from home on occasion, then there is definitely something wrong with this picture." He went to the pantry for the olive oil. "That's it." He spun to face me, some magnificent revelation reflecting in his eyes. "You're calm, relaxed, maybe even happy. For the first time since we met, you actually seem comfortable in your own skin." He put the container down and leaned against the counter. "You haven't wasted your breath berating my choices or unilateral decisions in," he checked his watch, playing up the dramatics, "the last five days. I'd definitely say that means you've found some inner peace."

I snorted. "Are you telling me I've actually learned to tolerate you?"

"Perhaps." He went back to preparing dinner. "But whatever it is, I'm glad you seem content. It's a nice change from the way you normally carry the weight of the world on your shoulders, always so grim and morbid."

"I think you're delusional." But I contemplated just how true his words were. "The reason I'm so relaxed is because someone finally rubbed those kinks out of my neck and back. Thank you, by the way."

We bantered and playfully flirted through dinner and dessert. It felt normal. It was the perfect evening, and it was something I was glad to have the memory of in the event I was cast into a long-term assignment with no contact. The first time I clipped on the badge, I didn't have any personal ties. I didn't have a family to worry about, and my only friends were on the job. This time, things were different, particularly since I couldn't tell him what was about to happen.

The next morning, he watched as I packed my

belongings into my weekend bag and conducted a final check for anything I might have left behind. Normally, I wasn't too worried, and he sensed the difference. His brows knit together in confusion, but he remained silent.

As we sipped coffee, he assessed my clothing – white button-up blouse, black slacks, and a suit jacket. Nothing out of the ordinary for corporate work.

He cleared his throat. "Next month, I have an event to attend. It's for charity, and I need a plus one."

"I don't think I can make it."

"I haven't even told you what day or time yet. How do you know you can't make it?"

"Does it involve a fancy dress and dancing?"

"It's black tie, and I'm sure they'll have a dance floor." He enjoyed torturing me with matters I found irritating.

"Sorry, but I definitely can't make it." Dressing up and being gawked at like arm candy wasn't on my to-do list.

"We've been dating for over a year, and you want me to go to a party alone?" He tended to get into trouble at social events. Once, he was arrested on suspicion of murder, and another time, his ex-fiancée assaulted him, using her lips against his mouth. "Aren't there additional perks that come with being in a committed relationship?" His green eyes danced. "Aside from the obvious, which I believe you benefitted from multiple times last night."

Blushing, I glared at him. "Fine. I'll try to swing it." Catching a glimpse of the time, I swallowed the rest of the coffee in one gulp. "E-mail me the details because I'm gonna be late if I stay here for another minute."

"Good luck, sweetheart."

"Hey," I pulled him close, "we'll figure something out. Maybe Bruiser has a dress hanging in the back of his closet that he's been dying to wear someplace fancy."

Martin ignored the quip, and I went down the stairs and to my car. Pulling onto the main road, I took a deep breath. The two day hiatus was over. Now the real fun could begin.

Giddy with nervous energy, my fingers tapped a rhythm against the steering wheel as I took the familiar route to the federal building and parked in the garage. Taking the elevator to the OIO level, I poked my head into Mark's open office door.

"You look rested," he said, tearing his eyes away from a stack of case files. "I barely recognize you without the dark puffy circles underneath your eyes."

"Thanks a lot. Am I reporting to you or Director Kendall?"

"Go see Kendall first. Then I'll meet you in the conference room once I get this sorted out. It looks like I must have drawn the short straw, seeing as how you'll be reporting to me again, Agent Parker."

"Just like old times." I swallowed, my eyes involuntarily darting to my former partner's desk. Even though I finally came to grips with his death and stopped blaming myself, it didn't make it hurt any less.

Mark saw the sobered look on my face and gave a curt nod. "Go on. We don't have all day."

And just like that, I went down the hallway and knocked on Kendall's door. He looked up and motioned me inside. My personnel file was on his desk, my reinstatement papers were signed and dated, and the case file was awaiting my perusal. He finished going over a few final points concerning my job, the updated mandatory requirement for periodic, unannounced drug testing since I failed one the last time I tried to be reinstated, and a few other hoops that needed jumping through. Then he passed me off to Special Agent in Charge Steve Cooper, whom I had worked with in the past.

"Parker," Cooper greeted, extending his hand, "I thought you swore you were done."

"I was, but obviously, the government had other plans for my retirement." I thought back to the mafia don who threatened my life and the lives of my friends if I didn't back off. "Whatever I'm embarking on now better not involve Vito."

"It doesn't. Kendall has you as far removed from the organized crime unit as possible."

"So what am I doing? Please tell me I'm not playing the role of hooker with a heart of gold."

He laughed politely. "I forgot what it was like to work with you." He led the way to a conference room and opened the door. "This was originally my op, but our assets were compromised, so the FBI turned it over to its more specialized branch, the OIO. Originally, we thought the DEA might want to take a crack at it, but this isn't one of their typical cartels."

"Drugs?" I already didn't like it.

"Among other things. This is mainly about smuggling, but we have yet to determine the source."

"International?"

"Obviously." But before he could say anything else, Mark stepped into the room. "Jablonsky will be your handler. You're running point from the inside, and anything you need will be coordinated directly through him. We've already established your new identity, but you should expect a slow insertion. We have to be careful not to raise suspicion."

"I'll take it from here," Mark said, shooing Cooper away. When the door closed, he rubbed his face and leaned back in the chair. "Here's your cover. Read through it first and then we'll get down to the basics."

I flipped open the manila folder, reading the first few lines. This seemed to be rather run-of-the-mill. It wasn't much different from the assignments I handled in the past. I continued reading, flipping page after page.

Alexia Nicholson had a fairly extensive rap sheet. She was a junkie who happened to get mixed up with the wrong crowd. The people she had been running with were dealers. When the group disbanded after a particularly gruesome bust, she was convicted of possession with the intent to distribute and was charged with felony murder. But the judge showed leniency, hoping to reform rather than incarcerate. Apparently, my cover identity had been expected to turn her life around, and her sentence was lessened with time served, mandatory rehab, and parole. But from what I gathered, there wasn't much chance she kicked her heroin habit.

"We have a few former tattoo artists who will airbrush you with semi-permanent makeup. It'll be less of a hassle than having to create realistic looking track marks every time you show up for a meet," Mark said when I questioningly held up my cover's rap sheet. "Also, we've worked out plausible reasons why you are suddenly taking up residence in that neighborhood. New job and new digs."

I continued reading. Alexia was recently hired as an exotic dancer. The information on my new career was mostly blank, meaning it had yet to be established. "Looks like my rehab isn't going to stick."

"Once a junkie, always a junkie," Mark said, sounding more cynical and jaded than ever. "But on the bright side, it'll explain your transient nature and unstable lifestyle. We've established an apartment, but until things get underway, you don't have to stay there permanently."

"Let me guess, this is the real reason for the mandatory random drug testing." I shook my head, sighing at the irony. "You do realize after being drugged once and dealing with the horribleness that accompanied it, I have no desire whatsoever to become an addict or use recreationally."

"No kidding. Frankly, that's probably why Kendall picked you for this one. You're the most strait-laced agent we have when it comes to substance abuse, and it shows exactly how much faith and trust he has in you."

"Plus, if the hacker actually discovered my file, and my cover has been compromised before we even get started, at least it adds a real dynamic if I have to talk myself out of a worst case situation."

"There won't be any worst case situations." His eyes bore into mine. "I won't allow it."

Too bad the feeling of impending doom settled like a bowling ball on my chest. This was a mistake. "You don't know that." I continued reading, attempting to ignore the look I was getting. When I couldn't take it anymore, I dropped the file on the desk. "Shit happens, especially when I'm here."

"Alex, I understand if you have cold feet, but if your head isn't in the game, back the fuck out before it's too late."

"No," I said resolutely, "I want to be here. I want this. I just don't know how to do it."

"It's like riding a bicycle. It'll come back. You never stopped investigating. This is the same thing, just from the inside. We'll review the protocols, catch you up on procedure, dead drops, code words, everything you'll need to know. You'll be fine."

"What about backup?"

"For the first couple of days, agents will maintain eyes on you and monitor the situation from a distance, so in the event there's trouble, they'll be nearby. If everything goes as planned, they'll be gone within the week, and it'll just be you."

"Thank god." I offered a bittersweet smile, surprising him with that sentiment. "At least no one else will get killed because of me." His eyes darkened, prepared to berate me or possibly confiscate my newly acquired credentials. "What? It's true."

THREE

It had barely been a week since I walked into the OIO building for the briefing on my undercover assignment, but already I was bored and exhausted. The tedium added to the fatigue, but boring was better than the alternative. Letting myself into the crappy apartment in the unsavory neighborhood, I flickered the overhead lights twice to indicate I was inside.

My only company on this op was a surveillance team posted outside in a laundry truck, and after today, they'd be gone too. Radio communication was too dangerous given the fact that the nearby gang and drug lords monitored police frequencies with their numerous scanners, so most things were conducted using visual cues.

When I arrived at the apartment, I'd signal. If company showed up, I'd flash the lights again. If I needed tactical support, it was three quick blinks. And if all else failed, my cell phone was my best friend. For this project, I had an unregistered throwaway with shoddy service and an encrypted app for text messaging, but it would do in a pinch.

I made my first appearance five nights ago, arriving around nine p.m. in questionable attire and appearing skunked out of my mind. I was loud, raucous, and made quite a scene. In tight little ghetto neighborhoods like this, people talked. And by the following evening, I noticed the silent stares and quiet observations. That night, I stepped up my act, arriving in ripped jeans, a revealing tank top, and covered in my newly airbrushed track marks and a few makeup created bruises. Alexia Nicholson was trouble, and hopefully, my new name and vices would be noticed by the local dealers.

Every night, I arrived loudly, trashed out of my mind. Shuffling inside, I'd conduct surveillance until the next morning. I'd leave between eight a.m. and noon, drop my nightly report and any surveillance footage at the established dead drop five blocks away, and continue to the bus stop. From there, I'd go to the business district, hail a cab, and go home. Undercover sucked, but the added precautions and countersurveillance measures were encouraged by the OIO. For once, I wasn't being my usual paranoid self. Instead, the paranoia was actually protocol.

I just stepped out of the shower, noticing the smudged marks on my makeup covered arms. I'd have to remember to do a touch-up with dark eyeshadow and hairspray before going back tonight. Drying my hair, I barely heard the phone. It was Mark.

"Hey, stay away tonight," he said. "I just finished reading your report. You haven't been approached yet, so we're thinking you're too predictable for a junkie."

"Maybe I'm a junkie with a day job."

"Stay away tonight," he repeated. "We're keeping eyes on the apartment. Who knows, maybe someone will decide to take a look around." He let out a sigh. "Is everything still out in the open?"

"Needles, spoon, burnt foil, and some empty prescription pill bottles. Did I overlook anything?"

"Nope, that should do it. How are you holding up?"

"I'm fine. But if we keep moving at this rate, waiting for the dealers to make an approach, we might be doing this for the next hundred years. When can I get a little more proactive?"

"Patience, grasshopper. We'll stagger your appearances. Once your comings and goings become more sporadic, you can inquire about a small buy. Let's shoot for the end of next week."

"Do you really think they'll make a move before then?"

"They might, if they believe you're itching for a fix. Just make sure you keep the cash on you. You don't want to be caught unprepared."

"Are you afraid someone will want to barter instead of accepting payment in dollars and cents?"

"You know how this goes. The dealer might want cash and ass if he has free time on his hands. Plus, most women are much more compliant when they're stoned out of their minds or desperate."

"Well, it's a good thing we don't have to worry about that." Drugs, sex, and violence tended to travel together in a disturbing package. "I can handle myself, Jablonsky."

"I never said you couldn't, but we don't need to worry about this for a few days. Enjoy your night off. But drop by the agreed upon meeting place tomorrow morning for an official debrief and strategizing session."

"You mean this didn't count?"

"Parker," he snapped.

"Yes, sir."

He hated it when I called him that, and he let out a disgusted sound and disconnected. At least I had the day off to remember how to be Alexis Parker. And the first thing she wanted to do was get some sleep.

When I woke up, I went for a long run, followed by an extensive strength training session. No longer excessively sore, it was obvious I was quickly bouncing back from my injury-induced hiatus. After washing up and dressing, I began the tedious task of researching smugglers and contraband, hoping to find some leads.

The OIO had their sights set on DeAngelo Bard, also known as Shakespeare. The guy had a rap sheet a mile long, and that didn't include his juvie record. He was twenty-seven years old and ran the KXDs, a gang that controlled most of the south side. He controlled the neighborhood where my cover identity's apartment was and the surrounding areas. Every drug runner and prostitute in the area worked for him.

When some other gangs tried to encroach on his territory a few years back, it turned into all-out warfare. And despite the dozens of homicides and drive-bys, the police never collected enough evidence to shut him down. He was too well-protected, and no one would turn against him for fear of retaliation.

However, after the gang wars ended, Bard tried to rebrand himself to keep some of the heat off. Going legit was something many mafia dons had done, and maybe this poor kid from the wrong neighborhood thought he could do the same. Perhaps he watched *The Godfather* and *Scarface* one too many times; although if that was the case, he failed to learn the deeper meaning – crime doesn't pay.

Now, on paper, it looked like he was removed from the gang life, even if the KXDs still controlled the neighborhood streets and he still controlled the KXDs. But he had branched out, made connections and contacts, both foreign and domestic, and seemed to be our best bet for the smuggling. Given his gang affiliation, guns and other armaments were likely being smuggled in, along with drugs and a possible human trafficking element. No wonder the FBI wanted this stopped. The only reason other government agencies weren't stepping in after the breach was because the facts weren't enough. The bulk of his business was too localized for the DEA, DHS, and ATF, especially since most of these suspicions were unsubstantiated.

The compromised operation into the KXDs had been running for seven months, and since the source of the security breach had yet to be identified, the Bureau pulled their current undercover agents, pending an investigation. Of course, just because the system was hacked, it didn't mean government agencies went on holiday and crime would take a vacation. So the FBI sent in the B-team to fill in until this mess was sorted out.

When my research hit the wall, I gave the computer a dirty look and shut it off. I spent the past week reading through the OIO files on the KXDs, Bard, and the lesser known players. Nothing was particularly helpful, and my personal search through the criminal databases and internet search engines didn't lead to any new discoveries. Deciding to explore my only remaining untapped resource, I picked up the phone and dialed one of the few numbers I had memorized.

"Hey, Parker," Detective Derek Heathcliff of the major crimes division answered, having read my name off the caller ID.

"Are you working tonight?"

"No, I get off in a couple of hours. Is everything okay?"

"Absolutely, which explains why I haven't seen you in a while and thought we should catch up." Realizing his investigative instincts would determine there was more to the story than meets the eye, I quickly covered by adding, "I was thinking of having poker night at my place."

"We've never played poker."

"Would you rather play Old Maid?"

"I didn't say that. What time?"

"Whenever your shift ends. I'll even splurge on the pizza and beer."

"Okay. I'll see you later."

Heathcliff used to work narcotics and would potentially possess some unofficial insight into Bard and his drug affiliation, but since I couldn't divulge the reason I needed these facts, I'd have to improvise. And now it looked like I needed to make a few more calls. My second call was to Detective Nick O'Connell, also in the major crimes division. With any luck, the rest of my cop brethren would provide some additional answers on the gang wars and smuggling issues.

"I thought I was your favorite," Nick said. Obviously, he must have been on shift with Heathcliff and heard the news before I could ask the question. "Shouldn't you have called me first? What would you have done if I was busy?"

"Saved a few bucks on beer. I take it you're in."

"Yep."

"Thompson too?" That was O'Connell's partner.

"I'll ask, but I'm sure he'll say yes. Is Martin joining us? We need someone to pad the pot with actual cash instead of crumpled IOUs."

"Um..." What the hell, a couple of civilians might keep

the detectives from interrogating me on my current job and interest in drugs and smuggling. "Hopefully, he'll be able to swing it. Why don't you ask your wife if she wants to come too?"

"Jenny and I will be there," Nick assured. "She'll want to know if there's anything we can bring. What should I say?"

"Tell her if she's good with pizza and beer, then I have it covered." I paused. "Do you think this will get us off the hook for date night?" The O'Connells and Martin and I typically met once a month as an excuse to get out of the house and appear to be members of the civilized world. Nick and I hated it, but that was the price we had to pay for being involved with civilians.

"Only if Heathcliff and Thompson showed up with dates, and you know that won't happen." Protests rang out in the background.

"Maybe they could be each other's date," I suggested before disconnecting in order to free up the phone and extend an invitation to Martin.

If this wasn't a fact-gathering mission, I would have asked Mark to join us, but there was a good chance he would chew me out for unofficially requesting this type of information when I was under strict instructions to keep my cover a secret from everyone. But asking innocent questions didn't pose a threat, especially when it came to the three men who had my back no matter what.

*　　*　　*

"All in." Thompson shoved his stack of chips toward the center of the table. I threw my cards down, leaving Nick and Thompson to duke it out.

Jenny was puttering around the kitchen. She had brought a large toss salad that could have fed an army and a tray of brownies. How a full-time ER nurse managed to be the domesticated happy homemaker was beyond me, but I wasn't protesting.

Martin had yet to show up. He was busy with work, and if he managed to free himself from the invisible shackles, by the time he got here, everyone else would be on their way out. It wasn't that he didn't get along with my cop friends, but he was a workaholic and a tad competitive. A friendly game of cards with set limits probably wasn't one of his priorities for a weeknight.

I'd been dancing around the issue most of the evening, but no one had given me any straight answers. Heathcliff had recently concluded an undercover assignment that involved the gangs, narcotics, and major crimes units, but it seemed unrelated to DeAngelo Bard and the KXDs. Taking out the hard liquor and a few glasses, I started pouring.

"What? You're hoping to get us liquored up so you'll be able to win back some cash?" O'Connell asked, his eyes never leaving Thompson as the two continued their standoff. It was nothing more than posturing since Thompson already announced all in, but the boys wanted to play. So they could play.

"Shh," I hissed playfully, "everyone doesn't need to know my secret strategy."

"Speaking of secrets," Thompson shot a look in my direction, "where've you been lately? I was just getting used to you popping up every couple of months and reminding us what a pain in the ass you are. What gives?"

"I'm working somewhere steady. Office, suit, paperwork."

"You aren't back at Martin Technologies, are you?" Jen asked, returning to the table.

"No. And I'm glad Martin isn't here for that comment." I rolled my eyes. "We shouldn't work together."

"That's because you hate taking orders," O'Connell mumbled, finally flipping his cards. He had a pair of fours. Thompson had a flush. "Dammit."

O'Connell took the cards and dealt another hand while Thompson scooped up his winnings. Derek's eyes were on me, and I gave him a look. He glanced at the inside of my forearm. Inadvertently, I had rolled my sleeves up during the course of the evening, and now some of the airbrushed bruises were visible.

"How'd that happen?" he asked.

"I don't remember." I pulled my sleeves down before he

could continue the scrutiny. "So any big cases in the works?" I hoped to derail his questioning look. "Y'know me, always looking for some consulting work."

"Nothing major. Well, it's all major. We are major crimes," O'Connell supplied, focused on the game and his drink.

"Some lunatic's been doing some horrible shit in the metro tunnels," Thompson responded. "But we have evidence and a BOLO out on the guy. It's just a matter of catching him." He shrugged. "Imagine, we seem to be functioning just fine without you."

I studied Derek, but he wasn't speaking. He just continued the visual assessment. "You look thinner than normal," he said after a time.

"Thanks, I guess."

"Not quite sickly thin but close. Have you been feeling all right? You should eat more. It's not like we're asking you to go undercover as a model again." That happened the first time the two of us worked together. His eyes flicked to the half-eaten slice of pizza on my plate. "Any reason you don't have much of an appetite? And why didn't you pour yourself a glass of the hard stuff?"

"Oh my gosh," Jen piped up, "leave Alex alone. Unlike the rest of you, she probably actually gives a damn about how unhealthy this food really is. And she's naturally svelte." She assessed me. "But you could stand to eat more, particularly since you haven't tried one of my brownies."

"Gee, thanks." I sighed. "I've been working out a lot more. Having a boring job and regular hours leaves plenty of time for other things. That's it. What's with the inquisition? It's not like I've been grilling you about your current assignments or the one you just finished." Trying to spin the conversation back to useful information, I took a chance since Heathcliff seemed more suspicious about me than my job. "So with all this free time, I've been reviewing some old cases and news stories from years ago. Do you guys remember the gang wars involving the KXDs?"

"God, that was a bloodbath," Thompson said. "I didn't work it, but Heathcliff must have. You were still in narcotics then, right?"

"Yeah." Derek didn't look completely convinced that everything I was saying was true, but he let it go and began spilling his guts.

For the next few hours, we shared old war stories. Even Jen joined in and spoke of some of the crazier things she had seen in the emergency room. By the end, I had some new intel and answers to a few of my questions.

FOUR

"How'd you hear about that?" Agent Cooper asked. He was sitting in on my debrief. "From the notes and your reports, I didn't realize you made contact."

"I didn't. It's old news. We're talking about what occurred five years ago. I'm sure it's in one of the files." I gestured to the two boxes worth of intel. "Plus, it was never substantiated, and from what I gather, it fell through. It looks like Bard's number two, Francisco Steele, is quite the entrepreneur. Based on the rumblings, he encouraged the KXDs to expand and brought the international connection to Bard."

Mark had that look that said 'I know where you got your information, and I don't like it', but I ignored it. He continued to glare in my direction as a few of the agents who had originally been stuck in the surveillance van began sorting through the hundreds of accounts and notes that were made over the years.

"So the KXDs tried to merge with a Mexican cartel in order to control the city's drug trade which is what led to the gang wars," Cooper finally said. "It's not surprising. The balance of power would have shifted, and no one wanted that. Not the cops, the neighboring gangs, or even the larger syndicates." He paused while his mind finished processing the current dilemma. "What is surprising is that the DEA and Customs didn't pounce on this after our breach. Then again," he skimmed the tabs on the files piling up on the table, "maybe they did intervene when this originally happened, and that's why the KXDs are still small potatoes. In gang life, a few years is practically ancient history." He opened the FBI's latest file on Bard and the KXDs. "We heard rumors of a new supply line and were asked to determine if the allegations were true and to shut down the source if they were. Like I said, it appeared to be international smuggling, but the current investigation never indicated ties to a cartel."

"But since Bard tried to merge once, he might be trying again," Mark added, "which adds an even stronger basis to our allegations of drug running, weapons dealing, and human trafficking."

"It can't be a big operation," I interjected. "If it was, another agency would have shut it down. And I'd guess the KXDs' south of the border contacts abandoned them five years ago when things turned bloody."

"Maybe Bard is looking for a connection farther south. The Colombians used to be the number one supplier of cocaine. Maybe they want to get back on top since Peru dethroned them. Then again, we don't know exactly what the primary staple is for the KXDs to peddle. But we will find out," Mark said. "Is there anything else you'd like to report, Agent Parker?"

"No, sir. But I need a touch-up. My track marks are starting to fade."

He rolled his eyes, fearing I would say something controversial and insubordinate, but I was already in enough trouble. "Fine, we'll get you outfitted." Mark focused on the other agents monitoring surveillance and compiling information. "How come none of you reported the failed cartel merger?" The team looked up but couldn't provide an explanation for their lapse, so Agent Cooper stepped in to berate them and review the gathered information while Mark led me out of the room.

"Don't you think that could be important?" I hoped to

avoid the ass-chewing I was about to receive. "It could make or break the case. And since I'm undercover, I need to know everything."

"You'll get the condensed report before you go back tonight, but I'm guessing you already know everything inside that box a lot better than anyone else in that room."

"I do my homework."

"Yes, you do. And after reading through every piece of information the FBI compiled, you decided to get some extra credit. Who'd you talk to? O'Connell? Heathcliff? Moretti?"

"It was poker night. They had a few drinks, and we talked about ancient history."

"Do they know you've been reinstated?"

"No. I didn't break cover. You said I couldn't tell anyone, including them. But I really don't see the point. I trust them. Shit, Jablonsky, you trust them too."

"Yeah, but in the event there's another security breach, they don't need to get blamed or investigated because you opened your big mouth. Understand? It's for their protection as well as yours."

"Fine." I brushed my hair back and took my jacket off, rolling up my sleeves. "Any idea how to get the airbrushing to last longer?"

"You could stop showering. It might help you blend in better in that neighborhood."

"Ugh," I cringed, "that apartment is rank. I saw a cockroach in the hallway and nearly screamed bloody murder. The building is disgusting, and people have to live there. It's heartbreaking."

"So besides an exterminator, what else do you need?"

"I could use a few more puzzle books. It's so boring, staying there for hours at a time with little to do except count the cracks in the wall, play swat the bug, and listen for sounds of gunfire. Until my role becomes more proactive, I'm going stir crazy."

"Alex, I know it's boring, but do not let your guard down. Are you sure you don't want a partner? We could give your cover some romantic entanglement which would explain another agent spending the night at the apartment."

"No partner. Right now, this is just recon and surveillance, and we've already established the reason for Alexia Nicholson's move. We don't change the play. You know that. Are you afraid I can't handle it?"

"Well, you and boredom do not get along. And I don't want to hear reports of weapons discharge because you decided to play shoot the cockroach."

"I really hate bugs."

He laughed. "Go get your makeup done. I'll check and see how far they've gotten on updating our intel. Then why don't you grab some lunch and pick up some magazines or whatever to keep you occupied in between maintaining eyes and ears on DeAngelo Bard and the KXDs." He dug a couple of twenties out of his wallet and put them on the table. "I'll get reimbursed. This should be on the government's dime."

"Thanks."

After spending almost an hour watching some former tattoo artist who was now receiving a government paycheck perfect the look of frequent heroin user on my arms, I took the stairs down to street level and emerged from the side door, glancing around for signs of a tail. The OIO was using a partially empty office building as our meeting place in order to keep my cover intact. If anyone were to notice my arrival or departure from the building, they'd probably think a junkie was using one of the abandoned levels as temporary shelter while getting her fix. Thankfully, the men in suits blended in well with the insurance firm on the second and third floors, and by taking the elevator to the lobby and going out the front door, no one would ever be clued in that they were federal agents. At least that was the plan.

Inside the nearby convenience store, I grabbed some pre-made sandwiches, browsed the magazine racks for word searches and crossword puzzles, picked up a few bottles of water, and paid the cashier before heading back to the building. We were in a different neighborhood, and there was no reason for the extra precautions, but regardless, I ducked back into the alley where the side door to the building was and leaned against the dumpster for the next ten minutes, watching traffic and pedestrians to ensure no repeat offenders popped up before entering the security code on the hidden keypad and going inside.

Setting the plastic bag down on a desk, I selected a turkey on white and waited for Mark to return. He and Cooper came into the room just as I was taking my third bite. Mark went to the bag, found a sandwich, and slumped into the chair.

"Lunchtime," he bellowed to the few remaining agents.

Cooper and I exchanged a quick glance, and then he handed me an envelope containing surveillance photos from the vicinity of my cover's apartment. Mostly, the photos were of key players in Bard's ranks, but a few appeared to be nothing more than scenic shots of the nearby dumpsters and alleys.

"Was someone learning how to use the camera?" I asked. "I know they have telephoto lenses, but isn't it just point and shoot?"

"Agent Parker," Cooper always sounded monotone, but there was a formality to his posture which signified we were getting back to business, "your first week was basic. You've created a presence for yourself. You frequent an apartment on a mostly regular basis. The other tenants have noticed you. And your planted background was reinforced the other morning when we sent a parole officer to the apartment."

My eyes flicked to Mark. No one mentioned that. And it was scheduled intentionally when I wouldn't be present.

"The point was to make sure everyone knows Alexia Nicholson is a junkie with a record. Don't worry, the cops aren't clued in to our operation. But that doesn't mean we can't call in a favor from time to time. Professional courtesy, gotta love it," Mark said, brushing crumbs off his tie.

"We've been surveilling Bard and the KXDs for several months. It's time we change the play. You need to earn their trust in order to infiltrate their ranks," Cooper concluded. "We've discussed the possibility of making a small buy to start the ball rolling. Authorization has come through, and that's the first step toward reaching our much larger goal."

I spread the photos out. "So which one of these bad boys am I approaching?"

"One of the nameless low-level dealers," Mark replied. "Start small and slow. These pushers are a dime a dozen. Turnover in the KXDs happens quickly, so it doesn't matter who. It's just a start. Eventually, you'll work your way up to one of Bard's lieutenants, but we can't rush this, no matter how badly you want to get away from the cockroaches."

"But since I'm new in that neighborhood, how do I know who to approach or what to buy?"

"We have a general idea where you can look since they frequent the same locations." Cooper pointed to the photos of the alleys and dumpsters. "So use your best judgment. Whoever you think is a safe bet. But since you're new, they might expect you to use in front of them if they don't believe your planted background."

"So don't ask for anything I can't fake," I surmised.

"And don't do it tonight," Mark warned. "Study the photos, see who you spot from your apartment, and determine the least dangerous person and position for your approach. The surveillance team won't be circling anymore, but we'll have agents on standby in case something goes sideways. Just keep in mind, they'll be at least ten minutes out since we can't risk tipping the KXDs off that you're a federal agent, so it's all on you."

"Don't worry. I won't blow this. Well, I might buy some blow. We'll see how the mood strikes me."

"We'll finish reviewing the old information and work on the intelligence angles," Cooper assured, getting up from the table. Since this had originally been his operation, he was coordinating the data collection and analysis. "She's all yours, Jablonsky."

"What else is new?" Mark studied me for a moment before diverting his attention to one of the untouched sandwiches. "So what are you planning to do this evening, Parker?"

"Show up at the apartment, get a more thorough lay of the land, keep my eyes peeled for danger, and wait for morning."

"Where are your credentials?"

"What?"

"Just in case something goes south, you need them close by, but keeping them on your person in the event you're searched isn't a great idea either."

"You do realize this isn't my first undercover assignment, right? Pretty far from it, actually."

"Okay. I just want to make sure you're being careful. Boredom leads to complacency, even in the best agents, and without backup on-site, I need to know you're taking every precaution imaginable."

"Stop worrying so much. I'm a paranoid lunatic. I even think the doc wrote that on my latest psych eval." I collected the photos and the condensed file Cooper left on the table. "What time should Alexia make her appearance tonight?"

"Shoot for ten. Leave after noon tomorrow, got it?"

"Great that gives me another four hours to read the funny pages." I held up the files. "It's only been a week, but I get the feeling we'll be having another conversation just like this one six months from now."

"You knew it was long-term when you agreed to come back. Should I remind you of *The Tortoise and the Hare*?"

"Slow and steady. Aye, aye, sir." I took a deep breath and went to the door.

"And, Parker, no more poker nights."

Grumbling a response too low for Mark to hear, I let myself out of the building. Always vigilant for signs of trouble, I took a bus to a much more pleasant neighborhood and then grabbed a cab to my apartment. That left just enough time to review the materials from my briefing, eat dinner, and alter my look to ghetto junkie. Why did I love this job so much? At times like this, I couldn't quite remember, or maybe that was from too many hits to the head.

Arriving a few minutes to ten, I knew the cold winter air held the promise of an impending snowstorm. With any luck, the heat in the crappy apartment wouldn't give out. Trudging up the steps in an opened parka that revealed a pair of short shorts, ripped fishnets, and thigh-high boots, I wasn't sure if my attire screamed stripper or hooker. Then again, there wasn't always a differentiation between the two. As long as it yelled desperate in big bold letters, I was off to a good start.

"Yo, Ms. Nicholson," a woman around my age called when I made it to the fourth floor, "a man was looking for you the other morning. You in trouble or something?"

"Nah." I watched her push a young boy back inside her apartment. She was smart enough to leave the security chain on, and optimistically, I figured maybe her watchful attitude was to keep the riffraff away from her family. "Just got some times and dates confused. No biggie. You have yourself a good night. I know I will." I lifted up the brown paper sack I was carrying. It looked like it could have come from a liquor store, but all it held was my rolled up crossword and word search puzzles. Wow, I was lame, even in this neighborhood.

She narrowed her eyes and slammed the door, muttering something derogatory about hos. At least my cover was shaping up nicely. Too bad I might freeze my ass off. Making a note to reconsider the slutty outfits or invest in a long, down coat, I closed myself into the disgusting apartment, locked the door, flipped on the lights, and checked every inch for signs of a disturbance or an infestation. No reason not to be thorough since I was checking anyway. After concluding the apartment was tamper free, I slipped into something more practical, checked the windows for outside activity, and set up the surveillance equipment to monitor the area.

FIVE

I rubbed my eyes and got up from my perch. The long hours of monitoring the surrounding area for activity was beyond boring. It was a snooze fest, and despite the fact I needed to be alert and vigilant, it wasn't humanly possible to do absolutely nothing but stare out the window all night. Knowing my own limitations, I made sure the feed was recording and rinsed out a cup before filling it with bottled water and microwaving it. Adding a packet of instant coffee, I stirred the contents, checked the other three windows for signs of life, and slumped onto the air mattress in the corner.

Furniture wasn't exactly a priority for the federal government or crack whores, so aside from a kitchen table and chairs, a few TV trays, and an air mattress, the place was barren. The camera equipment was set up on each tray, and signs of drug abuse littered the floor. I glanced at the tips of my fingers, reminding myself to cover them in soot since the burnt foil always left residue on a heroin user's fingertips.

After a fifteen minute break that consisted of staring at the ceiling and working on a word find, I repeated the process of checking each camera location and dragged a chair to a different window to continue surveillance. A partner did come with some benefits, like conversation and the ability to get takeout, and briefly, my mind wandered to my late partner, Agent Michael Carver, and soggy pizza. Nope. It wasn't worth it. I didn't need to be entertained every minute of the day. Taking a final sip of coffee, I paced back and forth, keeping my eyes trained on the ground below.

The snow started around one a.m., and by now, everything was covered in a light layer of white. It was bitterly cold, and the weather was acting as a decent deterrent to keep crime down. Admittedly, this was a good thing, but of course, it didn't make my job any easier or my night any less tedious.

Around six a.m., the sounds of the city waking up began. Stretching from the position I'd been sitting in for the last two hours, I picked up a slightly used trash bag that contained nothing more than some crumpled paper towels and went to the dumpster. It was one of the locations Cooper had pointed out, and I wondered if I'd find some sign of a dead drop or if this was one of the normal spots the KXDs used to hock their illegal wares. And since no one was around at the moment, it was the perfect time to snoop. Unfortunately, nothing presented itself as useful knowledge or evidence.

Just as I tossed the bag into the dumpster, I heard someone shuffling down the sidewalk, out of view. I palmed the taser in my coat pocket and emerged onto the street, keeping my face turned away from the falling snow. In the brightening sky, the accumulated snowfall reflected the light, illuminating the area more than normal for this early hour.

A man I recognized from the photographs as Francisco Steele, Bard's top lieutenant, was leaning against the building, hunched over as he lit a cigarette. I walked right by him, knowing it would be stupid to make an approach this early in the game.

"Just getting in? Or are you going out, chica?" he asked. "It's a strange time to be outside, isn't it?"

Great, he was already suspicious. I continued walking,

ignoring him and going up the steps to the front door of the apartment building. Saying nothing would probably be more effective than saying something.

"What's a matter, pretty lady? Cat got your tongue?"

"The cat's got something," I replied. As I went up the steps, I listened for footfalls behind me, but he didn't follow. That encounter didn't amount to much of anything, except an elaborate explanation on the paperwork I had to file.

Back inside the apartment, I gave the place another once over for signs of any unwelcome guests, smashed a spider hiding in the bathroom, and returned to the window. Below, Steele found someone else to talk to. I used the camera to zoom in, but I didn't recognize the other man. Taking a few snapshots and making a note to run him through facial recognition, I contemplated how some worthless stripper junkie, a.k.a. me, was supposed to get into DeAngelo Bard's good graces. One step at a time, and first, we had to work on orchestrating a buy.

The men outside continued their conversation for the next twenty minutes, but neither of them had any visible contraband. Working the kink out of my neck, I checked the other vantage points, but nothing exciting was happening. A few minutes after I resumed watching the exchange below, the unidentified man walked away, and Steele came inside the apartment building. Did he live here? I went to my front door and pressed my eye against the peephole, but if he resided in this building, it definitely wasn't on this floor.

With nothing else to do, I wrote my report, a thorough description of the men I noticed and encountered, a preliminary summation of the dumpster which proved worthless, and checked outside again. By now, it was after eight. The kids were off to school, the hardworking adults who had fallen on hard times were off to work or employment agencies, and everything quieted.

For the next four hours, I fought to keep my eyes open. The building and surrounding areas were lifeless with the only exceptions being traffic and the occasional siren or blaring car horn. Shaking off the boredom and fatigue, I worked my way through a few dozen Sudoku puzzles, stowed the surveillance equipment in the false back behind the locked closet, and made sure the place still looked like it belonged to an addict who had no intention of recovering. Alexia Nicholson might have heroin and cocaine on her rap sheet, but that didn't mean she didn't dabble in pills, alcohol, and whatever else she could get her hands on. Hopefully, the KXDs would find that believable.

Stuffing my handwritten report, surveillance notes, and the memory cards from the cameras into an envelope, I sealed the flap and stuck it inside the inner lining of my coat. As another precaution, I had hollowed out a place inside the lining to transport materials. This way, in case I was ever stopped or searched, my actual identity wouldn't be as easily discovered.

Locking my cover's apartment, I went down the steps and out the front door. Half a block away, the voice from earlier sounded again. "Now where you headed?"

"Fuck off, creep. I have a killer hangover and a million things to do. Go harass someone else."

Francisco didn't say anything, but his eyes narrowed. I continued down the street, barely hearing the amused snort that rang out a full minute later. At least he wasn't pissed. He was entertained. That could make things interesting in the future. Maybe I found a way in. Too bad it wasn't with some nobody dealer. Jablonsky would be agitated by this new turn of events, but it could speed up the process and get this op on a more manageable timetable.

After leaving last night's intel at the dead drop, I considered my options. It would have been nice to go to the federal building or the precinct and dig up Francisco Steele's background and look through the mug book for his known associates, but that wasn't an option. Instead, I took the crosstown bus to one of the larger terminals, got out, and stopped at the closest diner. Once lunch was ordered, I glanced around and pulled out my burner phone, dialing Mark.

"I want to go back," I said.

"When?"

"In an hour or two, depending on how long it takes to eat lunch and catch a bus to the neighborhood."

"Jesus," Mark exhaled, irritated, "we just picked up the intel twenty minutes ago. We haven't had time to analyze it yet, and you already want to go back. What happened?"

"One of the strays spotted me. He might be hanging around the rest of the day. Maybe it's time for an introduction."

"Don't push for a buy." He sounded exasperated. "Are you sure you're up for this?"

"We're establishing a rapport. It can't hurt. Worst case, maybe he found a place to get out of the cold, and I'll end up heading out a couple of hours later than planned."

"If this is happening, we'll have to get the rest of your cover established sooner, just in case someone checks up on you. So unless you hear otherwise, don't give any hard details."

"I never do."

"Yeah. We're gonna talk about that in the future." He hesitated, and I thought he might hang up. "Parker, be careful. And give me a call once you're alone inside the apartment."

"I will."

Disconnecting, I worked my way through lunch as my mind wrapped around the feasible options. My support team wouldn't be particularly happy about the change in plans. They liked to have extra time to prepare, and if Steele was still outside, we'd be going from zero to sixty. Then again, it was possible he went home or to work, assuming he had some type of legitimate job, which I doubted. Closing my eyes, I knew I read his profile, but no address was listed. Was he one of my neighbors? Maybe his attempt at a conversation this morning was the KXDs' version of the welcome wagon, and the gift basket would be a nice arrangement of uppers and downers since they didn't strike me as the Jell-o mold types.

I took the bus to the closest stop and trudged through the snow to the drafty apartment building. The frigid air and my lack of sleep only aided in solidifying my cover, causing my skin to appear paler than normal on account of the dark circles and windburns. I rounded the corner and spotted Steele sitting on the freshly shoveled stoop, rubbing his hands together and waiting for something.

"God, the last thing I need is a stalker," I growled, carefully maneuvering around a patch of ice to get to the front steps. Although I was speaking aloud to myself, it had the desired effect of causing him to strike up a conversation.

"Finished with your errands?" His tone matched the weather, and the hair on the back of my neck stood up. Maybe he was annoyed by my insolent remarks. "You're new around here. I'm guessing that's why you don't know to be more respectful."

"Just another tough guy." I rolled my eyes, clearly too strung-out to care. "Whatever. I'll leave you alone if you leave me alone."

I moved toward the door, but he stood, blocking my path. He was over six feet tall, strong, and broad. His look was fierce, meant to earn obedience and fear, and I made sure to act appropriately, cowering slightly and stepping away from him as I cast my eyes downward. Submissive wasn't in my wheelhouse, but it would be in Alexia's. Women like her dealt with plenty of bullies and had to know when to pick and choose their battles. He put a finger under my chin and brought my face up. My muscles tensed, but I didn't move.

"That's better." A slight smirk played across his face, and his eyes darted over my body. "You look like you're feeling pretty miserable right about now." He jerked his chin upward the arrogant way people do when they want to nod a greeting but don't seem to know how. "Bet I can make you feel better."

"Lots of men say that. Very few actually can." *Don't push, Parker.* Mark's words reverberated in my head, and I swallowed, stepping closer to the side railing. "I'm fine. I just need to sleep this off."

He studied my eyes. "Whatta you got under that coat, chica?"

"Nothing." Unsure of where this was going, I stepped farther away from him. "C'mon, man, I just want to go upstairs. I'm not looking for any trouble."

"Hey, I'm just watching out for my neighbors. I've been here a long time. We don't take kindly to new faces, particularly if we can't trust them. Y'know what I'm saying?"

"Not really." I knew what he was saying. They didn't want anyone around who would call the heat in to deal with disturbances or narc to the authorities. And they really wouldn't like an undercover federal agent taking up residence in the slums. "I have enough of my own problems. I'm not looking for any more. Hopefully, I won't be here long. This is just temporary until I get back on my feet."

He narrowed the distance between us, pinning me against the wrought-iron handrail. "Open your coat."

"No." So much for afraid and submissive.

He yanked the zipper down and roughly shoved the coat off of my shoulders, grabbing my wrists in each of his hands and pressing his hip against me. He tugged my arms to the sides and studied the bruises and track marks.

"Please," I said, pulling my hands free, "I just want to go upstairs and crash." His hands explored my torso, feeling for a wire. Underneath the thin material of the tank top I wore, he felt every curve, but the only wire he discovered was part of my bra. "Please," I begged, my mind occupied with the various methods of inflicting maximum damage with minimal effort, "don't."

"I wouldn't." He reached down and lifted my coat off the ground and put it back on me. "Like I said, in this neighborhood, it's important to know who can be trusted."

"Sure." I scurried toward the door.

"Chica," he called, just as I stepped inside, "you ever need something to make you feel better, I can hook you up."

Turning, I opened my mouth as if surprised, shut it, and proceeded to the stairs, making sure to keep the smug look off my face until I was locked inside the apartment and positive that I was alone.

"I hit nothing but green lights on the way home," I said once Mark answered. It sounded stupid speaking in code, but it never hurt to be cautious, particularly since I just found a way inside the KXDs.

SIX

Remaining at the apartment the rest of the day, I was too keyed up to sleep, and it was too bright to risk setting up the surveillance equipment in the windows. Instead, I replayed my encounter with Steele over and over. Obviously, he must have noticed me and spoke to the neighbors about the building's newest tenant. Of course, my rent was paid in dirty one dollar bills, one month at a time. And my lease agreement didn't disclose an occupation. This wasn't exactly your typical housing arrangement. Rent was cheap, and the roaches came in two varieties, six legs and rolled in cigarette paper. Based upon my outfits, late nights, and party hardy attitude, it would have been easy enough to jump to a few conclusions. But the lack of johns knocking on my door probably meant I wasn't a hooker, particularly since my parole officer liked to make random checks, so random, in fact, that I didn't even know about them. Sighing, I tried to let that go. There must have been a reason Jablonsky failed to disclose ahead of time. Maybe it wasn't a surefire thing or still in the works during my debrief. Who knows?

As the sky dimmed, I gave the place a final glance to make sure nothing incriminating remained, and then I left.

My days and nights just flipped, and there was a good chance I'd have to make an appearance in the early morning hours, based on this new schedule. Heading out the door, I spotted a group of adolescent men huddled near a trashcan they had set on fire. They made a couple of catcalls and lewd comments, providing the perfect reason to glance in their direction. Memorizing as many of their faces as possible, I continued on my way.

Half a block later, their voices began to grow louder. They were following me. *Think, Parker*, my mind urged as I forced rational thought to keep the panic away. The taser was still in my pocket. My nine millimeter was in my purse since I was afraid carrying it in a holster would blow my cover. Unfortunately, my purse was zipped underneath my coat because I didn't want to make myself a target for muggers. *Real brilliant*, my mind berated as the footsteps sounded closer.

There was a good chance I could outrun them, but they were from the neighborhood. And I'd be back eventually and so would they. I could call 911, but that seemed utterly pointless. By the time anyone arrived, the situation would be resolved in some fashion. A thought crossed my mind. Maybe it was asking for trouble, but with limited options, it was worth a shot. Turning around, I faced them directly.

"What?" one of them asked, surprised, while the others exchanged confused looks and the occasional grin as they surrounded me. "What's a matter? Cat got your tongue?"

"Dammit, that's the second time today I heard that. Did you ask for permission to use that line?"

"We don't need permission," one of them hissed, pawing at me. I elbowed him in the chest then dropped to the ground and performed a sweeping leg kick, rising and stepping back into a defensive stance. With the icy patches, the first guy went down easily, landing on his ass. Two of his buddies laughed, and the other two lunged. "Teach that bitch a lesson," said the guy on the ground.

One of them grabbed me from behind, and I screamed, catching the attention of everyone else on the street. It was a little after seven. Traffic was fairly heavy, and making a scene was the smartest course of action. The worst thing someone could do was hide in a secluded area. The more populated, the better.

The punk tried to clap a hand over my mouth, and I jerked my head back, hitting the side of his jaw hard enough to rattle his teeth. Disoriented, he let go, and I pulled the taser, giving the second guy a jolt that immediately reduced him to a quivering blob.

"Now who's the bitch?" I kicked the original asshole hard enough in the jewels to greatly decrease his chances of ever procreating. He let out a high-pitched yelp, vomited, and perhaps passed out. Spinning to face the remaining two guys, I took a breath, reestablishing my stance. "You want to keep going?"

Their focus shifted elsewhere, and a voice sounded from behind. "Take off. We'll discuss your behavior later."

Swallowing, I turned and came face-to-face with Francisco. He yanked the taser from my hand and studied the dial. Adjusting the setting to the lowest possible choice, he handed it back.

"You said you weren't looking for trouble," he stated in a tone that gave nothing away.

"I'm not." The five guys I just fought off were clowns, and from the way Steele carried himself, it was apparent he could fight. It was also apparent he could probably inflict quite a bit of damage before I could escape or subdue him. "But that doesn't mean I'm down for getting gangbanged. Do you have a problem with that?"

"Do you turn tricks?" he asked, his voice as hard as his name implied.

"No." I made sure to dart my eyes off to the side. Maybe I was lying, or embarrassed, or selling my cover identity. There was no way for him to know.

"Hmm," he continued to look down at me, "not ever?" His eyes grazed my covered arms. "So I won't find you selling yourself on the corner in my neighborhood?"

"Hell no." His neighborhood? What would his boss have to say about that?

"If you were to change your mind, you'd need someone to protect you from the creeps."

"I'm not a whore." Plus, why would I need protection?

Didn't I just demonstrate how well I could protect myself? "God. I can't do this. I can't fucking do this. What are you? Some pimp? That's why you were offering to hook me up, isn't it? Shit." I fidgeted, letting the nervous energy show. Forcing the adrenaline-induced tremors to appear more pronounced than usual given the circumstances, I still wasn't sure what he was thinking or what he planned to do. "Just because I'm an exotic dancer doesn't mean I turn tricks. That's what those bastards at work think, and that's what..." I shook my head. "That's not something I want to do anymore." Giving him my best damsel in distress look, I begged, "Please, just leave me the hell alone. Don't force me into this. I can't. I can't go back to that. I can't go back to jail. I just...I can't." I let out a loud, pathetic gasp, as if tears might spill at any moment. "My PO's already snooping around. He probably realizes I can't get clean and now this." Gesturing at the sidewalk as if it explained everything, I wiped at my nose and bounced on the balls of my feet.

"Chill," Steele said, and something passed behind his eyes. "Get going. It's fine. They won't bother you again. No one's gonna bother you. Just forget this happened." The way he said those words made the situation feel like a test designed to see how I'd react. Would I offer services for a fee? Call the cops? Or curl into a ball and wait for it to be over? My reaction had been none of those things, and I wondered if I passed. "You're okay. They were just messing around with the new girl in the neighborhood. Don't give it a second thought, chica."

"How am I supposed to do that? They...almost..." I stuttered and shook, clawing at my arms and jacket like I was being attacked by fire ants.

He stepped closer, dropping a tiny baggie into my pocket. "That'll take the edge off. Now go on. You're off limits, and I'll spread it around. Like I told you before, I take care of the people in this neighborhood. You got a problem, just tell them Francisco said to back the fuck off, understand?"

"Ye-yeah," I said, sounding unsure before darting down the street toward the arriving bus. Taking it all the way to the main terminal, I got out and found a restroom, locked the door, and dialed Mark. "We need to meet."

I wanted to go to the federal building, or home, or even to Mark's. But none of those were appropriate meeting places. Instead, I found myself sitting in the back corner of some horrible dive bar near one of the universities. No one from the neighborhood would venture this far out or want to deal with the uppity, barely legal smartasses who thought they knew everything there was to know about the world. God, I was getting old.

Washing up in the tiny restroom, I couldn't manage to shake the look of death warmed over. Lack of sleep could do that to a person, not to mention fending off a group of men who may or may not have planned on committing a violent sexual assault. Burying the thought away, I returned to the bar. As soon as the booth in the back corner became vacant, I slid into the seat, rested my back against the wall, and waited for Mark. He arrived fifteen minutes later, attempting to hide the cheap suit underneath a down jacket and baseball cap.

"You look like an idiot," I said when he sat down.

"And you look like hell." His eyes searched for possible threats or familiar faces. "This isn't how we're supposed to do things. What's going on?"

"Go order us some dinner. This might take a while." I jerked my chin at the bar, and he gave me another cursory glance and went to order whatever was on the menu. The best thing about college bars was they always offered food and cheap beer. He returned a few minutes later with a platter of cheese fries and two longnecks. "Am I off duty?"

"You tell me," he said, taking a swig and pushing the plate across the table.

After shoving a handful of fries into my mouth, I slipped out of my coat and used a napkin to pull the baggie from my pocket. I laid it on the table in front of Mark, and he picked it up with the same level of care, examining the single pill inside.

"I told you not to push for a buy."

"I didn't buy it. If it was cash, I'd call it hush money. But it's not, so I don't know what to call it. Maybe a happy pill to make the horrors go away." My eyes must have shown something disconcerting because Mark suddenly looked uneasy. "I'm okay. Nicholson's still in play. Green lights, baby. Green lights."

"Alex," he watched me uneasily, "what happened?"

Snorting, I picked up another fry and explained the last twenty-four hours in extreme detail. My story ended before the fries did, and I continued to eat while Mark mulled over the ramifications of my words.

"Do you want out? I can pull you."

"No. Frankly, it might have been staged. After my early morning encounter with Steele and his declarations about keeping things in the neighborhood, taking care of the community, and not calling the cops, I think it was a test. It sure as hell seemed like one with the way he appeared and told the guys to get lost."

"Yeah, and maybe he also wants to use you to make some money. And this," Mark pointed to the napkin that was keeping the baggie out of sight, "was just the incentive to get you started." He glanced around the room again to make sure no one was paying any attention to us. "I don't like the fact he searched you for a wire either. What would even make him think you would be wired?"

"He's paranoid."

"Are you sure that's all it is?"

"Perhaps. What does Steele's history look like? Oh, and I need to run through Bard's known associates and the KXDs' lineup again to see who I can pinpoint. Depending on their priors, it might prove that Steele staged it."

"That's a lot of ifs." He stood, going to the bar to get another beer and his order of boneless wings. "You need a partner," he said when he returned.

"No."

"Alex."

"No," I repeated. "That's a deal-breaker, especially now. Francisco's either suspicious or paranoid. He barely trusts me, and he won't trust anyone else who starts hanging around, especially after today."

"Dammit," Mark stabbed a piece of chicken, "this is why I warned you not to approach any of the top dogs. You were supposed to work your way up from the bottom."

"I didn't do it. Didn't you read the report? He approached me. What was I supposed to do?"

Mark rubbed his face. "Fine. Stay away from there until everyone's up to speed and we get the rest of your background solidified. I need to figure out a way to get eyes on you without anyone knowing."

"Okay, just say the word, boss, and I'll go back in."

He was used to my flippant attitude, but he softened. "No one's gonna bat an eye if you want to be pulled. I'll say it was my idea. After all, I'm your handler. The decision falls on me."

"I'm all right. I can take care of a few creeps."

"Are you sure?"

Nodding, I speared one of the wings from his plate, and we ate in silence. When we finished, he closed the tab at the bar, and I put my coat back on and rummaged through my wallet for some cash to cover a taxi home. Whatever drug Steele slipped me would be analyzed by the techs, and I was scheduled to show up to that drafty office building again tomorrow for a more thorough debriefing.

"Can I bum a twenty?" I asked when Mark returned to the table. "All I have are singles, and it annoys the cab drivers when you hand them a fist full of dollars."

"It's the least I can do." He handed over some cash, pocketed the baggie, and jerked his head at the door. "Ladies first. You had a long day."

"Night, Mark," I said, not needing to be told twice.

Exiting the bar, I scanned the vicinity, didn't notice anyone noticing me, hailed a cab, and went home. When I unlocked my front door, the tension left my shoulders, and I relaxed. Alex Parker was safe and sound, and a part of me never wanted to go back to that horrible neighborhood and be Alexia Nicholson ever again. Too bad I still had a job to do.

SEVEN

"Those three," I pointed to the mug shots, "but I don't see the other two."

"It's a start." Jablonsky rummaged through the stack of files for the corresponding rap sheets. "Assault, B&E, armed robbery," he skimmed the pages, "nothing domestic or sexual reported." He met my eyes. "You do realize not everything gets reported."

"True, but I'm choosing to believe they were told to scare the crap out of me. Steele was watching. He wanted to see how I would react."

"Which means either he thinks you're undercover or that you might cause trouble for him and the KXDs in the future."

"Well, now he knows. Plus, if he thought I was a cop, why'd he slip me a little something to take the edge off? Wouldn't I have busted him right then and there?"

"He didn't sell it. It's harder to make a case unless an actual transaction occurs, but I agree. It would be stupid." He pulled another folder from the stack. "That little pill is classified as a Schedule I controlled substance. It's some designer concoction, think some seriously souped-up version of Xanax meets opium. Talk about calm. You'd practically be in a coma."

"Great way to advertise. So when do I make another appearance?"

"Are you sure about this, Parker?"

"Yes, Agent Jablonsky, I'm positive." I narrowed my eyes and lowered my voice in order to prevent the support team from hearing our conversation. "Would you be asking this question if it were someone else, like a full-fledged agent?"

He fought the urge to say something we'd both regret. Instead, he glanced across the room. "Lucca, you got a minute?"

A man I didn't recognize approached the conference table. Clean-shaven, close-cropped hair that screamed military wannabe, and a crisp white shirt underneath a black suit and skinny black tie. Maybe he was the poster boy for the FBI. He practically stood at attention, waiting to be given orders. As I studied him, aghast at the brainwashing and horrified by the thought that's what I used to be like, he glanced in my direction, offering a slight nod and smile.

"Who's the boy scout?" I asked, suspecting this OIO agent was my new partner, despite my protests.

"Eddie Lucca, ma'am. Nice to meet you," he replied in a rehearsed, perfunctory manner.

"Give it time. I'm sure you'll rethink that last statement."

"Parker," Mark snapped, and I took a breath, "he'll be your on-site support. The two of you will never have to interact, but in case you need additional eyes or ears, he'll be positioned close enough to respond within minutes should you need him."

"Fine." Running a hand through my hair, I forgot how horrible it was to be forced to take orders, follow orders, and have no free will in most matters. The private sector ruined me. "Welcome aboard. Sorry about the bitchiness, and fair warning, it happens frequently."

"Lucca's been picking up your reports from the drop site," Jablonsky continued. "He's also been compiling the intel and analyzing the changing trends in the neighborhood. He's up to speed on the key players and pertinent facts."

"Great." I forced myself to stop grimacing at the thought of working closely with another agent. "What's your take on what happened yesterday?"

"Steele's feeling you out," Lucca replied. "He needs to know you're not a plant and you're not a tattle. From what I've read, it seems you handled the situation masterfully. That was unexpected." His right eyebrow twitched slightly, and the corner of his lip trembled, amused by the dig. Apparently, the boy scout could dish it out just as well as he could take it.

"Eddie," someone called from the adjacent room, and Mark dismissed him.

"So I was right, or at least that's what the analyst thinks," I said. "Does that mean I'm going back tonight?"

"Tomorrow morning. I want you to show up after the sun rises and get the hell out before the sun sets. You got that?"

"Yes, sir."

"Your instincts are still some of the best, Parker. But drop the attitude. It'll get you into trouble."

"I'll try." I leaned back in the chair and took a deep breath. "What excuse do I have for my sudden disappearance?"

"If someone asks, you worked through the night and crashed with a friend because you were scared to go home. There's been chatter about an incoming shipment. It sounds like the KXDs are getting a new supply of drugs in the next few days, so we're sending in an exterminator to spray your building and a few of the other apartment buildings in the area. And while we're getting rid of the bugs, warrants have been signed to plant a few of our own."

"Thanks for the heads up. Should I expect another appearance by Nicholson's PO?"

"No. We can't risk tipping off the locals. They don't know we're operating in the area, and I'd like to keep it that way." He slid the stack of documents across the table. "Here's some light reading before you leave."

"Thanks."

I opened the first folder, and Jablonsky left me alone with the reports. By the time I finished reading and memorizing faces, names, and prior convictions, the entire floor had cleared out. The actual agents went back to the federal building, and I was ready to go home.

Since I had an early morning appearance to make, I returned to my apartment, spent several hours working out and practicing basic combinations, ate something healthy, and went to bed. Sleep didn't actually come easily, but I forced myself to remain in bed, mentally reviewing the information I read today. The investigation was still in its infancy. Contact had only barely been made with one of the KXDs, and I couldn't push. Right now, the safest and most reasonable course of action would be to avoid Steele and his minions until he made another approach. Then we'd take it from there.

*   *   *

When I arrived back in the ghetto late the next morning, the sidewalks were practically empty. The snow had stopped, and whatever accumulated had been shoveled into large, dirty heaps. At least it was quiet. My eyes darted around, casting wayward glances at nearby buildings and down side streets and into alleyways, but I didn't spot anyone of interest.

As I entered the building, I offered a slight nod to one of my neighbors who was emptying her mailbox and continued up the steps. Francisco was seated next to my door. At the sound of my footsteps, he tilted his head in my direction and stood up. Based upon the sea of red surrounding his irises, he was probably on something or coming off something. Neither conclusion was particularly comforting.

"Now what do you want?" I leaned against the wall with the doorframe separating us.

"Just making good on my word."

"Didn't you already do that?" I wondered if he expected some show of gratitude. I didn't tase him. That should have been more than enough.

"What's your name, chica?" He already knew. I knew he did. But it didn't hurt to play along.

"Alexia."

He smiled. "I'm Francisco."

"Yeah, you mentioned that yesterday after your friends tried to welcome me to the neighborhood. Kinda funny how you just happened to show up when you did."

"Fortuitous." His eyes drifted from my head to my toes and back again. "You gonna stand in the hallway all day, or are you gonna go inside?"

"I don't invite strange men into my house."

He took a step forward, closing the space between us, but I remained leaning against the wall with my arms folded across my chest. "That's smart, but I'm not a stranger. We just had a lovely introduction, and I did give you a gift yesterday."

"That was some good shit." I exhaled as if relishing in the memory. But he didn't budge, and I didn't want to see how he planned to force the point if I didn't oblige. Thankfully, my purse contained a handgun, courtesy of the federal government. The serial number had been filed off just enough to make it untraceable to the casual observer. "Is that supposed to make us BFFs?" I maneuvered around him to unlock the door.

"I don't know yet. We'll see how things go, chica."

Inside, the place was just how I left it. The surveillance equipment was locked away in a hidden compartment behind the false back of the closet, and the rest of the room looked like a cross between Oscar Madison's apartment and a crack den. He followed me inside, silently taking in the scene before him.

"If you're hoping to collect for the chill pill, I don't have much cash."

"That was on the house." He picked up one of the empty prescription bottles from the floor, reading the patient name, Alexia Nicholson. "Do you still have a hook up?" He held up the bottle.

"No." The bottles were dated six months ago. "After I got pinched, my contact at the clinic cleared out."

"What'd the cops get you on?"

"Tax evasion, just like Capone," I teased. He turned, narrowing his eyes and expecting a real answer. "Possession."

"That's it?"

"With the intent to distribute and felony murder."

"Did you do it?"

"I was there when it happened." I let out a huff and turned away. "Prosecutor wanted blood, but the judge was lenient. Mandatory rehab, a couple stints at a few halfway houses, and parole which led to a job and this place. Minus the random check-ins with my PO, I'm more or less free. Well, just as long as I can continue to find creative ways to pass the drug tests." I spun to face him. "So since this is sharing time, what's your story, Francisco? Fancy yourself as Robin Hood or something?"

"Like I said, I take care of this neighborhood. I grew up here, and we gotta take care of our own. The cops think we're nothing more than lowlifes who deserve to die on the street like a bunch of dogs. They don't help us or respect us. So our crew takes care of things."

"The same way you took care of those guys yesterday?"

"Just watch," he stepped close enough that I could feel his breath on my face and his finger tracing a line from the back of my hand to my shoulder, "they won't hassle you again."

"I hope not." I looked into his eyes. "I wouldn't want to cross you."

He stepped back. "Good. That's the point." He gave the room a final glance and went to the door.

Just as he was turning the knob, I asked, "In case I have another rough day, how much next time?"

"We'll work it out," he met my eyes, "but I'm guessing you might be interested in other stuff, like some H."

"Don't you know it?"

As soon as he left, I went to the door and locked it, shoving one of the chairs underneath the doorknob. Not that it was going to do much, but it made me feel better. I didn't like one of Bard's lieutenants snooping around inside my apartment. And I really didn't like that he decided I was his new pet project. What did he want? At least I laid the right cards on the table. Now it was up to the powers that be to determine what my next course of action was. Things were moving a lot faster than anyone at the OIO intended. And I knew Jablonsky would think it was on account of my doing, but it wasn't. Was something off, or had my luck finally changed?

I took the handgun from my purse and placed it on the counter while I made some instant coffee. Then I took a seat at the table, leaving the gun within reach as I wrote out a report detailing as much of the conversation verbatim as I could remember. Once that was complete, I spent the rest of my time burning daylight by working my way through a few dozen crossword puzzles before calling it quits.

With any luck, the listening devices would be planted soon, and I could return to working evenings and conducting surveillance. It seemed like a better way of spending my time than doing nothing productive to aid in the investigation. When I left, a few familiar faces lingered on the street corner, but no one made a sound or attempted an approach. Circling around the city in a haphazard fashion, I made the drop, went home, listened to a few voicemail messages, and returned Mark's call to assure him I made it home safe and sound. Someone needed to remind him he was my boss because he was overstepping his boundaries, but given our history, I understood why.

EIGHT

The rest of the week was quiet. Not a single person approached me. Steele remained aloof and distant. I spotted him once or twice, lingering near the dumpster or on the front stoop of the building, but he didn't wait outside my apartment. The exterminator came to clear out the infestation and left a few mechanical bugs in their place. While I kept an eye out and continued to conduct surveillance, Cooper and his team ran point at the airports to check on incoming shipments. So far, nothing had panned out, but the word on the street was cross-border shipments supplied the KXDs with drugs. Then the raw materials were cut and mixed locally into some designer product, labeled, and distributed. Drug running was a business just like any other.

"Agent Parker," Jablonsky called, stepping into the conference room, "the rest of your cover is solid." He held out the updated paperwork. "You're waitressing at the Black Cat."

"Thank god. I was afraid you expected me to take center stage on the pole." I skimmed Nicholson's work history. "And for the life of me, I can't figure out how to calculate tips into my taxes, but then again, anything earned while performing a job for the federal government is government property, right? Hell, maybe Congress should pass a bill to employ an entire stripper brigade in order to get the country out of debt."

"Shut it," Mark growled. He wasn't in the mood. "This is your background. No one at the club knows you're undercover. We had to squeeze one of the managers to put you on the books and then make sure he took a nice long vacation. So everyone's in the dark. Make sure you keep it that way since there's speculation Bard owns a lot of the titty bars in the area. And if this is one of his establishments, we don't want to tip him off to the investigation."

"So I'm alone in the lion's den?"

"No, considering the environment, we'll be able to plant other agents on the premises. At the moment, there's an inside man. He's been inserted as a bouncer in case things get too rough, but he's there in a limited capacity."

"What's the play?" I asked, wondering why I needed a fake job to go with my fake apartment.

"Your cover was pinged in a database. The IP traces back to the neighborhood. Apparently, Francisco's been checking up on you. And from what we know about him, it wouldn't be surprising if he shows up at the club to see if you're telling the truth, which means you have to make this convincing."

"He's curious because I haven't approached him to make a buy. The last time we spoke, he asked if I still had a dealer. And I told him no."

"Then it's time you get a fix." Mark shook his head, never expecting those words to come out of his mouth. "Don't screw this up. Don't be arrogant. And don't ask for more than enough to get through the night."

"Okay."

"Why'd it have to be Bard's main guy?" Mark muttered to himself.

I pretended not to notice, instead turning my attention to SAC Cooper. "Any updates?"

"TSA and the DEA are monitoring airports and freight lines. They're reading us in, but so far, no shipments have been confiscated. The DEA's been asking questions.

Apparently, they've decided the FBI investigation into the KXDs might be bigger than they realized, and they were hoping to set up a joint task force," Cooper said, causing Jablonsky to utter a string of expletives.

"How soon do they plan to take over?" I asked.

"Director Kendall is dealing with that mess," Cooper replied. "We've been compromised once. I doubt he'll let another agency risk our security again."

Mark collected the files and went to the door. "I'll find out. If something changes, you'll be the first to know."

"Anything else?" I asked, anxious to mentally prepare for the evening.

"Here," Cooper reached down, grabbing a black tote bag off the adjacent chair, "your work schedule and uniform. Have fun."

"Fair warning, if you mention this to anyone or someone gets confused about how to focus the surveillance cameras and photos get spread around the office, I will hold you personally responsible."

"Agent Parker, I'm nothing but professional." And if those words had come from anyone else, I would have thought they were sarcastic, but Cooper was far too monotone and serious to joke like that. The last time I worked with him, he proved to be a reliable agent, even if I spent many a day inside a conference room, forcing myself not to go into a coma from his discourses.

"Thanks." I stood, unhappy with the new prospect.

"Be careful. If anything goes sideways, call it in. Casualties are not acceptable on my watch. By the way, Parker, it's nice to see those credentials back where they belong."

"Too bad the badge clashes with my new outfit."

*   *   *

The sun set an hour before I ventured back to the apartment complex in one of the shadiest neighborhoods in the city. There was no point in being afraid of the dark. Much scarier things walked these streets, and with any luck, I was one of them. I carried a mini duffel bag which held my clothing for later, my wallet, a wad of cash, and a government-issued firearm. What more could a girl need?

I spotted a few of the guys I encountered the other evening, but there was no sign of Francisco. As I continued past them, no one acknowledged my presence. Apparently, Steele's word was as good as gold. Continuing toward the building, I finally laid eyes on him near the dumpster in the alleyway next to the apartment building. He was whispering to someone in the shadows. Interesting.

Hurrying up the front steps, I burst into the building and ran up numerous flights of stairs to my apartment, unlocked the door, and gave the interior a quick check before rushing to the kitchen window that overlooked the alley. By then, the other man was gone, but Steele was still there.

Taking a deep breath, I put my game face on, grabbed the cash and my keys, and went back down the steps. This time, I emerged slowly from the building. Steele was now speaking to a couple of guys. One of them must have tipped him off to my presence because he turned just as I cleared the few steps from the building to the sidewalk. He turned back to the group briefly, muttered something, and approached me.

"Didn't you just get in?" he asked, eyeing my shoulder as if wondering where my bag went. "Now where are you going?"

"I was hoping I'd run into you," I replied, watching as a few of the men scattered. Two remained, and I suspected they were poised permanently at that position, perhaps to keep tabs on the comings and goings in the neighborhood or to act as spotters in the event there was police activity in the area. "It's been a rough week. I could really use a pick-me-up."

He smiled, his eyes practically closing as he let out a snort and wrapped an arm around my waist, guiding me into the alley. "Step into my office." Once we were out of sight, he backed away, leaning against the edge of the dumpster. "I wondered if you'd reconsidered."

"C'mon, man," I rubbed my face, "I have to be at work in an hour. I just need a hit of something to take the edge off.

Not a lot. Just a little something."

"What'd you have in mind?" he asked, not offering any suggestions. It was too soon to determine if this was because he feared entrapment or if he wasn't a pushy pusher.

"Maybe some H." I reached into my pocket and produced the wad of cash, peeling off the greasy, creased dollar bills one at a time. "Half a gram of powder." I continued to count the money. "Is that a problem?"

"No, but I don't carry things like that on me, and since you're in a rush and a new customer, it's gonna be two." He jerked his chin at the hundred I separated from the rest of the stack.

"Shit." I considered my options. "One fifty."

He sighed heavily. "Fine, but only because I like you." He brushed past me, earning a confused look. "Not here. I'll stop by your place in twenty."

"Do you always do home deliveries?"

"That doesn't matter. I'm doing one now, unless you don't want it."

"I do."

"Good. I'll see ya soon." He left the alley and crossed the street.

Nothing would have made me happier than to follow, but that would jeopardize the operation. Instead, I returned to my apartment, unlocked the door for the second time in the last ten minutes, checked the entirety to make sure nothing damning was in the open, and pulled out another fifty dollars. This would have been better if we could make the deal in the hallway in front of one of the surveillance cameras, but I didn't have enough time to figure out the most logical reason behind a move like that. So instead, I laid my uniform on the bed and pulled out my makeup bag, full of glitter, eyeliner, concealer, and foundation. With any luck, he'd believe I was planning to cover my track marks.

I began applying my makeup while I waited. Ten minutes later, the doorknob turned, and I spun, inching slightly closer to the bag with my gun. Steele entered, shutting the door behind him. Once he was certain we were alone, he held up a tiny baggie.

"Do you have the cash?" he asked.

"It's on the table." I returned to my current task, adding a tremor to my hands. "Dammit." I wiped at the smeared mascara. Abandoning the makeup, I went to the table. "You're a real lifesaver. I hope you know that. And obviously, in more ways than one." Lifting the baggie, I held it up to the light, examining the contents. "Is this as good as that miracle pill from the other day?"

"Sample it if you want." He was distracted by the money. "Is this the cash?"

"Yeah."

"All in one dollar bills?"

"Cash is cash."

He turned, his eyes focused briefly on the mattress, and my mind flittered to the knife I kept tucked underneath in case of emergencies. It never hurt to be prepared. But his eyes were focused on the black sequined triangle bikini top. Maybe he liked shiny things. After pocketing the cash, he glanced at the skimpy outfit again before going to the door.

"Have a good night, Alex."

The door shut, and I froze. My heart hammered in my chest. How had I introduced myself? I was positive I hadn't said Alex, but he had done his research on my cover. Maybe he couldn't read, or he was shortening the Alexia. Wouldn't Lexie make more sense? Calm down. I took a deep breath. There was no reason to jump to conclusions. None. I was out of practice and nervous to be on my own. That was it.

Ready to distance myself from Steele and the neighborhood as soon as possible, I finished my makeup, changed into the black sequined boyshorts and matching top, put my street clothes on over the uniform, slipped the drugs into the hidden compartment of my coat, locked up, and ran for the bus. Arriving seconds before it departed, I slid my transit card through the slot and took a seat in the corner closest to the door.

Near the front was one of the neighborhood regulars, but I made a point not to notice as I leaned back in the seat and jittered my leg and fidgeted for the rest of the ride, hoping to convey some of the typical signs of frequent drug use. It seemed to work well with a couple of older women who casually moved up a few seats to get away from me. Either that or they were offended by the glittery lotion slathered over whatever skin was visible and the ridiculously thick eyeliner I wore. If I were them, I'd probably move away from the skank in the back too.

Tugging on the line, I slid my bag diagonally across my chest and stood, waiting for the bus to stop. The airbrakes squealed and let out an exhale seconds before the doors popped open. Exiting into the cold night, I noticed the punk from the neighborhood get out when I did. Pretending to be oblivious, I went down the street at a fast gait. He followed at a reasonable distance. When I turned left, I saw the neon pink silhouette of a cat. Almost there.

Half a block later, I brushed my hair out of my face, turning just enough to see he was still behind me. Amateur. Continuing the pretense of being oblivious, I went around the side of the building to the employees' entrance and opened the door. One of the agents from the surveillance van stood in the hallway, and I nodded to him, continuing straight to the sign marked 'employees only'. This would have been easier if I had visited this lovely establishment before tonight, but since when did I ever do anything easy?

Finding a locker room full of women, some of whom obviously had rough lives and probably should be wearing a bit more than the required uniform, I found the locker labeled 'Alexia' and stripped down. My co-workers cast questioning looks in my direction. A few scoffed. And one slammed into my back, shoving me face first into the locker. Clearly, I was already making friends.

"Bitch, out of my way."

"Sorry," I muttered, not bothering to turn around.

"What?" she taunted. "You think you're better than us? I've never seen you around here. When'd you get hired?"

"Look," I spun, holding my arms down at my sides but with my palms out, so she'd see the barely blurred track marks, "I'm required to have a job. This is the only one I could find. Do you have a problem with that? 'Cause if you want to start something, we'll start something." I didn't want to start anything, and I hoped she didn't either.

"Whatevs. Your skinny ass won't last here. The manager has a zero tolerance policy."

"Is that so?" I narrowed my eyes, reading the name tag clipped to the top of her shorts. Veronica.

She rolled her eyes, huffing like a steam train and stomping off with more attitude than I'd ever witnessed from anyone firsthand. The door to the locker room slammed shut, and I turned back to the locker, making sure my belongings were secure and palming the baggie of heroin in order to slip it into the miniscule pocket of my shorts without anyone being the wiser. There was no way I was leaving it inside when I was dealing with such a friendly group of people.

"Don't mind, Vee," another woman said. "She's been here the longest and gives everyone hell." The girl smiled and offered her hand. "I'm Sasha."

"Alexia," I replied, studying her, "please tell me you're twenty-one and blessed with amazing genetics."

She laughed. "Twenty-three actually. And thanks." I heard a ding, and the loud music changed. "Gotta go. That's my song." She disappeared, and I realized she was one of the dancers, as if the bright red top and matching thong hadn't been a complete giveaway.

Taking a deep breath, I clipped on my own name tag and followed the narrow hallway out to the main area. The other undercover agent was now stationed at the front door, looking as menacing as the rest of the bored bouncers. Meandering through the closely packed tables, I made it to the bar. The bartender looked up, glanced at my name, and jerked his chin at the opening.

"Welcome. We're not much for training here. So this won't take long," he shouted over the music. "I'll give you a crash course, and then you're on your own." That sounded just about right.

NINE

The rules were simple. Take orders, serve drinks, and don't step in front of someone who is enjoying the show. Pay attention, wait for glasses to be half empty, and then approach to offer another. In most circumstances, make sure the patrons pay as they go. This was a cash-only establishment, and the ATM machine in the corner was busier than the bathroom. The tips were nice; the comments were not.

Gritting my teeth as another drunk slapped my ass, I buried my natural inclination to respond and continued to the bar. Touching was off limits. But most of these pricks didn't seem to care, and neither did the bouncers. I caught the eye of the other undercover agent as I went around the bar, but he wasn't going to jeopardize his cover for something that was nothing more than a pain in the ass. Snorting at the pathetic play on words, I refilled a few glasses and balanced out the tray. I needed a life.

"You ever wait tables before?" the bartender asked. "You're a natural at this."

"Didn't you read my résumé?"

"What résumé? The manager left a note saying he forgot to mention he hired a new waitress and to show you the ropes. You mean to tell me you turned in a résumé with your application?"

"Hell no." I smirked, glad to know what the official line around the gentlemen's club was. "And to answer your question, I did waitress once for a very short amount of time in a place similar to this."

"What happened?"

"Another story for another day."

I placed a new round of drinks at a table of out-of-town businessmen, wondering briefly if Martin ever entertained clients at a place like this. Maybe I'd ask whenever I felt a bit more self-destructive. One of them shoved a few crumpled tens into the side of my shorts while the rest stared slack-jawed at the main stage. Extricating myself from the group, I pulled the money out of my waistband and returned the empty tray to the bar.

The punk from the neighborhood had been lurking at the fringes of the club. He had spent some time leaning against the far wall, sitting at a few of the back tables that weren't in my section, and making frequent trips to the restroom. Apparently, he must have gotten up the nerve to make his move. He went to the bar, taking a seat at the end and swiveling on the stool. Joe, the bartender, immediately went to him and filled a glass from the tap.

Pretending not to notice, I went behind the bar and hopped up on the back counter, crossing my legs rather provocatively considering the boyshorts, and waited for Joe to open the register and cash out my latest table. Hopefully, this would provide plenty of intel for the neighborhood kid to report back to Steele or Bard. *See, the girl who knocked you on your ass is just a junkie stripper wannabe*, my mind screamed in his direction.

"Here," Joe handed back a hefty sum that was my remaining tip from the stack of tens, "did you just give someone a lap dance without me noticing?"

"Maybe," I purred, glancing at the mostly empty section of tables. "How come this place is clearing out so early?"

"Darling, it's after one a.m. We're only open 'til two during the week."

"Time flies when you're having fun." I hopped off the

counter. "I'll start to clean up."

Ten feet from the bar, the punk grabbed my elbow. I jerked away, uttering the management's line about touching and groping. He smiled, holding his hands up. Something sleazy was in his expression, like he wanted to establish dominance and let it be known he could get to me anytime or anywhere, but his words conveyed nothing but apologies.

"I know you from somewhere," I said, narrowing my eyes and playing dumb. He was the man who had been lucky enough to be introduced to my taser.

"Absolutely," he winked, rubbing his fingertips together and watching the transferred concealer blend into his skin. "You should probably hide the bruises a little better. You wouldn't want someone to get the wrong idea and tip off your boss or parole officer, would you?"

Oh, so now he was threatening me. This was an interesting turn of events. Cocking my head to the side, I stepped away from him. "I don't know what you're talking about."

"Yeah, you do." He crinkled his nose playfully and gave a toothy grin. He moved forward, forcing me backward against one of the booths. I remained calm, seeing a few bouncers take notice. His hands came to rest on my hips. "I'd suggest you don't mention any of this to Francisco if you don't want any more problems, chica." Practically spitting the last word, his hands began to travel.

"Sir," one of the bouncers said, grabbing him by the shoulders and pulling him backward, "we're gonna have to ask you to leave. Now."

"I'll see you around." He blew a kiss while two of the bouncers hauled him to the door.

Once he was outside, the other undercover FBI agent approached me. "Everything all right, miss?"

"Hell if I know." Taking a breath, I noticed Joe watching our exchange. "I wouldn't mind eyes on my way out."

"No problem." He returned to his position near the front door.

"Congrats," Joe said when I finished wiping down the empty tables in my section and returned to the bar to wait out the rest of the patrons, "you just popped your cherry."

"Excuse me?"

"First night and already the bouncers had to kick someone out for harassing you. Happens to all the girls. Shit, you don't even hold the record, but the first night is still fairly respectable." He twisted the top off a beer and slid it across the bar. "Cheers."

"Salut," I replied, taking a small sip.

The club closed thirty minutes later, and by 2:30, I was back in the locker room, putting my street clothes on over my uniform. The dancers had already cleared out, and Veronica didn't say another word. As I zipped my coat, I spotted two waitresses divvying up a bag of blue pills and cash. Great. The girls were selling or using ecstasy, probably both. I slammed the locker and went out the back door. That wasn't my problem.

When I hit the street, headlights flashed briefly. Nodding slightly, I continued on my way, knowing that someone had my back. At the bus stop, I pulled out my phone and dialed Jablonsky's burner. His throwaway couldn't be traced, and it held my paranoia at bay by providing an untraceable line of direct communication.

"I have a million things to tell you," I said.

"Can it wait until morning?"

"It'll have to. I can't just stay out all night, can I?"

"No. Go back to the apartment, wait until ten, and we'll meet at the office building around twelve."

Sighing, I disconnected and dialed a cab company. The last bus ran an hour ago, and walking twelve blocks in the freezing cold wasn't on my list of things to do, particularly after being hounded by that punk. When the cab arrived, I climbed in, gave the driver the address, and watched the judgmental look play across his face. *Screw you*, I thought but kept the sentiment to myself.

Arriving outside the apartment, I paid the cabbie, not bothering to give him a decent tip. He squawked at the dirty, crumpled handful of one dollar bills I tossed into the front seat, but his protests remained unanswered. Slamming the door, I wasn't in the mood for games or this bullshit.

One of the two gangbangers stationed near the trashcan let out a choked whistle, like he remembered half a second too late to mind his manners. Glancing down, I noticed my coat was still unzipped from paying the driver, and my shirt had ridden up, giving him a view of my midriff.

"Really? Is it the glitter or the milky white skin that has you so hard up?"

"Why don't you come over here and find out?" He blew a kiss in my direction and made a crude gesture.

"Enough," Francisco bellowed from his usual position in the alleyway next to my building, emerging just far enough onto the street that I could make out his silhouette. "Don't start shit you can't finish, Cesar." The whistler shut up, slinking back into the shadows. Francisco turned to me. "I stuck my neck out for you once, and you said you weren't asking for trouble. This is asking for trouble, so shut your damn mouth and get inside."

I snorted, rolling my eyes. "Yeah, right. You think you have some power over these guys. Sure, fine." I went past him to the door, catching my first glimpse of DeAngelo Bard. Bard leaned against the wall, next to the dumpster. Apparently, they were having a meeting, and I interrupted. "Whatever." Now wasn't the time to mouth off to Francisco, but I already committed to this course of action.

"What the fuck is that supposed to mean?" Francisco chased me up the steps and jerked my arm. He spun me around to face him, pinning me against the doorjamb. It was part of his posturing in front of the boss, and insolence would not be tolerated. If he hit me, it would hurt, and fighting back would make things worse. "Speak, Alexia."

"Nothing." I turned my head, glaring at the ground.

"Dammit, woman, what is your problem?"

"You. Your guys. This shit." I met his eyes. "Let's just pretend this didn't happen. Hell, forget everything about me. I don't need more of your buddies showing up at work and threatening to narc on me or worse. Whatever. It doesn't even matter. I can take care of myself."

His eyebrows arched in confusion, and for the briefest moment, I wasn't positive the punk hadn't followed me on his own accord and not because of Steele's orders. Then

Steele's lips curved into an omniscient smirk.

"You need to work on learning some respect, chica. But obviously, I already have your trust." His fingers trailed from my earlobe to my chin, holding my face steady to maintain my gaze. "Go to bed. You look wrecked."

The man he sent to rattle me at the club was a ruse. But I shouldn't be sharp enough to connect the two, especially at this time of night after my alleged hit of H earlier in the evening, so I shrugged, shaking my head as if trying to make sense of things, and trudged up the steps. Once I cleared the first flight, I picked up the pace, going inside and locking the door. After ensuring the coast was clear, I unlocked the closet, removed the false back, and grabbed the surveillance equipment and directional microphone.

Beneath my window, Steele and Bard were in the midst of a serious discussion. Thank god I arrived home when I did. Some of the words were garbled, but it sounded like the two men were speaking in code. Luckily, it was being recorded, and the powers that be could decipher it in the morning. But a few key facts were easy to discern. A shipment had arrived, and the raw materials were being cut and mixed. That meant the KXDs had a drug den somewhere, perhaps a stash house, and even a lab. After making a mental note to check property titles and request permission to establish additional surveillance to monitor Steele and Bard's movements, I allowed my thoughts to drift back to earlier in the afternoon.

Francisco had gone somewhere close by to pick up the heroin. It was within walking distance and probably guarded. What if the gangbangers near the blazing trashcan were keeping tabs on the entrance to the stash house? That would make sense. Propping the mic on the sill so it pointed at the men below, I shifted around in order to peer out the adjacent window.

From this vantage point, I could see the building across the way. What were the two lookouts monitoring? A few dozen doors, a side street, an alleyway, and steps leading down to a few basements were clearly in view. It really could be anywhere. Or they might be doing nothing more than keeping eyes on the street for signs of police or rival gangs. Picking up a digital camera, I took a few shots of the possible targets then zoomed in, hoping for some graffiti or marking to indicate what property belonged to the KXDs, but I came up empty.

As I scribbled down a few notes, someone pounded against my door. Shit. Francisco and Bard were gone. Silently, I disconnected the surveillance equipment. Just as I grabbed the digital camera and my notes, the banging started again.

"Chica," Steele bellowed.

This wasn't good. Throwing everything into the false back of the closet, I shoved the boards back into place, shut the closet doors, and turned the key, locking the door. Stowing the key underneath the loose tile in the kitchen, I groaned loud enough for him to hear from the hallway and went to the door.

"What?" I asked, leaving the security chain on as I opened the door. "You told me to go to bed. I went to bed. Is that respectful enough for you?"

"Let me in."

"Why should I?"

He held up another baggie, practically identical in size to the one I bought from him earlier, and regardless of how I spun it, there wasn't a chance in hell Alexia wouldn't let him inside when he came bearing gifts like that.

"Fine." Unlocking the door, I stepped away. My mind went to the kit in the bathroom. Inside was a syringe, a spoon, a lighter, and other items common in every heroin addict's arsenal. Underneath all of that was a second syringe filled with saline in the event shooting up was necessary to prove my conviction. God, I hated needles.

"You've been a good girl," he said when the door opened. "I knew the moment I laid eyes on you that you were precisely what I was looking for."

"How much?" I asked, pretending not to notice his running commentary and keeping my mind on a single track.

"We'll work it out."

I licked my lips, as if I could practically taste it, and swallowed. "No. I'm not whoring myself out for a fix. Cash.

That's all I'm offering."

"I'd be lying if I said I didn't want your body but not as a bartering tool. Things get messy that way, and we don't do messy."

"We?" My gaze flicked from the drugs to his face.

"The KXDs."

"Shit," I rubbed my face and stepped away from him, "I didn't realize. I didn't know. Shit."

"Relax, chica. We're what keeps this neighborhood running."

Wow, delusional much? I backed away as if I were still afraid. "What do you want?"

"You'll see." He shook the bag. "But first, let's just enjoy the moment."

TEN

Remaining curled on my side, I fought to keep my breathing slow and deep. Francisco had split the contents of the baggie between us and snorted his share. Electing to cook mine, I had barely managed to distract him long enough to switch the syringes before the euphoria hit and he collapsed onto the bed, pulling me along for the ride. The other syringe containing the drug was now out of sight beneath the air mattress. The good thing about the lightweight bed was the ability to easily shove things underneath it.

Now Steele was pressing against me, his hand tracing the curve of my hip. I made no move to stop him. My mind ran through the defensive options available. The knife was close by. My nine millimeter was inside my bag approximately six feet away, and I wasn't above stabbing the KXD lieutenant in the neck or chest with the unused syringe if the situation warranted such action. Thankfully, he seemed contented enough by the bump to do nothing more than run his fingers over my skin.

"You good?" he asked, spooning me, and I let out an affirmative hum, shifting my legs slightly in the event I needed additional leverage and placing my heel against his shin. He was lit, and that made him unpredictable.

My heart hammered in my chest, and it was a struggle to keep my muscles from tensing. However, in his current state, he didn't seem to notice my internal battle. Time passed slowly, and it felt like hours before he moved or spoke again. He propped himself up on his elbow to observe me, but my face was obscured by my long brown hair. He removed his hand from my hip to brush my hair away and trace the path his fingers took with his lips. I fought the urge to cringe as his mouth pressed against my neck just briefly, and he leaned back.

"Your pulse is racing. Is it a bad trip?" He sounded slightly more sober than he did earlier.

"No," I remained still, afraid he might realize something was amiss, "too much of a good thing today. I need to slow down. Rehab didn't exactly work, but being clean for a while," I let out an exhale, "makes overdosing seem much more likely."

"Have you ever ODed?"

"No."

"I did once. Shakespeare had to drag my ass into the shower. I remember cold water and pain. I've been careful since, making sure to use high-quality shit that's been properly cut and just enough. I'm more of a dabbler now."

"So you don't sample your wares?"

"Occasionally, like now." His hand traveled back to its previous location. "Have you ever moved product?"

"The cops say I did." It wasn't an answer, but it sounded good. "I'm not a mule or a dealer. I've hooked some people up. Friends of friends, y'know. Nothing major."

"You don't deal. You don't hook. And apparently, you don't strip either." The last part sounded accusatory, and I shifted farther from him, closer to my means of protection. "That's the word on the street. You serve drinks at the Black Cat."

"I'm not up to stripper snuff."

His hand came into contact with skin as he slid my shirt up. Underneath was my uniform, but it was still a question of how far I was willing to let this go. When he reached the crook of my elbow, my position didn't allow for him to raise my shirt any higher, so his hand trailed downward.

"I'd say you are." His palm traced my ribs, stopping below them near my back. "You've been shot before." The wonderment in his words made my stomach flip. Apparently, he found this prospect rather delectable, and that wasn't good.

"Like I said, I didn't quite make the cut."

He let out an interested hmm, urging the story onward while his fingers continued to trace my scar. Most people didn't realize what it was on account of its strange appearance, but Francisco Steele wasn't most people. He was in one of the most ruthless gangs in the city, and he recognized what amateur surgery on a GSW looked like.

"A deal went wrong. I was there. Someone got killed. I got hit. My boyfriend cut the bullet out, but it ended up infected. A couple days later, I collapsed and woke up under arrest in the hospital," I said.

"That was the felony murder you told me about?"

"Yeah."

"It sounds like you could have named names and gotten yourself out of trouble." Again, he was testing the waters.

"I would never. This is the life I chose. This is it, waiting tables in my underwear." Laughing as if this was hilarious, I rolled onto my stomach, ensuring the damning items were still beneath the bed. "And it pays for this fabulous apartment and mama's dirty little habits."

"Don't hate yourself. Embrace it," he said in a thick, raspy voice. He grabbed my shoulder, flipping me onto my back and placing his lips to mine. "It led you here. To me."

"Francisco, no." I'd kick him in the groin, then the stomach, then go for the gun. That was my plan, but by some strange turn of events, he backed off, flopping down beside me. "I can't, not after what happened the last time I got involved with my dealer."

"Shootings," he said, as if he understood, "they can be rough. My mom was killed by her loser boyfriend. He was her supplier, but she couldn't pay. And he decided the money was more important than getting some ass." A growl emanated from deep in his throat. "That asshole told me with enough cash, ass was free, and even with a little cash, you could buy some fine ass. And then I blew his brains against the wall." Steele shrugged. "That just goes to show, money ain't everything."

Swallowing, I didn't react, but the federal agent instinct was at odds with my undercover persona over this revelation. Part of me wanted to arrest him, but the other part knew this was just the tip of the iceberg.

"How old were you?"

"Fourteen." He laughed. "Stupid motherfucker." Considering my options and the point of this mission, I reached for his hand and gave it a supportive squeeze. "You're crazy, chica, if that doesn't scare you."

"You've come to my rescue. I don't think you'd kill me. But I am afraid of what you expect in return."

"The first time we met, I told you I wouldn't take advantage. And I meant it." His voice was harsh. "But I could use you to run drugs at the club. The business is expanding, but not everyone got the message. Other gangs have been encroaching on our territory. It's time we make a stand and take back what's ours, starting with the clubs."

"And I work at a titty bar." Whichever analyst picked this club ought to get a bonus and a few extra vacation days because damn he was good. "How do you know you can trust me not to sample the product or take off with the cash?"

"Because I've been watching you since the moment you stepped foot in this neighborhood. And who's taken care of your problems?" He smiled. "Plus," his hand released mine, tracing the airbrushing on my inner arm, "your tastes seem much harder and more singular than what you'd be selling. I'll keep you supplied in exchange for your services. It's a quid pro quo."

"What about that creep who threatened me tonight?" Before I could launch into an explanation, Francisco waved my concern away, snickering at the melodrama.

"I sent Vega to the club to scare you. I needed to know you would come to me for help, and you did." He shifted onto his side. "I'm gonna crash here. I have places to be in a couple of hours, and all this business talk wasted a good deal of my high." It wasn't a question, and I turned away from him. Without asking permission, he scooted closer until my back was against his chest, and he remained still for the next few hours, letting out contented mumbling sounds while I fought to remain calm and appear asleep.

As soon as dawn broke, he stumbled into the bathroom. Not wasting a moment, I took the full syringe and shoved it inside my bag. Grabbing the hand sanitizer from my purse, I dispensed some onto my fingertips and rubbed both of my bottom eyelids. Immediately, my eyes stung from the burning alcohol. At least my pupils would be swimming in a sea of red. And with any luck, I wouldn't go blind. Then I went back to bed.

When Francisco emerged, I sat up. "When?" I croaked, making my voice gravellier than it already was. "When do you expect me to start moving product?"

"Soon. First, you'll have to meet someone. Give me your digits?"

"Sure." I rambled off the number for my burner phone, and he input the information into his device.

"I'll be in touch." He leaned down, grasping a fistful of hair at the base of my neck and tugging so I was forced to look up at him. "Are you coming down hard?"

"Not too bad."

"Okay. If you need something, I'll be around."

After he left, I locked the door and went to the sink to rinse my eyes. I really didn't want to go through that again. I glanced at the mattress, and my stomach flipped. Though that was the most anticlimactic reaction I could have had considering I spent the night cuddled up against a self-professed killer and known drug dealer and gangbanger. What did I get myself into this time?

I peered out the windows for signs of illegal activity. The streets were clear, so I tidied up the apartment, sealing the drugs into a larger plastic bag and hiding them inside the ripped lining of my coat. Then I went to the closet, took out the surveillance tapes, memory cards, and notes from last night, finished writing my report, and waited impatiently for ten o'clock. The sooner I could get away, the safer I'd feel. But Steele confirmed something else last night. He had been watching since the beginning, which meant my movements were probably being monitored now. I'd have to be careful and even more cautious because he'd end me without blinking an eye, despite his misplaced affection.

Once the coast was clear, I left the apartment, taking a convoluted route involving numerous transfers to the rented office building. Sneaking in the side door, I went up the steps, listening to the echo of my footfalls in the cinderblock stairwell. Opening the door, I was greeted by the sight of perfectly coifed agents in suits and ties. A few gave me a second glance, probably thinking some homeless woman wandered in off the street.

Returning a few good mornings in a gruff fashion, I went down the corridor and let myself into Mark's temporary office. He wasn't here yet, and that brought my frustration and exhaustion to the forefront. Without thinking, I slammed the door, shed my coat, placed the evidence and surveillance on his desk, and found my go-bag underneath his desk. While I was in the process of stripping out of my attire, the door opened.

"Don't you ever knock?" I asked, not turning around as I slipped a hooded sweatshirt over my naked torso. "If I had been facing the door, things between us could have gotten awkward real fast."

"It's my office. Why are you changing in here? The bathroom is just down the hall."

"Because it seemed like a brilliant idea. Almost as brilliant as agreeing to come back to work at the OIO." Once I was appropriately covered, I turned to face him. "In case you haven't figured this out yet, I'm just bursting with brilliant ideas."

"What happened?"

"It'd be easier to ask what didn't happen?" I paced back and forth while he picked up the plastic bag on his desk.

"You made a second buy?" He held up the syringe containing the cooked heroin and the untouched baggie of powder.

"No, just the one, but Steele showed up with another free taste. He wants me to move product at the strip club in exchange for a steady fix. He also sent that loser to spook me."

"I heard about that from Agent Wolfe, our undercover

bouncer." Jablonsky narrowed his eyes, skimming the details of my report while I filled him in on everything that transpired. "I'm only asking this as your supervisor because I'm required to make a note in my report. Did you shoot up?"

"Only saline."

He watched as I paced. "Submit to a drug test before you leave today."

"Mark," I protested, but he held up his hand.

"It's policy. You have a probationary status, and because of that psychopath who dosed you that one time, there's a note in your file. You know this. And I know you, but it won't help our case if some defense attorney decides to question any of your findings. And I don't want some AUSA chewing me out because of it."

"Yes, sir."

His eyes shifted to the closed door. "Off the record, what's wrong?" We'd spent years working together. And he could read my body language and facial expressions better than anyone.

"I spent the night with Francisco Steele." I could still feel his hand on my hip. "He's extreme and unpredictable. And for whatever the reason, he likes me. We need a full workup. I want property records, financials, taxes, his rap sheet and juvie record, everything we have."

"Does he pose a threat?"

"To the op? Or to me?"

"Both."

"For now, I've earned his trust. He wants to use me, and I think I can convince him that he needs me. But if my cover gets compromised, he won't think twice before sanitizing the situation."

"No wonder you're so keyed up. Are you sure you have this under control?"

"I hope so." I stopped pacing, no longer able to evade the thought that had been haunting me since Francisco showed up at my door last night. "But I can't go home. I have to stay there and commit to Alexia Nicholson if there's any chance of infiltrating the KXDs."

"Alex," the way he said my name was a dead giveaway I

was right, "you can use my phone. Take a minute while I get the rest of the team up to speed."

"Thanks."

ELEVEN

The only person I called was Martin, and he was in a board meeting and couldn't be disturbed. After hanging up, I dialed his home phone and left a message, telling him I loved him and I was working and wouldn't be stopping by for a while. It was vague, but none of the lies I came up with sounded feasible. Pressing end call, I wondered if he'd be suspicious about the unfamiliar number on the caller ID. Oh well, Mark would just have to deal with that issue.

Detouring to the ladies' room, I found my reflection in the mirror shocking. I really did resemble some strung-out junkie. No wonder Francisco was convinced. If I didn't know me, I would have thought I was using too. Failing to pull off some semblance of professionalism, I gave up the struggle and went down the hall to the conference room.

"Parker," Cooper greeted, "here's your packet." He held out a zippered bag containing ID, a few credit cards, a gym membership, locker combination, and a motel room key. Each of the items was registered to Alexia Nicholson. "I didn't realize you would be needing this so quickly."

"Neither did I." I held up the gym membership. "Are you trying to tell me I have no business parading around in my underwear? Because I wholeheartedly agree."

"It's a safer location for our dead drop. The KXDs won't be able to follow you inside. You can leave reports and evidence in the locker, and we'll send another agent to collect them," Cooper said.

"Plus, it's obvious you keep in shape. Steele wouldn't have any reason to be suspicious," Jablonsky added. "The motel key is for your sanity. If it gets to be too much, you can hide out for a couple of hours. Hell, I'll send another UC to keep you company, and you could say you're having an affair with a married man or something."

"Leave the adlibbing to me." I sighed. "I'd like to pick up a few things from home, but I'm not sure I want to risk it."

"Buy whatever you need," Cooper insisted, nodding at the credit card. "And after today, limit your appearances at this office building. Worst case, we'll send someone to meet you at the gym or motel if you need a face-to-face."

"This is really happening." This wasn't supposed to happen, particularly not within the first few weeks.

"Are you positive you can handle this, Agent Parker?" Cooper asked, interrupting whatever Mark was about to say.

I nodded. This was the job. And I knew how to do it. The only problem was I didn't want to be in deep cover.

"Then let's get to it," Jablonsky said, ushering a tech inside to administer my drug test before the team was brought up to speed on recent developments and Francisco Steele's history.

Francisco Steele's name was on half a dozen apartment leases in the neighborhood, but he didn't have a set address listed anywhere. On paper, he had a day job as a bike messenger. It served as the perfect cover for drop-offs and pick-ups for his illegal exchanges. It also explained how he tended to loiter around at all hours of the day and night.

But that was only part of Francisco Steele's paper trail. Before Steele turned eighteen, he was accused of murder, armed robbery, aggravated assault, and possession, but not everything stuck. He spent a few years in juvie, from the time he was fourteen to eighteen. His lack of parental guidance, the extreme circumstances surrounding his mother's murder, and his age at the time must have influenced the judge who gave him a slightly easier way out. But once he turned eighteen, Steele returned to the neighborhood and was forced to find ways to fend for himself with nothing more than a GED and a history of violent crimes.

Six months later, Steele was arrested and brought up on possession with the intent to distribute. The charges were dropped, and he continued to be a frequent flyer in the court system. His sentences ranged from a few months to a couple of years. Amazingly, he avoided three strikes sentencing due to jurisdiction and changing legislation. The lucky bastard managed to benefit from ex post facto.

"When did he start running with the KXDs?" I asked, tired of reading through the extensive court proceedings.

"Realistically, I'd say it started after his mother was killed. Francisco Steele needed a family for protection, so he sought out the only other family he ever knew, the gangs," Agent Lucca said. "At the time, Bard was in the process of creating the KXDs which explains how Steele became so highly placed among the rank and file. Timing is everything."

"Steele was there from the get-go. He was just some badass kid with a huge chip on his shoulder and a lot to prove. And frankly, he had absolutely nothing left to lose," I said, realizing it explained the reason Francisco was who he was.

"Parker," Jablonsky said my name sharply, "you can't manipulate someone like that."

"Wanna bet?" But manipulation wasn't my intention. Turning Steele wasn't possible. He was loyal to Bard and the KXDs. Even if it were possible to sow some seeds of distrust, he wouldn't see a conspiracy surrounding him. He'd simply excise the malignant members of the gang and stop the cancer from infecting the rest of the KXDs. That's why infiltration was so dangerous. "Francisco's not our weak link, but someone has to be. What do we have on the unidentified man we ran through facial rec?"

"Lyndon Khary," Lucca said, grabbing a folder from the bottom of the stack and opening it so the four of us could see it, "real estate developer. He owns four of the six apartment buildings in that neighborhood."

"He's a slum lord," Cooper said. "Originally, he was on our radar, but we never had him under surveillance, nor did we observe him in proximity to any of the KXDs."

"Either he's getting sloppy, or he's not involved," Jablonsky said.

"They keep a supply somewhere nearby. Steele doesn't carry enough product on him because he fears the potential ramifications if he were caught," I pointed out.

"We're looking into property records, but we have a problem. At last count, there were over thirty members in the KXDs, not counting the new recruits and wannabes. Each of them has at least one apartment. Bard has his own business, and he has partners and associates that we still aren't aware of," Lucca said.

"Which means you don't know where to look," I said.

"That's precisely why we've had an agent monitoring the situation for several months," Cooper snapped, agitated by the wasted time and nearly scrapped operation. "It's why you have to get close to Bard."

"Yes, sir."

We spent the next couple of hours reviewing the intel, my changing role, and the way the new drop site and interaction with the OIO would work. Whenever my gym membership card was scanned, an agent would arrive, provide some cover surveillance, and procure whatever I left in the locker once I cleared the area. Every night I went to work at the club, someone would be there to keep tabs on me and the situation. It was nice to know there was backup, but it didn't alleviate any of the issues at the apartment.

After hashing out the finer nuances, Lucca and Cooper vacated the conference room, heading back to FBI HQ to update Director Kendall on recent developments, submit requisition forms, and gain approval for the additional manpower needed to ensure my safety and the sanctity of the operation. Giving the files a final glance, I leaned back in the chair and shut my eyes. Maybe Mark would let me stay in the office building for a few hours to sleep. That would be the most challenging part of this mess, achieving the optimal level of comfort and exhaustion to sleep in that roach infested hovel while gang members dealt drugs a few feet from my front door. Yeah, that really wasn't going to work. And I thought I had insomnia before. Ha.

"Alex," Jablonsky lowered his voice, even though we were alone, "do whatever you have to in order to stay safe. I don't care what it is. We will deal with the aftermath later."

"Mark," I opened my eyes and looked at him, "I'll be fine. I'm not about to shoot up or screw Francisco's brains out in order to stay that way." A thought crossed my mind, and I grabbed a sheet of paper and pen. After scribbling down a few words, I folded the paper, stuck it inside one of the empty manila envelopes, and sealed it. "But just in case, give this to Martin if I don't make it back."

"What did I just say?"

"Don't worry. There's no reason in this world why this will ever be opened." I shrugged. "It's like insurance. You pay for it, but it's not because you plan to use it. Basically, you're just throwing money at some nameless, faceless corporation in case the what ifs happen."

"So now I'm nameless and faceless?"

"You have to be in order to watch my back."

* * *

The rest of the week was hell. Maybe it was more than a week. I couldn't remember. I'd barely slept in far too many days to even count. My routine was simple. Go to the apartment, conduct surveillance, stop by the gym, leave the reports and corresponding feed in the locker, go to the strip club and silently observe a few members of the KXDs scattered throughout, then head back to the apartment.

Francisco's promise of an introduction had fallen to the wayside. There was no reason for him to doubt the veracity of my cover, but he was standoffish after the night he spent inside my apartment. Then he practically disappeared. When I searched for him outside, I didn't see him, and since he didn't give me his phone number, I had to wait for him to make the first move.

By now, Nicholson should have been dying for a fix. And I was dying for a reprieve. It was Tuesday morning. I'd returned from another night at the Black Cat on the verge of giving in to my irrational, homicidal thoughts. If one more disgusting excuse for a man slapped my ass, I would kill him. It was time for a break. I grabbed my belongings; the sun wasn't even up when I left the apartment, entered a waiting cab, and went to the motel.

The room key unlocked a door on the third floor, and after performing my due diligence to check outside for signs of a tail and inside for any malicious tampering, I flopped onto the bed. Even now, sleep was elusive, but within an hour, I conked out. And when I opened my eyes again, the sun was just setting. It was obvious I couldn't do this much longer.

After cautioning another glance outside, I picked up the burner and dialed Mark's disposable. He picked up, and I gave him my location and expounded on my frustration at Francisco's disappearance. He offered to check with the police and hospitals to see if Steele had been arrested or admitted. With no other angles to work, I stayed at the motel for another hour, watching mindless television and decompressing. When it was time to leave, I changed into my Black Cat getup and called another cab.

Arriving at the strip joint, I went in the back, changed in the locker room, noting the hard stares and angry glares traveling in my direction. Having no idea what caused the sudden hostility, I ignored it as long as I could, but when Veronica walked in, barking at the others to leave, I had no choice but to react.

"What the hell is your problem?" I asked. Luckily for her, I was well-rested. If I wasn't, we'd be exchanging more than heated words.

"You moved in on my territory, and you need to learn your place."

"What the fuck are you talking about?"

"Francisco."

"What about Francisco?" How did she even know Francisco or about my connection to him?

She stomped forward, invading my personal space and

backing me against the lockers. Striking out wouldn't be conducive to getting my questions answered and would likely result in me being fired. And strangely enough, I needed this job, or at least Alexia did. Instead, I held her gaze and my tongue. She grabbed my arm and yanked it up.

"I got myself clean, but instead, he wants another dirty crack whore to do his bidding." She scowled, baring her teeth. "The asshole says he can't trust someone who doesn't use what they sell. But truth be told, it's because he doesn't have power over me, and he knows it. He can't control me anymore." Despite her empowered words, she was pissed I replaced her. "I'd give it a month before he turns you out on the streets." She sneered. "And I'm gonna laugh my ass off when that happens."

Shoving her backward, I turned back to my locker. "You're crazy. He would never do something like that." I slammed the door shut and spun to face her. "And how the hell do you know anything about him or me?"

She slapped me, losing one of her fake acrylic nails in the process. "You don't get it. But you will. And you'll regret it."

TWELVE

When I exited the locker room, my eyes were immediately drawn to Francisco. He was alone in a round booth near the back corner. On the table sat a few empty shot glasses, but he seemed far too serious for someone who should be enjoying a moderate level of nudity. His appearance also explained Veronica's sudden hostility. Her shift started two hours before mine. Whatever he said to her must have struck a nerve. However, I still couldn't determine their connection.

Nodding hello to Joe, I headed straight to Francisco. His eyes remained focused on the center stage, and he didn't bother to look at me until I was next to him. He shifted in the booth, scooting sideways.

"Where've you been?" I asked, sounding annoyed.

"Around." His eyes continued to dart from the stage to me and back again. "So this is where you disappear every night?" He made a wide gesture, encompassing the room.

"It pays the bills. Well, the tips pay the bills."

"But you don't dance." His eyes studied me for a few moments. "So how much money in tips does a waitress make?"

"Depends on the night. Around a hundred, sometimes

two."

He nodded, sliding out of the booth. He stood up, lingering close but not quite touching me. "I can cover that and your expensive habit. Remember what we talked about?"

"Uh-huh. What do you want me to do? And what does any of this have to do with Veronica?"

He snickered. "Damn, that woman has a big mouth. What'd she say to you?"

"She said I'd regret this."

His hand ran up my side. "Have you regretted anything so far?"

"No."

"Good. I'll be at your place tonight when you get home. Get cleaned up before you leave here. There's someone you need to impress." Without another word or hint as to what was going to happen later, he dropped a thick stack of dollars on the table and went to the door.

As soon as he left, I scooped up the money, realizing it was the same stack I used to pay for the heroin. The undercover agent acting as a bouncer caught my eye, and I hoped to convey my utter confusion with a fleeting glance. He moved off to the side and spoke briefly with one of the Black Cat's patrons, yet another agent. The good news was we had plenty of eyes inside, but the bad news was Steele was no longer on the premises.

An hour into my shift, Veronica went home. She claimed to have a migraine, but I didn't believe it. More importantly, I still couldn't pinpoint the connection between her and Francisco. This seemed like something Agent Lucca or another one of the analysts should have determined, but no one knew anything, unless they just didn't bother to share that intel with me. The sooner we could connect this club to the KXDs, the better off we'd be. From what Francisco led me to believe, the KXDs wanted to expand and sell out of the clubs and titty bars, but some other entity had taken over or tried to. Since I currently lacked government resources, I would have to get creative and use the other means at my disposal to piece things together.

"She seriously bitch slapped you?" Joe asked as I sat on the back counter behind the bar, wallowing in self-pity. Realistically, I was scoping out the clientele and keeping the handsier patrons from pawing at me. At least two punks from the neighborhood were at the Black Cat, and I assumed it was so Francisco could keep tabs on me. Thankfully, I wasn't stupid enough to jeopardize my cover that easily. "Dude," his eyes lit up, "that's like every guy's fantasy. Two strippers going at it."

"First, I'm not a stripper. And second, I don't think a slap fest is what comes to mind when they think of two girls going at it."

"Fine. But still, it'd be a main event to have two women fighting in their underwear. I could sell tickets." My eyes narrowed, and he smiled. "Shit, I'd referee too. Don't worry. There'd be no hitting below the belt or in that general boyshort region."

When I first met Joe, something seemed off about him, and it had taken a night or two before I realized he was playing for the other team. He wasn't exactly in the closet, but he probably wanted to downplay his own sexuality in this type of environment. I didn't blame him. I was in the midst of perpetrating my own deception.

"So do I actually have something to worry about?" I asked, shifting the conversation back to serious. During my rendition of what occurred, I left out most of the key details, but maybe he'd still have something to spill on Francisco Steele.

"Vee's all bark and no bite from what I hear. But she's accusing you of stealing her man, so that could make her claws come out."

"Have you ever seen her with anyone? We're told to flirt, but I never noticed her spending extra time with anyone special."

"She does her job the same as you. I don't follow the gossip much. The dancers have a lot of stories to tell, but typically, there aren't that many tales from the waitresses, aside from the occasional lap dance or drunk manhandling them. You've been here long enough to know how it is."

"Yeah." The question on my mind wasn't one I should

be asking, but I couldn't help it. "Hey, Joe, have you ever heard about anyone dealing out of the club?"

His eyes shot up, and the look on his face said he did. "No," he replied forcefully. "And you don't know anything about that either, understand?"

"Not in the least, but I'll take your word for it."

"You better." His tone was cautionary, not threatening. "Bad things happen occasionally. My advice is to keep your nose clean and mind your own business."

"Does Veronica listen to your advice?"

"No, but she should have." He placed a tray of drinks on the counter. "Now get back to work, Alexia. I'd hate to have to call the manager and tell him the newest hire isn't pulling her weight around here." He offered his hand, helping me down from the counter. I picked up the tray, and Joe smacked my butt, earning a round of whistles from the men at the bar. He smirked in an attempt to lighten the mood when I turned to give him my best drop dead look.

The next few hours flew by in a mess of glitter, cash, and booze. Unfortunately, nothing useful was gained concerning the KXDs, Veronica, or whatever it was Joe wasn't saying. When I went to cash out for the night, Joe kept busy to avoid further conversation, and I had no choice but to let the matter drop. He didn't want to talk about the drugs running in and out of the club, and pushing too hard would make someone suspicious.

Returning to the locker room, I was layering up in preparation for the bitter cold when Sasha entered. She took a seat on the bench next to me and hiked up her leg to undo the strap on her stiletto. On the seat between us, she laid a hefty stack of cash.

"Looks like you had a good night," I said.

"Depends on your definition, but a few hundred for a half hour in the private room isn't too shabby." She dropped a shoe to the ground and repeated the process with the other. "I heard something about you and Vee getting into it again today."

"Apparently, I've stolen her man or some shit like that. Who knows?"

"Francisco?" She tilted her head, indicating she already

heard the story. "It's a small club. Word gets around." She stood, opening her locker and pulling out a sweatshirt and leggings. "Just be careful."

"Veronica doesn't scare me."

"That's not who you should be afraid of." She closed the door. "I'll see you tomorrow. Night, Alexia."

"Night."

Okay, what the hell was going on? I sent a brief encoded text to Mark's burner with information on my impending meet and a request for backgrounds on every Black Cat employee. Things weren't what they appeared. And I didn't know if I was the only one in the dark or if we were all fumbling around blind.

When I arrived home, there was no sign of Steele. The usual gangbangers were still at the corner, but they pretended I didn't exist. So I returned the favor. Once inside, I changed into a sweatshirt and jeans. It wasn't impressive, but Nicholson's closet only consisted of two styles – lounge and party wear.

The sudden rapping at the door made me jump. It was followed by Steele's voice requesting that I open up. When I complied, he looked anxious.

"Grab your keys. We're going," he insisted.

"What? Where?"

"Keys." He reached inside and snatched them off the table, flipping the lock, and grabbing my arm.

I barely managed to grab a hold of my parka on the way out; everything of any use was still inside the apartment. The hollowed out lining was empty. My cell was inside my purse with my arsenal of self-defense tools. Right now, backup and a support team would have been a reassurance. Why was I so stubborn?

I didn't like being unprepared. The fact that my nine millimeter was inside my locked apartment made my stomach clench, but Francisco didn't hear any of my protests or questions as he dragged me out of the apartment building and into the frigid night. A half a block later, he came to an abrupt halt and released his grip on my arm.

The street was empty. "Am I missing something,

y'know, besides my purse and phone and everything?"

"Listen," his voice was low and gravelly, "don't mouth off inside. Shakespeare likes respect and silence. Do what he says."

"Shakespeare? Seriously? What kind of name is that?"

"It's a nickname. And that's exactly what I'm talking about. Quiet, got it?"

I pantomimed zipping my lip and throwing away the key. So I was getting to meet Bard for the first time completely outmanned and outgunned. This wasn't what I envisioned happening. Francisco snorted in amusement and wrapped an arm around my shoulders. Opening the latch on a metal gate, he led us down a walkway to a hidden staircase. Two gang members were stationed near the stairs, and another stood in front of the doorway to the basement apartment.

"Yo, Steele," the one at the door said, bouncing slightly, "you gotta stop by, man. I just got number six, and damn, we be blowing some shit up."

"Yeah, later," Steele said. "Maybe you need to ease up on the caffeine chasers."

The guard laughed hysterically. Based on the way he looked, I'd guess his heart would probably give out within the year from too much speed, but I wasn't a doctor. And my current concern was aimed more toward discovering exactly what was being blown up. Making a mental note to question Francisco about it later, I followed him into the darkened basement, colliding against his back when he came to an abrupt stop.

He chuckled. "Afraid of the dark, chica?"

"I'm only afraid of what happens in the dark."

"Good answer," a voice said from a few feet away, and a second later, the lights clicked on. DeAngelo Bard sat in a chair in the middle of the living room. Another man stood silently in the corner. From what I gathered, the rest of the apartment extended outward from the two doorways to the left and right of the fireplace. "So this is your solution?" Bard asked Steele, who had stepped away and was now blocking the opening to the foyer. "She doesn't look like much."

"She has an attitude problem, but we can use her," Steele said.

Being trapped and unarmed caused a feeling of nakedness and claustrophobia to settle in the pit of my stomach. But I wouldn't show fear. Instead, I assessed the room, Bard's minions, and glanced uneasily at the automatic weapon sitting atop the mantle. There were ways out, but escape wouldn't be easy.

Bard got out of the chair and approached. He smelled of aftershave, metal, and something chemical and toxic. "My boy says you can fight," he said, circling. "Why's that?"

"Have you ever walked around the neighborhood in nothing but stripper heels and a trench coat? It leads to plenty of unwanted attention. A girl needs to be able to take care of herself."

"Or maybe you should just wear something underneath the coat." His eyes blazed. "Do you have anything under that jacket?" I unzipped, letting my parka fall open. It was hot inside on account of the fireplace. "Damn, I was hoping." His gaze darted off to the side, and Steele pulled the coat free from my arms and handed it to Bard's minion who checked the pockets and lining. For the first time, I was thankful there was nothing hidden inside. "Now take off your sweatshirt."

"Excuse me?"

"It's either this or being submerged in the bathtub. You decide."

"What? You think I'm wearing a wire? Are you insane?"

"Alex," Steele whispered huskily, "do what he says."

"Fine." I pulled the sweatshirt over my head, and Bard made a circle with his finger, indicating that I spin. "I feel like I'm modeling. Are you planning to take a few glamour shots too?"

"Just like you said." Bard spoke to Steele as if I were an inanimate object. "That scar looks pretty nasty, and that feistiness could lead to unwanted attention. You're taking on the risk, Francisco. You got me? I'm not shouldering your blowback this time."

"No sweat, Shakespeare. I can handle her," Steele said.

"What about the other one? She started causing trouble

and tried to jam you up. How are you taking care of that?" Bard asked. "Because I'm not dealing with it when your whiny ass comes back here, looking for help."

"Already handled," Steele said, watching as the other KXD member yanked some stuffing from the rip in my coat. "Are you finished playing with that, Seth?"

Bard nodded, and the man shoved the stuffing back in place and handed my coat to Francisco. "When's the last time you used?" Bard asked me, studying the faded bruise patterns on my arms.

"A few days." Mentally, I made certain to keep the level of fidgeting the same so as not to tip him off that it was only due to the power of suggestion. "Francisco disappeared, so I had to wait longer than I wanted."

"You must be pretty hard up for a hit." Bard went to the coffee table and picked up a packet. Licking my lips, I focused on the item like it was a million dollars. How the hell was I going to make this look convincing? Thoughts ran through my head, and the only thing I could come up with was a little ridiculous. "How 'bout I cook it up for you?"

"I don't use strange needles. My kit's at my place. I would have brought it if Francisco told me."

"Too bad. Make an exception." Bard was not one to be argued with.

"If it's pure enough, I'll snort it." My only option was the straw trick, but I hadn't practiced it that much. If I didn't pinch at the right time, I'd either end up inhaling that shit or Bard would realize it was a ploy. But it was the only thing I could do.

"Excellent." Bard dropped a small pad of paper on the table next to the drugs. "Sorry, but I don't trust you with a rolled up hundred. Too many people have sticky fingers."

Laughing, I went to the table and knelt down. "So what's this costing me?"

"Francisco covered it. You'll work that out with him." Bard's words were ominous, and I cocked my head up at Francisco as I unzipped the baggie and dropped the powder on the table. Bard smiled. "Are you that anxious with everything?"

Ignoring him, I took the edge of the paper and made a neat line. Then I tore off the top sheet and started rolling it into a tight tube. My heart rate kicked up three notches, and my mind ran through the possibility of getting out of this room alive if I didn't continue with the ruse. The odds of that weren't great. My life, career, and the crux of this case rested on a sheet of paper and my ability to create a temporary vacuum within the makeshift straw. Everything might be over in the blink of an eye.

"Cheers." I bent down, letting my long hair obscure my actions from view. Tilt, inhale, pinch. *Don't try this at home, kids*, the sarcastic voice in my head said as I leaned back, dropping the paper to the floor and rubbing the back of my hand against my nose. Something burned, and panic shot through me. How much did I accidentally snort? It was imperative I play it off, and I shut my eyes and let my head fall back. Tilting forward, I made sure the powder that collected in the paper was dispersed into the carpet, and I swept my knee over it to grind it deeper into the fibers as I struggled to stand up, intentionally wobbly. "Damn," I exhaled, keeping my eyes partially closed to help my pupils appear to be dilating.

"You passed. Now get dressed and get out," Bard commanded. Tugging on my sweatshirt, I intentionally lost balance and slumped against Francisco who offered my parka and put a hand on my back to guide me to the door. "And Alexia, if I regret this, you will too."

What was up with people and making threats tonight? Sheesh.

THIRTEEN

"Your blood work came back clean," Mark said, and I exhaled a sigh of relief. "Any particular reason you wanted another drug screening so soon?"

I didn't tell Mark exactly what happened at the meeting with Bard since he was a supervisory agent and needed plausible deniability. Instead, I gave him the condensed version and focused on my ever-changing position of favor with Francisco. After leaving Bard's, Steele came back to my place, and I spent the rest of the night in a faked euphoria while he spoke about dealing ecstasy out of the strip joint.

"I'm in close proximity to a lot of this shit. It's best to make sure I'm clean and not accidentally getting high off residuals. Plus," I rolled up my sleeves, "if we keep this up, I won't need those tattoo artists to airbrush the bruises and lines anymore." Checking the time, I sat on the bed and pulled my legs to my chest. There was no reason to pace when I'd be spending the rest of the night walking around in stripper heels while serving drinks. "It looks like I'm an honorary member of the KXDs. Alexia Nicholson, low-level dealer at your service."

"When is he giving you the product?"

"He's bringing it by the club tonight. We're planning on doing a handoff in one of the private rooms. He said it wouldn't be more than what I can move in one evening, but he didn't say exactly how much that is."

"I'm not fond of his vague attitude." Rubbing his face, Jablonsky flipped through a few pages of notes the analysts had given him. "You said you spotted a couple of the girls dealing already. Are they working for the KXDs?"

"I don't know. What did their profiles say? The only one who admitted to having a connection with Francisco was Veronica, and clearly, she's never been my biggest fan. She was adamantly opposed to my alleged drug use, but last night, she let the cat out of the bag about her former addiction."

"We're still digging for deeper connections, but the majority of the dancers have records for solicitation and possession. Lucca is still looking, and Cooper is reviewing the files. But none of the girls have connections to the KXDs or the neighborhood that we've found."

"So what's the link between Francisco and Veronica?" I asked, even though he didn't know.

"Your guess is as good as mine, but maybe you should just ask."

"Might as well." I took an uneasy breath. "Am I seriously distributing narcotics tonight?"

"Steele's paranoid. He keeps testing you, and it seems he picked up this annoying habit from Bard. So you don't have a choice. But we're tapped into the club's security system, so once we know what's going on, you'll pass the product to our people without anyone being the wiser."

"Great."

Jablonsky glanced at the clock on the nightstand. "Get going. It takes an extra twenty minutes to get to the club from this motel, and you don't want to look suspicious." Climbing off the bed, I slipped on my parka and grabbed my bag. "Be careful, Alex."

"Always." I tossed him a smile and went out the door. Tonight would be interesting.

Inside the club, the locker room was filled with a flock of scantily clad women in the midst of exchanging gossip. Not

G.K. Parks

paying much heed, I unlocked my locker and began stripping off the extra layers of winter clothing. Just as I was shoving my bag inside, something caught my attention. The locker three away from mine no longer had a lock, and the masking tape label was gone.

"Who are we missing?" I asked, turning to Sasha who was rubbing oil on her legs.

"You didn't hear?"

"What?" My radar pinged, and a quick scan indicated the missing label belonged to Veronica.

"Last night, Vee was mugged. She's in the hospital."

Quickly turning back to my locker in order to compose myself, I swallowed the bile and anger before facing Sasha. "Is she okay?"

"She won't be spinning around the pole anytime soon." Sasha closed the tube of oil and fastened the straps on her heels. "From what I've heard, she's not coming back. So Cindy cleaned out her locker and brought her stuff to the hospital. Vee was cut up pretty badly in the attack. It's no wonder she quit. Scars don't equate to tips." Sasha pressed her lips together, unsure of what else to say, gave a slight shrug, and left the locker room.

If this was how Steele handled that situation, I'd hate to see what he'd do if he found out who I really was. However, if Veronica was out of Francisco's good graces, there was a chance we could flip her. Tabling that thought, I took a moment to fall back into character. Alexia Nicholson had too much to worry about without focusing on Alex Parker's dilemmas. Right now, the only thing that needed my attention was Steele and selling some E.

It was business as usual at the Black Cat. Focusing on serving drinks and flirting a little more than usual, I made sure not to pay attention to the few private rooms. Joe was giving me the cold shoulder, and I wondered if he thought I had something to do with Veronica's assault. Obviously, I worked all night, so there was little reason for him to suspect me. If he suspected anyone, it should be Francisco.

"Alexia," one of the other waitresses said my name, and I spun, "the guy in the side booth is looking for you."

"Thanks." Leaning across the bar, I caught Joe's

attention. "I have a frequent flyer. You might need to get someone else to cover my section for twenty minutes. I'm not sure yet."

"Wow, your first lap dance." He chuckled, pouring a vodka tonic. "If things get out of hand, the security call button is next to the light switch. Have fun."

Sauntering over to Steele, I made sure my cover persona snapped into place. I was Alexia Nicholson. Smirking, I leaned against the table. "Can I get you something, sugar?"

"Someone's in a good mood. Are you ready for this?"

"Absolutely." Taking his hand, I pulled him away from the booth, leading him toward the row of rooms on the side. Each one was fairly small, enclosed by only a curtain. Inside was a free-standing pole, a chair, side table, and a security camera planted in the upper left corner. "Did you want a drink before we get started?" I asked, pushing him down into the chair and reaching for the curtain.

"Not yet." He was enjoying this take-charge stripper attitude. And once we were obscured from view, he grabbed the belt loop on my boyshorts and yanked me to him. "However, I would like a lap dance." His eyes darted to the camera, and I understood his unspoken message.

Kneeling on the chair over him, I did my best to mimic the movements the other dancers and waitresses occasionally used. Unfortunately, this was uncharted territory, and Francisco seemed to pick up on it. Adding to the awkwardness of the situation was the fact that he hoped to be obscured from the surveillance camera, and I wanted everything to be caught on tape. Finally, he grabbed my hips, forcing me into the position he wanted.

"Sorry, I'm a bit nervous," I whispered in his ear, running my hands from his neck down his chest.

"It's okay." His hands were still on my hips, and he slipped something into my pocket. "We'll start with twenty. You should be able to handle that. Last night, we talked about how to move it. Do you remember?" Nodding, I leaned back, continuing the gyrating motions. "I'll meet you outside the apartment building when you get home, and you'll give me the cash."

"What about a little something for my troubles?" I

asked. Our words had been quiet, not loud enough to be overheard or caught on tape with the pulsing music raging in the background.

"Let's see how you do first," he said. I stepped backward, but he grabbed my wrist. "Now finish the dance." For the next ten minutes, I grinded and danced against him, feeling his fingers play across my skin as he lined the waistband of my uniform with dollar bills. "I'll see you tonight," he whispered in my ear once the music stopped, and he disappeared through the curtain and out of the club.

Now that he was gone, the façade was slipping. Feeling slightly nauseous, I went back to refilling drinks. At my break, I went into the ladies' room, counted the pills, calculated how much cash I would need to cover the street value, and returned to the bar. It was time to start dealing.

Considering my dancing left something to be desired, I expected the same to be true of my drug dealing skills. Oddly enough, that wasn't the case. Steele's system was simple. While waitressing, I'd take drink orders, ask if they needed something to make things more fun, and hint that some items weren't listed on the menu. Apparently, word was already out on the street, probably since at least two of the other girls had been dealing, and if a customer wanted a hit of E, he'd tear off the corresponding number of corners from the coaster to indicate how many pills he wanted.

On my next trip to the table, I'd deposit the pills into a front shirt pocket or carefully leave them on the table underneath a napkin or new coaster. The money was slipped into my waistband, and I'd continue working with no one being the wiser. The scary fact was the system was already established which meant this had been going on for a while. And despite my best efforts to remain in the moment as Alexia Nicholson, I still couldn't shake my years of training and investigative tactics. What were these already horny men doing with drugs that would further exacerbate the situation?

Only one possibility came to mind. They planned to mindlessly hump someone or something. It was the same reasoning idiots used when dropping E in dance clubs and at raves. And my gut said that meant the KXDs had prostitutes working outside, or they were pimping out some of the strippers. And based on the profiles and arrest records Jablonsky had pulled, both possibilities seemed highly likely.

Thankfully, I was able to move most of the pills to undercover agents. Six pills remained, and the value could easily be covered by the tips I'd made. So I took another fifteen minute break, placed the remaining evidence inside the barrel of an empty ink pen, and went back to the bar. For my next trick, I planned to attempt a clandestine handoff with the undercover bouncer, and I needed a volunteer from the audience.

Tonight seemed busier than usual, or maybe it was on account of the lack of exchanging friendly chitchat with Joe. As he continued to serve the men at the bar, I grabbed a few longnecks from the cooler and filled a couple of glasses with ice. Loud and noisy would do just fine.

Adding a swing to my step, I went to the first table and took the empties, replacing them with the fresh bottles. As was the case every night, someone swatted my ass, and acting surprised, I dumped the entirety of the tray and ice onto the closest guy. Drunks were typically less forgiving than your average human, and since he was on his fourth in the last hour, he behaved as I suspected.

"My beer," he growled, brushing the ice off his pants.

"I'm so sorry, sir," I apologized, picking up a stack of napkins and dabbing at his pants. "Oh, I'm sorry." I dropped the napkins, pulling my hand away as if I realized my actions were inappropriate.

"You missed a spot," he slurred, grabbing my wrist and putting my hand on his crotch.

By the time I looked up to call for help, the bouncers were already on their way across the room. One of them apologized for the spilled drinks and my faux pas but reiterated club policy about touching the girls. While he explained this, the man argued how I made the first move. As the commotion continued, I made eye contact with the other UC and brushed against him, dropping the defunct ink pen filled with ecstasy tabs into his pocket. He nodded slightly and broke up the argument before it could escalate into a fight. Mission accomplished. Now all I had to do was survive the rest of the night.

At the end of the evening, I cashed out at the bar, returned to the locker room, and changed back into weather appropriate attire. The room was empty since I was the last to leave on account of being selected to clean the bathrooms. We all took turns, and for some reason, tonight was mine. Since the coast was clear, I went to Veronica's empty locker and opened the door. A few pieces of trash lingered in the bottom, and a layer of glitter covered everything. But there was no flashing neon sign indicating drug dealing or gang affiliation.

Before I could close the door, someone cleared his throat. Slamming the locker shut, I found Joe standing in the doorway. "I know what you're doing."

"I just wanted to make sure Cindy grabbed everything for Vee," I said, repeating what Sasha had said earlier.

"I'm not talking about that."

"Okay. Well, whatevs," I retorted, dropping back into Nicholson's persona.

"Twenty-four hours ago, I told you to keep your nose clean. And I wasn't talking about you snorting blow." His eyes traveled to my arms, but they were concealed by the jacket. "Although, that wouldn't surprise me one bit."

"You're crazy. How much did you drink while you were serving?"

"What were you selling tonight?" he asked, holding up a discarded coaster with a few torn corners. "E? H?"

"Are you going to break out into a chorus of *Old MacDonald*?" I spat, unsure of how to proceed with the confrontation. When in doubt, deny everything. "I don't know what the fuck you're talking about."

"Stay away from that world. And don't do it again. You're asking for trouble, Alexia. And no matter how tough you act, you can't handle it. Vee's tougher than you, and you heard what they did to her."

"She was mugged."

"Bullshit." He shook his head. "Why should I even care

about some junkie whore like you anyway?" And he turned and left without another word. At least someone bought my cover story.

FOURTEEN

Walking home that night, I wondered if Francisco would be pleased by tonight's sales. Then again, this was probably one of the many types of drugs he moved this evening. So far, I knew he sold illegal prescription pills, heroin, and ecstasy. Normal small-scale drug operations had limited options. It wasn't like they were some factory emporium, but the KXDs seemed to be. And I wondered what else they were cooking, cutting, and manufacturing. And now with the added indication that they were involved in prostitution, the small time gang just made the leap into crime syndicate. Therefore, the contraband being smuggled in and out was probably equally grandiose. Why couldn't this just be a dozen street kids who were surviving by making a pathetic attempt at some illegal entrepreneurial endeavors?

"Alex," Steele hissed from his usual spot in the alley, "how was the rest of your night, chica?"

"Easy." I reached into my pocket and pulled out a rolled stack of money.

"Good." He removed the rubber band and thumbed through it. "Nice job." He turned away, indicating our meeting was over.

"One of the girls from the bar was attacked yesterday. It was Veronica."

"So?" He didn't bother to turn around.

"Did you do it? I thought you said you were here to protect the people in this neighborhood."

He spun, pissed by my inability to leave well enough alone. "She's not from this neighborhood. Now stop asking so many questions and go home."

Muttering to myself, I continued down the sidewalk and up the steps to the apartment building. Once inside, I pulled out the surveillance equipment and monitored Steele for the rest of the night. He made a few deals, handed off the money to Bard, and hung around until five a.m. before calling it quits. After that, the streets were devoid of any action. I must have dozed because when I woke up, the sun was shining in my face.

Hurrying to take down the equipment and hoping no one noticed a reflection coming from the lens poking between the blinds in the window, I locked everything up and cautioned a few glances outside. The mornings and early afternoons were typically pretty dead, and aside from the usual lookouts, I didn't spot any of the higher ranked KXDs hanging around the neighborhood. Maybe they didn't notice.

Later that afternoon, Steele dropped by with another baggie of pills for distribution. He wasn't much for small talk. Obviously, the previous chattiness had been a ploy to convince me to do his bidding. And now that he had what he wanted, I was just another cog in the machine. The less squeaky I was, the happier he was, so I kept my mouth shut and did what I was told. It was a new one for me, but Alexia Nicholson said she didn't want to cause trouble. So we were going with her gut instincts. Damn, a few more days like this and I'd end up developing multiple personalities.

On the bright side, Veronica wasn't around to make my life miserable. The other women at work quickly forgot about their mugged comrade, far too busy raking in tip money to care. Watching the situation a bit more closely didn't lead to discovering who the prostitutes were or which KXD member might be acting as their pimp. Bard made sure his people were careful; it explained why Steele was the way he was. It also demonstrated precisely why this investigation had been going on for several months and no arrests and little progress had been made. The FBI must have missed something, and the same was true of the OIO.

Joe avoided me as much as he could, only speaking when it became imperative for work. His eyes darted to the cardboard coasters, as if he were keeping tabs on the number of missing corners. Despite his watchdog attitude, my actual ecstasy sales and the coasters did not correspond. I sold a handful to a few men I recognized from the neighborhood, but the rest were being taken off the streets and brought to some evidence warehouse for collection whenever this operation actually turned into a case. Optimistically, that would be soon.

When my shift ended that night, Francisco was waiting outside the Black Cat. He glanced up when I exited in torn jeans and my raggedy parka. I pretended not to notice his waiting presence, and he let out a shrill whistle to draw my attention away from the ground.

"Do you have my money?" he asked.

"Yep, so there's no need for you to mug me. I'll willingly hand it over." My words were a direct dig in relation to Veronica's assault.

He held out his hand, and I removed the money from inside my bag. "Don't start that again," he said, counting the crinkled bills. "That's none of your business."

"Except she was dealing for you, and something happened. Now she's in the hospital, and I'm her replacement. That kinda makes it my business." I met his eyes. "It's not like I have health insurance, so I have plenty of reasons to worry."

He snorted. "You're funny, y'know that?" I continued to glare at him, but he slung an arm around my shoulders and lead us down the street in the general direction of the apartment building. "Anyway, the reason I showed up tonight is 'cuz I have to take care of something out of town, and I don't need you moving product for the rest of the week."

"What about my fix?" I asked, reminding myself that would be Nicholson's primary concern.

"It's covered." He slipped a baggie into my pocket. "Don't use it all at once."

"Where are you going? And when are you coming back?"

"Why?" His tone sounded suspicious. "Are you gonna miss me?"

"I'll miss the benefits of having you around, like the presents you keep bringing me."

"I'll be back next week. Monday or Tuesday, depending on some factors that are out of my control. Then I'll need you to step up your game at the bar. Right now, I'm barely making a profit after that gram and a half I just slipped you."

I turned, acting anxious and delighted.

"Be careful with it. I'd hate for something to happen to you," he warned. We came to an abrupt halt at a busy intersection, and he threw up a hand to hail a cab. "Go on home. I'm getting out of here."

I still didn't know where he was going or why he was going, and both of those things could be key to our investigation. "Francisco, hold up," I said. "What about the guys in the neighborhood?"

"What about them?"

"I'm not exactly Miss Popularity, or maybe I am. Either way, I won't feel safe walking by them without you watching out for me."

"They won't bother you."

"And if they do, what am I supposed to do? C'mon, give me your number so I can call if there's a problem."

"Fine," he grabbed the cell from my hand, pressed a few keys, and handed it back just as a cab rolled up. "I'll see you in a few. And keep that ass in shape because when I get back, things are picking up." He slammed the door, and the taxi drove away.

Not risking acting strangely, I continued home, let myself into the apartment, and conducted surveillance for the rest of the night. The man who had acted as Bard's personal guard was now stationed in Steele's usual spot. Based on the vague details Steele had provided and the chatter Agent Cooper had heard, the shipment should be arriving soon. Maybe it was already here, and Steele had to pick it up. But why would he be gone for the next four days?

Pacing the expanse of the apartment, I sent a few coded texts to my handler and waited for permission to take a brief hiatus from the undercover assignment. Going from undercover to deep cover and back to federal agent all within the span of a couple of weeks would lead to whiplash. But any reprieve, even brief, would be welcome.

Around two p.m. I received a text granting clearance for a temporary exit. After my shift at the Black Cat, I'd go to the motel instead of the apartment, make a quick change, and exit through the adjoining room. No one would be the wiser, and if my absence was reported to Francisco, my excuse would be I was staying with a friend because I didn't feel comfortable in the neighborhood without him there. Or more realistically, I was blitzed on the shit he gave me and couldn't find my way back.

That night at the bar was more of the same. Naked women spinning on poles, handsy men trying to cop a feel, and Joe continuing his cold shoulder routine. However, there was a slight undercurrent of electricity coursing through the club. Maybe it was the larger crowd, but two different fights broke out that night. The bouncers had to break them up, and at least three different men were booted out on their asses, one of which was a low-level KXD punk. When the cat's away, I suppose. Chalking it up to a full moon, I couldn't wait to get out of the sequined underwear and into something dignified. Alex Parker was itching to make a comeback.

Calling for a cab ahead of time, I went out the alley exit, moved to the parallel street, and went across to a convenience store which I listed as the address for the pick-up. It never hurt to be careful. Darting inside the car, I waited until we were a few blocks away before telling the driver my destination. He eyed me through the rearview mirror. Ignoring the questioning look on his face, I stared out the window and at the sliver of side mirror I could see, watching for a tail.

"Do you work at the Black Cat?" he asked, too curious to hold his tongue.

"The what?" I pretended to be clueless.

"Never mind." His eyes returned to the road, but his gaze would flick briefly up to the mirror.

"Is that a usual pick-up spot for you?"

"Sometimes." He studied me again, ignoring the red light that he just drove through.

"What is it? Some kind of jazz bar or coffee shop?" I asked, hoping he believed me, even though I had been half a block away and covered in residual glitter when he picked me up outside a convenience store.

"Women dance there."

"Oh, a club. That sounds like fun."

He laughed. "No. Men pay to watch women dance. Understand?"

"Oohhh," I said, exaggerating the word. "So the girls you pick up, are they hooking?" What the hell, it was worth a shot. He tilted his head to the side in a noncommittal gesture. "And they ask to go to the same motel I did?" My eyes went wide as I tried to act flabbergasted.

"No, no, no," he said emphatically. "They stay closer. Three blocks away at the Maritime."

"You mean Merry Time," I joked, making a note to run that by Jablonsky and Cooper. He smiled and continued driving, paying more attention to the road now that he no longer believed I was a commodity that was rentable by the hour. "Sorry to disappoint, I'm just visiting some friends and needed a cheap place to stay."

He nodded, bored with the conversation. When the car stopped, I stepped out, making sure not to pay with the stack of dollar bills that were in my pocket. With any luck, he wouldn't remember me, and I made a point not to overtip or undertip in order to be less memorable. After he drove away, I circled around the exterior of the motel, making sure no one had me in their sights. Then I went up to the room, used the keycard to open the door, and nearly had a heart attack when I found Mark waiting inside.

"Jesus Christ, what is wrong with you?" I shut the door and slid the security bar over. "You know better than to sneak up on me."

"Alex, we need to talk," he said, ignoring my dramatics. He jerked his chin at my go-bag that he must have taken from the office. "Get changed. We need to hash everything out before you leave tonight."

"I thought my hiatus was approved." I took my bag into the bathroom. The welcome smell of commercial-grade cleaner and shiny white porcelain practically brought tears to my eyes, but it wasn't until this moment that I ever considered motels to be particularly clean or inviting. Damn, I really was living in a disgusting apartment and working at an even more grotesque bar. "Am I going back to that apartment tonight? Because if the answer is yes, then I'm handcuffing myself to the pipes and dropping the key down the drain."

"We'll see."

When I emerged, wearing a button-up shirt, dress pants, and having washed off as much of the oil and glitter as possible, Mark already had surveillance photos, case files, and copies of the current warrants spread across the bed. At least the rest of the team was hard at work. Being stuck in some hellhole by myself had made me question their commitment to this assignment, but obviously, that thought was misdirected.

Three locations were under tight surveillance. One was the international airport, the other a train station, and the third was a private airstrip. Based upon chatter from a few confidential informants and the buzz from our sister agencies, we knew the shipment was already on the ground, but we didn't know exactly where or when it arrived. Our options were narrowed to three possibilities, and each location was under surveillance.

"Why don't you just track Steele?" I pulled out the disposable and found his contact information. "I convinced him to leave his number."

After handing the phone to Mark, I leafed through the paperwork on the bed. The ink had dried for a wiretap, so accessing the phone's built-in GPS shouldn't be out of the question. Thankfully, I thought to relay the information to Mark when I texted earlier.

"We already are, except the sly bastard must have turned off his phone. The KXDs are more paranoid than you and a hell of a lot more careful. As soon as he turns it back on, the techs will notify us, but until then, we're stuck waiting."

"I thought we were planning a raid. Agent Cooper has a team salivating on standby. The sooner we blow this thing out of the water, the better off we'll be." And the sooner I could go back to my life and my apartment.

"We are but not until we know what's going on and who the players are. Don't you remember how we do this job? Big fish, not guppies."

"Steele's a big fish."

"Bard's bigger," Mark insisted. "Plus, this is about more than dismantling the KXDs. We need to find out what is being smuggled into the area, the types of drugs, and who the overseas connection is. From what you and Agent Wolfe have reported about the Black Cat, the KXDs are involved in drugs and prostitution. And from Cooper and Lucca's threat assessments, DeAngelo Bard is probably trafficking in illegal firearms too."

"Assault weapons and automatic rapid-fire handguns," I said, rubbing a hand down my face. "Bard had one in the apartment."

"Does he have more?"

"I don't know."

"Alex, he has plenty of men. With enough weapons, he could build his own personal army to take out the competition and the police force. He's already controlling that neighborhood. He could control half the city. That's why we've been trying to get someone on the inside to find out what is going on, so we can stop it."

"Have you tried to flip Veronica?" I filled him in on the details surrounding Vee and the alleged mugging.

"The police have questioned her. I spoke with Lt. Moretti in major crimes to find out what they've learned. But she won't talk. And if we approach her at the hospital, someone might notice."

"Who cares? She knows a lot more than she's letting on. Bard was worried about it because he wanted Steele to take care of it."

"I'm not jeopardizing a UC by talking to her in such a public place. We don't need anyone to connect you with our investigation, and like you've said, she doesn't like you. But once she's released from the hospital, we'll pick her up for a chat."

"She doesn't know enough about me to assume I'm connected to the investigation. Plus, they're convinced I'm a junkie. The government doesn't employ heroin addicts." I winked. "That's why I keep getting to go through these fun drug screenings."

He sighed, slumping into a chair and leaning back. "Alex, what is your honest assessment of the situation. You're the only one far enough inside to have perspective. So what call would you make?"

"I don't call the plays, Jablonsky. Shit happens when I do."

"You're not in charge, Parker." He slipped, using my last name despite the fact that it wasn't supposed to be uttered outside the office walls. "I just want your opinion."

"As soon as we determine a location, we commence the raid, scoop up everyone we can, and work them over until we have enough evidence to arrest Bard."

"It won't stop the influx of the contraband, and someone else will step up in the ranks, probably Steele."

"Then I have to get in deeper." Swallowing, I already knew it.

"Not tonight. Not while Steele's gone," Mark said. "Before you got here, there were fifteen different 911 calls to that neighborhood. The place is going crazy."

"Bard must be gone too. He's in charge, and Steele's his second. Without the two of them, the dogs are off the leash." I met Mark's eyes. "It's not gonna be pretty."

"That's for the PD to handle. We have our own problems. Now let's finish this assessment so I can get you home. Marty's been driving me crazy, asking if I have any idea where you are or when you'll be back."

FIFTEEN

We worked through the night. Jablonsky and I had spent years analyzing data, speculating, and developing pragmatic strategies, so this was nothing new for either of us. An hour before daybreak, we decided a relocation was in order. It involved a blonde wig, maid's uniform, Mark's sunglasses, and complicated maneuvering and doubling back before we arrived in the garage beneath the federal building.

Normally, I despised being inside this building, but today, I welcomed it. Ditching the short blonde locks, I took a seat on the sofa in Mark's office and continued dithering on about Joe, Sasha, and the other girls at the Black Cat. From the latest intel, it was obvious the women were working for the KXDs. Veronica had been running drugs, and my suspicions concerning the ecstasy and the cabbie's words from the night before only furthered my theory.

"Drugs and girls," Jablonsky declared, swiveling in his chair as he typed something into the computer. "I'd blame you for making this more complicated than it needs to be, but for once, it's not your fault."

"Gee, thanks." I stifled a yawn. "So are they involved in

human trafficking too?"

"I wouldn't be surprised, but I really hope not."

"Me too." We fell silent as Mark caught up on the morning's memos, and I continued to postulate which of the three locations seemed the most likely. "Francisco said he would be out of town for three or four days, so I'm guessing the pick-up location isn't local."

"The extended absence could be explained by cutting and processing the drugs before distribution," Agent Cooper said from the opened office door. "Agent Parker," he nodded, "nice to see you looking a bit more normal."

"Aren't you a charmer?" I retorted, but he seemed confused by my wittiness. Maybe I was losing my touch. "So where do you think the pick-up location is?"

Cooper shrugged, and Mark gestured him inside. "Close the door, Steve." Once it was shut, Mark began again. "We've read through your initial investigation, our current theories and findings, and reviewed all known leads, so what are you talking about?"

"Agent Lucca and I spent the morning with the DEA. Apparently, shipments have been coming into the state via rail. Somehow, items are being smuggled across the border and then being loaded onto train cars. The government has tightened border controls, but contraband is still slipping in, and once it's on a passenger car, it's easily moved across the nation."

"They're not using freight?" I asked.

"Too much scrutiny. Weight and contents are checked, but with passenger transportation, no one gives it much thought. Rail isn't particularly popular, and the companies are happy to get whatever customers they can," Cooper said.

"So what does this mean for our investigation?" Jablonsky asked, fearing the DEA would take charge.

"It means we're now assisting on determining the international source, but our main focus has shifted to infiltrating the KXDs, stopping their illegal sales, and getting DeAngelo Bard to oust his connection," Cooper said.

"In that case, monitor Steele's and Bard's financials and

phones. Maybe we'll get lucky and discover they've been on a train recently," Mark said.

"It's already being done. So far, we haven't gotten any hits, but only one of our suspected locations is a railway depot. And since the DEA is determined to move in, we're piggybacking on their team. Lucca is updating Director Kendall before briefing the response unit," Cooper said. "It looks like we'll be moving in tonight."

"Count me in," I said.

"No," Jablonsky declared. "You will not be anywhere near this mess. When this shit backfires and blows up in our faces, your cover needs to remain intact. Do you hear me, Parker?"

"Yes, sir." That's why I planned to wear full tactical gear, including gloves and a ski mask to obscure my identity. However, I knew that tone, and there was no reason to argue since his mind was made up. "So what am I doing in the meantime?"

"You're taking the day off." Jablonsky rubbed his face and looked at the time. "Cooper, phone me two hours before we're set to move," he ordered, shutting down the computer and putting on his jacket. "And get me a set of keys to one of the witness vehicles." When Agent Cooper returned a few minutes later, Mark thanked him and dragged me out of the room and back to the garage, ignoring my protests.

"Where the hell are you taking me?" I asked, hoping he didn't decide I needed to be in witness protection for the duration of the DEA's raid.

"You wanted a break, and you said you can't go home. So I'll do you one better." He smiled. "Plus, you promised Marty a plus one for the evening."

"Crap, that's tonight?" I let out a sigh and dropped my head against the back of the seat. "You mean to tell me I've been undercover for a month and we still don't know jack? And now the DEA is calling the shots after you spent the night telling me we couldn't execute a raid?"

"Say thank you and be quiet. I've been up the entire night dealing with a particularly difficult situation and a pain in the ass undercover agent. I think I've been through enough."

Mark took a careful route, doubling back numerous times to ensure we weren't followed before he finally arrived at Martin's. Only after the garage door was closed and the security system was reactivated did he let me exit the vehicle. And he thought I was paranoid.

"The techs cloned your phone the other day. So in the event the KXDs are smart enough to hack into it, they'll think you're still at the motel. I've covered all the bases. You should be safe. Marty's circles don't overlap with anyone or any location that might be under suspicion. But be careful. Bruiser doesn't know the situation, but he knows that he should be on alert."

"What do I tell Martin?" I asked, suddenly apprehensive to see him.

"Stick to the same story you already gave him. You're working at a home security firm. Maybe you've been conducting surveillance to thwart burglars. Be vague. Make it sound boring."

"I don't know if I can do this. Can't I hide out at your place instead?"

"Alex, the longer you have to be Nicholson, the harder it will be for you to return to your life when this is finally over. Take this opportunity to prepare him for the possibility this could drag on for a few more months. And just try to be you."

"Who else would I be?" I asked, feeling uncertain of the answer.

"I'll call when it's time to go back. Until then, limit your public appearances, and if Steele contacts you, let me know."

Nodding, I went up the steps to the main level. By the time I emerged on the second floor, the garage door lowered and the security system reengaged. Now what was I supposed to do? Was it possible I'd forgotten how to be me?

Taking a deep breath, I scanned the area for signs of Martin, but he was nowhere to be seen. Maybe he was out, and I could avoid the situation a little longer. Just as I started to relax, his voice traveled from one of the floors above, and given the way it sounded, he was annoyed about something. Bracing myself for whatever was to come, I went to the downstairs home office, found an envelope, slipped my federal agent credentials inside, and hid the sealed item in the guestroom that served as my home away from home. With the damning evidence concealed, I squared my shoulders and headed up the steps.

Martin was in his personal workspace on the fourth floor. From the illuminated button, I could only assume he was on speaker with someone from Martin Technologies. The paperwork that accompanied the laptop and tablet added to my suspicions, and when he started speaking again, it was obvious it wasn't to me. Waiting patiently for a pause in the conversation, I knocked gently against the doorframe once the opportunity presented itself.

He spun, surprised by the intrusion. "Hang on while I grab those projections," he said, hitting mute on the phone. "Alex," his voice came out breathy, and he crossed the room to me, "what are you doing here?"

"You should really consider changing your security codes," I replied, turning my head to avoid a kiss and feeling myself go rigid in his arms. Putting my arms around him in a perfunctory manner, I hoped he wouldn't notice anything amiss.

He buried his face in my hair and then kissed from my jaw to my lips, giving me no choice but to reciprocate. He stepped back, holding me at arms' length before running his thumb across my cheek.

"I've missed you. Where have you been? We haven't spoken in two weeks."

"Well, you skipped out on poker night," I replied, feeling defensive toward his interrogation. "I told you I had to work. Out of town conferences and conducting surveillance can be a hassle, and I haven't had much downtime to make phone calls or exchange e-mails."

"But you had enough time to talk to Mark?" he said, indicating he had been in contact with Mark about my absence. That was the problem with having mutual friends.

"He has access to government resources. It was a work call. Speaking of," I jerked my chin toward the speakerphone, "I didn't mean to disturb you." Trying to smooth the waters and appear less frazzled and neurotic than I felt, I offered a congenial smile. "But I couldn't just leave you hanging when you had some fancy party to go to and were in dire need of a plus one. So I dropped everything and rushed over. Surprise." He looked skeptical, so I continued. "However, in the name of full disclosure, I could be called back to work tonight."

Those green orbs stared at me, scrutinizing every mannerism and fidget. Finally, he cracked a smile. "I'm glad you're here." His gaze shifted back to the phone. "I'm sorry, but I..."

"No problem. I could really use a minute alone." It was the truth, but the words must have stung from the pained look that passed over his handsome features.

"What's wrong? Are you okay?"

"I've been up all night. I'm just tired."

"Get some sleep. We aren't expected until eight."

Tossing a glance at his bedroom, I decided it was still too close for comfort and returned to the second floor. The guestroom was a place of solace. The closet and drawers were full of my clothing and other necessities. Opening the nightstand drawer, I removed my backup nine millimeter, which had been there for the past month, field stripped it, cleaned it, and reassembled it. The muscle memory of such action and the familiarity of the cold steel were comforting and helped pave the way back to Alexis Parker.

Disassembling and reassembling the handgun two more times eased the anxiety that began to build since entering Martin's house. It was stupid to be nervous in such a familiar setting and with the one person who meant the world to me, but for the last month, I had been constantly on edge. Time and distance had a strange effect, and it was an affliction many UCs dealt with. Up until this point, I'd never had anyone back home, so nothing in my past prepared me for this.

Fake it until you make it, I suppose. So I changed out of my work clothes and into one of Martin's shirts. Pulling down the covers, I crawled into bed and instantly felt like I was in heaven. The mattress was just the right level of firm.

The sheets had a thread count with at least three zeros, and the blankets were plush and clean. That air mattress in the apartment was my own personal hell, and the motel bed was barely a step up with its scratchy sheets and stained blankets. This was what I'd been missing: Martin, a real bed, and a modicum of security.

Drifting off to sleep, I was barely aware of my body contorting into a tight, protective ball. It was how I slept on those rare occasions I managed to sleep inside the apartment. Always curled tightly and always at the edge of the bed to be closer to the knife and unregistered gun resting two feet away.

My dreams were a mix of faces and movement, and as I stared at Francisco, watching his mouth move but unable to determine why his voice wasn't his own, something touched my back. Acting reflexively, I rolled away, landing hard on the floor.

"Alex?" Martin peered down at me from the bed above.

Groggily, I sat up, tangled in the bedclothes. "Didn't the bed used to be bigger?" I asked. He broke into a fit of laughter that he'd been trying to hold back since my swan dive off the edge, and I glared, tearing free from the bedding and throwing the balled up blanket at him. "Don't laugh. This is your fault for startling me."

"I said your name a few times, and you mumbled something. I thought you were awake." He helped me up and pulled me toward him, hoping to demonstrate a proper apology but remembered the time. "It's after six."

"Can't we stay here instead?" I asked, attempting to manipulate the situation. "I thought you missed me?"

His eyes smoldered, but when his hand moved to my side, I couldn't shake the image of Francisco or those sleazebags from the strip joint. A shudder traveled through my body, and Martin let go, confused and worried.

"Are we okay? I've barely seen you, and you flinch every time I touch you. You're not okay, are you? You look," he struggled for a word, "different."

"We're fine. I've just been busy. It seems you've been busy too. Conference calls on a Saturday. Social gatherings that are really informal business meetings in disguise." I went to the closet and flipped through the hangers. "And the different is called long hours of boredom, but I'm fine."

"Are you sure?" He came up behind me and pulled a black cocktail dress from the corner.

"I'm sure." I took the item from him and examined it, glad to distract him with the less serious topic of fashion. "This isn't mine. And it looks too small to be yours."

"I'll admit I've missed you but not enough to wear your clothes. I sent Marcal to do some shopping. If you don't like it, you can always wear this." He pulled out a designer purple dress, also from one of Marcal's trips to the store. "But it's a bit formal for tonight's function."

"I do have my own dresses."

"Yes, but they're at your place. Now if you made this house your place, then they'd be here too. And I wouldn't have to send my valet to shop for you."

Despite the topic, this felt like the first normal conversation we had. Smiling, I wrapped my arms around him, dropping the dress to the floor and kissing him. He returned the kiss, and for the first time since stepping foot inside the house, I felt like me again.

SIXTEEN

"Dammit," he cursed at the ringing phone.

"Go," I urged, collecting the discarded dress from the floor. "I need to shower and get ready, anyway."

He cast another curious look in my direction before letting out an unhappy sigh and leaving the room. Once he was gone, I grabbed the necessities and locked myself inside the bathroom. Get a grip, Parker. This hot and cold routine that I was exhibiting was driving me crazy, and I was sure he was suffering from the effects of whiplash too. Maybe I was losing it.

Emerging, showered and dressed, I went to the nightstand and fastened my thigh holster underneath the dress. Then I holstered my nine millimeter and focused on the sealed envelope containing my credentials. Leaving them here didn't seem like a great idea, but there was no place to hide them underneath the dress. And if I put them inside my purse, there was a good chance they'd be revealed at some time during the course of the night. Tucking the envelope inside my bag that contained Nicholson's attire, I carried it out to the living room and took a seat on the couch.

As I flipped through the channels, Martin came down

the steps. The phone was no longer attached to his ear, and he somehow found the time to change into one of his fancier suits. Turning off the TV, I stood up, smoothing the wrinkles from my dress.

"Can you tell I'm wearing a gun?" I asked.

"You're beautiful, firearms notwithstanding." He twirled his pointer finger, and I obliged, spinning in place and fighting against the memory of performing this precise action for DeAngelo Bard. "Okay, I have no idea where this alleged gun is supposed to be."

"Great. Then we're good to go." I moved toward the door, reaching for my bag.

"Hey," his voice was soft, and his fingers brushed against the inside of my arm, "what happened here? That looks painful."

"Oh," I glanced down, "I must have hit it against the corner of the nightstand or a doorknob or something. It doesn't hurt." I pulled my arm away and grabbed the coordinating wrap that went with the dress, making sure to conceal the remaining airbrushed bruises and puncture marks. "Are you ready? We don't want to be late."

"Since when do you care?" he challenged, going into the kitchen. "There's one other thing before we go." He came back with a black velvet box. "I thought you could use this."

"Silver bullets?" I asked, wary to see what was inside. "I'm not planning on hunting any werewolves."

He opened the box and removed a necklace. The only adornment to the platinum chain was a solitaire diamond. Before I could protest, he moved behind me to fasten the clasp.

"Martin, no. It's too expensive. I don't need this. I rarely wear jewelry, and this," I gestured toward the diamond that felt like a noose, "is too much."

"Well, we could have the stone placed in a different setting that could be worn elsewhere, but that seems like a conversation we should be having when you aren't armed and dangerous."

"I'm always armed and dangerous. But this is too much. Take it off."

"No," he said in that infuriating tone he only uses after

reaching some unilateral decision, and his eyes twinkled. "We missed quite a few holidays recently, so that should just about cover it."

"I'm not..." I stopped, realizing I was about to say his property and go off on a tirade about how he couldn't supplicate me with pretty things just so he could use me in whatever manner he saw fit. Geez, that was how Nicholson felt working at the Black Cat and interacting with Francisco. That wasn't how Parker felt, particularly when it came to Martin. "I'm not sure what to say. But thank you." I offered a smile, determined to do my best to shake off Alexia's hang-ups for the rest of the night. "Can we please go? I'm absolutely starving."

The ride to the banquet hall was mostly in silence, except for the constant text message and e-mail notifications that kept sounding on Martin's phone. Whatever was going on at Martin Technologies seemed major, and already I knew the rest of the evening would be spent watching him work. But that was fine. I always insisted we put our careers first, and that's all I'd been doing for the past month. Now it was his turn.

His driver dropped us off and promised to remain in the garage across the street, so we could leave once business and the proper amount of schmoozing were completed. Taking Martin's offered arm, I snuggled against him. Truth be told, I missed him almost as much as I missed being myself. Mark was right; tonight was the break I needed.

We were seated at one of the larger round tables, and after a round of greetings, business was the only topic discussed. Vivi pulled her chair closer to mine. She was the wife of one of the board members and the only other person who didn't seem interested in the business aspect of the evening. The conversation was light. The food was good. And sounds of a dissolving merger played in the background.

After the plates were cleared, the mingling began. This event was a charity function with the price of the meal supporting one of the local homeless shelters and soup kitchens. Martin was philanthropic, and whatever the CEO of MT did so did most of his competitors. The nearby tables boasted the head honchos from Wallace-Klineman Industries, Danya International, and Hover Designs – Francesca Pirelli's company. She was also Martin's former fiancée whom I had consulted for on a security breach before the encounter had turned awkward and vindictive. Needless to say, I wasn't a big fan of the Harvard alumna, and she wasn't too keen on me either.

Excusing myself from Martin's current discussion with Wallace-Klineman's head of research and design, I took a seat at the bar. Obviously, my previous fear that Martin would shirk work because of me was unfounded. He was poised to strike.

Soon, more people joined the conversation. He and a few others were having a heated debate concerning which corporation owned the intellectual property rights to the recently sold product line. Once the debate began, I remained perched at the bar, my thoughts drifting to Bard and the impending raid. After checking my phone and Alexia's half a dozen times, I focused on the discussion taking place across the room.

Not seeing Martin in his element had made me forget how fierce he could be. While his words remained hushed, his body language demanded attention. Whenever the group finally came to an arrangement that suited everyone, a round of handshakes was exchanged and promises for paperwork to be drawn up and signed by Monday were made. And this was supposed to be a party. I stifled my internal smugness as Martin searched the banquet hall for his prize.

"I wondered where you disappeared," he said, coming to stand in front of me.

"I was watching the fight." My eyes sparkled. "You're one hell of a contender." I shifted my gaze to the other businesspeople, who by now were mingling and relaxed. "But I'm sure I'm not supposed to know what any of that was actually about, so I thought I'd keep Gus company."

"Gus?"

"The bartender."

He rolled his eyes, unsure if I made up that last part. He stepped closer so as not to be overheard. "We were just determining who owns the proprietary rights to Hover Designs' recent product line. They signed with us, but when we dissolved the merger, they relinquished their specs as part of the deal."

"Shrewd." I leaned in. "And I thought you made a bum deal on account of some unfortunate circumstances."

"I told you not to worry." That was the business trip he cut short on account of a certain news story that might have featured footage of me running into a hostage situation. "And now I'm all yours," he purred. "Come on, I promised you a dance."

"I hate dancing." I leaned against him. "Wow. I didn't realize talking business could get you that excited."

He smiled and whispered in my ear, "I believe what you're feeling is the gun strapped to your inner thigh."

"Shh, don't ruin my fantasy. How about you pay off the coat check girl, and we can play seven minutes in heaven instead?"

He cocked his head to the side, confused by my suggestion. I was never that forward about sex and most definitely not in public. "While I'm sure I could make you scream my name in seven minutes or less, I'd prefer not to be rushed." He pulled away, taking my hand and leading me out to the middle of the room. "We have all night for that. Just one dance, and then maybe we can duck out early." I crinkled my nose at him. "I know why you hate to dance. It's because you can't follow a lead."

Chuckling, I shook my head. "Do you realize what you just said? *I* can't follow a lead? I'm pretty sure that's one of the only things I actually know how to do."

"Well then, you simply refuse to follow mine. Now stop with the wordplay and being so snarky." He held me close, whispering countless romantic sentiments in my ear as we swayed back and forth. It wasn't exactly dancing, but it was an acceptable compromise. Just when I was starting to enjoy myself, I heard the clacking of stiletto heels approaching fast.

"Jamie," her tone was sharp and annoyed, "I need to have a word with you."

"I'm sorry," he whispered before turning to the cause of

the intrusion. "Francesca," his voice remained professional, but I detected a weary annoyance to it, and since they had a history, she probably picked up on it as well.

She glanced at me, barely acknowledging my presence, before grabbing his forearm and dragging him to the corner of the room. Their words didn't carry, but from her emphatic gestures, it was obvious she was pissed about the proprietary rights that Martin Technologies now possessed. After all, she's the one who signed the deal. It was her fault she screwed over Hover Designs, and briefly, I wondered if the company would force their COO to resign. Frankly, the farther removed from Martin she was, the better. But that was the small voice in my head that was jealous of the woman who had bedded my boyfriend a decade ago. She wasn't a threat, and I knew it. But that didn't mean I had to like her. However, on the bright side, I didn't have to dance.

I returned to my seat at the bar and drummed my fingers against the countertop. Fifteen minutes passed, then twenty. By the time I looked at the two of them again, they were still arguing, and it was an hour later. So much for sneaking out early.

I took another sip of seltzer, wishing for something a bit more potent, but I could be called away at any moment. Steele might want to meet if his supplies ended up raided, or Jablonsky might call to let me know we were performing evidence collection for the rest of the night. And there wasn't a chance in hell I'd jeopardize the operation after spending the last month undercover inside that roach infested hovel.

Picking up my phone for the umpteenth time, I noticed the signal strength was a bit weak. Maybe I should step outside and make sure I didn't have any missed messages. Grabbing my purse, I went down the steps and out the front door. As soon as I hit the sidewalk, I received a text message from Steele. Talk about a sixth sense. Not bothering to return inside to interrupt Martin from his hundredth business meeting of the evening, I scurried across the street to the parking garage and found the black town car on the second level.

"Hey, do me a favor and put the privacy screen up," I said to Marcal. "I need to change."

"Where's Mr. Martin?"

"Inside. He's working, and apparently, I need to do the same." Once the dark tinted glass was in place, I unzipped my dress, shimmied out of it horizontally in the back of the car, unhooked my gun, and pulled on the ripped jeans and black tank top from inside my bag. Luckily I grabbed the one with the shelf bra because the dress I just discarded wasn't conducive to practical undergarments. Opening the door, I stepped outside, zipped the dress into a garment bag I found in the trunk, and hung it from the hook, tossing the necklace into the bottom of the sealed bag for safe keeping. Then I grabbed the rest of my belongings that had been inside the trunk, shifted my gun to my shoulder holster, and slipped into my parka. "Tell Martin I was called away," I instructed.

"Sure thing. Be careful, Ms. Parker."

"Thanks. Have a good night." Darting out of the garage, I hoped to find a cab outside the event hall. This was a busy area with hotels, restaurants, and bars. Finding a cab shouldn't be challenging, but it was Saturday night.

"Alex," Martin said, catching up to me on the sidewalk, "where are you going?"

"To work." I noticed Francesca at the top of the steps, waiting for him to return. "I told you I might get called in tonight."

"But it's Saturday. And we've barely seen one another." He swallowed. "Is this because I've spent all night doing business?"

"No." I threw my hand up, and a cab came to a halt. "I'm sorry, but I just got called. And I have to move. Home invasions don't wait for anyone." At least that was the cover story I fed him.

He narrowed his eyes in disbelief. "Call in sick. Let someone else at the security firm handle it. You said you should have the night off."

"Martin," something about his tone made me think he didn't believe me and with good reason, "you know I can't do that." I jerked my head toward Francesca. "Go finish your conversation. I have to go, but we'll talk soon."

The cabbie beeped, annoyed by the holdup, and Martin leaned in to tell the guy to wait a minute. He also handed him a twenty. When he surfaced, I stepped into the open car door.

"I don't have time for this right now."

"You haven't had time for anything lately."

"Well, neither do you," I snapped. "What happened to putting our careers first?"

"Don't start that again." He let out a huff and released his grip on the door. "Just go. But try to pencil me in for sometime this year."

"I'll see what I can do. But it looks like I'd have to make those arrangements with your secretary." I didn't know why we were fighting or why I was suddenly so angry. Honestly, I think the lies and deceit were getting to me. But it was for his protection. No one could use him or hurt him if he didn't know anything. That's why he had to stay out of the loop, except that meant I was hurting him which in turn hurt me which made me bitchy. "I'll talk to you tomorrow, if we can both somehow manage to swing it."

"You're not coming home tonight?" The surprise was hard to stomach.

"Probably not. It sounds like an all-nighter. Stakeouts are a pain." I grabbed his tie and pulled him down to my level, kissing him goodbye. "Hey, we'll figure this out. But you need to get your work stuff straightened out, and so do I."

"Yeah, right." He shut the door and went up the steps to Francesca.

SEVENTEEN

On my way back to the motel, I texted Jablonsky to advise him of the current developments. The joint DEA and OIO raid was set to commence, and for all I knew, it might already be underway. Was that why Francisco texted me? His message was vague, simply listing an address and time. Hopefully, Mark could shed some light on the situation.

After a few more encrypted messages back and forth with my handler, I replied to Steele's message, asking why he was back so soon and why we weren't meeting in the neighborhood. In response, he reiterated the time and place and said he'd explain in person. I didn't like it. Getting out of the cab, I paid the driver and went up to the motel room. I had about an hour until my rendezvous with Steele.

As I mentally prepared myself, the motel phone rang. It was Agent Cooper. Jablonsky was reviewing the intel, so I'd been passed off to another member of the dream team. Pacing as far as the phone cord allowed, I listened to the updated plan.

"We didn't find anything," Cooper said. "We searched high and low, but there was no sign of a shipment. They must have moved it before we got there, or we had the wrong location. The fact that Steele wants to meet with Nicholson doesn't bode well. We're scrambling a backup unit to the designated location. If things go south, we'll pull you out."

"Do the KXDs know about the raid?" If they did, it was possible they assumed I was a mole. But then again, it wasn't like Nicholson knew where Steele had disappeared either.

"We don't know enough at this point to speculate. Just be careful and keep your eyes and ears open. You do remember the signals, right?"

"Yeah. Let's just hope we don't need them." I rubbed my eyes, remembering I needed to alter my makeup before the meet. "The agreed upon location is a twenty-four hour diner. It'd be stupid for him to make a move in public."

"Still, don't let your guard down," Cooper warned.

When we disconnected, I added a few additional layers of eyeliner and dark lipstick. It helped my skin look paler and more like an addict's. Then I stowed my credentials into the space inside the lining of my coat, left my gun where it was, and hoped I wouldn't need to use either of them. Maybe Martin's night improved now that I was gone.

Fidgeting with a loose thread, I bounced slightly on the balls of my feet, working on the jitteriness. Studying my reflection in the mirror, it took some practice before the right amount of anxiety bled through my gestures and motions. Once I felt certain I had crawled back into Alexia Nicholson's skin, I locked the motel door and went down the street.

The motel was a good distance from the apartment and almost as far away from the Black Cat, but it was still in a sketchy area. Luckily, it was fairly early for a Saturday night, and plenty of people were out. I considered flagging down a cab, but Nicholson wasn't made of money. And I didn't want to arrive early. The longer I could drag this out, the more time the OIO team had of getting into position, so I waited at the bus stop.

After performing a transfer six blocks away, I was close to the diner. Thinking back, I couldn't remember ever using public transportation this much. It posed too many risks and didn't necessarily leave many options for timely escapes, but Nicholson didn't have a choice.

By the time I pushed the diner door open, my face and hands were numb, so the warm blast of air was appreciated. Scanning the interior, I didn't spot any familiar faces. Where was Francisco? The two back corner booths were occupied, as were most of the tables near the windows. That meant my only option was the counter with my back facing the door. Instead of risking it, I smiled at the waitress, ordered a coffee, and continued on a path toward the restrooms. There wasn't a chance in hell I was painting a bull's eye on my back.

After washing my hands in warm water, I sent another text to Steele, asking where he was. The lack of response did nothing to calm my nerves, and I palmed my secondary phone, having forgotten to leave my personal cell at the motel, and considered sending a message to Cooper. Just as I began typing the text, Nicholson's phone beeped. Steele was here. Suddenly, there was pounding on the bathroom door, and in my haste, I did the only thing I could think of and tossed my phone into the wastebasket.

"Jesus, can't you read?" I barked, unlocking the door to find Francisco leaning against the jamb. "Ladies only."

"Then why are you in there?" He offered a grin. "Come on. Let's go."

"Where? I just ordered coffee."

"Alexia, let's go." He grabbed my arm and pulled me out of the bathroom and toward the back door. From where we exited, we were obscured from the street. There was no way the surveillance team would spot us. My heart beat faster. "It's too crowded inside, and I wanted to get you alone."

"Why?" I shivered, unzipping my coat slightly in order to tuck my hands inside without him noticing I was moving closer to my gun. "Where have you even been? And since when do you text? Don't you normally just holler at me or show up at my apartment?" I made a pretense of thinking. "You said I was off the hook for four days. What gives?"

"You ask a lot of questions," he said, his tone accusatory. "And plans change, chica." He led me down the dark alley, away from the front of the diner, and to the back door of some other building. He knocked a particular pattern, and the door opened. "After you."

He pushed me forward as I tried to determine where we were. The hallway was dark and narrow. I didn't see any other entryways, but he continued to press against my back, urging me onward. The blood pounded in my ears, and I feared my cover had been blown. Where was he taking me? Thoughts of torture chambers and crack dens came to mind, and frankly, I didn't know which would be worse. Either could easily lead to my demise.

"Francisco," my voice sounded shaky, and I didn't know if that was nerves, the cold, or my best rendition of how Alexia would react, "why did you want to get together tonight?"

"You'll see." Both of his hands braced my shoulders, halting our procession. "Hang here for a minute. Don't go anywhere."

Suddenly, bright fluorescent light flooded the dark hallway, and an unseen door opened and closed. With Francisco gone, I was alone in the dark. I leaned against the wall, my eyes slowly readjusting. Vaguely, I spotted a red dot near the top corner of the corridor. Wherever we were had security cameras. Turning around to face the way we came, I saw a green keypad on the wall. Someone must have let us in. And getting out would be equally tricky without the proper code.

Pressing my back against the door, I pulled my hands free from my jacket, zipping it up with one hand while I ran my other palm against the wall, feeling for a doorknob or latch, but there wasn't one. Only upon closer inspection did I feel the seam of the doorway and notice the tiniest hint of light seeping out from the edges. Where the hell were we? And what was inside that room?

After what felt like an eternity, Francisco emerged, bathing me in the harsh, bright lights. I threw up a hand to shield my eyes and caught the briefest glimpse of the KXDs' operation. Numerous women were inside, wearing nothing but surgical masks and their underwear as they processed, cut, and packaged illicit drugs.

"Just making a pick-up," he said, looping an arm around

my waist and hauling me back toward the door. "How do you feel about moving more than just E?"

"What's in it for me?"

"Five percent plus a regular fix."

"I'll have to think about it."

"What's to think about?" He blocked my view of the keypad while he entered a few digits, and the sound of a locking mechanism moving out of place echoed inside the walls. Obviously, it was a reinforced steel door. "You move product, same as before." This wasn't a debate.

"Fine, but I want a cup of coffee before I agree to anything. It's freezing out here," I protested once we were back in the alley. There had to be some way of convincing him to return to our agreed upon meeting place that was still under surveillance by the OIO team.

"Have you always been such a pain in the ass?" He led the way back to the diner at a much faster clip. "Fine, I'll get you some coffee if you quit bitching." Just as relief washed over me, he turned, ignoring the back entrance to the diner and emerging on a side street. "I know a quiet place where we can discuss these things in more detail."

Unable to provide a valid argument against the change of venue, I kept my mouth shut and moved next to him. Easing myself closer, I used the pretense of trying to get warm to determine if he was carrying. At the small of his back was a handgun. There was something hard and metallic in his pants pocket, and from the sound of crinkling plastic, whatever package he picked up was tucked inside his jacket.

We walked for a few blocks in total silence when he suddenly stopped and pinned me against a building. His hands came to rest on either side of my head, and his body pressed into mine.

"What are you doing?" he hissed.

"Huh?"

"Are you hoping for a taste?" He backed up, unzipping his jacket just enough so I could see the concealed brick of cocaine. "Or have you been missing me?" And I realized he was suspicious about my need for maintaining such close proximity.

"I wouldn't mind a taste," I laughed, "but actually, I was just trying to keep my hands warm."

He zipped his coat and took both of my hands in his, holding them to his mouth and blowing on them in a somewhat sensual way. "Better?" He stared into my eyes.

"Yeah, thanks."

He remained still for a few seconds longer, glancing behind him to make sure no one was watching or following us, and then he led the way to a tiny dive that smelled like sweat and burnt coffee and had a scattering of semiconscious people who appeared to be stoned out of their minds. He called across the counter to someone named Danny for two cappuccinos and took a seat at the corner table.

"You don't strike me as a cappuccino guy," I said.

"Why not? Don't you think I like nice things?" His eyes surveyed my body. "Because you're looking pretty damn nice tonight. Y'know, I could use some TLC. What do you say?"

"I don't put out on first dates. And coffee is about as first date as it gets." I cocked my head to the side, jerking my chin at his chest. "Is that why you wanted us to get together tonight?"

"To take you on a date?" He practically laughed in my face. "No. I just needed someone to accompany me on the pick-up."

"Why?" It didn't make sense.

He shrugged, refusing to answer the question. His eyes focused on something outside that I couldn't see, and he shifted in the chair. "No reason to worry about that."

"Whatever. So is that what you want distributed at the Black Cat?" We made eye contact, and I dragged my focus to his chest and the concealed brick.

"No. Strippers and blow are an urban myth, at least in these neighborhoods. Plus, this is high-end product. I'm just delivering it to someone who has a fancier clientele." He pulled out his phone to check the time. "He'll be here in a few to take it off my hands." He smiled, grabbing a plastic spoon off the table. "Maybe we should make sure it's primo."

Danny came around the counter with two paper cups and placed the cappuccinos on the table. Francisco emptied a sugar packet into one. Then he disappeared into the men's room, only to return a minute later after replacing one white powdery substance with another.

"Shit," I whispered, "aren't you afraid of getting caught? You know I don't want to go back to jail."

"Relax. Everyone here is cool." He poured the cocaine out of the packet and onto the table, using the flat edge of the spoon's handle to make two lines.

"Don't be stupid. It's a risk. Anyone could be an undercover narcotics officer. This place practically screams out illegal substances."

"Suit yourself, chica. It's only sugar." He held up the empty packet and then snorted both lines before downing a mouthful of cappuccino, which struck me as odd. "Are you going back to the apartment tonight?"

"I don't know." How did he know I hadn't been there? "I've been crashing with some friends."

"You have another connection you're not telling me about," he said, leaving no room for my protest. "You're gonna have to stop that sometime soon, but for now, I'll let it go." He blinked slowly as the euphoria hit. "Trust me, I'm the only one you need. Anything you want, I can get."

Before I could respond, the bell above the door chimed, but no one came in. I assumed someone realized this place was far too seedy to risk entering, but Francisco stood and dumped the rest of the coffee into the trashcan.

"That's my guy. I'll see you later, chica. Monday, things are gonna change. Be ready for it."

He darted out the door, and I gave the room an uneasy glance. No one seemed to notice me, except the barista. As Danny continued to fiddle with the coffee machine, I pretended to drink the cappuccino. Luckily, I kept the lid on it, so no one could tell I had yet to take a single sip.

After an appropriate amount of time passed, I dumped the cup into the trash and went out the door. It was after midnight, and I hoped to backtrack to the diner to pick up my discarded phone. Ditching it had been a mistake. I panicked, and if Jablonsky found out, he'd be so far down my throat he'd pop out my ass. Plus, the surveillance team was probably still out front, awaiting visual confirmation of the meet.

But as I began the trek back, I felt someone watching me. Cautioning a glance, I didn't see anyone. So I picked up the pace and strained to hear footfalls coming from behind.

Without warning, something slammed into me, knocking the wind from my lungs. I gasped; the same force spun my body around, shoving my back against the brick so hard my skin scraped through the thick parka. Slightly dazed, I made a move to push my attacker aside but stopped when I felt the barrel of a gun pressed against my temple.

EIGHTEEN

"Where is it?" the attacker asked. He was barely out of his adolescence, and a quick glance confirmed that he wasn't alone.

"Where's what?" I replied, sizing up the four gangbangers. Estimating their ages, I'd say two were still minors, the one who introduced me to the wall was probably twenty, and the last was a little older, covered in scars and missing an eye.

"Don't play dumb, bitch." He yanked me toward him just so he could throw me backward into the wall again. "We know you made a pick-up, so where are the goods?"

The weakest link was probably One Eye. He had an obvious impairment. The two youngsters were just punks, but they might be undergoing an initiation or possess an immortality complex which made them dangerous. They'd be the first to shoot their mouths off, but hopefully, that's all they'd be shooting off.

"I don't have anything. I don't know what you're talking about," I said slowly in case he was mentally impaired. To choose this life, he ought to be.

"Fine." He tossed a look behind his back. The punks stepped closer, each seizing one of my wrists and holding me in place. Mr. Talkative unzipped my parka, probably hoping to find a brick of coke. Instead, he found my holstered nine millimeter. "Then why are you packing heat?"

"Really? Packing heat? Who says that?" I queried, throwing him off guard with the sarcastic remark.

He was probably trying to come up with a smartass response when my knee slammed into his balls. He doubled over, and I used the distraction to perform a side kick. My intended point of impact was a kneecap, but I underestimated the strength of the punk's grip and fell short, landing a glancing blow to one of his shins. It was just enough of a distraction to free one of my wrists, and I reversed course, spinning away from the wall and using my momentum to circle around the punk who still had a firm grip on my other wrist. I wrapped our joined arms around his neck and ended up behind him with my nine millimeter in hand. He dug his fingers into my skin, scraping up my arm, but I held tight. With any luck, they wouldn't shoot since I had their buddy for protection.

One Eye moved toward us, causing me to back step into a small side street. Tossing a quick glance behind me, I saw car lights in the distance and wondered if an audience would encourage my assailants to take a hike. Just as my focus returned to the men in front of me, the ringleader pulled a piece and began a rapid-fire staccato. A few shots went into the punk, and I dove out of the way. A cry of pain rang out, followed by a gurgle, and I knew he was dead.

"Shit, Bobby, what the fuck?" the other teenaged punk yelled, but the ringleader's gaze was focused on me.

Drawing my nine millimeter, and I knew I could take him. My eyes remained fixed on his trigger finger. Even a slight flinch and I would shoot. The only problem was One Eye and the teenaged punk were attempting to flank me.

"Where is it?" the ringleader asked again, continuing the approach.

"I don't have it."

"Shakespeare's guy must have kept it on him," the teenaged punk muttered, tossing a worried look at his fallen friend. "When word gets out that we missed the target, we're screwed."

"Shut it," the ringleader growled. "So the KXDs are risking their girls in order to make sure their drugs stay safe?" He let out a harsh laugh. "It's funny how fast they changed their tune." He shrugged. "Fine by me. You're gonna deliver a message for us."

"I don't think so." I continued to step backward until my back came into contact with a dumpster. "Now, I'd suggest you lower your weapons and get out of here while you still can."

"Grab her," the ringleader growled, and One Eye closed the gap between us.

I shifted my aim to the left; the punk grabbed me around the waist and lifted me off the ground. I kicked out, using the dumpster as leverage to push upward, flipping myself over his shoulder. My back pulled at an odd angle, but the slight twinge wasn't nearly as devastating as the concrete. Thankfully, the punk took the brunt of it, landing hard.

During the acrobatics, I lost hold of my gun and didn't have enough time to recover it before One Eye launched himself onto me. We scuffled for a bit. His hands wrapped around my throat, and I clawed at his one good eye to no avail. Finally, I got the heel of my hand under his chin and shoved his head up. He faltered backward, losing his center of gravity, and I rolled to my side, into his blind spot, and twisted his arm at the perfect angle for a break.

More shots rang out, nicking the concrete next to us, and I scrambled toward the dumpster. Running in a crouch, I found my discarded nine millimeter and slid across the asphalt, feeling bits of broken glass and gravel cut into my legs and arms as I scooped the gun up and took cover between the building and the dumpster. The metal vibrated as the ringleader emptied his magazine into the side wall. Once the gunshots stopped, I fired blindly in his direction, keeping track of the number of bullets remaining.

Edging closer to their positions, I couldn't afford to continue returning fire in this manner. Cautioning a glance around the corner, I spotted One Eye attempting to sneak around to box me in. Without hesitating, I popped up, firing in his direction, but the punk had recovered and was only a few feet away. Upon my emergence, he rushed forward, cracking the butt of his gun between my shoulder blades. I howled, twisting to fire at him and crashing to the ground, slicing my parka and maybe my back on the sharp corner of the dumpster.

At point blank range, I didn't miss hitting my target, and he went down. Without waiting to see if he was alive or dead, I retreated into the space between the wall and the dumpster. There wasn't a chance in hell I was coming out again. Maybe I was boxed in, but if they came for me, I'd kill them before they could get to me. Reaching into my pocket, I grabbed my cell phone, dialing 911 and waiting for the two remaining gangbangers to make another attempt.

Who were these people? They obviously weren't part of the KXDs. A rival gang perhaps? But what the hell were they doing following Francisco, and why would they think I had the drugs?

The car lights from before grew brighter and larger, and an SUV screeched to a stop a few feet away. Automatic weapons discharge sounded, accompanied by agonizing screams, and just as the sound began to dissipate, tires squealed. And the smell of burning rubber filled the air. The lights came closer, heading right for my hidey hole, and I scrambled to escape before the SUV crashed into the dumpster.

Just as my torso cleared the narrow enclosure, the SUV hit the edge. The force knocked the dumpster backward into the space I had occupied. The SUV corrected course, darting into traffic and disappearing.

"Holy shit," I breathed, glad to still be alive. But now that the firefight was over, my body took notice of the damage, and I realized my left leg was pinned behind the dumpster. "Dammit." I reached into my pocket to see if my phone connected with 911, but it was missing. It probably landed behind the heavy immovable object.

My thoughts were jumbled. My only instinct was survival. Then escape. Now as the snow began to fall in thick, heavy flakes, I wondered if the four gangbangers were really dead or if they were only wounded. Who was in the SUV? Who opened fire? And would they be back to finish me? As the adrenaline continued to course through my system, I became more and more panicked. I needed to get free.

Twisting and tugging, I couldn't get my leg out. I was wedged in from just above my knee. Using my other leg, I tried to push off the dumpster, but the wet snow and patches of ice didn't provide much traction, and I slipped and slid. Think, Parker. I couldn't call for help, and I couldn't move the dumpster. If I were a fox, I'd gnaw my own leg off, but that didn't seem practical.

Something moved at the other end of the narrow street, but I couldn't see over the dumpster. So I became more frantic, pushing off and twisting with all my might. If I could just get my leg free, I'd be safe. Sweat collected on my brow from the exertion, but I was shivering from the cold. Zipping the tattered remains of my parka closed and pulling the sleeves down over my arms and hands, I twisted again, squeezing my other leg between the wall and dumpster in order to push it outward, and just as the metal trash bin moved a fraction of an inch, I lost my balance, wrenching my stuck leg.

White hot pain shot through my hip, and I screamed. Taking a few deep breaths, I tried to shift again, but the pain got worse. There was no way to get free. I'd just have to hope my call went through, and 911 dispatch was sending someone to check on the situation.

Bunching up as best as I could, I buried my face inside my collar and pulled my arms out of the sleeves and into the main compartment of my jacket, so I could wrap them around my torso to conserve heat. The snow was still falling, and everything was already covered in a layer of white. My teeth began to chatter, and the constant shivering made my hip throb worse. If I made it out of this mess, Francisco was going to pay.

My throat ached from breathing in the frigid air, and I was starting to fade. How long had I been out here? With no other option, I screamed for help. A bullet to the head would be faster than dying of hypothermia. Eventually, I stopped calling for help. I was too tired and too cold to keep it up.

NINETEEN

"This one's alive," someone said, and I opened my eyes to flashing lights, four police cars, a fire truck, and an ambulance. The female EMT hovering next to me was the one who spoke, and another EMT joined her. "But she's pinned."

In a matter of moments, a few firemen yanked the dumpster forward, and I let out a sharp exhale. The two EMTs assessed my injuries, grabbed a gurney, and lifted me onto it after immobilizing my leg. Was it broken? Dislocated? Would it be amputated?

One of the cops stepped in and began to speak, but I wasn't coherent enough to answer his questions. Soon, I was in the back of the rig, my parka was off, along with my soaking wet clothes, and the female EMT was speaking again. She had a needle and a vial.

"No drugs," I managed, coming out of the haze now that I was underneath one of those shiny aluminum foil blankets. What were they called? I couldn't remember. The shivering was worse, and I felt colder now than I did outside, probably on account of my body defrosting. Now I knew what it was like to be a Thanksgiving turkey. "I don't want anything."

"It'll make you more comfortable. Your leg–"

"No drugs," I repeated. And she replaced the vial in the cabinet and discarded the syringe, pulling out tubing to start an I.V. "What's that?"

"Warmed saline. It'll get your body temp up faster." She folded the blanket away from my arm, seeing the defensive wounds and the airbrushed bruises and punctures. "Oh." She paused. "I get it. If you tell me what you took, I can find a painkiller that won't interact."

"I'm not on anything. I'm," I was about to say a federal agent but got distracted by my missing parka, "missing my coat." She inserted the I.V. with a pinch, and as soon as the bag began to drip, the warmth spread.

"The police have it," she said, and I remembered an officer taking my belongings and asking if there was any chance I could escape while we were en route to the hospital. She began filling out the paperwork, and I realized I had two options. Divulge my cover and sacrifice whatever might be left of the operation or keep my mouth shut until someone with authority could get to me. "What happened back there? Four guys were killed, and you are the only survivor." I shrugged and shut my eyes. "What's your name?" Still, I kept quiet. "Are you allergic to any medicines?"

She continued to ask questions, and I pretended to be mute. When we arrived at the hospital, a few police officers were waiting to ask more questions, but medical professionals got the first crack. After an x-ray, it was determined there was no break. One of my tendons had a slight tear, and a ligament had moved over my hipbone in what was sometimes referred to as a partial dislocation. After an excruciating half a second, the shooting pain turned into a dull throb. And given that I was only exhibiting the first stages of hypothermia and somehow managed to stave off frostbite, there wasn't any reason for the hospital to keep me for too much longer which meant the cops could take me into custody.

"I want to make a phone call," I said. After refusing to give any of the hospital staff my name or information, they seemed anxious to find some way of determining who I was. After all, how else would they know where to send the bill for the ER visit and ambulance ride? "C'mon, it's not that big of a deal. Just one call. I'll make it quick."

"You can use the phone once we move you into a room," an orderly said, pushing the bed out of the ER and toward the trauma wing.

For the few minutes I was alone, I dialed Jablonsky's burner, but he didn't answer. It was six a.m. So I tried his house phone. Still no answer. Dammit, Mark, where the hell are you? Before I could dial his normal cell, which was an OIO number that could be recognized and potentially compromise the mission, a police officer entered the room.

"Miss," the officer began, "I need some information."

I rolled onto my side and stared at him. Sell it, Parker. "Please," I let out a gasp, wincing, "can you find the nurse?"

He studied me, determining if I was going to make a break for it. With the ice pack bandaged around my hip, it didn't seem too probable. Although, I would have been willing to give it a shot if I didn't think they'd stop me at the door. Unfortunately, hospital gowns weren't conducive to stealth escapes. If the cops didn't stop me, the hospital staff would.

"Fine, do you remember her name since you can't seem to recall your own?" His glare hardened, but I ignored it.

"Nurse Jen. Jenny-O, like the turkey." I didn't even know if Jen O'Connell would be working this early, but she was my best chance of getting out of here.

"Damn tweakers," he muttered under his breath, disappearing out the door.

I sat up, hoping to find something of use inside the room. My cell phone would have been nice, but my jacket would have been the next best thing. Unfortunately, my personal belongings were no longer in my possession. And if Jen wasn't working this morning, there wasn't a chance in hell I'd get out of this with my cover intact. Asking to speak to one of the major crimes detectives or insisting on someone phoning SSA Mark Jablonsky would blow the mission. That is, if it wasn't already blown. I didn't know. Going to ground was the only thing I could do until I made contact and found out what was happening.

Fifteen minutes later, Jen stepped inside the room. Thankfully, the officer remained outside, but he warned her I was potentially dangerous and to holler if she needed something. She did a double-take, surprised to see me like this. I shook my head and pressed a finger to my lips, hoping she wouldn't say anything. She looked back at the door and then stepped closer to the bed.

"Jesus Christ," her eyes roamed over the parts of me she could see, "what the hell happened?" Her eyes stopped on the numerous defensive wounds and track marks running down the length of my arms. "Alex, what is going on?"

"Is Nick at work?" I asked, desperate for the answer to be yes.

"His shift starts at seven." She grabbed the chart at the end of the bed and flipped through the pages. Most of the information was blank since I fought my damnedest to keep them from running any tests or shooting me up with anything. "Why didn't they give you something for the pain?"

"Jen," I focused on the door, hoping the officer wouldn't come inside, "I need you to call Nick. No one can know who I am or why I'm here. Just get Nick. Please." The urgency in my voice set her in motion, and she nodded, heading for the door.

The officer stepped back inside the room, and I slumped back on the bed, covering my eyes with my arm. He asked a dozen questions, but I remained silent, hoping he'd think I passed out. He was now threatening to charge me with multiple homicides if I didn't start talking. Luckily, Jen came back inside the room, throwing him out with the skill of any medical professional worth her salt. Once I heard the door click closed, I slowly moved my arm away from my eyes.

"He's on his way."

"Thank you. And thanks for kicking out the hound dog."

"Are you sure I can't get you something?" She glanced at the heart rate monitor that I couldn't disconnect or else they'd think I flatlined. "Your BP's through the roof, and I'm guessing it's because you're in pain."

"I'm fine."

She shook her head. "You're far from it."

With nothing else to say, I shut down, not speaking or acknowledging her. She didn't need to get involved. The less she knew, the better. It was bad enough I had to call Nick for a favor, but I didn't know how to safely get a hold of Mark under these circumstances.

Twenty minutes later, I heard voices in the hallway. The officer from earlier was explaining the situation to the detective who was attempting to take over. Apparently, it looked like a drug deal gone wrong. Four men were shot and killed in an alley, and one crack whore, that'd be me, was refusing to answer any questions.

"I'll take it from here," Detective O'Connell said, stepping inside the room. "Can I have a word alone with the patient, nurse?"

I sat up, and Jen tossed a worrisome glance my way before brushing past her husband, whispering something I couldn't make out before disappearing into the hallway. Once the door shut, Nick flipped the blinds closed and let out an exasperated sigh.

"You have to get me out of here," I began.

"Is it true?"

"That I'm a crack whore? No. That four men were killed in an alley and I'm the only one still breathing? Yes." He reached for one of my arms and assessed the airbrushed track marks. "They're not real." I jerked my head toward the alcohol swabs on the counter. "Hand me one of those." He did as I asked, and I rubbed off the semi-permanent makeup, hissing when the alcohol came into contact with one of the deeper scrapes. His brow furrowed. "I'm undercover."

"For who?"

"The OIO. My credentials are inside the lining of my jacket, and I need them back now. I don't know if I've been compromised, but if I haven't yet, I will be once your people start poking around where they don't belong."

"What do we know so far?"

"Nothing. I refused to give them any information. Unfortunately, they ordered a blood test, and it will come back negative for drugs. I'm running out of time. I needed someone with some pull in the department to get my medical files and belongings before they can be processed or taken into evidence."

"Where's your support team?"

"I lost them. Nothing like this was supposed to happen last night. It was a surprise ambush. I can't get a hold of Mark. I had to dump my phone, and the burner for the op was confiscated. I've been at this too long to let everything go to shit. I need your help."

"All right. I'll see what I can do. Stay put."

A few minutes later, Jen reappeared, pushing one of the medication carts. She came into the room and shut the door. Then she pulled an extra pair of scrubs and her winter coat from the bottom shelf.

"You can't traipse out of the hospital in one of the gowns that opens in the back," she teased.

"Thanks."

She unhooked the monitors, and I dressed while she guarded the door.

"I hope I don't get you in trouble," I said.

"No, Nick's handling it. The doctor didn't give you any crutches since you're prohibited from leaving. And I can't figure out how to sneak them in here."

"I'm okay. Everything's back in alignment, and the doc said the tear should heal on its own. It's not like my leg's gonna pop off like a Barbie doll, so I'm sure it'll be fine."

Nick knocked, and when the door opened, I noticed the officer was gone. "Thanks, honey." He gave Jen a quick kiss. "I'll see you tonight. Just remember, the detective in charge stole your patient."

"She was never mine, and I know nothing." Jen left the room, leaving us to devise the perfect escape plan.

O'Connell took my parka out of the evidence bag and handed it to me. Reaching into the tear in the lining, I felt around until I found the chain on my credentials and pulled them free.

"Did you want to see my badge?" I asked.

"Not particularly. Is that the most damning thing against you?" He put my parka back inside the bag and sealed it, leaving it on the bed for the officer to collect after our departure.

"My burner phone has a lot of numbers that most crack whores don't possess. Hell, I should have put your number in there under favorite detective," I joked, knowing I had Steele's number and Mark's burner listed, but that was about it.

"Don't worry about it. It was soaked, so it'll take time before IT can process it. Plus, it's already been sent back to the lab as evidence. I phoned Heathcliff and told him to grab everything that comes in on the multiple homicides but to maintain chain of custody. I assume one of your guys will take lead."

"Probably," I admitted. "How am I getting out of here?"

"Lucky for you, I said they pinched my CI, and it's in everyone's best interest if I get you out of here quickly and quietly." He glanced at the door. "So we need to go before that officer checks my story with the actual detective in charge."

Carefully, I slid off the bed. Pain shot through my hip, and I gritted my teeth. It was manageable. O'Connell slid underneath my arm and helped support my weight as we made it out of the hospital and to his cruiser. Once we were inside and on the road, he handed me his phone.

Dialing Mark's office number, I hoped the incident in the alley wasn't the result of another security breach. After all, I had no earthly idea who could have been inside the SUV. It didn't seem likely it was the KXDs or whatever gang One Eye and the three other dead men represented. Frankly, the OIO couldn't afford our operation to be compromised. They were already running low on agents.

When Mark answered, I gave him the briefest synopsis possible and disclosed O'Connell and Heathcliff's awareness and assistance in the matter.

"Fuck." His desk drawer slammed. "I'll tap into the DOT grid for surveillance footage. We'll start an investigation and figure out if you were compromised. If there's even a chance, I'm pulling you." I sputtered, attempting to voice a protest, but he continued on. "We don't know yet. So go to ground. Don't go home, just in case, and don't show up here or at the precinct until I sort this out. It's bad enough you have a police escort, but it sounds like O'Connell executed your escape quickly and with minimal fallout, so you should be safe."

"Martin?" I asked. This was the precise reason Jablonsky had been renamed my emergency contact. "If this is the result of a security breach, does anything trace back to him?" I couldn't remember.

"No. You were careful. We were careful."

"What if it was Vito?" I pondered the ramifications that the most powerful mob boss in the city might have a stake in the matter. After all, wasn't Bard encroaching on his racket? O'Connell turned at my words, concern etched his face.

"I haven't heard any chatter from OCU, but get your ass out of sight and make sure Marty's okay. As soon as I get this straightened out, I'll meet you at his place. And I'll call Bruiser and have him be extra vigilant," Mark promised.

"Thanks." I disconnected and passed the phone back to Nick.

"So how long have you been back on the job?" he asked, hoping to alleviate the tension.

"A month. Martin doesn't know. No one does. The FBI had a security breach, and quite a few inactive agents were called to fill in. I couldn't tell anyone. I wasn't supposed to tell you, but I didn't know how else to salvage the situation."

"Well, congrats, I guess."

"Yeah, unless I blew it somehow."

When we arrived, I gave him the security code, and he drove his car inside the garage. In the event there was a second breach and anyone determined my connection to Martin, the unmarked police cruiser wouldn't be able to add insult to injury. O'Connell killed the engine and opened his door. Before I could step out, he came around to my side of the vehicle and leaned down, lifting me out of the car.

"You don't have to carry me. I can manage," I insisted.

"It's not a big deal." We went up the stairs to the main level. "I'm just thankful I don't have to carry you up the six flights in your apartment building." He put me down on the couch and glanced around the room. "What's going on?"

"I can't tell you." I shook my head

"Parker, everything I've done in the last hour could jeopardize my career. Derek's too. So fill me in."

TWENTY

Nick shook his head and blew out a breath. Now he knew everything, and whenever word of this got back to Jablonsky, I'd be royally screwed. Then again, I'd been through hell in the last five hours, so nothing Mark could dish out seemed that bad.

Nick kept muttering curses, contemplating his next course of action and mine. "Why didn't anyone inform us about a federal investigation into the KXDs? We have a gangs unit at the precinct. Shit, Heathcliff just came back from helping narcotics identify a supplier. We have resources. We have our own ongoing undercover operations." He growled and stalked the walkway in front of the couch. "Why didn't *you* tell me?"

"I couldn't. I had my orders."

"Bullshit. This is us. We're practically family." He pointed an accusatory finger in my face. "How many times have I saved your ass?"

"Too many to count."

"That's right. And you've pulled my bacon out of the fire on numerous occasions too." He rubbed a hand down his face, softening. "I need coffee. It's too early in the day to be dealing with this."

"Help yourself." I jerked my chin toward the kitchen.

Checking the time, I wondered if Martin was awake yet or on another conference call. Hell, he might even be at the office by now. I considered getting off the couch and going upstairs to locate him, but stairs didn't seem like a good idea. As if reading my mind, O'Connell returned from the kitchen with an ice pack and wrapped an afghan around me.

"You should drink something warm. Jenny said you were borderline hypothermic when they brought you in."

"I'm also borderline crazy, but that doesn't mean I need to be institutionalized."

"Wow, and delusional too." He winked, returning to the kitchen and promising to make coffee for us both.

At the sound of footfalls, I turned, catching a glimpse of Martin bounding down the stairs in running gear. Apparently, he just woke up and was dressed for his early morning workout. He slowed his pace, eyeing me as he continued his descent.

"What time did you get here?" He sounded annoyed and studied the blanket and my position on the couch. "I'm not surprised you chose the couch over my bed. It comes second, right? Our jobs first. The couch second. Am I even a distant third?" I didn't say anything. I just stared at him. I forgot we were fighting. He threw his hands up, frustrated. "What is going on with you?"

O'Connell emerged from the kitchen, holding a coffee mug. "James, you might want to back off. Alex has had quite the night."

Martin swallowed, realizing something was wrong. It was the only reason O'Connell would be inside his house this early in the morning. Martin's eyes found mine. "Alex?" His mind was already working through the possible explanations, but I didn't answer, unable to formulate another lie to add to the growing list.

"Come on, we need to have a chat." Nick grabbed Martin by the arm and led him out of the room.

"Nick, don't," I warned.

"It'll be fine," Nick reassured. I shut my eyes and tried

to make out the muffled words. "Take it easy, man. She's in pretty bad shape. And you're making an ass out of yourself."

"What do you mean pretty bad shape? What happened?" Martin demanded.

"It was a freak thing. Just a random assault. She'll be okay, but we're still trying to identify the guys," Nick said, and I was thankful he had my back.

A few seconds later, Martin returned to the living room. His hand brushed my hair away from my face. And he studied my appearance, frowning at the dark circles and runny makeup underneath my eyes.

"Are you okay?" he asked, and I nodded. "I didn't realize." The blanket slipped, and he cocked his head at the scrubs. "You were in the hospital?"

"Not really. Just a quick check-up. It's police protocol." My eyes searched for Nick, who was unobtrusively sipping his coffee in the far corner of the room. "I should shower and change, so Jen can have her clothes back."

"I'll make a few calls while you do that," Nick said.

Carefully, I climbed off the couch, ignoring Martin's questioning look at the ice pack. I dropped it on the kitchen counter and continued down the hallway to the guest suite. After showering, I returned to the bedroom and sat on the edge of the bed, maneuvering into a pair of jeans. The thought of having to go through this process more than once was my rationale for the clothing choice. In all honesty, I either needed a few strong cups of coffee and to focus on work, or I needed to sleep. And the way I figured it, I could wear jeans while doing either of those activities. As I reached for my top, Martin knocked on the door.

He came inside, stopping midsentence, silenced by the cuts and scrapes. He brushed my hair over my shoulder, kissing the nape of my neck and the unmarred areas of my back with a feather-light touch. The bruise on my lower back was the most sensitive, and when he came close to it, I hissed.

"What can I do?"

"Hand me that shirt and bring those out to Nick," I said, pointing at the pertinent items. "I'll be there in a sec."

Pulling on the sweatshirt, I was glad to be warm and safe. The adrenaline surge and the freezing cold had sapped my energy, and the only thing I wanted to do was crawl into bed. But maybe Mark had other plans.

When I went into the living room, O'Connell was lingering near the door. "I'll sort things out at the precinct. Agent Jablonsky said he'd stop by to help us identify the assailants, so he'll probably be calling you in a few hours with an update. If not, Heathcliff or I will. Okay?"

"So I'm staying here until further notice?" I asked, wanting to make sure I understood.

"Yeah. Do you think you can stay out of trouble that long?"

"I'll try, but I'm not making any promises."

Nick nodded to Martin, and the two shook hands before Nick returned to the garage and Martin deactivated the security system and opened the door for him. I sighed and collapsed on the couch. My hip ached, and my muscles were tired and strained to the point where they'd tremble and give out without my permission. At least I could get some sleep. As I was considering curling up right here to nap, Bruiser came up the stairs.

"Good morning." He narrowed his eyes, having received a call from Mark that probably hadn't divulged anything. "I'm not used to hanging around when you're here since you like to be the only guard on duty." He was fishing for details, but I'd already spilled my guts far too many times today.

"But you're so good at bodyguarding. Plus, I went through an ordeal, and the nerves are a bit frayed. Just make sure the perimeter remains clear, okay?"

Martin returned from the first floor. "Do what she says, Jones." Then he came over to me. "You're not sleeping on the couch. So it's my room or the guestroom?"

"I'll just crash in the guestroom. The stairs aren't ideal right now."

Wincing as I pulled myself off the couch, he scooped me into his arms and carried me down the hall, laying me on the bed. "I'll keep you company as soon as I take care of a few things. Do you need anything in the meantime?"

"Just let me know if Mark or someone from the precinct calls."

He nodded, turning off the lights. "Alex, about last night..."

"Please, not now. Later, okay?" He moved toward the door, but I remembered something. "Did you get things sorted out with Francesca?"

"In a way. Hover Designs is suing. She announced it twenty minutes after you left. Legal will start on the paperwork Monday."

"I'm sorry," I said, but he waved the sentiment away with a flick of his wrist, running his hand through his dark brown hair.

"That doesn't matter right now." He seemed tormented and distant. But what did I know? Maybe that's always how he sounded, and I was just projecting.

After a few fitful hours of twisting and turning, never managing to fall too far into the unconscious realm, I heard Martin quietly return. I had been reliving the firefight, the close calls, and my encounter with Francisco. My mind was processing the events, trying to make sense out of the appearance of the four gangbangers and the SUV. Also, I couldn't help but think of the punk I killed.

Years ago, Mark had said never to assume someone was dead because of my actions, but I shot that guy at close range. He didn't give me a choice, and the other one that I had grabbed was killed simply because I tried to use him as a means for my escape. Granted, I'd do it again in a heartbeat, but the events still weighed heavily on my conscience.

"Hey," Martin said quietly, carrying another ice pack and the bottle of ibuprofen into the room, "Jen called and said you need to get the swelling down."

"What else did she say?" I shivered when the ice came into contact with my leg. Hopefully, she didn't say anything that would compromise my covert activities.

"That was pretty much it." He went to the linen closet to get another blanket. "No one else has called."

I nodded, closing my eyes and rolling over on my side. The mattress dipped down, but he kept his distance, remembering how I had reacted to his touch the day before. The near-miss several hours ago resulted in my personality displacing any remnants of my cover identity. Parker was back in control. She had to be because Nicholson was not equipped to handle these situations, and the only thing I wanted at the moment was comfort and safety. Curling against Martin, I was happy for the added warmth and the hard planes of his body.

"This is my fault," he whispered, placing his palm over the ice pack to keep it in place as I shifted closer to him.

"How is this your fault?"

"You were attacked."

"So?" Finally finding a comfortable position, I buried my face in the crook of his neck, ready to sleep.

His sharp laugh was full of loathing and disdain. "I practically forced that rock around your neck. I might as well have hired the muggers myself."

"Martin, the necklace is at the bottom of the garment bag with the dress. I left them in your car. This has nothing to do with you. Everything that happened is because of my job. I'm sorry. I wish I could explain."

"It's okay." He eased an arm around me, and the white noise led to unconsciousness.

The shrill sound of the telephone made me jump, and Martin reached for the phone. He glanced at the caller ID before handing over the offending object. It was Mark.

"What's the verdict?" I asked. Putting a hand over the mouthpiece, I asked Martin to make some coffee since I couldn't talk freely in his presence.

"It wasn't due to any breach, but I had no choice but to fill in Lt. Moretti since two of his detectives had to confiscate the evidence from last night's multiple homicides and release the only surviving witness and potential suspect. Director Kendall is going to have our asses for this. Shit, Parker, your casings and slugs covered that street. Yours. Not the unregistered weapon we gave you. We're bringing you in for a debrief."

"Is it scrapped?"

"No. Agents Cooper and Lucca are monitoring communications within the KXDs' network, but it doesn't

G.K. Parks

sound like they know anything went wrong. The PD identified the four bodies. They were members of the Lords, a rival gang." He paused. "Like I said, we need to talk. I'll pick you up in thirty, and we'll take it from there. Did you tell Marty?"

"No. He's under the impression it was a random attack."

"Gotcha. Have your gear ready in case we're sending you back in tonight." I hesitated, so Mark asked, "Are you able to go back in?"

"Yep."

"Okay. I'll see you soon."

When we disconnected, I freshened up and went into the kitchen. Martin was at the table, checking his e-mail on his phone. He offered a smile and pointed to the steaming mug.

"Mark's on his way. The police need some statements and information, and he's helping out. Look, I meant what I said before that this has nothing to do with you. I'm not very good at the juggling act, but I've warned you about this."

He looked up. "It's fine." But it wasn't, and we both knew it. "You do realize how screwed up it is that we can't even have an argument without something horrific happening. It's not fair. I shouldn't have to worry about things like this. It's not normal."

"No, you shouldn't. But it's always been my normal, hasn't it?"

"God," he smirked, "I'm beginning to think you aren't the only one who needs to consider going to therapy."

Slapping his arm, I made a face and took a seat at the table to drink my coffee and give my leg a rest. I'd be back at work soon enough, and last night was a major game-changer.

TWENTY-ONE

After performing a threat assessment, the OIO determined the events that took place in the tiny side street were not the result of a security breach. The gangbangers didn't know who I was. They had no intention of tangling with law enforcement. The only thing they wanted was a brick of cocaine.

The more relevant question was why did Francisco take me to the KXDs' processing facility. From the few comments the Lords' ringleader made, it was obvious this rival gang had a beef with Francisco and the KXDs. Unfortunately, I didn't know enough about who they were or how long they'd been keeping tabs on their rival. Closing my eyes, I put my feet up on the adjacent office chair and replayed the conversation and accusations that led to the firefight.

"Parker," Director Kendall said my name, and I moved to shove my feet off the chair and sit up straight, wincing at the sudden shift, "as you were." I relaxed back in the seat, waiting for whatever was to come. "You're not going back without support. Frankly, if we hadn't invested so much into this, I'd turn it over to the DEA. But that's not something I want to do. They're dealing with identifying the international connection, so we're handling things stateside."

"Yes, sir."

"You will rendezvous with Agent Lucca every afternoon at the motel before reporting to the Black Cat. Agent Wolfe is already stationed as a bouncer there, and once things die down, we will find a way to introduce a backup into the apartment building and neighborhood," Kendall said, skimming the files and reports. "However, we have more pressing matters to discuss." He jerked his chin, dismissing Lucca and Cooper. Mark made a move to leave, but Kendall put his hand out, indicating that Mark should stay. "Jablonsky, you trained Agent Parker. You've also kept in contact with her during her work hiatus, so I think you should be here for this." Kendall exhaled and turned to me, placing his palms on the table. "You broke protocol. You failed to communicate the change of plans. You ditched your phone. Shit, why did you even have any personal effects with you?"

"Sir," Mark interjected, "I told Agent Parker to take the night off. The raid was commencing, and she didn't need to get roped into that."

"Still," Kendall glared at me, "you've done this long enough to know better." He pushed away from the table, almost making his chair collide with the wall. "And don't get me started on the evidence against you at that crime scene. Furthermore, you broke cover to members of the police department. You jeopardized your own safety and the safety of every single agent tasked to assist and investigate."

"Director," I began, but his icy gaze forced my mouth closed.

"I'm not finished." He rolled his shoulders and sat back down. "And despite all of that, the best part is I have no choice but to send you back. Francisco Steele trusts you, which makes you a shoo-in with DeAngelo Bard. Hell, they even took you to a location we have spent seven months trying to find." He put a hand over his mouth, completely speechless. After a minute, he moved his hand. "Unbelievable," he muttered. "But this better be the last time you act recklessly. If I hear anything else, I will pull the plug. And so help me god if that happens." He left the room, slamming the door behind him.

"Wow, it's been a while since I've had my ass handed to me. I forgot what that was like," I said.

"I'd give you my own version, but you practically ripped your own leg joint out of the socket. So you've been through enough already today," Mark said, collecting a few of the files and going to find Lucca and Cooper. We still had a lot of information to get through.

Our first order of business was determining how much of last night to divulge to Francisco. My cell phone had been retrieved from the bathroom trashcan, and based on the level of garbage on top of it, it didn't seem likely the KXDs had discovered it. They trusted me, or at least Francisco did, which meant I should return the favor.

Once our bases were covered, Lucca was dismissed. He'd been on duty for over twenty-four hours, and it was starting to show in the dark circles and accumulated scruff. Our boy scout was beginning to look just as rough as the street punks.

Cooper exhaled, reviewing the few items that had been discovered at the train depot. "It should have been there. Our intel said the shipment was coming in last night. The DEA said the same thing. Everything points to the railway. So why wasn't it there?"

Regardless of the fact that he was speaking to himself, I offered my opinion. "It arrived earlier. We have to assume the brick Steele picked up was processed and cut from that shipment. And work like that takes time. It must have come in Thursday night. That's probably why Steele said he'd be gone for a few days."

"So why's our intel lagging?" Mark asked.

"The possibilities aren't good," Cooper said, mulling over a few disconcerting thoughts.

"You've been listening to chatter. Whose?" I asked.

"OCU and the gang task force have been hearing whispers about a shipment arriving. A bug's been put in our ear from confidential informants and other undercovers," Cooper said. "The DEA hasn't shared their sources, but I'm assuming they have a similar intelligence network. Hell, they might have some dealers wiretapped too. I know we do," he added, not bothering to glance up from the photo array and evidence notations. "Nothing was conclusive. The levels of residue and particulates weren't enough to definitively say drugs had been shipped through the area."

"Did you check the passenger trains that stopped here in the last forty-eight hours?" Mark asked, gnawing on a thumbnail. "We might have better luck searching the trains than the station and temporary cargo holds."

"I'll make some calls. With any luck, some lines have been taken out of commission, and if not, I'll notify the pertinent field offices to do a check whenever they make their next stops."

After Cooper left the room, Mark pushed Nicholson's phone closer. "You have to tell Francisco most of what happened. Just leave out the part about exchanging gunfire. We don't want him to question your tactics."

"Jablonsky, he's seen my scars. He knows I've been shot. I doubt returning fire would surprise him."

"Leave it out. There were enough men in that alley that you could have simply hunkered down and hid. Make sure he understands you want to know who was after you and whether or not you need his protection." Something crossed behind Mark's eyes, but he didn't say anything. Instead, he scribbled a note on the edge of a piece of paper, tore off the corner, and shoved it inside his breast pocket. "We need to figure out how to limit your time alone in that neighborhood. I don't want you out and about without some sort of backup."

"It's too late for that."

"We'll see. In the meantime, let's get the ball rolling. Give Francisco a call and tell him you need someone to pick you up at the hospital. DMV records show he has a vehicle. Maybe we'll get lucky, and you can lose a phone in the seat cushions. That way we can ping the cell's GPS and keep track of his movements."

"We'll need a few more burners." My face fell at the thought of ducking out on Martin again, especially after arriving in such disarray this morning. Anything could have happened last night, and he would never know the real reason for it. I had to tell him. He should know why I was gone and why I lied. I pinched the bridge of my nose, realizing that thought process was the result of fear and guilt. "Mark, before this goes any farther and you take me back to the hospital to wait for Francisco, I need to fill out some paperwork."

"Yeah, I knew you'd say that. Come on, I already filled them out for you. They're in my office, awaiting your signature."

After signing the forms, Mark gave me a few minutes to use his office phone, but since the documents had to work their way up the chain of command and get approved before I could open my mouth to a civilian, our conversation was full of lies and deceit. It's not like I planned to go into detail about the operation or my mission. I just wanted to tell Martin I was back at work. Life shouldn't be this difficult. I'd forgotten what a hassle the red-tape was.

"I promise I'll do what I can to improve my juggling," I offered as consolation for failing to explain when I'd be able to see him again.

"Maybe you need to bounce some balls around as practice," he said, the teasing evident in his voice.

"Maybe. But perhaps I should start with something easier."

"Like?"

"Like an apology for leaving the other night and showing up the way I did this morning and for barely speaking to you over the last month."

"You left out the two most important words." He was enjoying dragging this out.

"Oh, so now you're busting my balls. It's no wonder I suck at juggling." I laughed. "And I'm sorry," I added sincerely.

"Then tell me what's going on, sweetheart. The last time we were together, I mean really together, you seemed so different, happy and carefree, and now, you're distant and secretive. If I didn't know any better, I'd think you were seeing someone else."

In a way, I was. "I hate to break it to you, but work is my dirty, dirty mistress. And I have to keep a lid on things because of security. This job has the pinnacle of all nondisclosures. But I'll tell you everything I can as soon as I can. Do you trust me?"

An awkward silence filled the void for a moment too long, and then his voice sounded in my ear. "With my life. But don't push me away, Alexis. Don't disappear again."

"I'll stay in contact." And that was one promise I would find a way to keep. "After all, I need you, whether you realize it or not. You're brilliant, sexy, generous, and pretty damn amazing to put up with this." And he was male, which meant he needed my reassurance, even if he was one of the most confident people I'd ever met.

"Now you're just giving the ego a thorough stroking." He chuckled. "You know, there are tangible things that would benefit more from such actions." And there was the Martin I knew.

"I'll be in touch."

"Ooh, I can't wait." The devilish tone over the double entendre filled his voice.

Feeling better about the current situation, I hid my stupid grin and opened Mark's office door. It was time to get back to work. One of the technicians commandeered my attention and dragged me to the OpCenter. Jablonsky was giving whoever came on shift and missed last night's failed raid an update on the current situation. I listened in, and when he was done, I was handed another two burner phones, a replacement for communicating with Mark's burner since the last one was taken by the police and the other to leave in Francisco's car.

In addition to the GPS, the cell was outfitted with a listening device. Basically, Steele's car would be wired. The phone was blank and untraceable, and he'd have no way of knowing who planted it or when. So with any luck, he'd be willing to give me a ride, and we'd be one step closer to pulling drugs off the streets and determining who had an axe to grind with the KXDs, besides the federal government.

After another hour or two of briefings, filing reports, and reviewing the intel, bogus or otherwise, Mark gave me a ride to the hospital. But given my earlier escape, I was strongly cautioned not to go near the ER or trauma units for fear of being recognized. The police presence from this morning had been called away, and I owed O'Connell and Heathcliff my gratitude.

Picking up the phone, I dialed the number that sent the text last night. After three tries, Francisco finally answered. It was late in the afternoon, but from the sound of his voice, I suspected he had been asleep.

"I need you." My voice came out panicked and breathy.

"Alexia?"

"After you left the coffee shop, four thugs attacked me. God, Francisco, they're all dead. I'm surprised I'm not. There was a drive-by. Shit," I exhaled into the phone, "the cops were crawling around, asking questions, and making threats. I barely managed to sneak away. If they find out who I am, I'll probably end up in jail. That's providing I don't get killed beforehand. What have you done? How come men were following us last night?"

"Chill, chica." He sounded agitated and annoyed by my dramatics. "Where the hell are you?"

"At the city hospital."

"Get in a cab and get home."

"How? Everything I have is gone. I had to bribe an orderly just to keep my phone. What am I supposed to do?" I sniffled loudly. "Were you using me? Am I just a goddamn decoy?"

"Listen," his tone was cold and commanding, "hang tight. I'll pick you up outside the hospital."

"Really? You left last night. How can I be sure you won't abandon me again?"

"It's either me or the cops. Take your pick."

TWENTY-TWO

When Francisco arrived in a brand new, high-end, silver SUV, I was a little surprised. Granted, dealers made good money and the gang lifestyle could be prosperous, but a beat-up, ancient sedan with spinners and a killer sound system would have suited him better. He pulled to the curb, rolling down the window.

"I don't have all day." His focus shifted to the parked police cruiser which was always present at the hospital. Once I was inside, he pulled back onto the main road and into rush-hour traffic. "What the hell went down last night?"

I told him the condensed, OIO-approved version. As he continued to gaze at the road, I removed the outfitted throwaway phone from the front pocket in my sweatshirt and slipped it into the space between the seat and the center console, making a show of readjusting the seatbelt as I shifted one leg underneath me. He didn't seem to notice.

"Who were they?" I asked.

"Sounds like the Lords. They've been after our stash for a while. They tried to move in, but Shakespeare put an end to that a couple of years back. Obviously, they must have forgotten the lesson we taught them." Francisco didn't seem particularly interested in the thugs, and I wondered if Shakespeare had some retaliatory measures planned.

Swallowing, I forced the emotional turmoil back into the recesses of my mind. This wasn't the time or place. "What about the SUV? Whoever was inside mowed down the Lords and took off."

"I don't know." He laid into the horn, but the car in front of us was gridlocked just like everyone else. Tilting his head, he assessed me, unable to see the physical results of the fight. "You seem okay. What'd they do to you? Did they touch you?" he asked, sounding possessive and angry.

"A fight broke out, and they held a gun to my head." I stared out the windshield. "I ended up pinned behind a dumpster. I fought to get free and tore something in my leg. It's easier to call it a partial dislocation, but medically, it wasn't that severe."

"Where'd you get the clothes?"

"One of the nurses took pity on me and gave me some stuff to wear," I said, but he glowered at the sweatshirt, like it might have a tracking device implanted inside. "I was stuck outside in the middle of a snowstorm, literally freezing to death. Some people have hearts, unlike you and your Lord pals."

He released the steering wheel and grabbed my shoulder hard. "They are not my friends. Do you understand that?" I cowered, nodding. "Don't say shit like that, particularly around Shakespeare or the others. They wouldn't understand that you are just playing around."

"Aren't you Shakespeare's protégé or something? Why wouldn't he trust you?"

"It's best if you keep your mouth shut." Clearly, Steele wasn't much for discussing these details further.

When we arrived in the ghetto neighborhood, he parked illegally at the hydrant in front of my building. Stepping out, I hissed at the pressure and dreaded the four flights of stairs up to that horrible hovel. Francisco came around the car, scrutinizing me more severely than ever before. He didn't offer assistance, and I didn't ask.

Once inside the apartment, he blocked the door. "Show

me what they did to you."

"Do you think I'm making it up?"

He shrugged, so I pulled the sweatshirt over my head and turned around. When I completed a full revolution, he stepped forward, and I flinched.

"Easy, chica," his voice was soothing as he reached down and handed back the sweatshirt, "they'll regret this. I'll make sure of that."

"They're dead. There's no one left to pay back." The last thing we needed was a gang war erupting. "I just don't want to be used." I turned the anger toward him. "Was I your decoy last night?"

"No." But from the micro-expressions that crossed his face and the way his eyes darted to the side, he was lying. "I wanted you to see this is the big leagues, so you'd behave appropriately when hocking some crystal and powder."

"Last night, you said the cocaine was being delivered elsewhere."

"Things change."

And at that moment, I knew he didn't particularly trust me, and he also knew a lot more about the men from last night. Perhaps the attack was another test of my allegiance, but that didn't feel right. No, this felt more like a double-cross. He retreated to the door, uttering some sentiment about being in touch.

Locking the door, I examined everything inside the apartment. The hidden compartment in the closet was sealed, and nothing had been touched. Assuming my cover was still intact, I decided to forego the surveillance equipment for the moment. It was too early, and my gut said there might be other visitors stopping by this evening.

Over the course of the next few hours, the exhaustion set in. Sinking onto one of the kitchen chairs, I put my legs up on another and snuggled under the threadbare blanket from the air mattress. Aside from a few deals going down, the neighborhood was quiet. Perhaps too quiet. But I was in no condition to complain, and after the foot traffic reached a lull, I stopped fighting the urge to close my eyes.

Voices in the hallway woke me. My next door neighbor was having an argument with her husband. After listening to angry bellows for a couple more minutes, I returned to my perch, but screaming jolted me upright. I was definitely awake now.

Slipping the gun into my waistband, I pulled my sweatshirt down and cautiously opened the front door. The woman who had called me a whore and seemed protective of her son was on her knees in the middle of the hallway, crying and screaming. Her apartment door was open, and I couldn't quite determine what had happened.

"Hey, are you okay?" I asked as my eyes darted down the hallway, toward the steps, and back to her open apartment.

Her screaming stopped, and she looked up as if she'd never seen me before. Maybe I was overdressed. Unsteadily, she got to her feet, wiping her eyes with the back of her hand. Her confusion quickly turned to rage, and she spat in my direction, the glob of saliva landing on the hem of my jeans.

"This is your fault. They should have killed you."

Okay, playing nice just went out the window. "What did you hear? Do you know who those men were or what they wanted?"

"The Lords. And now the KXDs have to retaliate. Sean promised he was done with that life. That he was out. But when Francisco and Shakespeare came knocking, he went running off with them to defend the likes of some stupid cock-sucking whore like you. Stay the hell away from me." She shoved me and stomped back to her apartment, slamming the door hard enough that the flimsy walls rattled.

Returning inside, I picked up the burner and dialed Jablonsky. Someone needed to warn the PD an impending bloodbath was imminent. How did this happen? I felt like Franz Ferdinand right before World War I broke out. I wasn't responsible, but somehow, my attack was the catalyst for the beginning of bedlam.

Two hours later, the shiny SUV rolled up. Francisco, Shakespeare, and three other men I didn't recognize exited the vehicle. They appeared to be in one piece, but that didn't mean the Lords were. Shakespeare and two of the men went across the street and back to his apartment while Francisco and the other man entered my apartment building. A minute and a half later, voices were in the hallway, and then there was a knock.

"It's done," Francisco said, coming inside without an invitation. "I promised you they'd regret it. And they do."

"What did you do?"

"We had a nice little meet. They know not to fuck with us again. Last night, they lost four of their guys. Next time, it'll be more."

"What did you do?" I asked again.

"We gave them a warning. If you piss on our turf, we'll shit on yours." He smiled. "So now that I've demonstrated the lengths I'll go to in order to protect you, are you done doubting me?" He snaked a hand around my waist, locating the gun and pulling it free. "What's this?" He ejected the magazine and examined the barrel and filed off serial number.

"I was scared."

"There's nothing to be scared of." He put the gun on the table and hugged me. "You're one of us now, and we protect our own." I tried to break free, but he held tighter. "Listen, you'll start moving product for us on Monday, and I'm not talking E. If anyone messes with you, I'll take care of it. So leave that peashooter at home. Got it?"

"Yeah." I tried again to step out of his hold, but he didn't let go.

"Where'd you get it?" He kept a firm grip on my waist but leaned back in order to stare into my eyes.

"From a friend."

"I'm gonna need to meet this friend."

"He's nobody. Just someone from my past."

He studied my eyes, searching for the lie but not finding it. After all, the statement was true. "Regardless, set up a meet. Shakespeare doesn't like us hanging out with people outside the 'hood."

"I'll see what I can do, but we aren't in touch anymore. So did you kill anyone tonight?"

"What if I did?" He stepped closer, reaching for the discarded nine millimeter and putting the magazine back inside. He aimed at a fixed point on the wall before lowering the weapon and turning with a smirk. "Would you show some gratitude?" His fingers danced along my arm, tugging my sleeve upward to the crook of my elbow. "Or do you need another hit to convince you I'm not such a bad guy?"

"But you are a bad guy."

He smiled, a bright grin that crinkled the corners of his eyes. "That I am, chica." He winked. "And I'm guessing you have a thing for bad guys." Before he could say or do anything else, his phone beeped. He checked the display, cursed, and put the phone back in his pocket. "Dammit."

"Are you leaving?" I asked, feeling slightly more brazen.

"Got to. But maybe you'll be feeling a bit more grateful later. Call me if there's anything I can do for you." He gave me his best bedroom eyes. Then his gaze flicked to my exposed arm and the faked signs of heroin use. "I can meet all your needs."

"I'll think about it."

He nodded and let himself out. Too bad I didn't need anyone to take care of me, and quite frankly, I found the sentiment offensive. But that was neither here nor there. Returning to the window, I waited for him to clear the building before dialing Jablonsky. At least our two-way communication had improved since the attack, seeing as how he answered on the first ring.

"Did the GPS work?" I asked in lieu of a greeting.

"Like a charm. The audio's not great, but we could still hear most of what was said inside the vehicle. Agent Lawson, our tech genius, is cleaning it up, and I called Lucca back to analyze the data. Someone will meet you at the motel in the morning for an update."

"So this is happening every day?"

"Until I can get someone else on the inside. If something happens, leave a message at the locker dead drop. I only want you to use the gym from here on out. Our other dead drop was too exposed. You need to take more precautions. Have you encountered any problems since?"

"Nothing I can't handle."

"Okay." He paused, and a door slammed in the

background. "If it's life or death, get out of there. Call police dispatch or O'Connell or whoever. I don't want a repeat of last night happening. Do you hear me, Alex?"

"I think Kendall might have something to say about that."

"I don't care. Your safety is the first priority."

"That's not exactly how this works."

"It is now."

TWENTY-THREE

The next day, I woke around noon. It was the first time I'd slept in that apartment for more than a couple of hours. Obviously, after the ordeal Saturday night, I wasn't at a hundred percent. My hip was sore, and I knew it was important to follow doctor's orders. RICE - rest, ice, compress, and elevate. Too bad waitressing at a strip joint wasn't conducive to medical advice.

The R aspect was rather touch and go since chairs and air mattresses didn't really count as rest, but I'd been elevating and icing the injury as much as possible. Walking was slightly less painful today, but I shouldn't stretch, run, or otherwise engage in physical activity until the strains and tears had a chance to repair themselves. Deciding to do my best to take it easy, I grabbed my gym bag, dropped the memory card from the night before into the bottom of my sneakers, made sure I had my outfit for the club, and slipped my nine millimeter into my purse. Without the bulky parka, I couldn't conceal the handgun underneath my sweatshirt and risk Francisco discovering it again. After making sure everything damning was well-hidden, I slowly made it down the steps and out the front door. Francisco was waiting in the alley near the dumpster.

"Hey," he bounded up, "where are you going?"

"The gym. Then work."

"Did you forget what we talked about?"

"No, but I thought you were dropping the product off at the Black Cat like you did the other day."

"It's already there. Inside your locker. Additional instructions are written on a slip of paper."

"Okay." I shivered and hugged myself to keep warm.

"What happened to your coat?"

"The police took it as evidence."

"And your leg is pretty banged up," he commented, noticing the slight limp to my gait. "So why are you going to the gym?"

"I hate to break it to you, but I still have to keep the abs in shape. Clubs fire girls for flab. So I don't have much of a choice."

Continuing to the bus stop, I took a seat and tried to ignore his watchful stare. *C'mon, Parker, focus*, my mind ordered. Normally, I was better at reading people, but Francisco was far too contradictory in his actions to make his motives clear. He might suspect the untruthfulness of my statements, or he simply wanted to make his dominance apparent in every aspect of my life. Alexia Nicholson didn't need to account for every minute of her day, but Francisco failed to agree.

When the bus arrived, I climbed on board and took a seat at the back. I didn't recognize anyone, and after exiting at the proper stop for the gym, I checked again for signs of a tail. As soon as I was sure no one was following me, I ducked into the ladies' locker room and deposited the intel inside the agreed upon locker. Then I went into one of the empty changing stalls, pulled the curtain, and waited a half hour before leaving. After making certain the coast was clear, I hailed a cab and went to the motel.

Agent Eddie Lucca was inside, sitting at the table with a few files in front of him. At the sound of the key in the door, his hand came to rest on the government-issued firearm strategically placed beside him.

"Always prepared?" I asked, locking the door and glancing out the drawn curtain.

"Did you encounter any problems on your way here, ma'am?" His lip twitched slightly.

"Nothing to report." I bristled, knowing I shouldn't dish it out if I wasn't willing to take it. "What are we doing?" I eased onto the closest bed and propped my legs up. "Steele expects me to start moving coke tonight. I don't know what form it's in or precisely what is already in play. He had a system set up for the E tabs, so he must have something established for the harder stuff." I bit my lip. "The KXDs run the Black Cat. There's no other explanation."

"Are you sure you aren't the analyst?"

"I wish. Investigations suck far less than undercover field assignments. We could switch, and you can parade around in sequined underwear while I compile files and collect evidence."

He ignored my generous offer. "We should get started. The sooner you get back to work, the faster we'll nail these assholes." He flipped open a file, folding the cover backward and handing it to me. "Let's begin with the intel we gathered from the bug you planted inside the SUV yesterday."

The words were a bit garbled and staticky, but I could make out Steele's voice and Bard's. The other three voices on the recording must have belonged to the three men I saw exiting the SUV. Inside the truck, they had spoken of restaking their territorial claims against the Lords. There was some mention of rats and sellouts, but their words were guarded, even within the privacy afforded by Steele's SUV.

"After your call, we passed word along, and the PD scrambled a few patrol units to the Lords' neighborhood. No shots were fired. But I don't know what would have happened if there hadn't been an obvious police presence," Lucca concluded. "I'm guessing if it weren't for us, the ME's office would have been busy this morning. You did good."

"Doesn't feel like it."

"Moving on," he wasn't much for coddling, and that quality was one I could appreciate, "we've had more time to determine what went wrong with the raid. A couple of the passenger trains tested positive for drug residue. The drug dogs hit on it, and the evidence collection teams swabbed the area, discovering a mix of heroin, cocaine, and marijuana. Pills wouldn't show up on our tests, so we still can't be certain what other illegal substances the KXDs might be receiving from their international contacts."

"What about the other angles? Firearms and human trafficking?"

"Have you ever met a dog trained to detect guns?" he asked, and I rolled my eyes. "We didn't get a hit on any explosive residue, but that isn't telling us much."

"Well, at least they aren't moving bombs or WMDs." After skimming through the rest of the files, I didn't learn anything that I didn't already know about this assignment. "Okay, so what's our play for tonight?"

"After your near-arrest, the PD's been brought up to speed on the basics. Someone from narcotics division has an in with the KXDs. But the police brass isn't sharing their intel with us. From what I have inferred, they might have a few ongoing operations that overlap with ours, but they haven't been forthcoming, despite how hard we've been urging them to open up. We're hoping whoever you're supposed to pass the product to will be an undercover cop."

"And if it isn't?"

"We've tapped into the surveillance system at the Black Cat. Agent Wolfe is on-site as a bouncer. We'll follow the breadcrumbs wherever they might lead and coordinate arrests. With any luck, we'll scoop up someone a bit higher in the food chain than your average addict and get them to name names."

"And maybe afterward we can make friendship bracelets and hold hands," I said, and he gave me a look. "Optimism really isn't my thing." Rubbing my eyes, I just wanted this to end. "Hey, what happened to Veronica? Jablonsky said he wanted to bring her in for a chat once she was released from the hospital."

Lucca shrugged, standing and placing the files inside a briefcase. "He doesn't pass much information my way. He considers things like that above my pay grade." He glanced up from what he was doing and narrowed his eyes. "How come he lets you in on these little secrets?"

"Just lucky, I guess." I wasn't about to explain my history with Mark to the boy scout. Lucca nodded and went to the connecting door. Apparently, the OIO sprang for the adjoining room to lessen the chance of anyone realizing I was undercover. "Hey, what's the word on using the motel phone?"

"It's clean. You can call anyone. It's not a risk since the KXDs have no way of accessing phone records, and it's not a cell they could accidentally stumble upon or take from you." He paused at the door. "Is there someone at home you need to contact?"

"Maybe."

"Well, it's secure, so feel free." He unlocked the two sets of doors. "Good luck tonight."

"Yeah. Let's hope I don't need it."

Checking the time, I picked up the phone and dialed Martin. After a few rings, he answered, surprised and elated to hear my voice. "You actually kept your promise. Amazing. How are you feeling? I wanted to send flowers or chocolates or something, but you were pretty adamant that you were too busy working to even stop by your own apartment."

"I'm feeling better. Just working a stakeout, so please delete this number from your call log when we hang up, okay?"

"Sure," he replied, and we made small talk for a few minutes before I had to go.

At least I had some connection to the outside world, even if it would only make staying in character that much more difficult. Once we disconnected, I dressed for work, put a layer of clothing over the Black Cat's uniform, and took a cab to the strip club. Now that Alexis Parker's business was handled for the day, it was time to deal with Alexia Nicholson's issues.

Inside my employee locker was a brick of cocaine. Scribbled in barely legible writing were instructions to pass this off to a specific dealer after a complicated conversation that utilized key phrases occurred. Obviously, Steele must have thought he was an international spy with all this codeword nonsense, but I was just the middleman. However, it would be difficult to move such a large quantity out of my locker and into a single person's possession without drawing undue attention from my co-workers, specifically Joe the suspicious bartender.

On the bright side, at least I wouldn't be hocking illegal substances to a bunch of different people; however, I was supposed to pass it off to one individual who would likely do just that. At least from a tactical standpoint, making arrests would be easier. And the dealer could theoretically provide enough intel to trace back to the supplier or supply chain. It was progress, just like being taken to the location of the KXDs' stash house and processing center. Too bad Steele's instructions didn't fit into the OIO's plans.

Sliding the kilo of blow into my duffel bag to prevent premature detection, I slipped out of my street clothes and put on the stiletto heels, wincing at the added pressure and strain the shoes caused my sore tendons and ligaments. If I were really Alexia, I would have taken a bump of coke to dull the pain. Oh well, c'est la vie.

When I went to the bar to pick up an empty tray and order pad, Joe raised a questioning eyebrow. "What the hell happened to you?"

"Nothing."

He sighed dramatically and dragged me behind the bar. There was a makeup bag for emergency touch-ups tucked between the freezer and cabinets, and he removed the bag and sifted through the items. After pulling out a tube of foundation, he grabbed a piece of paper towel.

"Did you even bother to look in the mirror before walking out here? God, it's even worse in the back. Sit down and stop fidgeting. I'm supposed to be tending bar, not doing your makeup."

"My makeup's fine."

"I'm not talking about your face." He squeezed some of the beige liquid onto his fingertips and caked it on my back. "Is this why you weren't here the other night?"

"I wasn't scheduled to work."

"Right, because you were moonlighting as someone's punching bag." And with that comment, I realized I was still covered in defensive wounds and bruises. Looking down, I saw the scratches on my forearm and remembered Martin's lips on my back. I'd been too preoccupied to take notice. "It's not the best. Cosmetology wasn't my major," he said, sounding more flamboyant than I'd ever heard. "But at least you look less like a brawler." He handed the tube of makeup to me. "Maybe you should try to look less like an addict too." The bite was back in his words, and he wiped the makeup off his hands and threw out the paper towel.

After covering up the scratches, I grabbed a pen and began making the rounds. An hour into my shift, the limp was much more pronounced as I hobbled from table to table. Given my last encounter with Joe, I found it strange he was keeping tabs on me. And I wondered if he was working for the KXDs. Maybe he was their inside man. He knew about the coaster trick and confronted me about dealing. Mentally moving his name higher on my list of potential leads, I returned to the bar and lifted myself onto the back counter. I needed a break, and this was a good excuse to wheedle information out of Joe.

"Anyone ask for me?" I queried when he finished pouring a shot of bourbon.

"Like who?"

"I don't know. That's why I asked."

The buyer had yet to show, and I didn't spot any familiar faces from either the PD or the KXDs. The club was fairly empty. A few men were seated at the side booths, enjoying lap dances or other forms of entertainment. The stool at the far corner of the bar was filled, but the man was turned completely around. The only thing I could make out was a tattered leather jacket and about three days' worth of beard growth. I wouldn't have been surprised if he was the buyer, but he needed to interact with the waitresses if he wanted his product. And so far, he hadn't said a word to anyone except Joe.

"Get back to work, Alexia," Joe ordered after my ten minute break was over. He was back to being an asshole, and I couldn't determine the reason for his mood swings. Maybe he was PMSing. I went around the bar, hissing with each step. "Don't forget your tray." I leaned across to grab it, and the man at the corner stool pulled me onto his lap.

"Touching is off limits," I snapped, struggling against him.

He held on tight, chuckling. "You really need to stop ordering my girl around, Joe," the man said. Then he whispered in my ear, "Relax, Alex, it's me."

TWENTY-FOUR

Pulling back, I looked into his eyes. The voice was the same, as were most of his features, but Detective Derek Heathcliff was the most convincing UC I'd ever seen. And I'd seen a lot. Even on the few rare occasions that I'd needed him to play a badass, he never looked quite as threatening and disheveled as he did now. At work, he was spit-shined and clean-cut. His clothing was impeccable, and everything from his belt to his shoes to his badge gleamed. But here, he was dressed in ragged leather and chains. His premature beard made him look like a madman, and the way he carried himself read trouble in big, bold letters.

"What are you doing here?" I asked, realizing a second later that he must have been the UC narcotics sent to assist, except he didn't work in narcotics anymore. He was in major crimes and had been for the last five years. "I don't have time to talk. I have work to do."

"Yeah, I know. So figure out which of the private VIP rooms is empty because that sweet ass is about to dance for me," he growled possessively, sounding very un-Heathcliff like.

"Joe?" I asked.

"Take four," Joe said, and I caught a brief exchange between him and Heathcliff. "It hasn't been used all night."

I took Heathcliff's hand and dragged him through the club toward the curtained cubicle in the corner.

He stepped closer. "You shouldn't be here."

"Neither should you," I replied just as quietly. If the KXDs spotted me with a cop, I'd be done. And if I missed my window of opportunity to pass the coke off to the buyer because of Heathcliff's appearance, I'd be just as screwed. We made it to the room, and I pushed him into the chair, just like I'd done with Francisco. "Can I get you anything, babe?"

"I'd kill for iced lemonade with oranges."

I gaped at his words. Yes, they were ridiculously stupid. But no one would ever deem to speak like that in the real world, and the letters spelled K-I-L-O, making it the perfect key phrase. Derek was the buyer.

"I'm not sure exactly how to serve that particular item."

"Well, close the curtain, and we can figure the rest out together." After doing what he said, I moved toward him, barely able to stand, let alone dance. He pulled me forward, so I was straddling his lap. "Let me apologize now for anything that might accidentally happen," he muttered in my ear, holding me close so we could talk privately. "Mark called Sunday and said you were in a jam, and since I still have quite a few narco connections, this made sense."

"Now's not the time. But you're really the buyer Francisco told me about?"

"Yep. Where is it?"

"Down the hall, inside my duffel bag."

"Okay. Here's the plan. We'll stay in here for the next twenty minutes and convince that camera we're doing more than talking. Then you'll go back to the bar and tell Joe you aren't feeling well. He'll let you leave early. And I'll meet you outside, near the side entrance. I'll offer to carry your duffel, and we'll part ways when the cab comes to pick you up."

"Fine."

Speaking about anything other than the trade wasn't wise. Sure, the OIO hacked the feed, but since the club was

KXD property, Bard or someone else could eventually watch the security footage. Hopefully, our close proximity and hushed voices wouldn't be caught on tape.

The next twenty minutes were awkward, but we survived. My dignity was practically gone, and Heathcliff had his own reasons to be embarrassed. On my third step out of the room, I stumbled, landing in a clumsy heap on the floor. Derek's eyes met mine only briefly before he went out the front door. It was part of our ploy, even if my trip wasn't.

"Joe, I can't keep this up. Get one of the girls to cover my section. I need to go home," I said.

"I don't even want to know what the two of you just did." His eyes jetted to the VIP area. "Get out of here. You're no good to me when you're that wasted."

"Thanks." I went into the locker room and retrieved the bag.

Outside, Heathcliff was a few feet away from the employees' entrance. Without a word, he slipped an arm around my waist, leaning in close so I could put my arm around his shoulders and he could support some of my weight.

"You should have told me. That day in your apartment when I was grilling you about the bruises, you should have told me," he whispered.

"I couldn't."

"Sure, you could. But you didn't."

We continued toward the end of the street where there was more foot traffic before attempting to hail a cab. He reached into his pocket and handed me something. From the feel alone, it was a roll of cash, and I tucked it inside my purse. My eyes scanned the area, but he wasn't risking either of our covers by continuing communication or acting like we knew one another. When a cab finally stopped after my fourth attempt to flag one down, I climbed inside.

"I'll be around," he said, closing the door and tapping the side of the car.

Once the cab dropped me off, I pulled the roll of bills from my purse and put them inside my pocket. Waiting on the front steps of my apartment building were Francisco

Steele and DeAngelo Bard. There was no sneaking past or avoiding them, which clearly meant someone wanted the money and didn't trust me not to abscond with it.

"You're home early," Steele said, checking the time on his phone. "Did something happen?"

"No, but I had a crappy night." Reaching into my pocket and removing the cash, I closed the gap between us and slipped the wad of bills into his pants pocket. "That should do it."

"How do you know you passed it off to the right guy?" Bard asked, commanding our attention and snapping his fingers at Steele to give him the cash.

"Well, how many idiots would kill for some iced lemonade with oranges?" I retorted.

"Watch your tone," Bard ordered, removing the rubber band and thumbing through the bills. "At least you didn't get greedy." He tossed a glance to Steele before disappearing across the street, mumbling about mouthy bitches.

"Whatever," I sidestepped past Steele, "today was hell. I need to sit down."

"Chica," he grabbed my shoulders and pulled me backward, almost knocking me off balance in the process, "did you forget something?"

My mind ran through his instructions and orders, but I couldn't come up with anything. The only thought that raced through my mind was that he'd found the cell phone in his car. But if he did, I'd probably be dead by now.

"Apparently."

His hands slid across my waist and over my stomach, coming to rest inside the front pocket of my sweatshirt. "I told you I'd take care of you. A deal's a deal." He pulled his hands free a second later. "That ought to improve your night."

"Thanks, but I'll need a cut if you expect me to keep this up."

He emitted a noncommittal sound, so I continued on my trek inside and up the stairs.

Steele's present provided the perfect opportunity to hole up inside, fail to answer the door when he came knocking later that night, and to stay indoors and monitor the situation outside. After sending a few encrypted messages about my handoff to my handler at the OIO, I stretched out on the air mattress, bouncing slightly as the oversized balloon settled underneath my weight. But as usual, sleep didn't come.

When dawn broke, I removed the surveillance equipment and went back to bed. With the amount of smack Steele placed in my pocket, I could theoretically ride out the high for the next day or two. Sure, that probably wasn't his intention, but in order to continue the ruse, it seemed like an okay plan, particularly since I didn't want to go back to the Black Cat where more product might be awaiting pick-up. Addicts were unreliable, and I'd been keeping too strict of a schedule for the last couple of weeks. It was time to mix things up again.

When the boredom became too much to take, I climbed off the air mattress and did some light stretching, a hundred push-ups, and a few hundred crunches. My hip was feeling better, and the swelling was completely gone. It still hurt to put pressure on it, but taking a day or two off from sashaying about in my underwear would surely alleviate that.

After narrowly managing to contain a fit of hysteria when I found two six-legged friends showering with me, I returned to the main room. It was midday, but things were quiet outside. Probably too quiet. Trying not to think of the possible reasons for the lack of gang activity, I microwaved a frozen sandwich pocket and grabbed the last remaining crossword puzzle book. Jablonsky messaged earlier that I was to stay in the vicinity and inside the apartment if at all possible. For once, I was inclined to follow orders.

As the sky darkened and the foreboding clouds threatened to dump another foot of snow on us, Bard and a few of his personal guards exited the apartment across the street. Francisco was near the burning trash bin with the two usual lookouts. The men gestured wildly, and I would have loved to eavesdrop on the conversation. Unfortunately, my surveillance gear wasn't quite up to snuff for that. The discussion continued until someone else walked up.

From the distance, I couldn't tell who he was, but he offered his hand, pulling Bard and then Steele into a one-armed hug and clapping each man on the back. He fist-bumped the two lookouts and then pointed in the direction of my apartment building. Instinctively, I ducked down, studying the small screen on the camera from my crouched position. This newcomer wore a dark jacket, a scarf, and a ski cap pulled low on his head, making identification difficult from the tiny fraction of his face that was visible, but I recognized his gait. Derek.

Scrambling, I hid the surveillance equipment and pulled out the dark eyeshadow pallet, doing a quick update on my track marks and adding a fake puncture or two with some red lip stain. Shellacking the effects with a quick coat of hairspray, I hoped not to come under too much scrutiny by Steele or one of Bard's other lackeys. Finally, I dabbed the tiniest amount of peppermint oil on my cheekbones to make my eyes redden and tear just as the knocking sounded.

"Alexia, open up," Steele bellowed. I mumbled something that hopefully sounded like a euphoric grunt. He pounded against the door, making the floor vibrate. "Chica, I know you're in there."

"Hang on," I called softly, not moving from the spot. A minute later, I went to the door, slowly twisting the lock and opening it. "Huh?" I asked, fluttering my eyelids.

"You're gonna be late for work," Steele said.

"I'm not going. I'm sick."

I tried to shut the door, ignoring the posse of three men who accompanied him, but he stepped into the doorframe, using his foot to keep the door from closing. Pretending not to notice, I turned and stumbled back into the apartment, dropping onto the mattress and bouncing up. Heathcliff was in the hallway, and I wasn't too worried about annoying Steele with backup that close.

Francisco stormed into my apartment and yanked me off the bed. Remembering to act as if my limbs were made of gelatin, I let him shove me against the wall. "We had an agreement," he hissed, infuriated.

"I did what you wanted," I slurred, finding his shirt particularly fascinating and tracing my fingertips over the pattern. "And you rewarded me. I'm so fucking rewarded right now." Lolling my head backward against the wall and sighing, he saw the empty baggie on the table that I planted intentionally next to a syringe. I pretended to try to focus. "What's wrong? Was I supposed to do something else? Did you tell me to do something else?" He released my arms, and I sunk to the floor as if my legs didn't know how to function.

"You're useless." He turned to the men who remained in the hallway. "We'll have to get one of the other girls to do it for us." He cautioned a final glance my way before speaking to the two lookouts. "And keep your mouths shut about this to Bard, or you'll have to reckon with me." The two KXDs took off to enact whatever Steele wanted.

"God, I get put away for a nickel, and now that I'm back, it looks like things have really changed. But Shakespeare made it sound like you're still having the same problems as before," Heathcliff said, stepping inside.

"The Lords are trying to move in on our turf again. They turned a few of our girls." Steele ran a hand through his hair. "They're ballsy fuckers. They even made a move on our imports the other day, but we picked up the shipment early. So they came to our stash house. Did you see what they did to Alexia?"

"Hmm?" I barely lifted my head off my chest, watching the exchange from beneath my lashes.

"Oh, so that explains why she could barely dance," Heathcliff said, stepping closer and crouching down to examine my arm. "Was the blow part of the shipment you just received?"

"Yeah." Steele sounded suspicious, and Heathcliff stepped away. "Since when does stuff like that matter to you, Hotshot?"

"Since I need to know that your supply lines are secure." Heathcliff moved forward, standing toe-to-toe with Francisco. "There isn't a chance in hell I'm serving any more time, and pissing off the Irish is a surefire way to end up behind bars or in the ground."

"Then why are you acting like their lapdog?" Steele challenged.

"Because no one can move product at a markup that high without the proper societal connections, and we both know who has that racket. I'm not going back to pushing on street corners with skanks begging for a hit on trade or some other pusher knifing me in the back to clean out my pockets for a few dimes' worth of blow. I'm moving up in this world, Francisco, and you ought to consider doing the same," Heathcliff growled. "Now run along, unless you want word getting back to Shakespeare that you screwed up by not having someone ready to procure my product for tonight."

Steele looked torn, and for a moment, I was certain he wouldn't leave Heathcliff alone with me. Under different circumstances, it might have been considered chivalrous, so I needed to do something to convince him that leaving was a good idea.

"Babe," I pulled myself to my feet, "when'd you get here? Did you come back to finish what we started yesterday?" I purred, hanging on Heathcliff's arm and running my other hand through his hair.

"Take off," Heathcliff said again.

"If you do anything to her that she doesn't want, I'll rip your balls off and hang them from my rearview mirror. You got that?" Steele snarled. "You'll tell me if he hurts you, right, Alex?" I nodded, and he slammed the door shut behind him.

TWENTY-FIVE

"Looks like Francisco has a soft spot for you," Heathcliff said, "or a hard on. Either way, getting into his good graces is probably one of the few good decisions you've actually made lately."

"Bite me." Going to the door, I made sure to secure the locks and check the peephole for signs of lingering gangbangers. "It's not safe to talk here."

"How much MJ did you smoke? Because that's just called paranoia." He grabbed one of the straight-backed chairs from the table and dragged it to the door, shoving it underneath the knob. Then he led the way to the only separate room in the apartment – the bathroom. Once we were inside, he turned the sink and shower on full blast and shut the door. "Should I continuously flush the toilet too, or can we get on with this conversation?"

"Someone's in a crappy mood."

"Yeah. That's what happens when Eric "Hotshot" Hall gets pulled out of retirement. Since the story went that I was arrested and spending my days in the pen, it wasn't too hard to promulgate some misinformation about my release."

I flipped the toilet seat lid down and sat while Derek

leaned against the edge of the sink.

"You've stepped into the beginnings of a gang war, Parker. You refused backup. You didn't give the PD the heads up, and you're getting in too deep with the wrong bunch of people. Have you seen Steele's record? Or Bard's? They'll kill you without blinking an eye."

"That's only if they realize who I am. And they won't. Not if you keep your damn mouth shut." Taking a breath, I reminded myself Derek wasn't my enemy. "How much product is supposed to be moved out of the club tonight?"

"Another kilo. Don't worry. The place is getting busted in an hour for expired alcohol permits, and the girls will be brought in and grilled about prostitution. No one's saying a word about drugs, but hopefully, the brick will still be on the premises when the cops get there."

"That's why Mark told me to stay away. How come no one bothered to tell me the plan?"

"I did. Just now." Normally, Heathcliff and I got along great, but it was obvious he was upset about this assignment and my involvement. He scratched his beard. "We need to figure out how the drugs are being moved through the Black Cat and where they're originating. Any ideas?"

"Veronica was working for Steele, but she's out of the picture." I thought back to the two girls with the bag of ecstasy and Joe's suspicions. "Our best bet would be Joe the bartender."

"He doesn't know anything."

"How can you be sure?"

"Because I read his last report."

"Report?" My mind flashed through the inconsistencies. "He's a cop?" I asked, dumbfounded, and Heathcliff nodded. "Let me guess, he's not really gay either." Although, it provided an excellent excuse not to hit on the working girls. It also helped conceal the real secret Joe was harboring; he was an undercover narcotics officer.

"Not according to his girlfriend and their two kids." Some of his harsh exterior faded. "But I guess that means he had you fooled, which means he probably has the KXDs fooled too. If it makes you feel any better, he thought you were just another junkie," his tone hardened, "which is why the FBI should have informed us of their operation."

"Don't tell me we're working the same case."

"Like I said, you should have said something sooner. You knew I helped narco out a couple months ago on something big. Isn't this big enough for you?"

"Derek...Eric...shit," I sighed, "just read me in before this headache gets any worse."

"It gets worse." He glowered. "I'm willing to lay my cards on the table if you are. The brass won't like this, but I trust you, even if you've done nothing but lie for the last month or so." He met my eyes. "What do you say, Parker?"

"It's Nicholson from here on out. Agreed?"

He nodded. "You go first."

Silencing the voice inside my head that argued every word I said went against protocol and ignoring the fact that this voice also sounded a lot like Mark Jablonsky, I told Heathcliff everything from the FBI's suspicions concerning the smuggling of contraband to my own insertion into this neighborhood and attempt to infiltrate the KXDs. Occasionally, he would grunt out a response or nod, but for the most part, he was back to his still and stoic self as he processed this added information. As soon as I finished, he launched into his own tale.

Two and a half months ago, Detective Derek Heathcliff was asked to assist the narcotics division in making a bust. Despite the fact he had transferred to major crimes half a decade ago, he still had a long list of confidential informants, a few undercover identities, and numerous ties to local dealers at his disposal. He even had a few remaining connections to the gangs and crime syndicates that functioned in the dark underbelly of our city.

The police department had heard stirrings of a turf war on the verge of breaking out. The number of gang related deaths, drive-bys, and assaults had skyrocketed in the last few months. Originally, a task force was sent to deal with the gangs, but they quickly discovered that the reason for the violence traced back to a supply and demand issue. Illicit contraband was in demand, but the supply chain had dried up.

According to the research and intel the police department compiled, the DEA had taken a major stance against a preeminent Mexican cartel. The result of dethroning one of the major drug sources for the United States led to a sudden drought when it came to the influx of many illegal substances. And while the next bigwig supplier was scrambling to find a foothold in this wide open market, the street-level dealers were scrambling to stockpile what they could. Prices were about to soar, and everyone wanted to profit.

"It's basic economics," Heathcliff surmised. "Plus, the price of pills and prescription opiates skyrocketed. Morphine, oxy, hydros, everything went through the roof. And suddenly, a bunch of teenaged thugs are breaking into grandma and grandpa's house to empty out the medicine cabinets. It was a mess. So needless to say, narco needed a few extra eyes and ears to figure out who the biggest troublemakers were and to set them straight." He frowned and shook his head. "The sad part is once new supply lines were established, everything settled down. It had more to do with a fresh supply than anything we had done to stop it."

"People want what they want. Street drugs aren't just rampant in poor neighborhoods like this. The upper class want to experiment and escape too. And they'll pay through the nose for the shit they want to put up their nose."

"Heroin. Coke. Crack. Ecstasy. A plethora of hallucinogens. Marijuana. Pills. You name it, they want it. And don't forget about the designer stuff that gets cooked up in labs. And people say the sixties was a drug era. They need to look around at what we're dealing with now."

"I wouldn't know. That was before my time." I shook my head. "Yours too. But this isn't a philosophical debate. Drugs are here, and as long as we're enforcing the law, we follow orders. So after the violence died down, you went back to major crimes, right?"

"Yeah. But the department didn't give up on keeping the peace and getting as many dealers and drugs off the street. The Lords were still causing trouble, rattling their sabers and hoping for a fight. They wanted to absorb the KXDs' supply system into their own and become the primary distributor."

"So Bard is top dog." I didn't realize it, and none of the intel mentioned it. Then again, our intel focused on the overseas connections and not the distribution system already established within our city. "Is he moving anything else besides drugs?"

"Maybe a few guns to keep his guys armed and ready to throwdown. And from the whispers I've heard, he has a couple of prostitutes working in a few select locations, like the Black Cat. But he's careful about that. The hookers serve to pass around product and give the customer a little more bang for their buck. But the KXDs are careful not to step on any toes since the bigger prostitution rings are mafia controlled. Hookers and specialty black market items are mainly focused within the families." He narrowed his eyes. "Wasn't there a certain mafia don who threatened to kill you if you made a move against him?"

"Good thing I'm only working the drug angle then."

"Are you sure Vito would see it that way?" Heathcliff asked, but all I could do was shrug. "Just be careful, we have enough to deal with, and you have plenty to worry about after that SUV almost ran you down."

"Does the PD have any idea who was behind the wheel?"

"They're looking into it. Obviously, we're working different angles in the same case. And whoever it is will eventually fall into our sights." He paused to rub a hand down his face. "The FBI should have informed us. We could have exchanged intel months ago and already washed our hands of this mess. You wouldn't have been coerced into getting reinstated, and I wouldn't have been dragged back to my old division. Things could have been so much simpler." The accusatory look was back. "You should have come clean on poker night."

"Don't even, because I could blame you for not saying a word when you went to assist narcotics. Plus, I was private sector during the original investigation. This isn't my fault or my mess to clean up. I was dragged into this because of a security breach." Scowling, I reached into the shower to shut the water. This was getting ridiculous, and we were doing nothing more than pointing fingers. "Damn hackers."

"Alex," he pressed his lips together, "the two of us can work together. We have before. Let's cut through the bullshit so we can go home."

"Fine by me, but I have to run this new information up the chain of command. And you should probably do the same."

Opening the bathroom door, I went to my bag, searching for the burner. The reception was still shoddy inside the apartment, so it was actually a relief that most of the communication with the OIO was via text message. As I predicted, sharing sensitive information with the PD was frowned upon, but Mark had already bent the rules in order to keep my cover intact. So I ignored the curt replies and replaced the phone inside my bag. When I looked up, Heathcliff was conducting business on his end, except he had an actual cell phone with tons of capabilities and reception to match. He finished his brief conversation and squeezed the bridge of his nose.

"The Black Cat's shut down for the night. How long do you think it'll be before Steele or Bard come knocking?"

"It depends." My stomach clenched. "Probably too soon. And we can't help looking suspicious, especially me. I was supposed to be working tonight. Maybe you should take off. Don't you have some product to pass off to the Irish?" I made a face, wondering who in the world he was talking about or why the KXDs believed him.

"Not tonight. After Steele's blunder, you're my consolation prize." He pulled out a chair and surveyed the rest of the room. "Seriously, the OIO couldn't even spring for a television or couch. That's just cruel and unusual punishment."

"Nicholson's been staying in halfway houses, and couches and TVs aren't that easy to move. I should be thankful for the freaking air mattress and the table and chairs. They're better than the floor."

He tilted his head to focus on the far corner of the room. "Not by much. With a blanket or two, the floor doesn't look so bad."

"Yeah, well, I barely sleep as it is, so I don't plan on giving the floor a try." Sighing, I peered out the window at the snow covered ground below. Apparently, the storm had picked up again, and while we were discussing matters, everything ended up with a fresh coat of white. I shivered at the memory of being trapped behind the dumpster. "It's been impossible to check the KXDs' dead drops and pick-up sites with all this damn snow. Leaving tracks is too great of a risk."

"Speaking of tracks," he nudged his chin at my arm, "those are mighty convincing. Care to paint a few on me?"

"I can try, but the bulk of this was created by professional tattoo artists."

"Never mind."

He drummed his fingers on the table. Conversation was limited since talking about our real lives wasn't a good idea. The activity outside was nonexistent, probably on account of the raid and subsequent arrests, and there was no sign of Steele or Bard. I would have loved to rendezvous with my support team at the motel in order to find out what was happening, but that was out of the question.

Heathcliff checked his watch. "Warm coffee and cookies would be nice," he said, recalling words I'd spoken to him during our very first stakeout when I was nothing more than a private investigator.

"Did you bring any?" I tossed him a smile. "Because the only thing I have is instant, and it's pretty sketchy."

"Well, at least it fits in with everything else around here."

TWENTY-SIX

Twisting around, I buried my face in the pillow. As usual, my mind wouldn't turn off, and I wondered when I did laundry last. It had been five or six days at the most, before the incident with the Lords. That sudden image of the dead men and my near brush with fate resulted in a sharp intake of breath, but silence continued to permeate throughout the apartment. Fighting against the existential crisis that threatened to develop into a small-scale panic attack, I rolled onto my side and stared across the dimly lit apartment at the man in the opposite corner of the room.

Derek was slumped against the wall with his legs pulled up in front of him and his arms resting on his knees. He didn't move or speak, but I felt his eyes on me. Maybe I was imagining things. One of us should be asleep, especially at this time of night. He had suggested we take turns in case the KXDs came knocking, but after two hours of watching me twist and turn, he thought his presence was making me uncomfortable. So we were both supposed to be getting some shut-eye, except that plan didn't seem to be working either.

Not wanting to disturb him in case he actually was asleep, I resisted the urge to get out of bed. Instead, I shifted my position again. My hip had started to ache, and the mattress had a lot to do with that. Propping my head up on my arm, I stared at him, hoping he'd give some clue as to whether or not he was asleep. But he didn't move. The room was bathed in an eerie light that filtered through the blinds from the outside streetlamps, making it difficult to discern his level of wakefulness.

"Hey," I whispered, "are you awake?" He snorted, stifling his chuckle. "I'll take that as a yes." Hauling myself to my feet, I crossed the room and opened the freezer door, pulling out the ice cube trays and grabbing the dish towel. "Why don't you take the bed? One of us needs to be able to see straight in the morning."

"Fine," he agreed, "but only if you keep that leg elevated."

"Are you hoping to play doctor?" I quipped, but he ignored the remark and collapsed onto the air mattress with a slight bounce.

Leaning against the window sill, I studied the ground below. This was the first time since being stationed inside this pathetic hovel that the streets were completely devoid of life. Even when things had been quiet before, there would still be the occasional pedestrian coming home or going out. But tonight, no one stepped foot outside. It was like they knew a battle was brewing, and the first shots might be fired at any second. Hopefully, I was delusional. Lack of sleep had been proven to lead to insanity, and even on my best days, I always seemed a little closer to that line than most.

Convinced that recording the exterior was pointless tonight, I dismantled the surveillance equipment and put it away as quietly as possible. Then I returned to the chair near the window, propped my legs up on the edge of the table, and rested my forehead against the cold glass. I was waiting for trouble.

It was 6:30 and the sky had just started to brighten when Francisco's SUV pulled to a stop, and a chorus of slamming car doors rang out. Roused from my comatose state, I blinked a few times and sat up. From the looks of things, Steele was barking orders and making emphatic gestures.

Less than a minute later, another vehicle joined it. This one was painted matte black, and DeAngelo Bard climbed out. He opened the rear hatch, and the two lookouts who had just stepped out of Francisco's vehicle raced to the back.

"Derek," I said loud enough for him to jump, "grab your phone. We need to call this in."

He crossed the room, peering out the window. "We can't." He bit his lip and looked away. "You know what will happen if we do."

"But," I swallowed, "that man will die without help."

"We don't know that. Plus, that's one of Bard's lieutenants. The KXDs will do what they can to keep him alive."

The two lookouts hoisted the wounded man between them, carrying him by the arms and legs across the street and toward Bard's basement apartment. The dark crimson stains covering the man's torso didn't bode well, and I would wager they had been caused by multiple gunshot wounds. Then again, they might have been stab wounds, or maybe the blood belonged to someone else. I couldn't tell from here. My instincts said he needed medical intervention, and I turned to Heathcliff with a question on my lips.

"We can't just sit back and wait to see what happens."

"Even if units roll up, Bard will lie to them. We can insist on what we saw, but it'll ruin your mission." He sighed, shaking his head. "It's your call. If you want to make it, go ahead." He handed me the phone. "The KXDs protect their own. Gang members get dropped off at the ER all the time. Let them handle things themselves, Alex."

My mouth dropped, and I stared at Heathcliff, expecting him to have a different reaction.

He poured a glass of water from the sink, and the slightest shudder went through him. "Stop looking at me like that." His voice held bite, and red-hot rage shot from his eyes. "There was a reason I transferred." He took a sip, letting out a resigned exhale. "Situations like this are never easy. It's like trying to help a wounded animal. They'll rip your throat out if given the chance because they're afraid you'll take advantage of them in their weakened state."

"Fine. You can sit back and do nothing. I'm passing this along." Picking up my burner, I opened the encryption app and sent Jablonsky a text on what we witnessed.

My phone buzzed a response, and after reading the message, I dropped it on the table. Mark promised to send some units through the area and have paramedics on standby, but unless the uniformed cops witnessed anything or were flagged down to help, we were told to wait it out.

Rationally, I understood. From a security standpoint, I understood. But at the same time, someone was in pain, possibly dying, and I was to wait it out. That seemed ludicrous. And I paced, running through scenarios in the hopes of finding a solution. But nothing I thought of seemed feasible or safe.

"What if you're wrong?" Heathcliff asked. "Maybe he just killed someone and got wasted afterward. We don't know enough to intervene."

"Do you really believe that?"

"At the moment, I'm choosing too." He shut his eyes and inhaled deeply. This was bothering him too. "Once we know more, we can take the appropriate steps to resolve the situation, okay?"

"Okay, so how do you propose we find out more?"

"I'll have a talk with Steele."

Derek went to clean up, and I forced myself into a chair, anxious and jittery. My lack of sleep coupled with our current predicament left a queasy feeling in the pit of my stomach. The Black Cat was raided last night. So why was a bloody gang member pulled out of the back of an SUV early this morning? The war had already started.

Heavy footsteps echoed outside the apartment, making the floor vibrate, followed by loud banging against the door. Derek emerged from the bathroom and grabbed his Glock off the TV tray we were using as a makeshift nightstand.

Communicating silently, I nodded and called out, "Who is it?"

"It's Francisco. Open up, chica. This is important."

G.K. Parks

"Hang on, I'm coming," I yelled, unsure of how to proceed.

Derek concealed the weapon beneath his shirt, but that wouldn't fly. It was too early in the morning for him to be awake, dressed, and armed. Shaking my head, I crossed the room.

"Take off your shirt and get in bed," I ordered, yanking the sweatshirt I wore over my head. "And stick that piece somewhere no one can see it." His eyes read confusion, and I didn't bother to wait before tossing my shirt haphazardly across the room, unbuttoning my jeans, and going to the door. Casting a final glance behind me to make sure he listened and nothing damning was in the open, I yawned audibly, opening the door and running a hand through my tousled hair. "What time is it?" I asked, making a show of buttoning my jeans.

Francisco barged in, unfazed by my state of undress, but he stopped dead in his tracks when he found Derek in my bed. "You let him stay the night?"

"You've stayed the night too." I squinted at the clock. "Is the sun even up yet? What's so urgent that it couldn't wait until later?"

"Get your ass out of bed, Hotshot," Francisco said, ignoring me and kicking the corner of the mattress. "Were you here all night?"

"Every. Single. Minute," Derek replied. Slowly, he stretched, letting the blanket fall and leaving Steele to believe he might be naked underneath the covers. "If you don't want to start your morning by staring at someone else's frank and beans, I'd suggest you give me a minute to get dressed."

Francisco grunted and focused on me as I picked up my sweatshirt and shrugged into it. For the briefest moment, he actually looked hurt or betrayed. But as long as it was nothing more than a bruised ego, everything would be okay.

"You're one lucky bitch, chica," Francisco said, continuing to eye me. "That titty bar where you work was invaded by the po-po. They grilled the girls pretty hard about taking some side jobs. It's not like any of them would

- 199 -

fess up anyway. But it made Shakespeare nervous. And he doesn't like to be nervous. If you'd been hocking product for us last night, things wouldn't have turned out well." He spun to face Derek who was taking his time fastening his recently unbuckled belt. "Twenty-four hours earlier and you'd be back behind bars."

"Are you trying to say something?" Derek asked, crossing the room. "Because if you are, then just spit it out."

"Close call." Something flitted across Francisco's face. "How'd you get an early release? For the shit you got caught with, you should have been serving a decade or two. Not a nickel. Did you turn on someone? Cut a deal? Narc on us?"

Derek laughed. "Dude, that was five years of my life down the drain. If I'd turned on anyone, don't you think they would have gone down five years ago when I did? Shit, man, you've been smoking the ganja again, haven't you?"

Steele didn't look convinced, but no weapons were drawn. Instead, he cocked his head to the side and lifted his shoulders. "So you just happened to get lucky?"

"Damn lucky." Heathcliff smiled. "Plus, I couldn't pick up my brick yesterday because you botched that, remember? So last night I claimed my consolation prize."

Derek brushed past me on the way to the sink, letting his hand linger at the small of my back, slipping the blade from beneath the mattress into my back pocket. Tugging down my sweatshirt to conceal the weapon, I didn't react as he opened the fridge to search for something to eat or drink. Steele wasn't pleased, and based on Derek's actions, I couldn't be sure what he thought was about to happen. But a knife in a gunfight wasn't exactly a stellar idea.

"What happened to Sasha and Joe?" I asked, hoping to derail whatever suspicious thoughts were circulating in Steele's brain.

"Nothing. Like I said, the cops have nothing to go on. They're just snooping around, hoping for a bite," Steele said. "It's a good thing you called in sick."

"Well, that's only because someone paid handsomely for a favor." I winked at him, but he wasn't in a playful mood, probably because one of his friends was full of lead.

"I've heard enough," Steele growled out of the blue. "Let's go."

"Where? It's not even seven a.m.," I protested.

"Move it, chica." He grabbed my arm and yanked me toward him. "You too, Hotshot. Shakespeare wants a word."

"God, Francisco," I pulled my arm free, "what's with the manhandling? I'm sore enough as it is without you acting like some alpha male jerk."

He squeezed the crook of my arm harder and spun, so we were face-to-face. I caught sight of Derek tensing, and I kept my right hand low, signaling that he keep cool. Francisco and I remained locked in a staring match for thirty seconds, neither of us flinching. And then he backhanded me unexpectedly, keeping his grip tight so I wouldn't stumble.

"Do as you're told."

I opened and closed my mouth, licking my split lip. I wanted to spit in his face, but that was what Alexis Parker wanted. Instead, Alexia Nicholson broke eye contact and cowered. "Francisco, please," I whispered, and he released my arm.

Realizing what he'd done, he lifted my chin, and I flinched. He ran his thumb across my bottom lip and kissed my cheek. "I'm sorry. But no more of this. Everything's fucked up right now. Shakespeare's on the warpath, and I'm on edge because of it. Don't cross me again, understand?"

I nodded, and he turned an icy eye on Derek. "Do you have something to say?"

"Maybe later, when we're alone," Derek growled, maintaining his status by not cowering. Sometimes, it paid to have brass ones, but unfortunately, that wasn't my role. Thankfully, it was Derek's. "But if you hit her again, we'll be exchanging more than just words, chico."

TWENTY-SEVEN

When we arrived at Bard's fortress, the normal guards weren't stationed outside. The door was locked, and it was the first time I noticed the high-tech security system being implemented. Biometric locks, scanners, and keypads were positioned at the various entry points. Francisco keyed in a number and led us inside. I didn't spot a single KXD member, but voices traveled from a back room, deep inside the apartment. On the plus side, no one was around to pat us down, which meant the blade wouldn't be detected or questioned; although, I still wanted to ask Derek why he felt it necessary that I be armed with such an impractical weapon. We continued down a back hallway that had been hidden from view on my last visit, and the voices grew louder.

"Help him," Bard said, growing frustrated. At the moment, I still couldn't discern which room he was in or precisely where we were. The apartment was a labyrinth that spanned the entire basement of the apartment building. "If he dies, so do you."

I swallowed and glanced at Heathcliff, but he remained facing forward, exuding complete neutrality. Francisco stopped in front of a doorway, knocked twice, and then pushed the slightly ajar door completely open. Bard shot a glance in our direction and cracked a smile. It was disconcerting.

"Did Steele tell you what happened?" Bard asked, and before I could even fathom who he was speaking to, Heathcliff replied.

"Not in so many words. The police are breathing down your necks. It sounds like vice raided your club." Derek jerked his head at the downed gang member. "Did they do that to him? The Irish said the cops have been raining hell down on drug runners, guns, and girls for the last few months. Frankly, I didn't mind being otherwise occupied and missing out on that shit." He snickered. "But it looks like the fun's getting started again." He rubbed his palms together. "What do you need from me, Shakespeare?"

Had I not known who Derek Heathcliff was, I would have thought he was one of the KXDs or some psychopath. His familiarity with Bard, Steele, and members of different criminal organizations made me draw into question exactly what he had done in the past and what he was about to do now. Remaining silent, I shrunk back against the wall. It was tactically advantageous to limit the angles by which one could be attacked, but it also allowed me to maneuver around Steele and get a better look inside the room.

"Stitch my guy up before he bleeds out," Bard ordered. "Rocco's gonna end up killing him by the time he figures out how to thread the needle." Bard rolled his eyes. "Idiots."

Heathcliff nodded and crossed the room. Taking the first aid kit from Rocco, he pulled out a few items and set to work. Most law enforcement agencies required first responder training. But how did Bard know Heathcliff possessed such skills? And why was Bard confident Heathcliff could do a better job than Rocco?

"Alex," Steele hissed my name, and Bard snapped his fingers in front of my face, "who the hell attacked you after I left the coffee shop?"

"Don't you know? You said you took care of it, and no one would hurt me again. I thought you promised to protect me."

"I did." Steele glowered, annoyed. "But who were they?"

"I don't know."

"Yes. You do," Bard said, approaching and putting an arm around my shoulders and pulling me against his side. "Let's go someplace less chaotic and talk about this. Just the two of us," he added for Steele's benefit. The weight of the knife in my back pocket was the only assurance I had that he wasn't about to take me into another room and kill me for being an undercover agent. "Don't be afraid. Just tell me what I want to know, and you'll be rewarded." Heathcliff glanced up, but with four of the KXDs standing by, we were out of options. It was a good thing I could handle myself. "I have just what you like."

"I really don't know what I can tell you. I already told Francisco what happened." I tried to sound meek and afraid. Normal people would be upset by a man with a few bullet holes. Then again, the KXDs already knew I had experienced my fair share in the past, so it wasn't like Alexia was exactly normal either.

"Relax," he purred, "you're thinking too much." He kept a firm grip on my shoulder as we went down another darkened corridor. Stopping at a thumbprint reader, he pressed his finger to the screen, waited for the light to change from red to green, and opened the door. "Welcome to my humble abode."

The room was large, brightly lit, and actually felt homey. It had large couches, a counter and kitchenette, a television and gaming system, and another doorway that led to some other room. He released his hold and went to the fridge and came back with a can of soda.

"Your house is insane," I said, appearing awed. "So many hallways and rooms. What is this? The man cave?"

"No one comes in here without my permission," he said, as if I should be impressed or thrilled to be invited. "This is where I come to silence the voices." He opened the can and took a sip. "You need to silence the voices."

Hopefully, he was speaking metaphorically. Then again, I wouldn't be surprised to find out he had some diagnosable mental disorder. People who sought power and control and would go to such extremes to achieve that

G.K. Parks

grandeur often did. However, it could be argued that was just ambition and drive. But in Shakespeare's case, it might be more accurately depicted as ambition and drive-bys.

"There were four of them. They dragged me down this dark street. They wanted the blow Francisco picked up." I licked my swollen lip. "One of them looked really rough, like he had the shit knocked out of him one too many times."

"I don't care about them. I want to know about the SUV."

"It was black, I think."

"Who was inside?"

"I didn't see. I was pinned behind the dumpster."

He looked annoyed and pushed me onto the couch. "How were you pinned?" He sat uncomfortably close. The handle of the knife pressed against the small of my back, giving me another option for escaping the room, but I didn't take it.

"The gunfire terrified me, and I froze. By the time I decided to make a run for it, the SUV crashed into the side of the dumpster and pushed it against the wall. It nearly crushed me." He looked confused, so I continued. "My leg got caught." And suddenly, I realized what the point of this interrogation was. He couldn't care less about the SUV. He thought I talked to the police, and that's why they raided the Black Cat.

"And then what happened?"

Playing dumb, I continued with the story about the paramedics and escaping the hospital and calling Francisco for a ride. When I was done, he scrutinized my facial expressions, looking for some sign of a lie. I'd been trained to hide any obvious tells, but the body still had its own responses which could be mitigated and tricked through other means.

"I didn't talk to the cops. A couple of them questioned me, but I wouldn't even give them my name. You can't seriously think I'd turn on my girlfriends at work or Francisco. That's ridiculous."

He squinted. "But you'd turn on me?"

"I didn't say that."

- 205 -

He stood, towering over me, and leaned down, placing his palms on either side of my face. "So what did you say?"

"I'm loyal to them. I wouldn't do anything to hurt myself or my friends. And I'd be a fool to cross you. You control this neighborhood. When you were gone, the place went crazy." My answer must have pleased him because he smiled. "Are you satisfied?"

"We're good." He stepped away, downing the rest of his soda. "But there's just one more thing I'd like to know."

"What's that?"

"How do you know Hotshot?"

Dammit. If our stories didn't match, we'd both be dead. "I don't really know him. He picked up the brick at the club." Furrowing my brow, I cocked my head to the side. "Why didn't he just come to the neighborhood to get it? You guys seem tight."

"We are."

"That's not an answer," I replied, still too flippant for Bard's liking. Unfortunately, my personality had bled through Nicholson's exterior a time or two. I couldn't completely play the cowering damsel in distress, or he might realize it was just a ploy.

"You're not asking the questions," he said. Falling silent, I waited to see what would happen next. "And for someone you don't know, why was he still inside your apartment this morning?"

"We were finishing what we started at the club." Looking away, I hung my shoulders in defeat. "He's a smooth talker and a good tipper."

"It didn't look like there was much left to finish," Bard retorted, sounding sleazy and aroused. "Maybe I need to stop by and give you a nice, large tip."

My voice went hard as nails. "What happened the other night doesn't mean I'm willing to turn tricks for you or anyone." I stood up. "So are we done here?"

"I say when we're done." He shoved me back onto the couch and stormed a path across the room, muttering to himself. It was about power and control, so I shifted back into submissive mode, watching him from the corner of my eye as he considered what I said. "Get out of here and stay out of our way. If I so much as hear a murmur that you spoke to the cops about my enterprise, then god help you." He opened the door, holding it and waiting for me to walk out. "Go before I change my mind and put you out on the street where you belong."

My only course of action was to leave. And I hurried down the darkened, zigzagging hallway, back to the foyer, and out the door. Leaving Heathcliff inside wasn't ideal, but obviously, he could handle himself. The KXDs saw him as a comrade, whereas I was a wild horse that either needed to be put down or broken. Maybe lack of sleep was impairing my judgment and rationality, but despite the dozens of agents and police personnel working this case, I felt exposed and alone.

Once outside, I ran across the street and up the stairs to the apartment. When I opened the door, I found the place ransacked. The contents of my duffel were on the floor next to the air mattress. The handgun was on the bed, and I checked the magazine and went into the bathroom to make sure the intruders were gone. Then I opened the closet door, afraid of what I would find. The false back was still secure, and aside from a few towels crumpled on the floor, it didn't look like they discovered the surveillance equipment. My burner phone was on the table. The encryption app looked like a game, and my call history and text messages seemed like innocent chatter to innocuous numbers. I'd have to thank the tech department for their genius as soon as I had the chance.

Aside from the most damning pieces of evidence, the phone and gun, I was relieved to remember my credentials were still at Martin's. If they had found those, it would have been game over. The only thing left to worry about was my kit, and I opened the small box, finding the clean syringes, a vial of saline, and a rubber tourniquet. Thankfully, the items weren't anything odd for a junkie to possess.

Far too worried to take anything else with me for fear it was bugged, I examined the gun, ejected the magazine, removed each bullet, cleared the chamber, completed a full field strip, then reassembled it, grabbed my keys, and took off at a run out of the apartment. Panic clouded my senses, making clear thought difficult. By the time I made it down the steps, the federal agent instinct had kicked in. I needed to contact Jablonsky. Running away would make me look guilty, and Heathcliff was still with them. If Bard believed I was a rat, he might take action against anyone I was close to. And Heathcliff was the only one who came to mind.

Stopping at the door, I peered through the glass, but the only familiar faces I spotted were the two lookouts. I couldn't leave, but I couldn't stay. Remembering the bugs that had been planted in the building, I went down the dilapidated corridors, assuming the usual locations had been utilized to maximize surveillance.

Hunkering close to a floor-level air vent, I began talking to myself. No one was around, but if someone showed up, they'd probably just assume I was a crazy lady. And if the KXDs and their high-tech security gear were set up somewhere inside this crappy building too, they'd also assume I was nothing more than neurotic and unhinged. Quietly rambling about the man being shot, Hotshot having to sew him up, and Bard not trusting me, I hoped the message would be received and someone would find a way to advise on the current recommended course of action. After a few deep breaths, I trudged up the steps.

The cell phone that I didn't want to use for fear it had been cloned flashed a new text message. *Girl, just wait until tonight, we have the most amazing party planned. I'll text you the details later.* The good news was my handler got the message, but the bad news was I had to wait until someone found a way to make contact.

Blowing out a breath, I slumped into the chair and removed the knife from my back pocket. Turning it over in my hands, I thought about Heathcliff, hoping he was okay and wondering how deeply implanted he had been five years ago. He had a history with these gangbangers and numerous regrets to go with it. It was my fault he ended up roped into this mess. Now we both had to figure out the best way to collect enough evidence and information to make a case and still get out alive.

TWENTY-EIGHT

I remained silent and motionless most of the day. My eyes were glued to the building across the street, but no one ever came out. And if they did, I didn't see them. Replaying Bard's questions and threats, I couldn't help but wonder if he had seen the security cam footage from the private room at the Black Cat. Did Heathcliff or I slip up? We tried to make it look real, and we kept our voices low when we were inside the private room at the club. Surely, someone at the PD or OIO would have intervened if they realized we'd been compromised. No, the reason Derek was still inside that basement apartment was because Bard thought he was a vital asset. At least that's what I kept trying to convince myself.

Glancing at the time, I couldn't remember when I slept or ate last. My stomach growled, but the thought of eating was sickening. How could anyone expect me to remain undercover when the gang I was sent to infiltrate no longer trusted me? There had been too many close calls and questionable absences. Maybe I moved too quickly or been too eager to help Francisco.

I reconsidered every action and conversation since my arrival; the one glaringly obvious mistake was confronting the group of men on the street. The only problem was they didn't give me a choice, and Steele took me under his wing and vowed to protect me after that. But maybe I fought too hard.

A car parked illegally in front of my building, and someone wearing a pizza delivery outfit stepped out. From the angle, I couldn't make out any other details, but a minute later, there was a knock on my door. Agent Lucca held out a cardboard box with grease stains.

"That'll be eighteen dollars," he said evenly, but his brow furrowed in concern as his eyes darted around the apartment.

"Hang on, I have to find some cash. Can you just set that down on the table?"

He stepped inside, but before he could ask a question, I shook my head. Grabbing my purse, I pulled out a pen and wrote on a napkin. *Bugged?* Finding a twenty, I handed it to him.

"Did you get my order right?" I lifted the lid and found a plastic baggie with another disposable phone and a handwritten note taped to the inside lid above a mushroom pizza. "Looks like it." I swallowed, wishing he could stay. "Keep the change."

"Thanks, ma'am." He winked. "Have a nice night."

Once his car pulled away, I took the pizza box into the bathroom, shut the door, and turned on the faucets. Then I examined the room for signs of a hidden camera or surveillance equipment. As soon as I was positive the room was secure, I opened the box, took out the phone, and read the note.

Exterminators will be stopping by in the morning to check for any bugs. Your misplaced mobile phone has been a real eye-opener. We've found a few places to move on. Meet at our usual rendezvous tomorrow before work. If something happens, you have my number. Despite the vague nature of Mark's message, I had my orders. All I had to do was wait until tomorrow.

Returning to the main room, I opened my kit, removed the lighter, and burned the note over the sink. Then I choked down a slice or two of pizza, waited at the window until it was too dark to see across the street, changed into a ratty t-shirt and sweats, and lay on the mattress. As I stared through the dark, looking for any indication Bard had put my apartment under surveillance, I couldn't help but worry about Heathcliff. This was why I didn't want a partner.

When morning came, I climbed out of bed, showered, dressed, and drank so much instant coffee the Surgeon General probably should have issued a health warning. But it was the only thing keeping me upright. From my perch at the window, things looked normal. The typical weekday street activity commenced. A smattering of KXDs took up their usual positions near the dumpsters and trashcans, and Steele sat on the front stoop of my building.

A knock at my door signified the arrival of the "exterminator", and when I opened the door, I was relieved to see the OIO tech, Agent Lawson, in coveralls and carrying a huge container of insecticide. He began in one corner of the room, sweeping the entire apartment with a RF reader. After examining the fixtures, cracks and crevices, and even going so far as to check my belongings and me, he shook his head.

"Looks like our last visit cleared out the infestation. But it's policy for us to follow up once a month to make sure nothing returns," he said as we stepped into the hallway. "I'm sure it's a relief to know your place is free of critters."

"Thank you." I grabbed my bag. "I hate running into unexpected surprises, particularly in the shower."

"Bathroom's clean too. I'll finish checking the rest of the building, but unless we get another report, this ought to be our last visit."

He headed up the stairs to sell his act, and I went down the steps and out the front door. Francisco sat on the railing, somehow managing to balance his large frame on the tiny wrought-iron bar. We made eye contact, and he hopped down, reaching for me. I jumped back, and he frowned.

"I'm not going to hit you," he whispered.

"Shakespeare probably wants you to do a lot worse." I blinked and looked away. "What do you want, Francisco?"

"Nothing. I just want you to be careful. The cops are still snooping around, and you need to keep your mouth shut at work. Okay?"

"I didn't do this. I didn't say a thing to them. I wouldn't. Don't you realize what would happen if I did?"

He grabbed my arms and pulled me tightly against his chest, muffling my words. "Shh. I know. But in the meantime, you're not selling product or taking any side jobs, understand?"

"I don't turn tricks."

"That's not what Hotshot said."

"That was different," I retorted, wondering what the hell Heathcliff said.

"Doesn't matter. Shakespeare's not looking for any new talent right now, anyway." He released his grip, stepping back. "And stay clean for a couple of days. With the police hanging around, you don't want to get picked up for possession or public intoxication." He assessed my appearance. "Plus, from the looks of you, you must have had one hell of a night."

"Well, I thought your boss was going to kill me. And that wounded guy," I pressed my lips together, swallowing, "how is he?"

"He'll survive. Someone owed us a favor." He jerked his chin toward the bus stop. "That's not your problem. Now get out of here before you miss your ride."

Not needing to be told twice, I took the bus a few stops farther than I needed to go, backtracked on foot to the subway, and took a cab to the motel. The entire trip took over an hour, but I had to be careful no one was tailing me. Shakespeare's guard was up, and until I knew Heathcliff was safe, I couldn't risk blowing either of our covers.

Unlocking the motel room, I stepped inside to find it empty. After performing a quick sweep, I checked the time. It was two hours earlier than I planned. That was one of the only benefits of not sleeping; there were always extra hours in the day.

Locking the door and latching the security bar in place, I sat on the bed and picked up the motel phone. My first inclination was to call the precinct and convince Detective

O'Connell or Lt. Moretti to give me some details on Heathcliff's previous assignment with narcotics, but that would be violating both OIO and PD protocols. Then I thought about dialing Derek's number directly, but if he was still with Shakespeare, the last thing I needed to do was hand the head of the KXDs my safe house on a silver platter. Out of good ideas, I distracted myself by dialing an unrelated number.

"I just really needed to hear your voice." I curled up on the bed with the phone pressed to my ear.

"Should I be worried?" Martin asked. "It's rather early in the day for you to be fantasizing about me, isn't it?" His attempt at levity brought a smile to my face. "What's going on?"

"I showed up early for a meeting," I replied, stretching the truth just a little. "No big deal. Have you finished work for the day?" It was slightly after four, and even though I called his office phone, it was possible he had more business to conduct.

"More or less." As he spoke about his day and aspects of the lawsuit that he was able to talk about, my eyes began to droop. "Alex?" he asked.

I blinked and focused on the time, wondering where the last forty minutes went. "Sorry, I must have zoned out. I need to go. We'll talk again soon."

Just as my eyes closed, footsteps sounded outside the room, and the adjoining door opened. Jablonsky gave me one look, shook his head, and set a suitcase down on the foldable rack. Unzipping the luggage, he pulled a dozen files from inside and placed them on the foot of my bed.

"Let me guess, if I hadn't sent over the pizza, you wouldn't have eaten either," he scolded. "What have I told you about doing this job?"

"Sleep when you can. Eat when you can. You never know what's around the corner," I repeated, annoyed by yet another of his constant life lessons.

"Precisely. Which begs the question, why do you look like an anemic anorexic?"

"Bite me."

"I would, but I'd break my teeth. There's more meat on

a chicken wing." He cracked a smile. "What's the problem?"

"Where should I begin? Is Derek okay?"

"He's fine. That isn't to say the PD is being the least bit helpful. They don't seem to understand what the word transparency means." Mark rubbed his face and took a seat. "Tell me everything you know and everything Detective Heathcliff has told you."

During my debrief, Mark scribbled countless notes. After I finished, he returned the favor, clueing me in as to why the PD was involved and the progress that had been made since I planted the cell phone inside Steele's SUV. The tech department upgraded the power source, enabling the battery life to last between five days and a week. With any luck, the OIO would continue to gather useful intel for the next few days.

So far, we knew Shakespeare had met with the Lords three times since my run-in with the four gang members. The last visit occurred two evenings ago on the night the Black Cat was raided. From the comments Francisco made to the two lookouts on the drive there, it was obvious the KXDs believed the Lords were horning in on their territory and selling out their rival's drug dealing and prostitution to the police department. Even if the PD didn't favor sharing their intel with us, much the same way we had kept them in the dark, they had been running an operation for some time and were determined to shut down most of the drug dealing in the city. Heathcliff had said as much, but I didn't realize narcotics still had an ongoing sting operation in the works. Then again, my attention wasn't focused where it needed to be.

"I spoke to Veronica Kincaid, the stripper who was assaulted," Mark clarified. "She wasn't willing to divulge that much information, but she provided a few helpful details. The tech department's piecing together the assault, but maybe you can save everyone some time." He opened a file and removed a blown-up, black and white photo. "Do you recognize these two guys?"

I expected to see Francisco or maybe the lookouts from the neighborhood, but that wasn't who assaulted Veronica.

Sucking in a breath, I moved the photo into better light, convinced what I was seeing wasn't possible. Then again, it made sense.

"That one," I pointed to One Eye, "was part of the group that attacked me." Mark took the photo, squinting at it. "It's hard to tell, given the hood and angles, but it's him. I'm positive."

"So you weren't the first warning the Lords issued. That changes things."

A conversation between Shakespeare and Francisco played through my mind. "I thought Francisco was responsible. He was supposed to be taking care of mouthy bitches or whatever Bard was complaining about." I reexamined the few facts I knew about Veronica. "Do you have her medical records?"

"Only what the PD has a copy of when the assault was reported." He handed me another sheet of paper.

"Amazing. She was actually telling the truth." He looked confused, so I pointed to the toxicology screening. "She's clean. No drugs or alcohol. So she found sobriety and stopped dealing. The KXDs had no way to continue to coerce her to play by their rules, so they would have had plenty of reasons to attack her, maybe even kill her. So how come the Lords were responsible for the assault?"

"I'll continue to dig into her background, but my gut says the Lords are going after the weakest members of the KXDs' herd. Veronica. You. Fringe members and wannabes. It's probably about posturing and demonstrating their own superiority. But it backfired when Bard didn't rush off to her defense. He probably used it to his advantage to send a message to the rest of his followers not to cross him. It doesn't matter if you're in or out, you can't give up the gang life, unless it gives you up."

"Did they hire you to come up with that slogan?" I quipped, unable to make sense of this mess.

"Cute," he scoffed. "But that would explain why the KXDs didn't retaliate after her alleged mugging. They were sending a message to her and anyone else who might want out. If you leave, you lose our protection. It was probably enough to scare most of the rank and file to stay in line."

"The KXDs already fear Bard, probably Steele too. When the two of them left to make that pick-up, the neighborhood erupted in chaos. Bard's the power that keeps them safe from outsiders and themselves." Massaging my temples, I asked, "How does this happen?"

"We don't have time for lengthy social theories. It just does." He checked the time. "Let's focus on the headway we've made in the last seventy-two hours before you go back to serving drinks and shaking those bony hips."

The stash house Francisco took me to was under surveillance. Everyone who went near it was identified, and a log was being kept of the comings and goings. It wasn't much, but since I didn't witness the exchange firsthand or get a clear glimpse of what occurred inside that locked room, no judge was willing to grant a warrant for what he considered to be a fishing expedition. Obviously, several months and dozens of requests had caused the current operation to fall from favor in the eyes of the court.

Numerous train depots and cargo holds were being torn apart. Random checks were being conducted throughout the country on all passenger trains. Amtrak wasn't pleased, but so far, fifty bricks of cocaine, a dozen or so kilos of heroin, and plenty of marijuana had been confiscated. However, no one was talking, and the passengers who checked said bags didn't appear to exist. They bought a ticket, loaded their belongings, and disappeared somewhere along the route or disembarked before the train even left the station.

"Security has been tightened everywhere. It's just a matter of time before someone gets caught, and then it'll be like dominos – a train reaction," Mark announced, and I physically cringed at his pathetic wordplay. "What? You say crap like that a lot."

"In that case, remind me not to." I rubbed my eyes, but it did little for my headache. "When are you pulling me out?"

"Why? What happened?"

"I told you about the GSW victim. And while I was being interrogated by Bard, some of his minions ransacked Nicholson's apartment. He doesn't trust me. I'm not sure

Steele does either, not after Derek was naked in my bed." I held up my hand. "It's not what you think, but it was supposed to look like it."

"Steele's been using you from the get-go. He wouldn't be doing that if he thought you were an agent. See what else you can pick up on at the club. Those numbnuts at the precinct nearly wrecked everything with that raid. Sure, they claimed they were rounding up hookers, but it might have escalated the impending gang war. The rumblings are getting louder. It also might cause the KXDs' international connection to go to ground. Be careful. We'll see how things play out over the next few days, and I'll run everything past Kendall. I'd hate to pull you prematurely."

"Yeah, especially now that we have even more cooks in the kitchen to screw things up. Do you have any idea about Heathcliff's previous stint with the narcotics unit? Bard knows him. It's like they were good buddies back in the day. It's disconcerting."

"I'll wheedle what I can out of Lt. Moretti, but the police department is sticking to its guns in terms of officer safety. Not that I can blame them. I'd do the same thing to protect my undercover asset."

"How 'bout you give your asset a twenty and let her take a cab instead of freezing her ass off by prancing around in slutty attire?"

He emptied his wallet, giving me whatever cash he had. "Keep that new burner on you at all times. As soon as we have something concrete, I'll let you know. And text if you need to make a drop. The gym is open twenty-four hours."

"Oh, sure, now you tell me."

TWENTY-NINE

The Black Cat was quiet and subdued, even the volume of the obnoxious, raunchy music was lower. The clientele was practically nonexistent, so the servers were camped out at the bar, occasionally running back and forth to deliver a drink, while the actual strippers were left to dance to an almost empty room. I wondered if they preferred it that way. The twirls and stripteases lacked the usual level of enthusiasm. Everyone was phoning it in tonight. But I was ill at ease being treated like a pariah. Was everyone told to watch themselves or stay away? Granted, we didn't normally sit around, braiding each other's hair or exchanging hints on how to score generous tips, but when I returned from cashing out my only table, the surrounding area cleared out quickly.

After Sasha finished her number and walked off stage, expertly maneuvering the three steps in her five inch heels while fastening her top, she went around the bar, picked up a bottle of water, and took a sip. Slowly, I spun to face her, expecting her to avoid me too, but she held her ground.

"You should probably run for the hills. Apparently, I have a contagious disease. I hope it's not VD."

"Did you hear about what happened the other night?"

she asked.

"I heard the cops were sniffing around for some ass. Was someone having a bachelor party?"

"The skin squad questioned us and shut down the place. We didn't make a dime and had to spend hours in lockup while we waited to answer a bunch of pointless questions. And you weren't here."

"Great, so now I'm getting branded a snitch because my leg's screwed up?"

"No. Misery loves company. And you weren't miserable." She stabbed a maraschino cherry with a toothpick and popped it into her mouth. "The only thing worse than being felt up and scrutinized for hours by those pricks with badges is the cold shoulder you get when you miss it." She shrugged. "We go through this every few months. Give it a couple of weeks, and we'll forget all about it and treat you normally again."

"Can't wait," I replied sarcastically, and she snorted. "Joe's not even here to listen to my whining and bitching. Did they arrest him too?"

She looked around, asking one of the girls who was filling in behind the bar where Joe was. Her response was a shrug. Maybe the PD pulled him off this case after the raid or kept him for possession or something in order to make his cover look good. Who knows?

In the meantime, I was supposed to be gathering information and maintaining a low profile. Too bad no one wanted to talk to me, and no one wanted to visit a club that had dealings with the police department less than forty-eight hours ago. Tonight was just getting better and better.

Resigned to the evening turning into a wash, I busied myself with menial labor. After bussing the empty tables, wiping down every surface with disinfectant, and vacuuming the less trafficked areas, like the empty VIP rooms, I offered to clean the offices and restrooms. Since I was in the doghouse, I might as well act like it. Plus, it provided the perfect opportunity to snoop. The assistant manager seemed pleased someone was offering to clean, especially when it looked like we'd be shutting down just as soon as the last two visitors called it a night.

The first room I entered was the security office. One of the bouncers glanced up when I opened the door, dragging the vacuum along behind me. He didn't say anything, but I got the distinct impression he was enjoying the view. Perhaps I should have donned a French maid's outfit too.

Casting a few discreet looks at the monitors, I saw that cameras were set up in each of the VIP areas, at the bar, and near the back hallway facing the stage. Surprisingly enough, the offices, locker room, and changing areas were off limits. Who knew this place actually had some scruples?

Finishing in that room, I left the door cracked open and continued down the corridor, entering the locker room. As the Hoover remained in place, thoroughly sucking up the excess glitter on that particular patch of flooring, I checked the lockers. The ones without locks were empty, and everyone else had done a fine job securing their belongings. Picking each lock would have taken far too long and would have violated the Fourth Amendment. Damn, I'd forgotten how much it sucks to play by the rules.

Two rooms remained in the back hallway. One was the manager's office, and the other I wasn't sure about. I'd never stepped foot inside either. The nameplate read "private" which didn't exactly provide any insight into what was behind door number one, but before I could turn the knob, the side door opened directly behind me. It was the employees' entrance. Maybe someone was showing up late for a shift. Instead, the person who opened the door quickly pulled it closed. The brief glimpse hadn't been enough for an identification, and being far too curious for my own good, I went to the door, slowly turned the knob, and eased it open inch by inch. But whoever had been out there was gone.

I let the door close on its own. Something was off, and I didn't like it. Deciding that remaining alone in the back hallway wasn't the best idea, I returned the vacuum and cleaning supplies to the janitor's closet and went back to the bar.

The place was devoid of patrons. And within ten minutes, the house lights came on, and we were told to go home. I lost count of the number of angry glares that came my way as the women trooped past.

"I didn't do anything," I said, and for my trouble, I was shoulder-checked a few times. Not wanting to deal with the hostility, I waited until the outside door opened and closed half a dozen times before I made my way to the locker room to change.

A few derogatory slurs were whispered, but no one attempted to brain me with a stiletto, and for that, I was grateful. The current situation occupied my mind. And I waited for the club to empty before changing into my street clothes and lugging my bag outside.

I only made it a few steps from the door when a faint wail rang out. I assessed the area. The adjacent building didn't have any openings or windows facing my direction, and it was too slight of a noise to have traveled through the street traffic. Reconsidering the direction of the sound, I went back inside the Black Cat. The source of that howl had come from within. Unfortunately, the other undercover FBI agent wasn't on today's work roster, and with Joe absent, no one else was in a position to intervene or report a potential crime being committed.

Despite the fact it had only been a few minutes since closing, the club looked like a ghost town. It was dark and eerie with the emergency lights casting unsettling shadows across the floor and stage. Unzipping my bag, I removed my handgun. Stealthily moving down the hall, I strained to hear possible movement over my pounding heartbeat. The hairs on the back of my neck stood at attention, and muffled sounds and whimpers came from the door marked 'private'.

Pressing my back against the wall, I steadied my breathing and hands, and palming the gun in my right, I reached out with my left and silently turned the doorknob. I pushed the door open a few centimeters and stopped, waiting to see if my intrusion had been discovered. After ten seconds, I pivoted on my heel, keeping my shoulder against the wall and peered into the crack.

Chained to a chair in the middle of the office was Joe. Duct tape covered his mouth. His right eye was swollen shut, and the blood trickling from his temple had stained his collar. Two men were on either side of him, wearing dark hoodies and facing away from the door. One of them donned brass knuckles and swung, connecting with Joe's torso.

The sound of his muffled shriek was enough to set me in motion, but my own momentum was turned against me when someone clamped a hand over my mouth and pulled me backward, temporarily throwing my balance off. I threw an elbow, but it lacked the proper amount of leverage, and my captor seemed to expect it. His grip didn't loosen, and the hand against my mouth and nose remained tight enough to cut off my oxygen.

A rush of cold air hit my skin, and as I watched the exterior door close, words were whispered in my ear, "Alex, stop fighting." The hand didn't loosen until my mind had time to process the voice. "Don't make a sound," Heathcliff said, slowly removing his hand from my mouth. I took a breath, but he kept my back against his chest, facing away from him. "Get out of here."

I shook my head, turning in his arms. "Joe." The name came out a puff of breath in the freezing night sky.

"ESU's on the way. Get out of here."

But I didn't move. "We have to intervene. They're torturing him. They'll kill him." Something pinged in my brain. "He's been made. They know."

"In five minutes, this place will be surrounded. You have to get out of here before someone sees you. You know what they'll do to you."

"Five minutes in that situation is an eternity, and Joe might not have five minutes." Checking the slide on my handgun, I was prepared to go back in. Screw undercover and the op. There wasn't a chance in hell I was letting a cop get killed. Not on my watch. Not again. "We have to move in."

"No. You can't be here. We'll take care of our own."

"He doesn't have time to wait." I hated every second we spent arguing.

"He can handle it for a few more minutes. He knew the risks. And now you need to focus on the time crunch this puts us on. The KXDs will be covering their tracks, moving their stores, cutting ties. It's just a matter of time before they discover who we are too. You have to go."

I took a step away from Heathcliff, toward the door, but he grabbed me in a tight bear hug, pinning my arms down at my sides and lifting me off the ground, physically carrying me away from the club. He stepped in front of a cab, causing it to screech to a halt, and he threw me into the backseat, telling the cabbie I had too much to drink and giving him the address of the apartment. Instantly, we were in motion, and I did the only thing I could do – I texted Mark.

My phone rang immediately, and holding it up to my ear, I listened to the instructions I knew I'd be given. Back off and let the police department handle the situation. My cover was already questionable. Bard didn't like or trust me, and if the KXDs even had the slightest indication I was hanging around when the tactical unit responded, I'd be their next victim. Considering I was stuck inside a cab, I couldn't voice my protest. All I could do was agree to obey. I had to push my way inside the gang because if we had any hope of making a case, it was now or never.

Getting out of the cab, I was rattled and ready for a fight. My instincts were honed, and my senses heightened. My eyes scanned the area, coming to rest on Francisco waiting out front. His hands weren't getting dirty this time, but that didn't mean he didn't know what was happening in the back room of the club. Payback would have been fleetingly sweet, but I forced my hand to relax the grip on the gun and zip my bag. Faking any emotion other than what I was feeling would tip him off that something was wrong, so I stormed up the steps, pissed off and seconds away from throwing a few punches.

"What's up, chica?" he asked, pretending to be oblivious.

"We closed early. Tips were shit, and everyone's acting like the raid was my fault. Do you have any idea where they might have gotten an idea like that? Today's the first day the Black Cat's been back in business, and you'd think I was some fucking rat. Maybe Shakespeare's been talking to some of the girls and spreading rumors," I huffed.

Francisco moved to grab my arm, and I jerked away. "Don't touch me. I have done nothing but what you've asked. I've risked everything for you. My freedom, my life, every single goddamn thing. So don't you dare tell me to calm down or shut up because I'm tired of being calm, and I'm sure as hell not holding my tongue anymore. Whatever it is you're going to do to me, just do it because I'm sick of these mind games."

"You better watch your tone."

"Or what? You'll slap me again?" No, he'd probably permanently silence me, and given the neighborhood, there was a good chance he could get away with it right here in the open without anyone ever saying a word. "What do I have to do to prove myself to you? I shouldn't be treated like an outcast by absolutely everyone. This was supposed to be a fresh start, but it's more of the same bullshit. All you dealers are the same. You use people because you know we'll do anything for our next hit." Moving closer, I latched onto the front of his shirt, pressing against him. "Tell me what to do. What do you want? You want me to screw your brains out? Will that prove my loyalty? Or do I have to go through some initiation and kill a few of the Lords or whatever rival gang member steps foot on your turf? Is that what it takes? Because right now, I need a fix, and I don't know where else to go. I cut ties with my old dealer after we came to our arrangement, and now you're screwing me over." I pleaded with my eyes. "And to top it off, I'm short on cash. So what do you want in return?"

Something unsettling moved behind his eyes, and I wasn't entirely sure how to navigate the situation I just placed myself in. "I thought you didn't believe in trade."

"Well, you manipulated the situation in order to leave me with no other choice." I pretended to fight back the tears. "Did you learn that trick from your mom's dealer too?" I spat, squeezing the only pressure point he had.

He tensed, jerking away from my grasp before barreling forward. I flinched, expecting him to strike. When all else fails, assault charges are a great reason to arrest someone. The problem was they were more convincing when you didn't fight back.

THIRTY

Steele held me against the building. Only the tips of my toes brushed the ground. "Don't you ever say that again." He trembled with rage and drew in ragged, harsh breaths. "Don't. You. Ever." His fingers wrapped around my neck, squeezing hard. I gasped, clawing at his hands. He squeezed harder, but something shifted behind his eyes. And his grip loosened.

Groveling was not in my wheelhouse, but Francisco wanted what he perceived to be respect. It was more closely akin to fear or obedience, but I gave the man what he wanted – control.

"I'm sorry. I...I...shouldn't have said that. I didn't mean it," I stammered. He dropped his hands, and I collapsed to my knees, rubbing my neck for effect.

He was still enraged and took out the pent-up aggression on the front door, slamming his fist into it numerous times and giving it a few strong kicks, cursing and yelling. I didn't move. He'd lash out at a moving target. There was no doubt about it. Finally, when his rage was under control, he grabbed my ponytail and yanked, practically ripping my hair out and forcing me off the stoop and across the street to his SUV.

"Get in." He opened the door and shoved me inside.

"Where are we going?" I hoped the listening device attached to the cell phone was still transmitting.

"Shut your fucking mouth."

Well, that didn't leave much wiggle room for conversation. So I buckled the seatbelt, paid attention to the street signs, and devised a plan to get out of this alive. The only downside to that plan was Francisco would probably be dead because I would have to kill him.

My eyes never wavered from watching him. As the minutes ticked by, he calmed, moving from livid to pissed. Great, I screwed up again. Insulting my only chance of getting inside the KXDs was a ridiculous move, but I had been desperate and overstepped. The only thing left was figuring out where he planned to take me before he killed me. Finally, he parked in front of a no parking sign and got out of the SUV. He came around and opened my door, grabbing my wrist before I could even unbuckle the seatbelt.

"You wanted in, so this is it." He led the way to a back entrance of a laundromat and opened the door. "There's no backing out now. You'll do what I say, when I say. And if you piss off Bard, he'll end you."

"My god." My mouth dropped open as I took in the chemistry equipment. "You have your own lab." This was a major discovery. It was one thing to process and refine drugs into purer forms, but from the looks of this place, the KXDs were cooking up their own designer concoctions too.

"Stop gawking. This isn't even operational yet. But we've been using it to house the good stuff." He went to a large wall safe and entered a six digit code, retrieving a sack of premeasured dime bags. "You said you wanted to prove yourself, so this is your chance." He held up the bag, but when I reached for it, he pulled it away. "This is worth five large."

"The Black Cat closed for the night, remember?"

Steele laughed. "You really think it's that easy to become one of us?" My expression must have been one of bewilderment because his features contorted into smug satisfaction. "Shakespeare owns us. He controls that titty bar where you work. He has places throughout the neighborhood and around the city. So if you want to prove you're worth all the trouble you've caused, you need to branch out to some uncharted territory, chica."

"I didn't cause any trouble," I eyed the bag, "so stop wasting my time and tell me what you want."

"We're gonna make some deliveries." He smiled. "Well, you're gonna make some deliveries. No skimming off the top, and no sampling the product. If you finish by sunrise, you'll be rewarded with a taste."

"That's it?"

"Do you think you deserve more?" Something flashed behind his eyes, and he closed the gap between us, caressing my cheek with his free hand before dragging my chin upward and kissing me. "Because if you want more than that, then I deserve something in return, especially after the shit you said." His eyes turned cold. "I've let you get away with a lot. I've vouched for you when Shakespeare said you tipped off the cops. I've coddled you. I've given you exactly what you needed when you were pretty damn low, so it's about time you do something for me." His hand moved to my neck, and he wrapped it around my throat, squeezing slightly. "You had no problem showing some affection to that middleman I sent your way. And he did nothing more than pay you. I've protected you and put up with your disrespect. So if you want anything else from me, you'll have to demonstrate just how grateful you are after you bring in the cash."

"Why wait?" I asked, hiding my distaste masterfully. "I'd be more than happy to show you my appreciation right now."

He stepped backward, thrusting the bag into my arms. "You have to work for it, first."

He led the way back to the SUV, casting glances in my direction as if I might rip open one of the baggies and inhale the contents. Granted, that probably wouldn't be beyond the scope of my cover identity, but irritating Francisco again tonight wasn't wise by any account.

He drove out of the neighborhood, away from the usual spots and local watering holes, and to a nicer, upscale area.

The dance clubs and bars on this strip were popular and frequented by everyone from college students to business tycoons. This wasn't gang territory, and Francisco barely slowed the SUV to a stop before hitting the unlock button.

"Get out," he said.

"What?"

"You heard me. Get out. I'll pick you up in a couple of hours." He glanced at the clock on the dash. "Clubs close at four, but I'm sure you can find some afterhours places to visit if you haven't sold it off by then. Five Gs and not a penny less."

"Where am I supposed to conceal this?" I held up the bag, but he shrugged, reaching across and pushing open my car door. Then he shoved me out and drove away, the door slamming shut as he sped off. "That's just great," I mumbled.

Quickly, I stuffed the bag of drugs underneath my sweatshirt, wondering how in the world I was expected to move five grand of cocaine in a little over three hours. On the bright side, the fact that I wasn't a dealer would make this easier. Ducking into a nearby alleyway, I studied my surroundings for signs of KXD activity or a tail who might have been following Francisco.

Just as I began to dial Jablonsky, a faint green glow came through the cotton of my sweatshirt. Removing the plastic bag, I noticed a tracer inside. The son of a bitch was monitoring me.

This would make life a lot more difficult. Calling in for an exchange wouldn't fly, so I had to make this believable. The first step was getting inside one of the clubs, and jeans and a sweatshirt weren't conducive to that feat. Luckily, I still had my work clothes on underneath my current ensemble. Shedding my sweatshirt, I balled it up, keeping the bag of coke tucked out of sight. Then I sauntered past the crowd to the doorman outside the most popular hotspot on the street.

He raised an eyebrow. Outfits were daring and scandalous, but a bikini top in the middle of a snowstorm wasn't a sight he was used to seeing. I leaned close, grasping his bicep.

"One of the VIPs called for some private companionship. I'm sure he had my name put on the list," I whispered, distracting him as much as possible while I scanned the sheet in front of him for a name that wasn't checked off. "Is getting inside going to be a problem? Because he was hoping a posh place like this would allow some discretion." The doorman looked like he was about to say something regarding letting hookers inside the club, so I gave him a charming smile, rambling off a name on the list. "And just for the record, I'm only an escort." I batted my eyelashes. "Do you need to see my card?"

"Go inside, but tell your friend not to make this a habit," he warned.

"I assure you, it won't happen again."

Inside, I made my way to the ladies' room. The line to the restroom wasn't nearly as long as the line to get in, but it wasn't ideal. After five minutes, I managed to secure a stall of my very own. Closing the lid on the toilet seat, I sat down and examined the contents of the bag. Nothing else was glowing except a single packet. Pocketing that one, I did a quick count and considered my options. Surely, I could find somewhere to secure the evidence, but I needed the five grand.

Texting my handler, I waited for a response. Given that it took time to fill out requisition forms, get signatures, and access those types of funds, I didn't know if Jablonsky could pull it off within the next two hours and still make the exchange in time. While I waited, a few women chatted nearby. After they left, I listened for other sounds, but no footsteps echoed off the tile and porcelain. Stepping out of the stall, I moved in front of the mirror, relieved to have a moment of privacy. Something had to be done to improve my appearance. Digging around inside my purse, I reapplied my makeup, brushed my hair, and secured it into a messy knot with a pen. Then I considered the contents of my purse, deciding the only items I really needed were my gun and phone.

A few women entered the restroom, and I waited for the coast to be clear again. As soon as their prying eyes were hidden behind the stall doors, I dumped the contents out, replaced my handgun, and poured as many of the baggies inside as possible. Whatever didn't fit, I stuffed into my top, pocketed my phone, and went into the club, carrying my sweatshirt. I needed something else to wear, especially if I wanted to blend in.

Examining the layout, I found a narrow hallway in the opposite corner near the back of the bar and ducked into it. An employees only sign greeted me, and I pushed the door open to find a decent sized office. Hanging behind the door was a black dress shirt with the club's name embroidered on the left breast. Someone probably left it behind, but I could make do.

While I was ripping off the name patch, my phone buzzed. Mark needed a location and time, so I texted back the information, hit send, and continued working on my arts and crafts. The shirt was large, so I left it mostly unbuttoned, tying the bottom tight around my midsection and leaving my midriff visible with a good deal of cleavage showing. Then I folded up the sleeves until they were no longer covering my hands, made sure Mark was on the way with the money, and returned to the main area of the club, feeling nervous and exposed. Maybe it was the five grand of narcotics concealed on my person, the fact that I just stole some guy's work shirt, or that, in this setting, wearing a barely concealed triangle bikini top just didn't seem right.

"What are you drinking?" the bartender asked as soon as I slid onto an empty chair.

"Rum and Coke, hold the rum."

It took him a moment to understand what I said, and then he chuckled. "So you want a Coke?"

"Yeah, and toss in a lime wedge." I smiled. "Don't worry, I'm not pretentious enough to ask for an umbrella too."

Flirting with the bartender ought to secure my seat at the bar until closing time. It would also make it appear I might be dealing from the bar, particularly if I slid some napkins across to people, passed a few bowls of pretzels around, or talked to some lonely gentlemen who were placing orders. And given that the place was packed, it would look convincing. Furthermore, ever since I emerged from the back hallway, two guys had been keeping tabs on my movements. Maybe it was nothing, but by now, I knew how Francisco worked. And I bet he wanted to know how I worked too.

Over the next hour, I made it a point to whisper a few words to a few dozen people. It was innocent conversation, but a touch of the arm or a handshake could be anything, particularly to the untrained observer. The two men, who looked just familiar enough to be frequenters at the Black Cat, never moved from the high-top table in the corner. The only thing they did was study me. So I put on a good show. Sure, the fake junkie jitters and fidgeting were gone because I didn't want to come across that way to everyone I spoke to, but with any luck, they wouldn't notice the difference.

A couple minutes after last call was announced, someone bumped into my back, practically knocking me off the stool. He apologized profusely, righting me on the stool and slipping a three inch thick wad of cash onto my lap. Securing the money, I swiveled just slightly to acknowledge him.

"Five o'clock," I said, and he leaned back against the bar, taking in the view of the emptying dance floor. "Two at the high-top."

"No worries," Mark said, dressed in his wrinkled suit from work. He didn't exactly look like much of a businessman at four a.m., so he disappeared down the bar. And I quickly began chatting with the closest guy like nothing happened. With any luck, my two spotters missed the brief exchange.

After a few minutes and losing Mark amidst a crowd of last minute drinkers, I ducked back into the ladies' room, knowing he was tracking my path. Flipping the lock, I went to the handicapped stall, discovering the legally required baby changing table inside. Sometimes you have to love state regulations. Even if a baby in a club was probably in and of itself illegal, the changing table was state mandated.

Opening the contraption, I removed my gun from my purse, emptied my pockets and top, and stuck my cocaine-laden bag inside, securing the thick plastic vertically against the wall using the Velcro strap. After flushing the glowing tracer, I locked the stall door and slid underneath. I secured the gun behind my back, untied the shirt, retying it lower to hide the concealed weapon, and left the restroom.

Mark was lingering inside the men's room with the door cracked open. Casting a glance around, I didn't see the two men, but that didn't mean they weren't there. Mark didn't say a word, but our eyes met. He was concerned and anxious, and my mind which had been occupied with other things since encountering Francisco returned to the situation at the Black Cat. I didn't know what happened or if everyone made it out alive. If I wasn't concerned about Detective Heathcliff's safety, I would have been extremely angry with him for the way he handled me and the situation. But I couldn't think about that now.

"Stupid changing table," I griped just loud enough for Mark to hear and for the words to sound innocent enough to any unknown eavesdroppers.

Walking out of the club, I put my sweatshirt on over my stolen attire, checked the time, and went to wait in the same spot Francisco dropped me off. If I was right about the two men, they'd phone their boss, and the SUV would be pulling up shortly. If I was wrong and they were rival gang members, Agent Jablonsky would be close enough to handle the situation. Game on, bitches.

THIRTY-ONE

I didn't see the two men again. Perhaps they were a figment of my imagination or a hallucination from being in such close proximity to that much cocaine. Regardless, relief washed over me as I headed down the street. The traffic picked up as most of the clubs shut their doors for the night. Cabbies fought for the best locations to snatch up drunk partiers, and slews of people teetered down the sidewalks, finding twenty-four hour diners, getting into private vehicles, or taking a brisk, sobering walk in the middle of the night. By my best calculations, the streets would be empty within fifteen minutes, and if Francisco didn't show by then, I'd find another way home.

"Chica," he called from a parking space, "you're done?"

I didn't notice his arrival and wondered how long he'd been waiting. Burying the fear he had seen Mark arrive or spotted a government-issued vehicle, I dashed across the street and flung myself into his arms. He wanted affectionate gratitude, so I could play along for now.

"It's not hard when you have something everyone wants," I whispered, nipping at his earlobe and passing the cash to him. Thankfully, he was more interested in the new bulge I put in his pocket than the hard metal protruding from the base of my spine. "That was exhilarating. Now can we get out of here?" Giving him a wicked grin, I went around to the passenger's side and opened the door.

"I had my doubts." He put the car in gear, setting out for the neighborhood. "But if this is any indication of what you can do, then there's no reason for me to worry. Shakespeare will be pleased."

"So we're good?" I remembered his earlier aggression after my verbal blunder.

"Better than. And might I say, damn, you're looking fine in that tied up shirt."

"How do you know what I'm wearing?" I asked. He cast a quick look my way but didn't speak. "You were watching?"

"I've told you the KXDs have eyes everywhere. And I have some sexy stills of you passing product on my phone."

"Can I see?" I hoped Mark wasn't caught in any of them.

"Only if you plan on replacing them with something even more scintillating." He didn't offer his phone, but he dug into his pocket for half a gram of heroin. "Maybe you'll be more inclined once I give you what you're after." He dropped the tiny packet onto his lap. "You don't mind grabbing that, do you?" It was another test, and ignoring my personal distaste for him and the things he wanted, I reached onto his lap and searched for the baggie that dropped between his legs, giving him a gentle squeeze. "That's more like it."

When we arrived home, he led the way up the steps and past my apartment. On the level above, he went to the corner apartment and stuck a key in the lock, opening the door. Apparently, he lived in the building. I'd have to remember to update the OIO on this fact. The thought of Steele finding the gun behind my back was worrisome, especially after his insistence that I not be armed. Furthermore, everything I needed to fake taking a hit of smack was downstairs, as was the blade beneath my mattress. Things were about to get tricky.

"Are you anxious?" he cooed, still turned on from being fondled during the car ride home. "Fine, I'll let you take the edge off before we get started."

"My stuff's downstairs. I'll just run down and get it and be right back." Assessing the room for weapons or other means of escape, I played off my desire to leave by smirking at him. "I didn't realize you've been on top this whole time."

"Top, bottom, doesn't matter much to me, just as long as I have you exactly where I want you." He grinned wickedly, producing two sealed syringes from a drawer. "And there's no reason for you to leave. It pays to have a prescription for diabetes medication. All the clean needles a person could ever want." Well, there went one excuse down the drain. "Make yourself at home. I'll be right back." He put a lighter down next to the box of aluminum foil.

He disappeared into the bathroom, probably to do a few push-ups, but his absence gave me time to fill the syringe with water, liquefy the drugs, and dump them down the drain, leaving the smell of cooked heroin in the air and burnt residue on the foil. Stripping off my sweatshirt, I tucked my gun into the front pocket and rolled the sleeves around it, putting it on the floor at my feet. When he came back, I pressed the plunger down slightly on the syringe to get the air out and glanced around the room.

"Tourniquet?" I asked.

Smiling, he pulled a rubber strap from inside a box and handed it to me. Inhaling deeply, he watched through hooded eyes as I tied off my arm, just above the elbow, and found a vein. Needles were on my list of ten most hated things, and injecting some questionable water into my body was the purest form of torturous self-loathing. Thoughts like 'why the hell am I doing this' cascaded through my mind, but I held the determined look on my face until the needle went in, then I pressed the plunger down, counting to three before releasing my grip on the syringe and throwing my head back in sheer ecstasy. Sinking to the ground, I rested my head against the cabinet doors, leaving the needle in my arm and fighting the urge to cringe. My only comfort was the gun inside the sweatshirt at my back.

"I have something else you'll like." He knelt on the floor and kissed me, but I didn't respond. Maybe I could fake an overdose or a bad trip. A seizure might work too. When I failed to reciprocate his affections, he untied the tourniquet and pulled the needle out of my arm. A few drops of blood dripped onto his floor, but he didn't notice. He pulled his shirt over his head and unbuckled his belt. "Alexia, come on," he scooted closer, "we're just getting started here."

The next few minutes felt like an eternity as we kissed, and my thoughts focused on how badly I wanted to wash my hands in bleach. He didn't seem to notice I wasn't into this, which meant either I was pretty convincing or he didn't care. It was probably the latter, but my biggest dilemma was figuring a way out of this before I'd have to bleach more than just my hands.

He pushed my fingers away and began to untie and unbutton my shirt. "Francisco," I whispered, wondering what to do. In two minutes, things were gonna go from bad to worse. And before that happened, I would shoot him. So I needed a better plan and fast.

"Hmm," he murmured, pulling the shirt off of me and kissing along my clavicle. His fingers went to my belt, and I wondered how hard I'd have to hit him in order to knock him unconscious. The kitchen was sorely devoid of practical weaponry like knives, frying pans, and rolling pins. He pulled down my zipper and splayed his hands against my lower stomach, trying to push my jeans off. "Lift your hips." Maybe I could just knee him and put an end to his randy mood. As I moved into the perfect position to squish his berries, the phone rang. "Fuck," he growled, shoving me off of him and onto the floor, "hang on."

It quickly became apparent he was agitated with the caller and the conversation. While he continued to answer questions in the affirmative or negative and utter a mile long string of expletives, I remained in a gelatinous state on the ground, deciding on the perfect method of killing the mood.

"She's been with me all night," he said, and my ears perked up. "No, man." A long pause. "No shit." Another pause. "Now?" He grabbed his jeans off the floor and zipped them up. "Shit. No, I'll be there in five."

Now that he was dressed, it was safe to act interested again. I clawed at his leg as he went past, making a pouty face. "Francisco, what's going on?"

He knelt down and grabbed my shoulders, trying to force me to look at him, but I lolled my head back, afraid he'd catch on to my sobriety if he got a good look at me. "Did you see anyone strange at the club tonight?"

"No. The girls hate me," I whined. "I barely said two words to any of them."

He shook me. "No. At the club. Were there any strange men. Maybe some cops?"

"The cops raided two nights ago, and that's why no one was there tonight. That's why we closed early." Shakespeare must have heard about ESU handling the situation with Joe and the KXD enforcers. What was he planning to do now?

"I gotta go."

"What's happening?" I asked, making a show of struggling to my feet and grabbing my sweatshirt. "Why are you asking about the club?"

"It doesn't matter." He led me to the door. "Wait for me at your place. I'll be by later." He raced down the steps and out of the building, leaving me standing outside his locked apartment door. I needed answers.

Returning to my apartment, I opened the door and tensed. The sound of running water instantly alerted me someone was inside. Pulling the gun free, I aimed at the closed bathroom door, edging toward it. The faucet stopped, and the doorknob turned. Leveling the barrel at chest height, I cocked the gun and slowly exhaled.

The door opened, and it took every ounce of self-restraint not to automatically fire at the intruder. This was a lousy neighborhood with scary gangbangers. Whoever snuck inside must have a death wish.

"Easy, Parker," Detective Heathcliff said, raising his hands. "You already bruised my ribs. You don't need to shoot me, too."

"I should." I holstered the gun. "What were you thinking, shoving me inside that cab?" Heathcliff was alive, which meant my emotional meter just went from worried to irate. "How's Joe? What happened?"

"C'mon." He stepped to the side of the doorway, gesturing that I join him in the bathroom. This was quickly becoming our place, and I didn't quite care for it. As soon as I entered, I washed my hands in the sink. He turned the shower on and took a seat on the edge of the tub. The dark circles under his eyes, the way he held himself, and his unseemly appearance were indicators this job was getting to him. Once he collected himself, he let out a weary sigh. "Did you just shoot up?" He nodded at the trickle of blood running from the bend in my arm.

"Yeah. A few ccs of water. Well, I hope it was water." Shrugging, I slipped into interrogation mode. "Don't change the subject. Joe and the Black Cat. What's the deal? Did ESU get to him in time?"

"Uh-huh," Derek said, but his tone wasn't convincing. "The PD's raid was premature. It caused the KXDs to start talking. Apparently, Bard has plenty of pull at the Black Cat, and he has access to the security feeds. Despite the fact we've been piggybacking off their footage and I assume your people have been doing the same, Bard must have discovered Joe was undercover. Joe must have slipped up, and we missed it."

"How?"

"A few detectives are reviewing the footage, but from what we've seen, it has to do with the ecstasy tabs. There's footage of Joe collecting those coasters with the tearaway corners. It was the only suspicious thing on the tape, but since Bard's paranoid, maybe he thought they could be used as evidence."

"Why don't you ask Joe about it? The KXD enforcers were asking him about something. Maybe Bard didn't know for sure Joe was a UC." My thoughts scrambled to determining if we were blown or if this was Bard being a paranoid lunatic. Given his personal preferences for having top-of-the-line security, paranoia seemed a likely medical diagnosis for the KXD leader.

"We don't know enough yet. That's who I was on the phone with before you arrived." He glanced at the sink, indicating the reason for the sound of running water when

I entered.

"Can't Joe tell you what happened? Or did he have to get his union rep to intervene because IA is accusing him of something?"

"He can't talk right now." Pain contorted his features.

"Can't or won't?" My heart palpitated at the morbid thoughts traveling through my mind.

"Parker–"

"We should have intervened. You shouldn't have pulled me. Who put you in charge? You had no right, Detective. We are not in the same chain of command, and you will not make those types of calls again. Do I make myself clear?"

He bit back whatever remark he wanted to make, instead snorting incredulously. "You and your people waltz into the middle of a police investigation, practically blow it to kingdom come, and then blame us because you can't do anything wrong. Then you get annoyed when we don't share our intel or assets. And you want to ride in on your high horse and save the day, when things didn't escalate until it was your bacon in the fire." He shook his head. "It must be nice to be a Fed again." He stood up. "Jablonsky asked that I keep an eye on you since we have a history and you wouldn't risk anyone else's neck. If you went in like you wanted, you'd be dead now. Those KXD douches had machine pistols. Two members of ESU are in the hospital. Joe's sedated while they get him stabilized. So how the hell would sacrificing yourself have helped anyone?" He backed me against the sink. "I've already had one suicidal partner. I will not tolerate another one."

"We could have done something."

"I made the right call. At least one of us can see that." He opened the bathroom door. "Patch yourself up. We need to prepare for what's about to happen."

THIRTY-TWO

Heathcliff was in rare form. No matter how unemotional and by the book he tried to act at work, he always came to my rescue when I needed him. He'd defended me against his fellow officers and friends on numerous occasions, and he'd risked his neck more times than I could count. That's why the current situation was so frustrating. He was wrong. We should have moved in to help Joe. Until today, he'd never treated me like a damsel in distress or a liability, but apparently, now he thought I was both. And he called me the f-word. So what if I was a federal agent again? It didn't change anything. I was still me. He was still him. And we still had a job to do. This wasn't that different from any of the other cases we'd worked together, but from the heated glower that traveled in my direction, he didn't agree with that assessment.

"Steele just heard the news," I said. "He dashed out of his apartment like a bat out of hell. Whatever Shakespeare is planning to do, it's happening now."

"Great," Derek growled, dialing a number. He returned to the bathroom, turning on the sink and shutting the door.

Despite the fact my apartment wasn't bugged, the walls inside this building were thin. And we couldn't risk tipping anyone off. Bard owned this neighborhood and everyone in it. If someone discovered we were law enforcement, it would be a matter of minutes before that person gave us up.

I peered out the window. Steele's SUV was still parked outside. The streets were empty. Even the lookouts were gone. That seemed strange since Bard was under the impression the police department was keeping tabs on him. Why would he pull his spotters? Something didn't sit right, and an unsettling twinge nagged at the corners of my mind.

Heathcliff returned to the main room and joined me at the window after turning on the kitchen sink. "I'm to sit tight and see how this plays out. Once we know something for sure, I'll call it in."

"We haven't really talked since that morning Steele showed up," I said quietly, my eyes never leaving Bard's apartment building. "What happened after I was told to leave?"

"Do we have to do this now?"

"No, but if anything might be relevant, I'd like to know about it."

"Shakespeare and his guys got in an altercation with the Lords. You saw the aftermath."

"You stitched up that wounded KXD member." My own voice sounded foreign in my ears, and I couldn't be sure the words didn't come across like an accusation.

"Just to get the bleeding under control until he could get actual help." Derek continued to stare out the window, but he must have felt my eyes on him. "Don't look at me like that. You wanted us to save him. He's saved. Did he deserve it? Probably not." A grimace ran across his face before he could stop it. "Which makes every life he takes from here on out my fault."

"It isn't. And you know that." Swallowing, I wasn't used to Heathcliff wallowing. That was my schtick. "How..." I paused, unsure if I should push, and he glanced at me, waiting.

"Go ahead. Rip off the band-aid."

"How did Bard know you could help?"

G.K. Parks

"Because five years ago when I was originally assigned to infiltrate the KXDs, DeAngelo Bard was shot through the chest. And I saved his life."

"Derek." I couldn't get any other words out, even though I wanted to say something to remove the sour expression from his face.

"Yeah, my career is that fucked up. So don't think you're the only one with a questionable history because I'm certain I have you beat." He shifted his focus out the window, and we remained silent for a few minutes. "After you were sent home, Bard spoke about paying back the Lords for the trouble they caused. He was tightening up the ranks and sending outsiders and wannabes packing. I offered to leave, but given our history, he told me to stick around. He never mentioned Joe or the strip joint. He talked about shutting down the Lords for good by ending their dealers, stealing their working girls, and taking over their neighborhoods. After I left, I phoned the precinct and was given orders to report to narcotics. By the time I made it back here, it was too late. I was on my way to your apartment when I heard those two knucklehead lookouts talking about Bard sending a message to some guy at the club. After I discovered it was Joe, I knew we had to move in."

"And I got in the way?" I challenged, arching an eyebrow. "Because the way I remember it, I was prepared to get him out."

"They would have killed you. The second you stepped foot inside that room, it would have been over. You're the newest addition at the club and the weakest link. Nicholson's a heroin addict. By design, they aren't the most trustworthy or reliable people. Frankly, when I put you in that cab, I hoped you'd get home early enough that Bard and Steele wouldn't suspect you. But for all I knew, you might have returned to find a firing squad waiting. It was a calculable risk, and I didn't see another choice." His eyes flicked from Bard's apartment to me. "Do you think that's why Bard called Steele over? Do you think you've been made? You were snooping around right before ESU intervened."

- 243 -

"No. Steele trusts me, especially after I spent the night proving myself to him. In the last few hours, I've moved five grand of blow and let things get a little freaky upstairs." Heathcliff met my eyes, and I sighed. "Don't worry, I washed my hands." I turned serious. "Actually, the call from Bard was kind of a godsend because I was prepared to inflict painful and possibly permanent physical damage to Francisco's favorite body part."

"What are you going to do when he comes back? You know he wants some and doesn't seem the type to just let it go."

"I have no idea. Maybe he won't come back. Aren't your people supposed to roll in and arrest everyone or something?"

"Sure, now you want our help. And what exactly is your team doing?"

"We're working the supply angles. Office of *International* Operations," I winked at him, "the name says it all."

Remembering everything that happened in the last six hours, I stood and went to my phone. The OIO needed to know about the lab Steele had taken me to and a few other precious tidbits. Deciding now was an okay time to send a few encrypted messages, I left Heathcliff to monitor the situation outside while I fiddled with the phone.

The responses I received were brief, and I suspected Jablonsky must have called it a night after confiscating the bag of cocaine from the ladies' room. Lucca or one of the techs was probably on early morning watch, and they tended to keep information close to the vest. It was protocol to minimize the use of unsecured communications, and despite the encryption program, a throwaway cell phone was hardly secure. After changing out of my stripper clothes and into a basic t-shirt and jeans, I returned to the window.

"Did I miss anything exciting?" I asked, glancing at the water cascading from the faucet.

"A pigeon crapped on Steele's SUV," Heathcliff deadpanned, not bothering to tear his eyes from the window.

"Did anyone shoot it?"

"No."

"Then I guess I didn't miss anything exciting." I unsuccessfully attempted to stifle a yawn.

"Since there aren't any new developments, why don't you get some sleep?"

Truthfully, I was exhausted, and it didn't take much wheedling to convince me to climb onto the jumbo-sized balloon that called itself a bed, pop a few ibuprofens to counteract the inevitable ache that would intensify after a few hours of sleep, and curl into a ball. When I opened my eyes again, it was noon.

"They still haven't come out," Heathcliff said, immediately filling a mug with bottled water and popping it into the microwave. "Well, Bard and Steele haven't. The rejects are taking up space on the street corners."

"Any idea what they might be planning?"

I expected him to hand over the heated mug, but instead, he dumped a packet of instant coffee into it, stirred, and took a sip. Obviously, we weren't trading shifts at the window, so I did a few careful stretches, working the kinks out of my back and neck, and hoped that loosening up my legs wouldn't make my hip worse.

"The last time Bard holed up this long, he planned a large-scale assault, complete with military-grade assault weapons."

"Would he be stupid enough to declare war on the police department?"

"I don't know." Heathcliff sucked in a breath. "He's more likely to seek revenge on a rival. He knows the rules. If you kill a cop, every police officer in the city will hunt you down."

"But he tortured Joe. He doesn't care about that."

Frowning, Heathcliff considered my point. "He must have thought he'd get away with it without anyone discovering the connection."

That irritating gnawing at the recesses of my mind returned, buzzing a question through my brain. "What if he thought Joe was working for the Lords?"

"Where would he get that idea?"

"Steele's made mention that the Lords were out to sabotage the clubs. Veronica was attacked by members of the Lords, at least one of whom came after me. What was Joe's established background? Would it have made the KXDs suspicious?"

A noise in the hallway startled me, and I clamped my mouth shut. We didn't have the water running. I went to the door, but I didn't see anyone.

"We weren't talking that loud. It's fine," Heathcliff assured, watching as I checked my gun, holstered the weapon, and nervously paced. But for my sanity, he flipped the handle on the faucet. "I don't know much. No one read me in on our current UCs. But I've been doing this long enough that I know the men in the unit."

"What's that supposed to mean?"

"It means that I walked into the Black Cat, expecting to see one familiar face but instead that number turned out to be two."

The PD didn't tell Heathcliff they were working this either. Not only did law enforcement agencies refuse to share intel with others, but they couldn't even share intel within the same command structure. No wonder we couldn't stop this. The gangs and cartels were more organized than we were.

"Heads up," Heathcliff put the mug down and sat up straight, "Steele's coming this way."

"Great."

My stomach clenched tightly, and my mind raced through possible ways to thwart his advances. Using Heathcliff's undercover persona as a permanent love interest was probably my best bet, but it could endanger our covers and our lives. Mark's words echoed through my ears. *Do what you have to in order to survive.* But there were some lines I'd never cross because they'd jeopardize my morality and the investigation. Therefore, I'd just have to play this another way.

Steele pounded against the door, and I blew out a steadying breath, tossed a final glance to Heathcliff who didn't move an inch from the chair, and opened the door. Francisco didn't look particularly apologetic for running out on me, and he barged into the apartment without so much as a hello. Frankly, he didn't even seem surprised to find Heathcliff inside.

"Those bastards fucked with the wrong people." Steele crossed the room and sifting through my club wear. "They're like a cancer that we're gonna cut out." He ran his fingers over the black sequins of each of my tops but didn't find whatever he was looking for. He was on a rampage, so I stepped back and let him do what he wanted. Seconds later, he fished his cell from his pocket, tapped the screen a few times, and held it up to his ear. "Nothing. Like I said, it's not her." He paused, his back to us, but I didn't risk taking my eyes off of him. "Okay. Sure. I'll bring her too." He stuck the phone in his pocket and spun.

"What's up?" I asked, attempting to appear slightly cross.

"I could ask you the same thing." Fire burned behind his eyes. "But Shakespeare wants us." His eyes rested on Heathcliff for a split second. "Is this your new home? I guess since Alexia's around pussy all day, she's decided to take in a stray."

Derek produced a cruel, sadistic smile. "That's only because you aren't man enough to close the deal."

My eyes went wide with momentary shock. What did Derek think he was doing? Francisco's gaze was still trained on his competition, and he didn't notice my slip. The two remained locked in a staring contest for a solid minute, and then Steele narrowed his eyes and stepped toward Derek.

"Do you want to say that again?" Steele asked.

"You heard me the first time, Francisco." Heathcliff stood, moving to within an inch of Steele. "She's mine now. You've blown your chance. And if you try to lay claim again, it'll be the last thing you ever do."

Steele laughed, an ugly sound that rumbled through his chest. "Shakespeare won't protect you forever. He'll get tired of your attitude soon enough, and when he does," he lifted the gun from his waistband and pressed the muzzle against Derek's temple, "you'll regret this conversation."

THIRTY-THREE

Following the altercation in my apartment, Steele dragged me across the street to Bard's, ordering Heathcliff to stay away. My mind was reeling from that disgusting show of male dominance. My feminist attitude was offended by the entire situation, but I had to bite my tongue. For once, that mindset wasn't important. What was important was the fact Derek just painted himself as Steele's nemesis. And I wouldn't put it past the KXD lieutenant to blow a hole or two through his competition. But luckily, Bard ran the show, and Derek's heroics from five years ago had earned him a favored position with the head of the gang. It would be enough to keep him protected for now.

"Any particular reason you ran out on me? Or maybe you'd like to share why you were copping a feel of my work uniform," I said as we went down the icy steps to Bard's apartment.

"The Black Cat had a rat," Steele said, and I wondered if he was hoping to sound clever. "We were handling the problem, but someone must have heard the ruckus and tipped off the cops. The fuzz is turning up the heat, and the Lords think they're just gonna sit back and laugh their asses off while we scramble." He stopped. "That ain't happenin'."

"What does this have to do with me?" I wondered if I should have asked about the identity of the rat instead.

"Shakespeare and I spent the last few hours with the Black Cat's security footage, and now he wants to talk to you."

Shit. Forcing my breathing to remain steady, I narrowed my eyes. "Why?"

A growl emanated from his chest. "Stop asking so many questions." He keyed in the security code and opened the door to Bard's apartment. "Because I could ask you a few of my own, like how you could betray me again."

"I'm not your property. I can screw whoever I want, whenever I want."

"Spoken like a true whore," Bard said from within the recesses of the living room. He flicked on a light, adding to the dramatic effect, and gestured to a chair in the center of the room. "Take a seat." I hesitated, so he added, "I wasn't asking."

After answering his questions about the club, my interactions with the girls and Joe, and what exactly I'd been up to the rest of the night, Bard grabbed my wrist, manipulating my arm around and studying the most recent punctures and phony track marks. He must have realized they might be fake, and I didn't know if they'd hold up to his scrutiny. At least a few of the needle marks were real. He pinched the sensitive flesh on the inside of my elbow, and when one of the scabbed spots seeped blood, he was pleased.

"Congratulations, you've redeemed yourself," Bard declared, taking a step back and picking up a pipe from the mantel. After holding a lighter over the bowl and taking a few puffs of what I could only imagine must be crack, his upper lip curved into a smile. "And I thought you'd be the first person I'd kill." He snickered. "Funny how things change. Francisco says you know your way around a gun."

"I do."

"Good. You're gonna show me."

He barked out half a dozen names, and Steele grabbed my upper arm, hoisting me out of the chair. It was time to go. Francisco led our motley crew to his SUV. Three KXD members climbed in the back, and I feared what was about to happen. Another three joined Bard inside his SUV, and the two vehicles darted into afternoon traffic.

"They'll never expect this," one of the guys in back said. "I can't wait to see their faces right before we blow them off."

"Easy, Petey," Steele chided, "we're not blowing them off. We're leaving that up to the professional." He gave me a look from the corner of his eye, making sure the whore reference didn't go by unnoticed, but I remained silent. "Shakespeare wants to test out the fresh meat."

"I thought we were sending a message," another voice said. "Aren't we hitting those douchebag Lords where it'll hurt them the most? We should light up their stash house."

"We're gonna empty their stash house while Alexia distracts them." Steele actually met my eyes this time. "You'll want to keep them interested just long enough to shoot them." His eyes darkened, and his voice grew hard. "If you were smart, you would have used Hotshot as practice."

"Francisco," I hissed, realizing the backseat had grown uncomfortably quiet, "it just happened." Heathcliff's story and appearance ruined my declaration to show some affection and gratitude to the KXD lieutenant and any chance of finding my way back into Steele's good graces. "He was there. You weren't."

"Ooh, burn." Petey laughed.

"Slut," Steele muttered, but the rest of the ride continued in silence.

By the time we reached our destination, the sun was barely above the horizon. It'd be dark within the hour. Bard pulled to a stop diagonally behind Steele's SUV. The punks from the back seat emptied out of the car, and Steele barely cast a look in my direction before exiting. Just as I reached for the handle, one of the KXDs from the back opened my car door.

"Are you ready?" he asked, holding out a snub-nosed twenty-two. "Shakespeare wants me to point out the Lords you're supposed to target." I hesitated to touch the weapon, wondering what other evidence might be on it that would prove useful, but the man pressed it into my palm. "You'll lure them away from the door, maybe around the corner so no one will see, and then pop 'em." He pointed to three men huddled around the side entrance to a pizza joint. "Just be quiet about it."

"The acoustics are wrong." My eyes darted to the enclosed space. "The sound of gunfire will bounce off the buildings, causing a massive echo. It'll be loud enough to wake the dead." I turned my head, making sure my voice would be heard clearly on the recording device inside the SUV. "Everyone inside Gino's Pizzeria will hear the shots, along with every single Lord within four blocks."

"You don't want to do it," he sneered, "which is fine, but if you don't, I'm supposed to take care of them and you." Something slimy crossed his face, and I recognized him as one of the men who tried to jump me when I first moved into the neighborhood. He had recently grown a beard, but the dead look in his eyes was still the same. "And this time, Francisco won't rescue you." He glanced back at the rest of the group congregating together next to Bard's vehicle to work out a plan. "You're either fully committed or you're gone. What'll it be?"

"I'm committed." I reached inside the SUV and searched for something useful. Just as I was about to give up, I spotted a half empty soda bottle in the rear cup holder. "And luckily for you geniuses, I'm more afraid of serving hard time than anything you could do to me."

Pouring out the contents, I removed the knife from my pocket, cut the end off, and fashioned it into a makeshift suppressor. It wouldn't do much to silence the gunfire, but it was enough to demonstrate my willingness to become one of the KXDs. He rolled his eyes, as if this was the most ridiculous idea ever, which it was, and went to chat with the others while I pretended to search for something to secure the bottle to the barrel of the handgun. After a final glance to make sure no one was paying attention, I retrieved the cell phone I planted days ago, noticing the blinking battery light.

"Track and trap," I muttered, shoving the device inside

my pocket and hoping it was transmitting and the battery would last long enough for units to trace the GPS and roll in before the streets were splattered with blood. Now I just needed to find some way of killing three men without causing them any permanent damage. When did I become an illusionist because I didn't remember ever attending a course on this at Quantico?

"As soon as the sun goes down, you're up," Bard said once I joined the group. "I don't care what you have to do to get them away from that door. We need access to the restaurant, and it's not like we can just go in the front."

"What's in the restaurant?" I asked.

"Not in," Steele shook his head, "below."

"Just get them away from the door and don't think too hard about the rest," Bard commanded. "The only way we're getting inside is by putting those fuckers down." Bard eyed the punk behind me, but I couldn't turn around to see what his eyes were communicating. "Excellent," Bard said with such exuberance I couldn't tell if it was due to the drugs he inhaled or whatever nonverbal signal he just received. "We'll load up and be gone before they realize what hit them."

Francisco and Bard moved away, taking up positions inside the two parked vehicles, and started the engines. The six remaining gang members eased into the shadows, exchanging snickers and knowing looks. Obviously, I was up, and from the sounds coming from the peanut gallery, I wasn't sure if they were waiting to see my award-winning impersonation of a prostitute or if they were excited by the prospect of killing the Lords. Either way, I needed to think on my feet.

As usual, I wasn't dressed for the part. It seemed like Francisco took some kind of perverse pleasure in forcing me into situations like this completely ill-equipped. It happened last night when he wanted me to hock cocaine at the dance clubs while dressed in a baggy sweatshirt. Luckily, I had the Black Cat uniform on underneath and was able to make-do. This time, I was standing outside in the freezing cold in nothing but jeans and a t-shirt. Hookers, while dressed inappropriately, would have had the foresight to put a long coat on over their barely there skirt and tube top, and they wouldn't be caught dead working the streets in jeans and a t-shirt.

After taking a few steadying breaths, I turned onto the main street, hugged my arms around my body, and continued toward the pizzeria. Keeping my head down, I pretended not to be aware of my surroundings, but my five senses were on alert. The sound of car horns, the hum of engines, conversations, and televisions blurred into the background of noise pollution while I watched my exhales turn into puffs of frozen vapor in the frigid air.

I cocked my head to the side and looked at the men. One of them wore a red polo with the Gino's emblem on the left breast. The other two were dressed similarly to the KXD lookouts, smoking menthol cigarettes. Apparently, gang wear was a style all its own.

"It's freezing out here," I said loud enough to catch their attention. My presence didn't register on any of their faces, which meant they probably had no idea who I was, and if they did, they didn't recognize me without the sequined top and glitter. "Can I bum a cigarette?"

One of them shrugged, so I approached the side door. "Where's your coat?" he asked, pulling out a pack and flipping it upside down against the palm of his hand to make the cigarette fall free of the soft packaging.

"I was out late partying last night, and I can't seem to remember where I left it." I took the offered cigarette. Having never been a smoker, I wasn't entirely sure what to do with it, but it seemed like a good way to strike up a conversation. Giggling, I crinkled my nose playfully. "Oh," I covered my mouth with my hand as if embarrassed, "I think I left it on the floor of some guy's limo. Oops." I pursed my lips and cast bedroom eyes at one of the men. "Do you think there's any way I could persuade you to lend a girl your jacket in order to get home?" I put the unlit cigarette up to my lips suggestively. "I might freeze to death while I wait for the bus."

Polo guy let out a surprised snort and winked at his friends. "I'll meet up with you guys after work," he said and went back inside.

Okay, one down, two to go. That meant my odds were getting better. My nine millimeter was still tucked at the small of my back, and the twenty-two was shoved into my ankle boot. Without adhesive, the makeshift silencer was nothing but a useless piece of plastic which I abandoned next to Francisco's SUV.

Neither weapon was in a particularly secure position, but at least they weren't blatantly obvious to a casual observer. However, I couldn't just shoot these men, and I was lacking in gags and handcuffs. Knocking them out seemed like the only option. Where was backup when I actually needed it?

"Don't you want a light?" Cigarette guy asked.

Tucking the unlit cigarette behind my ear, I smiled at him. "I'd like one afterward. Come on, it's just a coat. I even promise to return it tomorrow to the restaurant. And you'll get a little something to keep you warm in the meantime. What do you say?"

The third man hadn't spoken since my appearance, and he clapped Cigarette guy on the back. "Go for it. I'll keep an eye out until you're done." He met my eyes. "Maybe I could interest you in a scarf or some gloves?" He wore a wool scarf over his leather bomber jacket with a matching pair of fingerless gloves.

"Maybe."

Taking Cigarette guy's hand in order to keep him from putting it at the small of my back, I guided him away from the side door, past the double doors for deliveries to the restaurant, and behind the dumpster. He was out of sight of his friend, and I shoved him playfully against the brick wall. A quick glance ensured no one could see us, and when I turned back, his fingers were already on his zipper.

Clamping my mouth over his, I ran my fingers through his hair, down to his neck, and eased them around, feeling his pulse point and identifying his carotid. Cutting off blood flow to his brain would put him out cold, and I leveraged my arm around, catching him unexpectedly and squeezing hard. His surprised gasp was muffled, and when he stopped flailing, I counted to twenty and then carefully released pressure, letting him crumple down the wall and into a heap behind the dumpster.

I needed to find some way to secure him in the event he gained consciousness faster than expected, but the only thing of use was his shoelaces. He wore a fancy, high-end brand of kicks with custom laces. They were thick, plastic coated nylon. Making fast work of his shoes, I unlaced each one and bound his wrists behind his back before tying his ankles together. The laces were extremely long, and I looped them enough times to increase the tensile strength and minimize the chance of him breaking free.

Then I mussed my hair, as if he'd been running his hands through it, and stepped away from the dumpster. From the looks of his pal, Wool Scarf, I'd wager that he'd been straining to hear what was going on. Pervert.

"Hey," I said, batting my eyelashes, "your buddy isn't quite up for the job. Do you think you can help him out?"

Obviously, this strange turn of events was too confusing for his tiny reptilian brain to process, so he smiled and abandoned his post, an obvious swagger to his walk. In a few more steps, he'd spot Cigarette guy, so I had to act now. Grabbing the ends of his scarf, I tugged, and he turned. I pulled the wool upward, over his mouth, like I planned to pull it over his head, but instead, I used the motion to spin around, grabbing him from behind and pulling the scarf tight around his neck. Then I made sure the bend of my elbow rested against the main arteries in his throat and squeezed.

He bucked, throwing his head back, but since he was six inches taller than I was, he hit nothing but air. He thrashed sideways, knocking my hip into the side of the dumpster, and I saw stars. My grip loosened slightly, and he reached around, continuing to squeeze and claw at my side while using his other hand to pry my arm from around his neck. From this position, it was obvious he planned to flip me over him, and when I couldn't get him to go down, I let him hurl me forward.

As I sailed over his shoulder, I swung my legs out, kicking him under the jaw. He faltered backward, losing his balance and landing on his ass. When he opened his mouth to stabilize his equilibrium, I took that opportunity to wrap my legs around his torso, holding him down and putting him into a chokehold with his back against my chest. Once he stopped struggling, I waited a full minute before releasing my grip and rolling him off of me. It was a good thing I'd insisted on refreshing my hand-to-hand combat skills.

Repeating the process of tying him up with his own set of shoestrings, I dragged him a few feet closer to his friend, put them back to back, and wrapped the scarf around both of their mouths, binding their heads together and hopefully silencing any sounds they might make once they roused. The KXDs still hadn't moved into position, and I didn't know how much time I had left. The longer I could delay, the greater the chance law enforcement would intervene. But as the minutes ticked past, I knew Steele would become even more irritated, and Bard wasn't exactly patient either. After another minute, I pulled out the twenty-two, firing four times into the base of the brick wall.

The sound of gunfire ripped through the alley, like I knew it would, and the eight KXDs appeared near the entrance, already moving inside. The one that was told to kill me if I failed gave me a cursory glance and jerked his chin toward the door. Apparently, I was one of them now. Moving inside, Steele bashed through the door immediately to our right and began moving down the steps. It was scary how well he knew what their competitor's fortress looked like.

Down the steps was the boiler room and just beyond that was a sealed door. This one was made of reinforced steel, but the lock was rudimentary. I could have picked it in ten seconds, but Steele pulled his gun, firing to the side of the knob and opening the door. Heavy footsteps thundered above. And I had been worried about making too much noise. Sheesh.

"The four of you stay here and keep those pricks at bay," Bard ordered, leading the rest of us deeper inside.

I didn't want to think about how many lives would be lost. With any luck, the only people checking on the basement would be gang members and not innocent pizzeria employees or curious patrons. Enough time had passed that a tactical team should have shown up, but they weren't here yet, which probably meant the battery was dead and they were still working on tracking the exact location. In the meantime, gunfire erupted in a nonstop barrage behind us, but Bard and Steele continued to move through the newly exposed room, taking in the sights of what must have been hundreds of bricks of cocaine, bags of pills, and sacks of marijuana. This was the largest drug operation I'd ever seen, and my blood ran cold to think the Lords' stockpile paled in comparison to Bard's resources.

THIRTY-FOUR

"Let's load 'em up," Bard ordered, pointing to a pallet of carefully wrapped product. "Grab the biggest ones you can carry and bring them out to the trucks." The two lower level KXD members complied while my brain attempted to restart after the obvious glitch. "You too," Bard ordered, tossing a bag with a few kilos in my direction.

Barely catching it before it hit the ground, I stood there, dumbfounded. The direction in which we had just come was blocked by gunfire. We couldn't go back that way, especially with thousands of dollars of drugs in our arms.

"Chica," Francisco said, appearing at my side with a large stockpile hoisted atop his shoulder, "there's a back door. Follow me."

At the far end of the room was a hidden doorway that led to a few narrow steps that brought us out on street level behind the building. The two SUVs were parked out back, waiting. Apparently while I was taking care of the lookouts, Francisco and Bard found two primo parking spaces. As we dumped the contents inside Francisco's SUV, I strained to hear sirens, but I couldn't hear much over the faint gunfire and my own beating heart.

"Where did they get this much stuff?" I asked.

"The cartels. Same as us," Steele replied, shoving the narcotics into the rear hatch. "As far as I know, they don't cut or manufacture their own shit. So we have a leg up on them. Two now." His eyes flicked to me. "And when we get back, both of your legs will be in the air. I don't care what Hotshot thinks. He doesn't own you. I do."

I swallowed, a cold chill traveling through me. "Is that it?" I asked as another KXD member exited with a handful of loot.

"No, go make a few more runs," Francisco ordered. "Shakespeare wants to clean them out. So don't stop until every last joint and dime bag is ours."

Edging down the steps, I wasn't in a rush to return. With only two exits, it wouldn't take much for the Lords to box us in. And with the limited hiding spots and vantage points, if they set up a crossfire, we'd be dead in a matter of seconds. Granted, Steele was outside, theoretically preventing such a thing from happening, but he was one guy.

The gunfire grew louder, and a single cry of anguish echoed off the walls. I couldn't let this continue to happen. I had to stop it; consequences be damned. For the most part, the constant vibrato wasn't interrupted by screams, indicating the bullets were missing living targets, pounding into the walls, and ricocheting off pipes and fixtures instead.

"Where are you going?" Bard grabbed my arm as I moved toward the door. "The exit's on the other side."

"Your people are dying out there. They need help."

"They're fine. The Lords are the ones dying. And if my people aren't good enough to stand up to some wannabe losers like the Lords, then they're getting what they deserve." His cold demeanor brought his ruthlessness to the surface, and I realized this was nothing more than a power play by a megalomaniac. Sure, Bard tried to be smart by legitimizing some business ventures and property acquisitions, but he was just another thug from the streets who wanted to prove his stick was bigger than anyone else's. Teddy Roosevelt should be rolling over in his grave. "Now move your ass."

Before I could say anything, a metal canister rolled into the room. I barely had enough time to realize it wasn't a pineapple before it spewed tear gas. From the sound of metal tinking against the floor, no guesswork was needed to know what was coming.

The air was heavy with chemicals that burned my eyes, nose, and throat. As if that didn't make it hard enough to see through the tears and choking, a few smoke grenades went off. The room was enveloped in thick clouds of darkness, and I dropped to my knees, hoping to avoid the gunfire that was likely to accompany it. Instead, heavy footfalls thudded against the tile floor, and through the blinding haze, laser sights lanced through the smoke.

"On the ground. Get on the ground." The words repeated in a chorus throughout the room. Flopping onto my stomach, I laced my fingers behind my head, hiding my face in the fabric of my shirt to lessen some of the abuse my mucus membranes were enduring. Rushed footsteps sounded from all around, and in my current state, I couldn't tell which direction they were traveling. The sounds of my own coughing and choking blurred out everything else. Gloved hands moved along my body, searching and removing my weapons, before cold metal secured my wrists behind my back. Instantly, my skin burned at the contact. "On your feet." Someone hauled me up and dragged me, sputtering and dizzy, into the hallway and up the steps.

Outside, the first breath of clean air felt like razorblades inside my lungs. Hacking up a few mouthfuls of phlegm and wiping my runny nose against my shoulder, I searched for a familiar face through my blurry, teary eyes but didn't see anyone I recognized. ESU, emergency services unit, had taken control of the situation. Using advanced tactical gear and methods, they neutralized the firefight and were taking everyone into custody. Questions would only be asked and answered in a much more formal setting.

A female officer was on scene, along with a dozen police cars, two ESU vans, and a couple of ambulances. After spotting me, she took custody, leading me away from the side door and to one of the squad cars. The entire time she recited my Miranda's while I choked on my own snot. Pushing my head down, she shoved me into the back of the car and closed the door.

What felt like eons later, she climbed into the driver's seat, turned on the lights, and headed for the precinct. Since my eyes were too sensitive to remain open against the burning and tears, I kept them closed. When it felt like the car finally came to a stop, I cautioned a glance.

"How many?" I asked, my voice hoarse.

"What?" She eyed me through the rearview mirror, and I leaned forward toward the glass barrier that separated us.

"How many dead?"

"I don't know. The coroner wasn't called." She seemed uncertain what to do or if she should answer. Her partner or TO was probably still on scene, but since I was the only female suspect, they must have figured she could handle me. "Do you want to tell me what happened, ma'am?" Her training was taking over, and soon we'd be going through the fun of booking.

"How many arrests were made?"

Her eyes turned cold, like I was trying to manipulate the situation. She removed the keys, slamming her car door and opening mine. "This way, ma'am." She pulled me from the car, and the desk sergeant buzzed us into booking. Next would be holding, and who knew how long I'd be there.

"If you don't let me wash these chemicals off and rinse my eyes soon, I'll make a formal request for medical attention. Then it'll turn into a complaint about police brutality. Do you really want to deal with that kind of paperwork and internal review?"

"Oh, so we have a frequent flyer," the desk sergeant mused, overhearing my words. "Take her to get cleaned up before she starts squawking to some shyster civil rights attorney. But keep your eyes on her and don't let her get away, y'hear that, Officer."

"Yes, sir," the arresting officer said, leading me toward the ladies' room. "Don't try anything, I'm not in the mood," she whispered in my ear, opening the door and pushing me inside.

It was an individual bathroom with a single sink and a

toilet. She stood at the door, watching me lean backward over the sink to turn on the water with my hands secured behind my back. Once it was on, I had to kneel on the floor in order to get close enough to the sink. Giving up on washing my face, I placed my entire head underneath the faucet, letting the water soak through my hair and run down my shirt. It was better than nothing. When the burning ebbed and my face felt clean, I stood up, dripping water everywhere.

"Y'know, I get it," I said, flipping back around to turn off the sink with my bound hands. "I can't say I wouldn't do the same thing, but the police department harps on respect for a reason."

She narrowed her eyes. "Thank you, ma'am. I'll keep that in mind." She wanted to appear tough, like she had something to prove.

"So when do I get my phone call?" I asked, letting her take charge as she opened the door and dragged me back to the desk.

"Once you've been processed."

A quick glance answered my question that none of the KXDs had been brought in yet. "Where's everyone else?"

"Don't worry, your friends will be here shortly, but they don't allow visitation among prisoners. But if you behave, maybe I'll let you say goodbye before we ship you out to a women's holding facility."

"Can I have some water?" I asked as she led me past the desk sergeant, and I caught the slightest eyebrow raise. I couldn't tell if he was proud of her or worried that I'd claim it was abuse. Either way, maybe I should work on making friends while I waited for someone to spring me, instead of annoying the officers on duty.

After being processed, I spent some time in lockup before getting moved into an interrogation room. At least in here I was given a bottle of water. It wasn't exactly cold, but the liquid helped soothe my throat. Despite the harrowing events of the last few hours, I was oddly at peace. My nerves were fairly settled, and the slight nausea due to the adrenaline, tear gas, and smoke grenades had faded quickly. Maybe I was becoming immune to this crazy shit.

The door cracked open, and I heard voices outside. "Here's the form for her transfer. We need to ask her questions in relation to our ongoing investigation. Once that's settled, we'll relinquish her back to you. I'll be waiting outside when you're through with her." Lucca? I strained to hear, but the voice wasn't loud enough to clearly decipher. "Is she shackled?" More garbled responses. "Make sure. Ankles too."

Oh, for god's sake. Biting back my anger, I took another sip of water, knowing an officer was about to enter the room, unhook the cuffs from the bar in the center of the table, resecure them, and then shackle my arms and legs together. With my luck, it'd be the arresting officer who I pissed off that would get to do the honors. She'd probably pour the rest of the bottle over my still wet hair and hope I'd freeze to death on the way to the federal building.

Instead, Detective O'Connell stepped inside. He didn't acknowledge that he knew me, and from the warning look in his eyes, I knew some of the KXDs must be nearby. He was hoping to keep my cover intact, and I gave a slight nod, acknowledging that I understood. As we moved through the precinct, the chains clanged, solidifying in everyone's mind that I was facing some serious charges.

Moving to the loading bay, Nick opened the rear door of a government-issued SUV and helped me inside. "Good luck," he whispered, making a show of securing the chain to the hook in the floor. His facial expression never faltered as he shut the door and returned inside.

Agent Lucca caught my eye in the mirror, but he didn't say a word until we were on the road. "Are you aware that phoning ahead would have been advisable?"

"I tried, but the battery was drained." My forehead creased. "You mean to tell me you didn't send ESU to intervene?"

His eyes darted back to the rearview mirror. "Track and trap? Is that really the operational phrase you were taught to use in a situation like this? Maybe you should have read up on proper protocol and codewords before we planted you in the apartment." He chuckled at the icy glare I cast at him. "But with that arrest, Nicholson's been burned. It looks like you'll have to hang up the g-string and pasties. Are you prepared to wear actual clothing and report to the office on a daily basis?"

"Ready, willing, and able. And from that playful tone, shall I assume that progress has been made?"

The boy scout actually smiled. "Ink's drying on a few search warrants. Arrest warrants are in the works, and the DEA's in the process of making their biggest international bust of the year, thanks to us."

"Wonderful, now how about passing a handcuff key my way?"

"Not until we're inside the OIO offices. It's possible you might run into a detainee, and we don't want to risk another security breach, do we?"

"Fine." I hated restraints. Agent Lucca stifled a chuckle, and if my feet weren't bound to the floorboard, I would have kicked the back of his seat. "But wipe that smirk off your face, Lucca, or the boy scouts will confiscate your merit badges."

"What makes you think I was a boy scout?"

"You love following the rules."

"So what? They're in place to ensure we stay on the right side of the law and our evidence and cases aren't thrown out of court. You'd benefit from being more of a stickler. This is the second time your cover's been compromised on this op. And you should have sent word of Bard's plans so we could have been lying in wait. I'd hate to be you when the Director hears about this?"

"All right, Lucca. You win. I won't call you a boy scout anymore."

"Thank you."

"Kiss ass."

THIRTY-FIVE

My go-bag had been stored in Mark's office, and after taking a shower and changing clothes inside the women's locker room, I was ready to get to work. The information I'd gathered only helped solidify our suspicions and strengthen our case. But most of what was about to occur was already in the works. Raids would commence on the locations Steele had taken me. At the moment, surveillance vans and tactical teams were positioned outside the KXDs' stash house behind the diner, at the lab we went to the night before, and throughout the neighborhood. Additional units were keeping tabs on the coffee shop, the Black Cat, and the club where Steele dropped me off to sell cocaine. In the meantime, arrest warrants were pending on Steele and Bard.

"Any word from Heathcliff?" I asked after spilling my guts to the room full of agents who'd been working this case since the beginning.

"Parker, Detective Heathcliff is not one of our assets," Jablonsky said, his tone silencing any other questions I might have asked. "The PD is still processing the dozen arrests they made and scouring the pizzeria and connected areas for additional evidence. They are too busy to share their intel with us."

"We'll grab their records in the morning, make sure there aren't any game-changers, and execute the search warrants simultaneously tomorrow afternoon," Cooper said.

"Casualties?" I asked, rubbing crusty gunk from the corners of my sore eyes.

"Parker, we don't have the police reports yet," Cooper repeated. "But we know DeAngelo Bard and Francisco Steele were not taken into custody." Remembering the rushed footfalls, I suspected Bard had made a break for it, and he and Steele must have escaped with thousands of dollars' worth of narcotics. Blanching, I shivered, breaking out in a cold sweat for some unbeknownst reason. Cooper scooted closer, casually placing a gentle hand on my wrist and nonchalantly taking my pulse. "Are you okay?"

"Yeah," I shook the cobwebs from my brain, "I just can't make sense out of what happened earlier tonight."

"Let's reconvene first thing in the morning." Jablonsky pushed away from the conference table. "These long hours are taking a toll. Unfortunately, there isn't much more we can do until the court orders are signed and the PD sends us their reports. Go home, everyone. We'll start fresh tomorrow at seven a.m."

"Eight hours from now," Agent Lawson muttered, but no one acted like they heard him. Hell, maybe I was hallucinating.

"Parker, hang back a minute," Mark said before I could stand. He waited for the room to clear before he spoke again. "Honestly, how are you?"

"I'm good." I felt like I had a cold, but other than that, I couldn't complain. Truthfully, the last twenty-four hours were a blur, and none of it had set in yet. "Maybe a bit numb."

He pressed his lips into a thin line; his expression looked grim. "C'mon, you need a drink and a ride home."

* * *

Upon waking, I was so congested I would have been a

shoo-in for a cold medicine commercial. Beneath my head was a balled up suit jacket, and I was covered in mismatched bedding. Where was I? Rubbing the grit from my eyes, I looked around the room, spotting Mark's furniture and questionable décor.

"You'll be happy to know you weren't talking in your sleep," he said, coming down the steps and making a beeline for the adjoining kitchen. "But you did everything else in your sleep. Scream, thrash, grunt." He set the coffeemaker to brew and grabbed a box of cereal from the pantry. "And you wonder why I've always hesitated to let you stay at my place." I stretched and joined him in the kitchen. "Just let me eat my breakfast. Then I'll drop you off at your place, and you can get ready for work."

I slumped into one of the kitchen chairs and propped my head up in my hands. "I'm sorry about last night. I didn't plan to crash on your couch."

He poured two cups of coffee and brought them to the table with his bowl of corn flakes. "You needed to stay somewhere safe." His eyes focused on me, looking for things he probably didn't want to see. "I get it. I've read your reports and reviewed the surveillance feeds. We've talked regularly enough, but I know what you've shared has only been relevant to making a case against the KXDs and identifying their drug supplier. And that's only the tip of the iceberg. What you've dealt with on a day-to-day basis has been much more difficult. You've been living in fear for the last two months."

"I wasn't afraid." But he saw through my lie. "Just anxious and confused. I've been in a state of flux and uncertainty since the beginning. Never knowing how to act or react. Toeing the line of getting close without being too close." My mind drifted to the Black Cat, Francisco, and the wounded KXD member. "You asked Detective Heathcliff to watch my back."

"After the Lords tried to make an example out of you, it was clear you needed on-site support. And if I sent in any of our agents, you would have found a way to make their covers irrelevant. You didn't leave me a choice."

"Do we know who gunned down the Lords the night I

was attacked?"

"We have our suspicions. Like Steele said, the bulk of Bard's drugs are coming from a Mexican cartel. We've pulled nearby footage and CCTV feeds, and after a thorough analysis, we think Bard asked the cartel to assist in sending his rivals a message."

"Okay, so any leads on the whereabouts of the SUV or its occupants?"

"Parker, we'll go over everything at the office."

"What about Derek? Francisco wants him dead."

"I thought they were on good terms. Heathcliff was supposed to be an honorary member of the KXDs or some shit like that."

"Steele's acting alone. Things got dicey, and I made some promises I couldn't keep. Before I could talk my way out of them, Derek provided the perfect excuse, except he's still undercover even though Nicholson's out of the picture."

"The PD has more irons in the fire than they've been willing to share. Heathcliff has his own agenda given to him by narcotics or the gangs unit. Regardless, he's been at this longer than you have. He'll be fine." After putting the cereal bowl in the sink, Mark secured the holster to his belt, double-checked that his credentials were beside it, and grabbed a fresh suit jacket which looked only slightly better than the one I had used as a pillow. "Let's go. We're already running late."

"It's 6:15."

"Yeah, that gives me forty-five minutes to drop you off at your apartment and get to the office. And don't think that means you get special treatment just because you were tackled by ESU and gassed yesterday. You're expected at seven a.m. sharp, just like everyone else, Agent Parker."

"Actually, we might be a few minutes late. My credentials and car are still at Martin's."

Mark glared but resisted the urge to reprimand me for the break in protocol. My government-issued firearm and badge were supposed to be on my person at all times, but undercover required some finagling and exceptions to be made. Although, leaving these items inside a lockbox at

Martin's was beyond the scope of acceptable. But since Mark discovered these facts while off duty, he could pretend to have plausible deniability. Or at least that's what I told myself while he conducted some rudimentary countersurveillance before flipping on the lights and sirens and heading to Martin's compound.

*   *   *

Slipping into the back of the conference room, I hoped my tardiness wouldn't be noticed, but as the door swung closed, all eyes turned to me. I gave a curt nod and took an unobtrusive seat at the far left corner of the table. Agent Cooper stood in front of the large monitor mounted to the wall, showing the images taken by ESU during last night's raid.

Five of the six KXD members that had accompanied Bard and Steele were now in police custody. And eight of the Lords were also arrested. Two of them had been discovered hogtied behind a dumpster. Another four of them had sustained injuries ranging from abrasions and contusions to gunshot wounds. Despite the amount of ammunition that had been expelled by the rival gangs, no one was dead or in critical condition.

The police department was investigating the turf war and the impetus that had been building. Heathcliff said this had been in the works for quite some time, but the only other agency the OIO was sharing information with was the DEA. Despite cries for transparency, interagency cooperation didn't exist by any stretch of the imagination.

Thankfully, misinformation was sometimes better than the truth. The single female who had been arrested was thought to be wanted for questioning in connection with a dozen or so previous crimes and was currently being detained by the FBI, or that was the cover being planted to explain Alexia Nicholson's disappearance. Neither the KXDs nor the Lords should believe any differently, particularly since the majority of the police department didn't know any better. Sure, Detective O'Connell was aware of the situation. But he wouldn't compromise our operation, and neither would Heathcliff.

From chatter that filtered into the OIO through outside contacts, it was apparent the PD's gangs unit was conducting random checks of known gang establishments. Instead of letting the gangbangers duke out their differences on the streets, the police commissioner must have thought there would be less bloodshed if he united the different factions against a single enemy – the police department. Thankfully, no shots were fired, but it had only been twelve hours since last night's raid. ESU's interference probably wasn't widely known yet, but once it was, it would be open season on our boys in blue.

"We'll use their random checks to our advantage," Cooper announced, drawing me from my reverie. "They know the police busted a stockpile of drugs last night. So we're hoping the KXDs will either move additional men to safeguard their stash or attempt to relocate their supplies. We already have units on the various locations Agent Parker discovered."

"Why haven't we moved in yet?" I asked.

Lucca glanced up from an open laptop. "The DEA wanted us to wait until after they storm the cartel's compound. From the updates I've been receiving, agents are positioned outside the cartel's base of operations. The exits are surrounded, and the Federales have been alerted. They're set to move right before daybreak." Lucca looked up at the clock, calculating the time zone difference. "T minus twenty and counting."

"And we're certain this is the international source of the KXDs' contraband?" I didn't want to sound skeptical. But my role had been to gather intel on the source, and I never did. Within the last two days, I started to make enough progress to get close enough to Steele and Bard, but I still didn't know much. So it made no sense how the OIO had obtained this information.

"The tip we received about the train system, Steele's disappearance, and the bags of drugs you've delivered have been instrumental in piecing this together," Jablonsky said. "Not to mention the cartel's intervention the night the Lords made a move against you."

"The cartel harvests its drugs from a specific region. Certain environmental elements are present at the molecular level, and others are more easily recognizable, like the tags on the packaging. Once we determined the method of transport, we followed the trains back to locations near the border. The DEA had already been investigating, and once we agreed to work together, they tracked the mules crossing the border, expelling the drugs, and shipping them via passenger rail," Cooper offered. "Our job's no longer identifying and stopping the international source. It's to stop the local trade. Bard has created an extensive web with dozens of dealers."

"The problem isn't just the drugs," Jablonsky chimed in. "It's the military-grade armaments. Those were also sent from Bard's cartel connections. But the more disconcerting fact is that a few months back, the PD's evidence locker was broken into. They kept this information in-house, but one of our friends mentioned a stockpile of Russian assault rifles, automatic machine pistols, and a dozen or so grenade launchers went missing. Agent Lawson and the rest of our tech team analyzed their footage." Cooper dialed up the grainy, security cam feed while Mark continued to speak. "Do any of these men look familiar to you?"

While their faces were obscured, I'd recognize Francisco's build and walk anywhere. "Steele."

"That's what we thought. Lawson ran a comparison, but it wasn't conclusive enough for a judge. So that's another reason we're being careful. We're set to move, but we don't know what we might be moving into. From Cooper's previous estimates on contraband imports, they might have had dozens of weapons at their disposal before they plundered the evidence warehouse. Now," Mark sucked in a breath and shook his head, "they could have hundreds. You've mentioned the labyrinthine way Bard set up his personal residence. Do you think he also uses booby traps?"

"I wouldn't doubt it. Bard is a security nut with a ton of high-end shit." Thinking back, I considered the weaponry I'd seen at his place and throughout the various KXD bases. "Here's everything I know." And I proceeded to divulge information on every location and interaction, drawing and diagramming on top of the blueprints that had been pulled for each of the four locations the tactical teams planned to raid.

THIRTY-SIX

"Are you sure you want to be a part of this?" Jablonsky whispered in my ear. We were in TacOps, getting outfitted with body armor, assault weapons, and raid gear. "You don't have to join us on this venture. You can hang back."

"Do you remember what happened the last time I hung back?" I reached for a black ski mask. "Don't worry, I won't compromise myself. I'm just another government drone sent to carry out a specific task. Plus, I'm the only one who's been inside. You need me on-site."

"Parker," Cooper called, and Mark jerked his head in that direction and clapped me on the back.

"Sir?" I asked, leaning over Cooper's shoulder to look at the diagram of the KXDs' lab.

"The most confusing location seems to be the basement apartment Bard inhabits. But since you've visited on multiple occasions, that's the location you will lead a team to breach. The lab seems pretty straightforward. The processing center behind the diner might be tricky, but from your report, it won't matter who goes in. We're basically blind, regardless." He flipped to the final location. "And the coffee shop will be a straight up bust. Once we make the arrests, we'll search for hidden rooms or underground areas, but I don't expect to find anything. If Steele hadn't taken you there, we probably wouldn't have realized it was a property held by the so-called corporation Bard created."

"How many assets does DeAngelo Bard possess?" I asked, speaking more to myself than the other agents, but Lucca answered anyway.

"You'd be surprised. A few of the accountants are reviewing it, but he's invested in real estate capital. Basically, his business exists only on paper. But it's allowed him to buy various types of locations and the buildings that house different businesses, like the diner and laundromat. His business," Lucca made air quotes around the word, "partially owns six other properties: the apartment building where he resides, the building where your cover lived, the diner, laundromat, a warehouse near the train depot, and the Black Cat."

"So you already knew the strip joint was KXD territory when you sent me in, but you didn't share?" I felt like I'd been jerked around.

"His business's name isn't anything recognizable. We only discovered it after checking into property records and commonalities based upon the locations you visited with Steele." Lucca read the question in my eyes. "During the previous seven months, a few CIs tipped us that the KXDs were dealing out of the Black Cat. It's why you were sent to infiltrate that particular club and how we knew to squeeze the manager into stepping down before you could be hired. We couldn't trust anyone inside that establishment, so we had to get creative."

"You didn't think I'd get hired on my good looks and natural rhythm?"

"Parker," Cooper interjected, probably forgetting my sarcastic streak, "there is no reason to discuss these matters now. Nothing indicates your cover was ever compromised. So may we get back to the matter at hand?"

"Yes, sir. Sorry."

"You are up-to-date on tactical maneuvers, right?" Cooper asked, assessing the teams assembled. After I nodded, he continued. "You won't be the first one through the door, but you'll be somewhere near the front. You'll instruct and divert the team as the rooms and hallways branch out. Okay?" I nodded again, and he stepped closer, lowering his voice so only I could hear. "You'll be fine."

"We'll perform a final radio check before reaching the locations. At precisely sixteen hundred hours, we'll commence the breach. Assume anyone you encounter to be hostile, but do your best to perform non-lethal takedowns if at all possible." Jablonsky fastened the OIO emblazoned vest over his dress shirt. "A lot is riding on this, so we're doing everything by the book. Are there any questions?"

No one said a word, so we disbanded to the different vehicles to make the trek to the scouted locations. Before the van even stopped, I pulled the mask over my face, making sure my vision wasn't impeded by the thick fabric. At least if I was gassed again, it would provide some protection; although, I really didn't want to have to relive that experience. My eyes were still sore and red.

"Hey, guys," I said as the pre-op euphoria kicked in, "before we breach, you need to know there's a potential friendly inside. Detective Derek Heathcliff is undercover as Eric 'Hotshot' Hall. His photo was passed around during prep. Let's try not to burn his cover or take him out with friendly fire. Okay?"

"Sure, Parker," one of the guys replied, "but all bets are off if he fires first." I gave him a glare, rocking back and forth as I rode out the adrenaline surge and false bravado that came with the ratcheting of half a dozen different slides. "We move in three."

I glanced out the tiny window on the back door. The two KXD lookouts weren't at their normal perch. Bard must have known someone was coming for him. He probably assumed it'd be the police. Not that it really made a difference. He was facing federal and state charges, and it'd be decades before he saw the light of day again. So it wouldn't matter who brought him into custody.

"Stay on my six," the tactical commander ordered, opening the back door and moving purposefully toward the staircase that led to Bard's basement apartment. Another man jumped out of the van, and I followed with three more bringing up the rear. The two in the back made sure no one snuck up behind us as we broke through the door and entered Bard's domain.

Immediately, an alarm blared. Obviously, the key code reader served a purpose besides decoration. As usual, the foyer was dark, and we moved down the narrow hallway. The close quarters forced us to bunch together, making the entire team easy pickings for a single grenade. Thankfully, the KXDs weren't that smart. Flashlight beams bounced off the walls and surfaces as we continued to move deeper inside.

"Two hallways lead out of this room," I said into the mouthpiece attached to the clip in my ear. And the commander signaled for the team to break up. Two men went to the right. I had never gone in that direction, but based on the blueprints, the OIO assumed it led to a kitchen and dining room. "Doorways on both sides," I said as we entered the left hallway.

Before we could begin clearing each room, light erupted at the end of the corridor. The man held a fully automatic handgun with an extended magazine and opened fire. We scattered, bursting through the doors on both sides of the hall.

Scanning the interior of the room while gunfire echoed in the hallway, I recognized it as the room where Derek stitched up the wounded KXD member. No one was inside, and I caught the eye of the other agent across the doorframe. He peered out the door, ducking inside when bullets ripped through the nearby wall. As soon as there was a pause in the gunfire, he leaned out the door, took aim, and fired three shots. Another three-shot burst sounded from the other side of the hallway, and then footsteps resumed on the previously intended course. So much for non-lethal force.

The two rooms we'd just used for cover were clear, and we repeated the process with another two rooms. From my recollection, we were nearing Bard's private quarters. It was almost like an apartment within an apartment within a maze. The blueprints were practically useless. Bard had customized the space for his own protection and security.

If he wasn't a bad guy and a paranoid lunatic, he'd be my kind of interior designer.

"Look alive," the commander's voice echoed in my ear as two of the men held a position in the hallway and another worked to decrypt the scanner to Bard's quarters.

A shotgun blast ripped through the door, narrowly missing the first agent who entered. Sliding to a cover position behind the sofa, I focused my aim on the kitchenette, positive I'd seen movement behind the island countertop. Scattershot pummeled into the couch, piercing the cushioning. Ducking, I rolled toward the kitchen while the other agent already inside moved deeper into the room. I lost sight of the two agents in the hallway as I crouched along the side of the island, partially in the line of fire of the shotgunner. Luckily, he was distracted, and I pressed my cheek against the wood, inhaling and holding my breath as I turned to aim.

The gang member hiding within the kitchenette didn't notice and stood up straight, preparing to take a shot at the tactical team member who had just neutralized the other gunman.

"Drop it," I ordered, my finger partially pressing the trigger. He spun, intent on shooting me, and I fired. The body armor he wore took the brunt of the impact, but the shot still knocked him off his feet. I stood over him, kicking his gun out of reach and aiming at his face. "Turn around."

He made a move for a handgun at his hip, and I kicked him hard enough to flip him over. Immediately, I knelt down, pressing the muzzle of my gun to the back of his neck and confiscating his side arm. Then I cuffed him. He tried to buck backward, and I hit him with the butt of my gun to gain compliance. More shots echoed through the room, and I dove back behind the counter, leaving the cuffed gangbanger dazed on the floor.

"Clear." The word reverberated through my earpiece, and slowly, I stood. Three gangbangers were cuffed on the floor. Another one was clutching his bloody arm. And one of our agents was down. "Ambulances en route. No sign of Bard," the commander's voice rang in my ear, but after the gunfire, the words sounded muted.

Two team members rounded up the KXDs, keeping them in a contained space until additional support and medical teams could arrive. The rest of our team appeared in the door, having cleared the other areas of the basement apartment and dragging two other gang members with them. The commander was on the ground next to the downed agent. I didn't know his name, but he was one of the tactical team. His shoulder, neck, and cheek were riddled with pellets, but the damage seemed minimal considering the vast majority of the shotgun round had impacted against the Kevlar.

I swallowed a lungful of air as the commander sat him up against a wall, ripping the Velcro away and examining the injury before applying pressure. That was close. Too damn close. I turned away, spinning on the group of KXD members who likely wore higher grade body armor than we did. "Where's Bard?"

One of them looked up and chuckled. "Wouldn't you like to know?"

"Damn straight." I grabbed the smartass by the collar and dragged him to his feet.

One of the other agents moved to intervene, but the commander called him off, "Stand down and let her work." We made eye contact briefly, agreeing to a silent pact that I wouldn't break the rules or this guy's face.

"We're going for a walk." I shoved him into the hallway. "Someone ought to install recess lighting. The place is pitch, and we both know plenty of bad things happen in the dark."

He snickered, amused. "You can't touch me. You're not allowed."

"We'll see." I led him back into the front room, the same place Bard had used to interrogate me. Divide and conquer. "Sit down." I grabbed his handcuffed wrists and pulled him backward, forcing him into a high-backed chair with his arms around the backrest. "Where's Shakespeare?"

He lifted his shoulders in as close to a shrug as he could manage from his current position. "Dunno."

"Did he run away like a little bitch and leave you and

your group of friends to take the heat?"

He glared but didn't respond.

"Bard has eyes everywhere, so here's what's about to happen. I'm gonna personally walk you out of here and make a huge show of giving you special treatment. And someone is bound to see it, especially in this neighborhood. And Bard will kill you because of it."

"You can't do that."

"Sure, we can," one of the agents said, stepping into the room. "We wouldn't want to risk violating any of your rights, so we'll make sure to take mighty fine care of you. Your friends in the other room are going to get suspicious the longer we keep you here. And we'll make it look real good. Trust us, we do this for a living."

The gang member started to fidget, cursing under his breath. He shifted his gaze, putting on an indifferent façade. "Whatever. No one will ever believe I was a snitch. I'm no snitch."

"Fine, take your chances." I watched the way his eyes followed me around the room, like there was something I wasn't supposed to find. "Then again, I'm guessing with the security measures Shakespeare utilizes, there's probably a hidden cache of drugs or stockpiled weapons on the premises. He might even have an escape route."

The gang member snorted, a grin erupting on his face. "You're about to find out."

Suddenly, a barrage of gunfire sprayed the room, and the other agent dove on me, knocking us flat on the ground, as bullets ripped through the air where I'd been standing seconds earlier. A wet, sucking scream filled the room, and the already dim lighting went completely out. A door creaked, and a group of men rushed out of a hidden alcove. Instantly, I was up and moving after them, my gun in front of me.

Bard, Steele, and two others were on the move. They cleared the front door before I made it past the foyer. Radioing for assistance, I knew backup was on the way, and if they were close enough, they might be in a position to stop the escaping men.

Focusing on Bard, I saw him slide behind the wheel of a

parked car while the other three continued on foot. It was diversion tactics 101, but I wouldn't settle with taking down his second-in-command. The men on foot split again, and I aimed and fired at the car, taking out the back window and two tires. Bard was barely out of the parking space when the rims squealed against the asphalt and flashing lights blocked his intended path.

Left with no choice, he launched himself out the passenger's side door and took off down an alley. I pursued on foot, hearing the radio buzz in my ear that we were in pursuit of a suspect. One of the agents trailed behind, but I had a greater head start and was on Bard within thirty feet. I grabbed the hood of his jacket. The tug caused him to slide on the accumulated slush. His momentum propelled him forward as his feet tangled up, and we tumbled together in a heap. He reached for his gun, and I wrestled his arm upward before he could fire. He knocked his forearm and elbow into the side of my face, but I refused to loosen my grip as we twisted on the ground.

Finally, I gained enough leverage to stand, performing a perfect arm bar to incapacitate him while the other agent cuffed him and hauled him back to the government vehicles. I remained silent, fearing Bard would recognize my voice. Hopefully, the tactical gear and ski mask disguised my true identity from the leader of the KXDs.

THIRTY-SEVEN

"We've had a very productive day," Jablonsky said as I swiveled in my chair, working out the nervous energy and nausea that always followed the adrenaline rush. "A couple of our agents had to get a few stitches, but there were no serious injuries reported on our end. We've confiscated sixty kilos worth of narcotics and discovered a cache of illegal firearms. It's been one hell of a payday, folks."

"I didn't realize you were planning to open your own drug running business." The words left my mouth without my brain considering their inappropriateness.

Mark frowned but refrained from dressing me down in front of the dozen agents in the room. "Between our coordinated efforts this afternoon with local law enforcement, twenty-seven arrests have been made. And DeAngelo Bard has been apprehended. Evidence cataloging is underway. The legal paperwork is in the works, and interrogations have already begun." He nodded at the group assembled. "It'll probably be a long night so go get comfortable."

Agent Cooper divided up the men, placing Agent Lucca in charge of the evidence collection. Everyone else was tasked with reviewing the results of the DEA's raid on the

Mexican cartel, questioning the arrested gang members, or coordinating with the police department. When almost everyone had their assignments, Cooper turned to me.

"Sir?" I asked, swiveling endlessly in the chair.

"I wanted to congratulate you on smoking out Bard."

Nodding, I tried to ignore my memory flashing to the raid. The KXD member I dragged into the front room and forced into the chair had been killed by Bard's firepower. Eight bullets struck his upper body. The man didn't have a chance, and if it hadn't been for the agent who threw me to the ground, I might not have had one either. It was a mess, but no one was talking about that. We were too busy celebrating the victory. Taking an unsteady breath, I stopped swiveling and faced Mark as Cooper quietly exited.

"Detective Heathcliff is in our interrogation room. He was with Bard and Steele when they decided to hole up in that hidden room. He claims he was unaware the KXDs were going to open fire, and he pursued them when they fled in order to keep tabs on Steele and the other KXD member."

"Derek was there?"

"He wanted Steele, but Bard's lieutenant escaped. Heathcliff arrested the other gang member and burned his cover in the process."

"So why is he in our interrogation room?"

"Because we have questions. The KXD member he arrested is in isolation. No phone. No interaction. We aren't giving him a chance to say boo to any of his buddies. We're trying to minimize the damage."

"And Steele?" I asked, dreading the answer.

"He's in the wind. The police have an all points on him, and we've issued a BOLO. But he's the only one left. The majority of the gang is in lockup either here or at the precinct."

"So you're holding Derek for an internal review? This is unbelievable."

"He's been close to them. He was there when they opened fire on federal agents and killed one of their own, and he helped them elude law enforcement by patching up that wounded gangbanger. You reported that yourself, if you don't remember, Agent Parker." The last two words were really turning the screws, and I fought to keep from saying as much. "It's not my doing. IA has to check into these things, and this way, his cover remains somewhat intact with the other KXDs we brought in. At least if narcotics or gangs need to send in a UC, he isn't completely compromised."

"Can I talk to him?"

"No."

"Then why did you tell me any of this?"

"Because this building and the situation are too hot right now. A few gangbangers are dead, and Bard still has power, even behind bars. As soon as he gets some footing, he'll be on the warpath to bring down the people responsible for taking him out. And I don't need him to make a connection between Alexia Nicholson and you."

"Guess what, that's part of this job."

"Yeah, so is protecting our assets and our people. The director agreed, so you're going home for the night." He fingered the discarded ski mask. "By tomorrow, this building will be cleared out, and you won't be risking anything by working on the information. But in the meantime," he pushed the mask toward me, "put that on and get out of here."

"You're being overprotective and ridiculous."

"Follow orders, or I will have you reprimanded," he replied harshly. "And since you're on probation, that won't go over very well."

"Bastard." I snatched the mask off the table and headed for the door. Pulling it over my face and tucking a few wayward strands that came loose from my bun inside, I spun on my heel. "If it weren't for me, Bard would still be on the loose."

"We appreciate your service, Agent Parker," Mark said. "Now stop being a pain in my ass and take the night off."

Marching out of the building and feeling like an idiot for having to disguise myself, I went to my car, turned the key in the ignition, and drove away, executing numerous turns before shedding the mask, pulling my hair loose, and driving home. After parking the car, I sat behind the wheel, staring at my apartment building. My apartment, not Nicholson's. And I realized the reason I argued with Mark about leaving wasn't because of some duty driven idealism. I didn't want to go home because I didn't know how to resume living my life.

I hit pause on Alex Parker nearly two months ago, and now I was supposed to go up those six flights of stairs and through the front door like nothing happened, like everything was still the same. But it wasn't. I wasn't. At least not yet.

After spending an indeterminate amount of time in my car, I collected myself and my belongings and ventured inside. My apartment was cold, dusty, and eerily quiet. I flipped on the lights, turned up the thermostat, and performed a check for signs of an intruder. Once I knew everything was secure, I unholstered my nine millimeter, glanced at the empty fridge, and hit play on the answering machine.

As the twenty-nine messages played, I stripped out of my clothes and headed for the shower. Telemarketers, a few forwarded calls from my P.I. office, and a dozen voicemails from Martin played while I strained to hear the majority of the messages over the running water. By the time I stepped out, the machine had given up its repetition. A cursory glance showed the latest call was made from the Martin Technologies building earlier today.

Frankly, it was a tossup between ordering delivery or dialing Martin. And honestly, neither of those options held very much appeal. Instead of calling for dinner, I chose the latter. And on the third ring, Martin answered.

"Funny thing happened today," he began.

"What's that?" I walked around my apartment, wiping dust off the furniture and examining the personal effects and other items to get a feel for the person who lived here. It sounded insane, but I needed to remember how to be me.

"My security system caught an intruder this morning on camera."

"Did you notify the authorities?"

"About a gorgeous brunette who waltzed into my home?

Nah." I could hear the smile in his voice. "They'd just assume I was insane. It's not like she took anything of value. Well, perhaps my heart and maybe my wallet."

"Did you check your pants pocket?"

"I was hoping you could come over and look inside my pants. You are a professional investigator, after all." He paused, hoping I'd fill the silence. Instead, I sat on the couch, placing my hands on the coffee table and closing my eyes to ground myself in the feel of being home. "Was there any particular reason you stopped by when you knew I'd be at work?"

"I needed my stuff."

"Alex, what is going on with you?"

"I wish I knew." I gave the main room another glance before getting up and going into the bedroom.

"The caller ID says you're home. Can I assume you've finished work?"

"Sort of. We'll talk about it soon. But not tonight."

"How about I come by?"

"No. I need to do some things first. But maybe one day this week."

He hesitated, the kitchen chair scraping in the background. "I miss you."

"Just give me two more days."

"I'll be counting the hours."

Climbing into bed, I left the lights on in my apartment, checked that my nine millimeter was on the nightstand, and opened the bottom drawer, placing my credentials and an extra magazine inside. Then I curled up on the corner of the mattress, realizing it would take more than forty-eight hours to shake the defensive measures I'd constructed as Alexia Nicholson. This was ridiculous, and I knew there was no reason for the way I was acting or treating Martin. I just didn't know how to stop. Even my outbursts at work were far from normal behavior. Tonight, I'd sleep in a comfortable bed inside my safe apartment, and tomorrow, I would force my normal behavior and attitude to take hold. And if all else failed, I'd just have to fake it.

*   *   *

"Wow, you've actually stopped being quite so cantankerous. Amazing." Jablonsky eyed me over the report I'd just handed him. "Did you hit your head or something?"

"Yeah, and I contracted amnesia." I took a seat in front of his desk, enjoying our moment of privacy. "I still can't figure out who I am."

"Undercover can be a bitch."

"Tell me about it. Where are we on the KXD bust?"

"The DEA shut down a big branch of the cartel. It's obviously not the only one, and they'll regroup and rebuild. But for now, a major drug supply source is wiped out. The gangs are scrambling to solidify their hold since DeAngelo Bard's been dethroned. With the number of casualties and arrests the KXDs sustained, they won't be controlling anything outside of prison walls for a long, long time. The police are rounding up assets and stragglers, and it seems the biggest dilemma is determining who's in possession of the civil forfeiture."

"Won't the OIO and FBI keep what was discovered during the coordinated raids?"

"Yeah, but the police had a dozen or so undercovers planted throughout the KXDs' network. They're squawking we invaded their territory and took credit for their busts."

"Don't blame me. I didn't ask for Heathcliff's help. You did."

"It wasn't just him. The bartender at the Black Cat was undercover, one of Bard's lookouts, the barista at the coffee shop, the waitress at the diner, and the guy running a nearby Stop N' Shop were all police officers tasked with monitoring gang activity and drug sales."

"How long have they been at it?"

"Four months. The FBI was keeping tabs first, and since that's our mother agency, we were here first. So the police department should've notified us. Not the other way around, regardless of what the commissioner or Lt. Moretti may think." Jablonsky sneered at his desk phone, and I suspected he'd already spoken to those men earlier today.

"I just have one last question before I get started on

these." I gestured to the giant stack of paperwork on his desk. "I was reinstated to identify the international source of the drugs and guns, but the DEA had that covered. And the PD was already dealing with the gangs. So what was the point of this?"

"Parker," he sighed, "you're back. It's done. Now get to work and stop overthinking things."

"You mean like how you really didn't need me for this."

"We did. You brought down Bard, remember? Just be thankful it wasn't as extensive as it could have been."

"Right, because instead of losing close to two months I might have lost two years." Pressing my lips together, I squeezed my eyes shut. "I'm not the person I was two and a half years ago. That gung-ho, do anything for the job, dedicated woman you knew doesn't exist anymore. She's seen and experienced way too much for that."

"Alex, I don't expect you to volunteer to become a long-term operative. This was just a way back in, and you knew that when you agreed."

"Yeah," I took a breath and collected the files off his desk, "I just didn't realize it would destroy my life." From his look, it was obvious that statement was a tad dramatic. "Has the paperwork cleared yet so I can talk to Martin about where I've been?"

"It should be back by Monday. His international holdings and affiliates have caused quite the delay."

"This is ridiculous. I finished the job before the background check even cleared. It shouldn't matter anymore."

"Hey," Mark sensed my frustration, "I don't care what time it is when we leave this building. We're grabbing a drink, so you can talk out whatever animosity it is that you've been harboring. And if you don't want to talk to me, then I'll put the company shrink on notice."

"You wouldn't dare."

"Drinks on me."

THIRTY-EIGHT

Mark and I spent a couple of evenings together that week, hashing out my anger issues with lemon drop martinis and Irish car bombs. It turns out I didn't quite care for the clientele at the strip club, constantly being on alert and in fear of being discovered, and there were some residual issues regarding the close call and subsequent shootout with the Lords. When the only people you can rely on are criminals, it makes trusting difficult and self-reliance a matter of life or death. Add that combination to my already loner-like existence and I was asking for trouble. Thankfully, Martin was too wrapped up in business, and the forty-eight hour moratorium was pushed back another seventy-two hours, giving me a few more days to get comfortable in my own skin.

In the meantime, my days were spent in the office. Working behind a desk and sorting through evidence and statements were welcome and familiar tasks. My resentment over this assignment was fading by the hour. Sure, I spent two months being objectified and used by pretty much everyone, the OIO included, but at least this was the tangible proof it hadn't been a complete waste. Or so I kept telling myself.

"I'll run by the hospital and get an official statement from Joe," I offered, leaning inside Mark's open office door. "He has some armed guards outside his room, but from what the hospital staff said, he's awake and alert and expected to make a full recovery."

"Just don't give the guy a heart attack," Jablonsky warned. "He might still think you're a stripper." He grinned, and I laughed. "It's good to see the old Alex is still in there."

"Yeah, well, we closed the bar last night. I'm probably too hungover to pretend to be anyone else."

"In that case, take Cooper or Lucca with you."

Something was still bothering me about the Black Cat. Maybe it was the girls selling ecstasy underneath an undercover narcotics officer's nose or Veronica's attack and disappearance from the club. Mark had explained the Lords were behind it, but she had been the KXD member Steele was supposed to handle. There was something more there, and that would be the first thing I'd ask Joe.

"Penny for your thoughts," Lucca said on the way to the hospital.

"Any clue where Francisco Steele might have gone, Mr. Analyst?"

"Being an analyst doesn't make me clairvoyant." I gave him a look from the corner of my eye, and he let out a dramatic exhale. "I can tell you Steele was orphaned in his early teens, but he has an aunt a few states away. Maybe he left town. We haven't had any sightings or heard any chatter. The KXDs were his family, but since they're incarcerated, maybe Steele took off. It really doesn't matter since Bard was in charge, and the KXDs are basically dismantled, unless you count gen. pop. as their new haunting grounds."

Upon entering the hospital, we flashed our credentials and were given directions to Joe's room. Outside, a few uniformed officers were keeping a close watch on visitors. We flashed our badges again, and after some scrutiny and not so friendly quips, Lucca and I gained access to Joe's room. The man I knew as a gay bartender looked up from the photos Detective Heathcliff was showing him and offered a smile.

"Wait outside, Lucca," I said, not giving the analyst any time to protest. He mumbled something under his breath about not having to follow my orders but stepped back into the hallway and shut the door. "Detective."

"Parker," Heathcliff said, standing, "allow me to introduce Officer Joe Aronne, narcotics division." He turned to Joe. "This is Alex Parker, federal agent or private investigator." He cocked his head to the side. "It's hard to keep track."

"Officer Aronne," I said, sticking with the formality for now. This wasn't the best time for Heathcliff to be busting chops, but I would deal with him later. "Do you mind if I ask you a few questions?"

Joe jerked his head toward the empty chair at the end of the bed. "It's good to know you aren't a coked-out whore. Because you had me convinced until this numbskull showed up and vouched for you."

"Well, I knew you were hiding something, but I thought you were in the closet," I replied, and he chuckled. "Obviously, you've done this enough to know how to cover one lie with another." I bowed my head and gestured as if to say, 'my hat's off to you, sir.' "Now, can we get down to business? I'm sure you don't want to spend the day answering questions you've already been asked."

Joe went into a vast amount of detail concerning the PD's interest at the club. It wasn't anything I hadn't heard or read before, but I let him continue with his rendition, just in case there was a new angle or something we'd missed while going over the various interviews and police files. Heathcliff would interject occasionally, but for the most part, he sat in the chair next to Joe's bed, silently observing. We hadn't spoken since the night Francisco stepped in, and I owed Heathcliff my gratitude for that dumbass move he pulled.

"Joe," I began when he was finished, feeling embarrassed for acting so familiar with this man who I didn't really know, "sorry, Officer Aronne, I know this is difficult, but can you go into further detail concerning your involvement with the KXDs?"

Heathcliff glared, but Joe waved him off. "Joe's fine, Alex, but I'm not sure what to tell you." He pulled his hand free from the blanket, and I saw three of his fingers had been cut off. "They determined I was a snitch and wanted to know who I was working for and who else was informing on them."

"I am so sorry. We should have done more. Acted sooner." The apology poured out, but Heathcliff's stern gaze caused my words to become clipped. "Sorry."

Joe had grown ashen, but he shrugged it off. Recollecting traumatic events was always difficult. I knew this better than most and shouldn't have gone down that road. "Was there anything else you needed for your investigation, Agent?"

"What can you tell me about Veronica?"

"That was no mugging. She was playing both sides and got caught."

"Both sides?"

"She was selling drugs for the KXDs and the Lords. From the way the KXDs started using you, I assumed Steele must have realized his girl had double-crossed him. Then she calls up, saying she's in the hospital and won't be back, so it wasn't too hard to put two and two together."

"How do you know she was dealing for the Lords?"

"Word travels, but I was always the last one to leave at night. It was necessary in order to check the locker room. One night, I found a label and an empty baggie inside her locker. It was a designer version of cocaine only the Lords sell." He shifted his gaze to Heathcliff. "It should be in evidence at the precinct since I turned it in the morning I found it." He scrunched his face in thought. "Maybe a week and a half before her attack, so that would be..."

He began calculating dates while my mind wandered to Jablonsky's interview with Veronica. My brain pinged on a few inconsistencies and only when Derek waved his hand in front of my face did I blink and realize I was zoning out.

"Let's let Joe rest. His girlfriend and kids are on the way, and we've monopolized enough of his time," Heathcliff insisted, ushering me out of the chair. "You take care of yourself, man. If there's anything I can do for you, just holler."

"Hey, Joe, thank you for watching my back at the club. I hope you feel better," I added, offering a warm smile over my shoulder.

Back outside, Lucca waited in a chair in the hallway next to the protection detail. Upon seeing me, he stood like a puppy waiting for his next command. Pretending I didn't notice we walked past him. Heathcliff led me down the hallway and out of earshot.

"We need to talk," he said but spotted Lucca bounding toward us, "off the record."

"That can be arranged. Are you on duty?"

"I'm riding a desk while IA concludes their review, but I'm off duty now."

"All right, just give me a few minutes to lose the boy scout."

I convinced Lucca to wait in the car while Heathcliff and I grabbed a cup of coffee from a cart outside the hospital. Derek was clean-shaven and spit-shined as was his norm. It was too cold to sit on the snow covered benches, so we huddled near the building.

"What happened after Steele dropped by to collect me?" I asked.

"I stayed in your apartment. I thought you would come back, and when you didn't, I began snooping around Bard's place. He and Steele returned with two SUVs filled with drugs. And they wouldn't let me leave after that. Steele didn't trust me, and it was making Bard suspicious. But you have to believe I didn't know Bard was armed or that he was about to open fire when your team breached his home." The sincerity in Heathcliff's eyes, mixed with his remorse over Joe, was hard to stomach. "It's my fault that man was killed and you were almost taken out. It's also my fault Steele escaped."

"Derek, don't do that to yourself. You're a good man and a good cop. This case has my head so twisted around, but it's okay. I'm glad you're okay. I didn't know what Francisco would do to you, especially after you stuck your neck out to get me out of a jam. But it's done. Bard's going away for a long time, and his empire has crumbled."

"Then why are you asking Joe about one of the strippers?"

"Something doesn't feel right. I can't put my finger on it, but something is off."

"I'll tell you what, I'll pull the records and do some digging into her history and known criminal ties, and you go have a talk with Jablonsky and find out what he knows." A car horn sounded, and we both spun to find Lucca gesturing wildly. "Looks like you're being summoned."

"Damn boy scout," I griped. "Unless something major surfaces, I'll drop by the precinct on Monday, okay?"

"Sounds good." Heathcliff hugged me, and for once, I didn't cringe quite so much at the physical contact. It was a side effect of working at the Black Cat, but I was getting past it. "And the next time you decide to do something as stupid as go undercover, give me the heads up."

"Right back 'atcha."

We parted ways, and Lucca attempted to make small talk the entire ride back to the office. I deflected on each count, and he finally gave up after threatening to inquire about the cause of my less than personable attitude to which I had replied that he do something anatomically impossible. At least the remark encouraged him to leave me alone while I wrote my finalized report.

"It's Friday night, Alex," Mark said, interrupting my filing. "Take off. The rest of that can be done on Monday. You've had a long week. Go home."

"Hey, I've been meaning to ask, where did you put the file on Veronica Kincaid?"

"She doesn't have a file. There're a couple pages of notes stuck inside the operation folder. We didn't arrest her because there wasn't much evidence against her, and we didn't want to risk tipping off the KXDs that we had a mole inside their organization."

"Well, I'd like to read through it again. The facts just don't jibe."

"It's probably because the PD hasn't shared everything with us, but I'll pull it and leave it in your desk drawer for Monday."

"I could work the weekend," I offered.

"You can't avoid Marty forever. The man is incorrigible, and he loves you. You need to see him."

"I need to tell him the truth."

"You can tell him Monday. Until then, I'm sure he'll be happy to spend time with you. It's been a couple of weeks since you barged into his house covered in bruises and with a police escort."

"Oh, god, as if things weren't bad enough, he'll expect an explanation about that too."

"Go home, Alex. This is nothing compared to what you've been dealing with for the last six weeks."

THIRTY-NINE

Cooking, cleaning, or perhaps hiding, those seemed to be the only three options currently available. Martin was supposed to be dropping by after work and staying the weekend. Okay, so maybe the weekend part was pushing it, but I couldn't tell him no. He made up a large part of my non-work life, and I wanted to see him. I really did. Conversely, I also wanted to avoid the situation and hope it would go away. The fact that I wasn't exactly a fan of physical contact at the moment was a problem, and the bigger problem was my absence over the last several weeks. Even now, I still couldn't tell him the truth. Our relationship had turned into deceit and lies, and that was my decision. Sure, I did it because it would shield him from danger, but maybe I just wanted to protect myself from the cross-examination he would put me through when it came to resuming the one career I swore against.

"Knock, knock," Martin called from the hallway, and I jumped, realizing if I was going to hide, my escape routes were now limited.

Without saying a word, I went to the front door, took a deep breath, unlocked the two deadbolts, slid the security bar out of the way, and opened the door. He was holding two grocery bags and had a bottle of wine tucked underneath his arm. His bodyguard lingered in the hallway, and I smiled at him.

"Ms. Parker," Bruiser said, returning the smile, "nice to see you again."

"You're just dying for a rematch, right?"

"Anytime you're ready."

"Well, it won't be this weekend, Jones," Martin said, stepping inside my apartment. "I'll see you at the office Monday afternoon. Enjoy your time off."

"Thanks, have a good night." Bruiser waved and disappeared toward the stairwell.

"You need to hire more staff." I closed the door as Martin attempted a kiss. Stepping away from him, I cleared off the counter. "Poor Bruiser's overworked and clearly underpaid." Martin was a generous boss, even toward the employees he had no interest in dating, and he let out a good-natured laugh at the comment.

"Yes, I'll make a note to stop being such a tyrant." He put the bags and bottle down and enveloped me in his arms. "Hey, gorgeous," he whispered. When he broke the kiss, he cocked his head to the side. "Is something wrong?"

"No." My gaze diverted to the bags. "What's with the groceries?"

"I thought I'd make dinner. Correct me if I'm wrong, but I'm guessing your fridge is empty."

"I have ketchup."

"Great. We can play spin the bottle." He stepped backward. "Maybe you'll get lucky and can kiss the toaster instead." He took off his jacket, shed his tie, and rolled up the sleeves on his dress shirt. "Would you care to explain why you go rigid every time I touch you? I won't hurt you, Alex. Not intentionally. Are you still scraped up from the attack?" His forehead creased, and thankfully, he began to unpack the bags, dropping the accusatory stare. "How are you, sweetheart? The last time we were together, you weren't doing so well."

"I'm fine. The leg's on the mend, but the cuts and bruises have healed." I took a seat at the counter and watched him unpack bags of leafy green things. "Work has been causing some anxiety."

"What kind of work is it? Home security or something?"

"Or something."

He washed his hands in the sink, reached below the counter to grab a pan, and poured some olive oil in it to heat while he chopped. "Is that why you look like you haven't eaten in a month?" I didn't say anything, and the chopping grew angrier. "Would you tell me if something was wrong?"

"Nothing's wrong."

The chopping stopped, and he looked straight in my eyes. "I'm not an idiot. I've seen the needle marks. Your face is sunken in. And if I didn't know you better, I'd think you were an addict, especially with the way you've disappeared for weeks at a time, avoided me, and are uncomfortable answering simple questions. What aren't you telling me?"

I stifled my laugh. My act was much more impressive than I ever realized.

"Are you okay? Are you sick? Did something happen? Is that why you stiffen every time I get close?" he asked. I glared at him, so he abandoned the inquisition. "Because I know something else that stiffens every time we get close." He smirked, adding some lighthearted, juvenile flirtation to the accusations.

"None of those things. I've been working. That's it. And I can't give you any other details until Monday." I searched my mind for something that would make sense.

"Why Monday? Why can't you tell me now?"

I snickered. "Because if I tell you, I'd have to kill you."

"Oh, so you're an international spy, and this home security firm you work for is just part of your cover identity?" He had no idea how close to the truth he was. "I heard the CIA was recruiting." He went back to chopping, casting the occasional glance at me. "A woman of mystery. Jane Bond or something like that?"

"Sure." Sliding off the stool, I went around the counter. "Do you find that sexy, Mr. Martin?" My pathetic attempt at a British accent earned a chuckle.

"I find you sexy." But he didn't sound pleased by the

delay in learning the truth. "But I'll give you space. That's what you want." He flicked his gaze to me, making certain that despite our proximity, we didn't accidentally touch. "And I promise not to make a single move on you, so if you're suddenly jonesing for some affection, you'll have to initiate."

"Stripper rules," I retorted, realizing Alexia Nicholson was still stuck in my head. He gave me a questioning look as he sautéed the vegetables. "Random question, have you ever been to a strip club?"

"That has to be a trick. So I'm pleading the fifth."

"Have you ever closed a deal at one of those places?"

"Alex, I haven't been with any strippers or prostitutes. What's this about?"

"I meant legitimate business deals. Speaking of, how are things concerning the lawsuit?"

"To answer your first question, gentlemen's clubs aren't conducive to a work environment. I have no intention of getting investors or possible business partners intoxicated on cheap liquor and fake tits just to sink a deal. Do you think I'm a whore?"

I held my thumb and pointer finger close together. "A little bit."

"In that case, you can't afford my hourly rates," he said, and I slapped his arm. "Normally, that's a little extra, but I'll let it slide just this once."

"Maybe we should get back on topic before I have to break out the handcuffs."

"Handcuffs definitely cost extra, but they could add a fun dynamic to enforce your no touching dictum." He gave me a sexy smile. "Well, more fun than you completely zoning out while I talk about business and the problems MT's facing with Hover Designs."

"I have a confession," I admitted. He stopped what he was doing and turned serious. "I didn't exactly zone out on the phone. I fell asleep."

He snorted. "Wonderful. My work and life are so boring that hearing about them literally puts you to sleep." Something disconcerting flitted across his face, and he went back to cooking. "I've been doing my best to keep it together and not pester you, but obviously, I'm out in left field. You have to confide in me at some point, Alexis, because whatever's going on has everything to do with you and nothing to do with me." His words resonated in my gut, painful and true. "The only thing I'm not quite clear on is where it leaves us."

"Hey," I took the spatula from his hand and pushed him away from the stove and against the island, suddenly needing to be close to him, "where do you think it leaves us?"

He rubbed his face. "I don't know. I can't do this forever, so at some point, you'll have to stop this twisted carousel because it's making me crazy." My fingers went to work on the buttons of his shirt, tugging on the fabric and pulling him closer. "Although, I don't particularly mind this type of delay tactic, but I should warn you that it's unlikely we'll be interrupted like we were last time. So are you sure you're not starting something you can't finish?" His eyes twinkled deviously.

"I trust you'll make sure that doesn't happen."

*   *   *

I woke with a start. My heart was pounding, and it took a few moments to realize I was in bed. Martin was on the other side of the mattress; only his fingertips grazed the ends of my hair. He was doing exactly what he said; he wasn't initiating any physical contact. Considering the fact he was sleeping soundly, the reason for my sudden wakefulness must have been the result of a bad dream that I just couldn't remember. But I couldn't shake the unease, and I sat up in bed, pulling my knees to my chest and reaching across to the nightstand for my handgun, another of Nicholson's habits.

My room was dark. Normally, one of the living room lights would filter in, but it was possible that in our haste we didn't bother to flip a light on. It was a miracle we remembered to turn off the stove.

After a few minutes of waiting for the hairs on the back of my neck to relax, I knew there wasn't a chance in hell I'd be able to fall asleep. So I slipped into a pair of jeans and a t-shirt, tucked the gun at the small of my back, and went into the living room. Maybe I could get some work done. Most of the Bureau's reports were accessible from any internet connected computer, provided the user possessed the proper log-in information.

Going to the end table, I pushed the switch on the table lamp, but nothing happened. The bulb must have burnt out. I moved to my desk, repeating the process, but still, nothing happened. Power outage?

Glancing into the kitchen, the digital clock on the microwave glowed blue, and a chill shot through my body. My instincts kicked in, and I reached for the gun. But a man wrapped his arms around me.

"Chica."

Steele. I tried to pull away, so I could grab the gun, but he felt it against his stomach and held me tighter in order to keep it lodged between us. My mind screamed that I relax and play it off, so I leaned against him, no longer struggling.

"Francisco," I sighed, "how did you find me?"

A growl rattled through his chest. "What did I tell you about carrying?"

He walked us toward the couch and coffee table. In the pitch black, I had the home court advantage and banged him against the arm of the loveseat. The move didn't inflict any damage, but it surprised him. He steadied himself, and his grip loosened slightly. I barreled forward, reaching behind my back and yanking the gun free.

He pounced, knocking us to the floor. The force of his momentum slid us across the hardwood, lodging my shoulder beneath the couch. Steele didn't waste any time and grabbed the coffee table, slamming it against the inside of my arm, pinning my limb between the couch and table. The impact loosened my grip on the gun, and it skittered just inches out of reach.

Steele's grin was deadly as he held my other arm down and knelt on my legs to keep me still. With his free hand, he reached inside his pocket and pulled out a capped syringe. Holding it between his teeth, he tapped the inside of my elbow, looking for a vein.

"Francisco, what are you doing?" If I could just get one leg free, I could kick him, wrap my legs around him, or throw off his balance in order to get myself out of this predicament. "Please, don't."

My begging stunned him, and he leaned back on his haunches, pulling the capped syringe from his mouth. "So it's true then?"

"What's true? What are you talking about?" I could play dumb with the best of them, and I needed to cast doubt in his mind to throw him off his game.

"Don't lie to me, Alexia. Hotshot's done enough lying for the both of you. You're working with the police."

"I'm not lying. You know me. How many times have you seen me use?" He wasn't convinced, and given that he was inside my apartment, it made sense why he wouldn't believe me. "What are you doing here? How did you find me? Did you come to take me home?" I asked.

"Shut your fucking mouth." He slapped me, making my teeth rattle. "You can't manipulate me anymore."

He leaned down, his face inches from mine, and I jerked upward, head-butting him. The abruptness of my move sent him reeling backward, freeing my legs from beneath him. I wrapped them around his torso, hoping he'd rear back so I could get my pinned arm free and put him in a chokehold. Instead, he threw his body to the side, twisting us together. He was on his side with the bulk of his weight on top of my uninjured leg. He placed his instep against my calf and yanked himself off the ground, forcing my legs open in the process.

The scream erupted from my lungs, and tears from the sudden blast of pain blurred my vision. He clapped a hand over my mouth, not bothering to hold me down as I writhed ineffectually on the floor. Focus, Parker, the voice in my head yelled, but it took precious seconds before I could think of anything besides the searing pain and what must have been another tear to my tendon.

Although from this new position, I just needed to roll onto my side and kick him off of me. Roll and kick, then push the table away, grab the gun, and fire. It wasn't that difficult, except my body seemed unable to function.

He removed his hand from my mouth and fumbled for the syringe. "The Alexia I know would be begging for a taste."

"Not like this," I gasped, struggling to free my arm from his grasp.

He pulled the cover off the needle and held my wrist in a death grip. "C'mon, you know you want it," he insisted, trying to make out my veins in the darkness. "And in a couple of seconds, you'll be feeling really good. That bum leg of yours won't hurt anymore. I'm gonna help you, chica."

"Don't." My life, my career, and our investigation could all be over with one injection. Assuming the heroin inside the needle didn't kill me, it would kill my career and make every single piece of evidence and every statement and report I made questionable. Steele wasn't stupid. He knew this, and that's why he was doing this instead of shooting me in the head. "Francisco, please."

"That's funny, chica. You should be begging for it."

I felt the prick, but before Steele could press the plunger down, he careened sideways over the coffee table, knocking into the couch so hard the furniture flipped over. Not wasting any time, I shoved the coffee table a few inches, carefully removed the needle from my arm, grabbed the gun, and got to my knees. It took another few seconds before I could stand and a good four steps before the pain in my hip became tolerable.

The sounds of flesh hitting flesh echoed in the apartment, and I trained my gun on the two men. In the dark, there wasn't a clear shot, and I stumbled toward the kitchen, intent on adding some light to the situation. When the light came on, Martin's eyes shot upward, and Steele knocked Martin backward. Spotting the gun aimed at him, Steele ran for the fire escape, evading the two shots I fired. One bullet shattered the glass, unintentionally aiding in his escape.

I ran after him, making it down three flights before giving up. He was too far ahead, already on the street. I knew I wouldn't be able to catch him, and I clutched the railing in desperate need of air.

Martin came up behind me, announcing himself before I could turn the gun on him. He was on the phone with 911, and I hugged him, asking if he was okay while he waited for the operator to come on the line. The fact that he was in my apartment the entire time didn't register until he threw Steele off of me. My mind had been singularly focused, but now it splintered in a million different directions.

"Alex," he clutched my face, bending to press his forehead against mine, "I've never heard you scream like that. Are you okay? Who was that guy? What's going on?"

"Not now." I took the phone from his hand, limping up the rickety metal steps. Whatever damage Steele inflicted to my already injured hip wasn't enough to prevent my mobility, and my first priority was his apprehension. How did he find me?

"911, what's your emergency?" the operator asked.

"This is federal agent Alexis Parker, ID number," I rattled off my credentials, catching the shocked, betrayed look on Martin's face. "Scramble units to begin a search. The suspect, Francisco Steele, was last seen heading south on foot. Consider him armed and dangerous. He's wearing a charcoal grey hoodie and jeans, approximately six four, and two hundred pounds. A BOLO's already been issued on him. Send additional units to my place." Something about Steele's words brought my anxiety to an all-time high. "And I need a location for Detective Derek Heathcliff."

There was a long pause while she keyed in some details. I used those brief seconds to check the rest of my apartment for any other KXD presence, put on my shoes and jacket, grab my cuffs and credentials, and slip into my shoulder holster with my backup nine millimeter.

"Ma'am, I can't seem to get a location on Detective Heathcliff."

"Send units to his place now." I disconnected, dialing Det. O'Connell.

"Alex?" Martin looked lost, and I noticed blood on his knuckles.

"Wash your hands and then stay in the bedroom."

He nodded. I'd forgotten how great he was during crisis

situations.

"Nick," I said as soon as he answered, "do you have any idea where Heathcliff might be?"

"No. What's wrong?"

"Steele just stopped by to say hi. And since I'm blown, Derek probably is."

"I'll call for units to his place."

"I already did. Do you have his address?"

"I'm texting you now."

"Okay."

I disconnected and dialed Mark's home phone, anxious to move on Heathcliff's place. If anything happened to Derek, it was my fault. He stepped in to save me.

Pushing those thoughts away, I circled through the KXD arrests. Steele shouldn't have been able to connect the dots, so what was he doing at my place?

Martin came back into the room, and I assessed him while I waited for Jablonsky to answer. "Alex," he sat on the edge of the bed and pulled on the rest of his clothes, "what's going on?"

"Apparently, work came home with me. It's too much to talk about right now. And the last thing I want is for you to be a witness or get dragged into this, but I don't know how to avoid that. The police are on the way. They'll have questions, so just tell them whatever you know. Once they get here, I have to go." Hanging up, I tried Mark's cell. Martin's knuckles were torn up, and his brow and lip were split. But the fight with Steele didn't cause any permanent damage.

"What about you?" He focused on my stance, watching how I favored one leg, but I shook my head.

"I'm okay, Martin." I held up a finger to silence him when Mark answered. "Steele just dropped by. Units are searching for him. Talk to Martin," I said to a very confused Mark. Then I handed back the phone.

Sirens grew louder, and knocking sounded at the door. I opened it, flashing my credentials at the responding officers and giving them a brief update before brushing past them. Someone had to find Derek.

FORTY

When I pulled up to Heathcliff's address, two patrol cars, a fire truck, and an ambulance were on scene. I raced inside and up the steps. The uniformed officer at the door blocked my path, and I shoved my badge in his face, never breaking stride. Blood spatter streaked the wall, still so fresh that a few drops continued to drip downward. A black tarp covered whoever painted the wall, and my knees threatened to buckle.

"Derek?" Two officers spun at my outburst. "Derek?" I called again, much more frantic this time. One of the officers shifted his gaze from the notepad to me. "Is that..." I choked, swallowing the thought along with the bile. "Where's Detective Heathcliff?"

One of them nodded to a doorway, and I moved deeper inside Derek's apartment. In the next room, I spotted him sitting on the edge of the couch while a paramedic monitored his vitals. He looked up, pushing the guy away and getting to his feet.

"Parker," he teetered but remained upright, "Steele knows the truth. I didn't tell them. Nothing in this world would get me to talk, but they took my phone. I'm so sorry.

I should have password protected my address book."

"Sit down, Detective," the paramedic ordered, and I moved closer, taking a seat on the coffee table in front of Heathcliff. "You took a nasty hit to the head. Stay put." Derek's hair was matted with blood, and welts covered what I could see of his torso.

"Who were they? What did they want?" I asked.

"Three guys. One was a KXD lookout, and I'm not sure who the other two were. They got the jump on me. When I came to," he blinked, shaking his head and rubbing his eyes, trying to focus his vision which I suspected was blurry, "I heard one of them on the phone. He was reading off your address. Apparently, Steele's calling the shots now."

"How did they find you?"

"I don't know." He took an unsteady breath. "I didn't get a chance to ask them any questions."

"What happened?"

"They must have figured three of them could handle me. But while they were knocking me around, I grabbed my Glock and put two of them down. I winged the third, but he escaped." Out of the corner of my eye, I saw the medical examiner arrive. Then I heard a few familiar voices. Agent Jablonsky, Lieutenant Moretti, and Detective O'Connell were vying for answers from anyone they could find. Heathcliff met my eyes, slumping backward into the cushions, too defeated to care. "Nail that bastard, Parker."

"Absolutely, just as soon as I know you're okay." I eyed the paramedic for reassurance.

"He'll have to go to the hospital for some x-rays and a head CT, but his chances are a million times better than the guys in the body bags."

"I'll be fine," Heathcliff insisted.

"You better be." I stepped away to find Mark as Lt. Moretti entered the room. O'Connell caught my eye and nodded. I mouthed 'thanks' and found Mark standing outside the front door, giving orders to the uniformed officers. "Shouldn't you be at my place with Martin?"

"He said you were on your way here." Mark studied me for a moment. "You really were desperate to work the weekend. C'mon, let's go. The police can handle things here."

"We need to find Steele, but first, I need to know Martin's safe."

"He's fine. Confused as fuck, but otherwise, perfectly healthy."

Nodding, I studied the interior of Derek's apartment. The blood spatter and bullet holes riddled most of the living room. Heathcliff said he winged one of them, and it was possible Steele might have gotten cut when he bolted from my place. It wasn't much to go on, but it was our only lead.

The paramedics moved Derek to a stretcher and rolled him out while O'Connell followed close behind. "Hang on, I have one last question," I said, halting their procession. "Where does Bard send his bangers to get stitched up?"

"A vet's office, Dr. Ovalon, over on Twelfth," Derek replied, and I nodded. "Do you think that's where Steele is?"

"Maybe or someone there might know where he is." I shrugged, and they hauled him away. "Meet you there?" I asked Mark, holding up my keys.

"Absolutely, but go quietly so they won't hear us coming."

I arrived first, parking at a hydrant half a block from the veterinarian's office. Before getting out of the car, I checked my gun, tucked it into my shoulder holster, made sure my jacket was unzipped, and my credentials were secure in my pocket. Then I scanned the neighborhood for signs of activity. Steele was nowhere to be seen. I got out of the car, pushing the door closed as silently as possible before making my way to the address.

The front door was unlocked, and I cautiously stepped inside. The bell above the door clanged. I held my breath, but the sounds of barking from within might have been enough to camouflage my entrance. After checking the waiting room and the area behind the front counter, I made my way to the exam rooms. They were empty, so I continued to the back where the sounds of barking and the smell of cat urine and wet dog grew stronger.

A few animals were caged, whimpering, meowing, and barking. Continuing down the corridor, I noticed blood on the beige tile floor. One doorway was slightly open, and I pulled my gun, sidling up to it and reading the word "office" etched on the frosted glass. Pressing my back to the wall, I peered inside. A man had his shirt off, and someone in a lab coat was making quick work with the sutures.

"Federal agent," I announced, holding my credentials in one hand and my gun in the other, "put your hands where I can see them." The doctor immediately threw his hands up, and I spotted a handgun on the table near the wounded man. "Don't do it." His eyes flicked from me to the discarded weapon, and he seemed to be calculating his chances. "Don't you already have enough holes in your body?" I eased into the room and edged toward the gun. "Let me see those hands." He lifted one, but the other clutched his stomach, just below his ribs where blood was seeping through his fingers. "Good boy."

I snatched the gun off the counter, cuffed the vet to the pipes, and stared at the KXD member. He sneered. "You're that stripper bitch."

"Wow, you recognized me with my clothes on." I approached him cautiously, pulling a plastic zip tie from my inner jacket pocket. "I guess that means you deserve a treat." I yanked his arms backward and hooked his wrists to a metal loop used to secure a dog's leash. "Where's Steele?"

"Who?"

"Don't play dumb." I glanced at the suture kit and picked up a wad of gauze. "You should really apply more pressure." I shoved the cotton into the bullet wound, and he shrieked. "That's better. Should we try this again?" The vet voiced a protest, but I ignored it. "Or maybe you'd prefer if I stitch you up."

"She'll do it," Mark said, entering the room.

"You can't do this," the vet protested again. "You're federal agents. We have rights."

"You have the right to remain silent, so shut the hell up." Mark unhooked the restraints, grabbing the vet and dragging him out of the room. Mark returned a second later without my cuffs, so the doc must have been detained in one of the exam rooms.

"Where's Francisco Steele?" I asked again.

"I dunno."

"You must know how to contact him," Mark said, taking over. This wasn't exactly good cop, bad cop. It was more psycho bitch cop, and I don't give a shit cop, but it worked for us. "Why don't you give him a call to meet you here?" It wasn't a suggestion.

Mark patted him down, finding a switchblade and a cell phone in the man's pocket. He searched the list of contacts, stopping on Steele's name and holding it up to the KXD member.

"Dude, I can't. Do you know what he'll do to me?"

"You almost killed a man earlier tonight. Do you know what I'll do to you if you don't call him?" I asked, jabbing the gauze in deeper. He howled again, gasping. "And so help you if you tip him off."

"Don't try anything cute," Jablonsky warned, pressing speaker and hitting the dial button.

"Is it done?" Steele's voice asked.

"Naw, man, he got the jump on us. I'm at Ovalon's. You need to get your ass over here."

"Fucking idiots," Steele griped, letting out a few exasperated huffs. "I'm on my way. Be ready to go when I get there. The freaking pigs are turning up the heat." Before the KXD member could say anything else, Mark disconnected the call.

"Now we wait," Jablonsky said, using his own phone to send a text. "The doc's out of the way. A team is on standby to move in once they spot Steele. We'll just have to hope he doesn't notice anything's amiss before we can grab him." He assessed the condition of our captive. "Eh, you'll be fine."

We took up strategic positions, waiting for Steele to arrive. When the bell above the door chimed, and the barking grew exponentially louder, I pressed my back against the wall, keeping my gun at my thigh. Mark donned a spare lab coat and turned his back to the door. When Steele stepped into the office, he didn't notice me until

Mark turned around, aiming his gun

"Hey, chico," I shoved him against the wall and patted him down while Mark kept his gun trained on him, "you left so abruptly I forgot to tell you something." I removed Steele's gun, jerking his arm behind his back so tightly that if he struggled, I'd break the bone or dislocate his shoulder. The standby team entered the room, providing support and dragging our other two detainees away. Steele didn't seem that tough in a room full of federal agents. "You're under arrest." A fellow agent handed me a pair of cuffs, and I clicked them in place, tightening them as much as possible before passing Steele off to someone else. "Maybe you and Bard can be cellmates."

"This is entrapment," Steele growled, and I laughed. He fought against the two agents who dragged him out of the building, but he didn't have a chance in hell of escaping.

"Good job, Agent Parker." Jablonsky led us out of the building. "So are you planning to get started on the paperwork now?"

"We might as well."

"How did I get roped into this mess when you were the one who wanted to work the weekend?" he teased, putting a reassuring hand on my shoulder. "By the way, you need to expound on what happened at your apartment earlier."

"Yeah, we'll get to that too."

FORTY-ONE

With the apprehension of Francisco Steele, the KXDs disappeared into the abyss. The remaining gangbangers would either be assimilated or picked off by their rivals. Optimistically, maybe they would get out of the life and become productive members of society. At least, that was what I hoped. Who knew my glasses were rose colored?

"Steele lawyered up," Jablonsky announced, entering the conference room. "So we're finished with him for now. I talked to the hospital. Heathcliff has a concussion and a few hairline fractures, but he should be okay. The police department is conducting an investigation to determine how he was compromised, but so far, they don't have anything conclusive."

"It'd be faster if Steele was willing to talk."

"Yeah, well, we can't go near him until his lawyer gets here." Jablonsky picked up my report and the corresponding police file. "It looks like he gained access to your apartment by bumping the lock. What happened to your deadbolts and the security bar?"

"Martin distracted me."

Mark held up his hand. "Besides that, the investigators found two broken light bulbs in your sink."

"That's probably what woke me. I don't want to think what Steele planned to do if I hadn't heard him."

"More than likely, he would have shot you up with heroin, and whenever we discovered your body, it would've discredited your investigation or the tips you were feeding to the police. It's still not clear if he thought you were undercover or just an informant."

"It doesn't matter." I watched Mark scan the report.

"They boarded up the broken glass on your fire escape. Thankfully, the damage wasn't that bad."

"Where's Martin?"

"He's giving his statement at the precinct." Mark flipped open another folder, pulled out a piece of paper, and signed the bottom. "Tell him what he needs to know. If for some reason Kendall has a problem with it, I'll take the blame."

"Thanks."

We worked through the rest of the morning, recording the events that occurred in the last twenty-four hours and solidifying our answers to whatever questions remained regarding DeAngelo Bard and his drug network. Agents Cooper and Lucca arrived around noon. So much for taking the weekend off. Cooper compiled a list of evidence collected for the prosecutor's office, and Lucca examined my report and the police reports that were filed within the last twelve hours.

"Parker," Lucca said, "the police just sent over the IDs of the men who attacked Detective Heathcliff." I swiveled toward him, wondering why he thought this was breaking news. "They're known enforcers for the Lords."

"What?" I kicked off the floor with my good leg, rolling my chair across the expanse to Lucca's desk. "Heathcliff said he recognized one of the men as a KXD lookout. Why would the KXDs be aiding the Lords?"

"The man you brought into custody," he pointed to a mug shot of the man from the vet's office, "is affiliated with the KXDs. But these two men," the photos were provided by the coroner's office, "were part of the Lords."

Processing the information, I stood, cursing again as pain shot through my leg. Hobbling to Jablonsky's office, I barged in. "Did Steele's lawyer arrive yet?"

"It's Saturday. What do you think?"

"In that case, I need to speak to Veronica Kincaid."

"Take Lucca," his eyes darted to the way I was favoring one leg, "and be careful."

Exiting Mark's office, I cast my eyes at the analyst. "C'mon, boy scout."

"I thought you weren't calling me that anymore."

"I changed my mind."

He drove to Veronica's address, filling me in on the DEA's bust and the cartel connection. Bard paid the Mexican cartel hundreds of thousands for opium, cocaine, marijuana, and whatever prescription drugs the cartel had access to. Since the drug business continued to be lucrative for both sides, Bard soon began importing firearms to safeguard his investment. The KXD dealers, enforcers, and lookouts were equipped with military-grade weaponry. And it acted like a deterrent to hold the rival gangs at bay ever since the previous gang war which occurred half a decade earlier. And since Bard was such a loyal customer, he used that connection to convince the cartel to help squash the Lords' uprising.

"The DEA checked into a list of travelers who entered the country around the time you were attacked. Four names came up in conjunction with the cartel. We're operating under the assumption Bard called them," Lucca said.

"That doesn't make any sense. How would they have known the Lords were planning something that night?"

"An educated guess?"

"Steele set me up. I know he did. I could see it on his face." I thought back to the night in question and everything that had been divulged in the last couple of hours. "The KXDs and Lords were working together." Lucca looked at me like I was crazy. "Not when Bard was running things, but with Steele in charge."

"Steele's never been in charge." Lucca pulled up to the curb. "Do you think Steele was planning a coup?"

"No. He wouldn't betray Bard. That's the only thing I know for certain. But maybe he wanted to merge the two gangs that way they'd control more than half of the city. Just imagine how much they'd stand to gain by doing that."

"Bard would never go along with it," Lucca argued. "And I'm sure the head of the Lords wouldn't either."

"Unless the Lords suddenly lost their hierarchical system and Steele planned to assimilate their dealers, stockpiles, girls, and other connections into the KXDs."

"What you're talking about would take precision planning, and quite frankly, I don't think Francisco Steele is capable of that."

"When he was a kid, Steele executed his mother's boyfriend, and ever since, Bard's the only family he's known. He would do anything to protect that family and to make Bard proud of him." I thought about Steele's beef with Heathcliff. On the surface that was about who had claimed me, but Steele resented the way Bard treated Heathcliff. Steele wanted to be the favorite and would do anything to maintain that position. "Veronica allegedly worked both sides, and we know she worked for Steele. We need her to cooperate."

"Then let me do the talking," Lucca insisted. "She doesn't like you." He chuckled. "I can't imagine why."

Veronica Kincaid didn't seem particularly interested in speaking with us, and I considered calling it quits after the front door slammed in our faces. But Agent Lucca wasn't as easily deterred. He spent five minutes speaking through the heavy door, finally coaxing her into opening up.

After enough promises and threats were made, she willingly agreed to come with us. Once inside the federal building, she insisted on seeing everything we'd agreed to in writing, and Lucca spent the better part of the day on the phone with various state and federal prosecutors trying to get them to agree. As soon as the ink dried, Veronica spilled her guts.

Originally, she'd been recruited by Francisco, along with a few of the other girls, to deal out of the club. She wasn't from the neighborhood, but once Bard acquired partial ownership of the Black Cat, it was easy to take some of the girls under his wing. Over the past few years, the KXDs used the girls to deal and turn tricks. Most of them became addicted to the products they were hocking, couldn't pay to cover their usage, and in order to work off their debt, Bard put them to work on their backs. It was the same plan Francisco had for Alexia Nicholson, but that didn't work out the way he hoped either.

"I got clean," Veronica said, playing with the handle on the coffee mug, "and Francisco didn't like it. He told me he didn't want me working for the KXDs anymore."

"So you went to the Lords?" Lucca asked.

"No. About a month later, Francisco pops up again. He says he misses me. That I was always his best girl." Her gaze lingered on me. "And he had a special job for me to do, but I couldn't tell anyone. He wanted me to deliver shipments to some dealers. They'd drop by the club, and either before or after shift, there'd be an exchange." She dropped her hands to her lap. "It seemed easier than the other things he had me do. And the pay was better."

"Do you think you would recognize any of the dealers?" I asked, pushing a mug book across to her.

"Yeah, I guess." She flipped the pages. "I thought it'd be safer that way, not having to go off with some john and do things." The pages continued to turn. "And then those men came at me. I was sure they were gonna kill me. They were pissed. They had no idea they were buying from the KXDs. They thought the bar was Lords' turf." She pointed to a couple of photos, and Lucca marked them. The men she identified were Lords' dealers. "And for the life of me, I couldn't figure out why Francisco would be selling to his rivals. After I was admitted to the hospital, he came to see me and told me not to say a word to anyone about what happened and to stay as far away from the Black Cat as I could get. That nasty son of a bitch nearly destroyed me."

When we exited the interview room, Lucca disappeared to work on the new angles. The fatigue was finally setting in, and I glanced at the time. I'd been going nonstop for over twenty hours. I needed to crash.

"Parker, my office," Mark bellowed, and I gave the coffeepot a forlorn look before reversing direction. Inside, Martin was waiting. "Take as much time as you need," Mark said, shutting the door and leaving the two of us alone.

"I'm so sorry." I dropped into the chair next to him and launched into the abbreviated version of everything that had transpired over the last two months, leaving out the details that were relevant to the ongoing investigation. The look of betrayal in his eyes was too much to stomach, so I focused on the cut above his eye.

"You should ice your hip," he said when I was finished. "A tear in one of your tendons or ligaments could require surgery, and I know you don't want that."

"That's the last thing I want, just like lying to you."

He bit his lip and looked away. "Sure."

I opened the door. Jablonsky was in the midst of an interrogation with Steele. The office was fairly busy for a Saturday night, but the focus seemed to be on paper-pushing. Cooper caught the confused look on my face and stepped inside.

"Agent Jablonsky said you can call it a night, and he doesn't expect to see you again until Monday. Understand?"

"What about the progress we've made?"

"Lucca and I have it handled. Enjoy your weekend, Agent Parker." He nodded to Martin and went out the door.

"It's been a long day, Alex. Are you staying with me, or should I call my driver to pick me up?" Martin asked.

I handed him my car keys. "I'll go home with you but only if you drive."

FORTY-TWO

By Monday, most things were finalized. Steele had planned to usurp the Lords' power by making them dependent on the KXDs for their drugs. It was also the impetus for attempting to pillage the Lords' stockpile of drugs the night the PD tear gassed me and made their busts. Steele was willing to explain his plans, snitch on the Lords and the cartel's hit squad, and plead guilty to the charges against him in exchange for a reduced sentence. Since no murder charges were pending against him, the AUSA and DA were willing to play ball.

The PD reviewed their findings concerning the breach of Heathcliff's cover, and upon a close examination of phone calls placed to the precinct, they discovered someone phoned for information regarding a police officer. The caller provided a perfect description of Heathcliff, and the idiotic desk sergeant gave them his name. It didn't take much for the caller to make the connection, inform Steele, and discover Heathcliff's address. From there, they searched Derek's apartment, believing I was his CI. And since he had no other Alex listed in his phone, they took a guess that I was one and the same. The two valuable lessons we learned from this were to use password protection and that I never wanted to go undercover again.

Director Kendall called me into his office, asking about permanent placement at the OIO. I told him I'd think about it, but he said he needed an answer by next week. This was it. I was either in or out. There would be no more sitting on the fence. I'd been back and forth numerous times to assist on investigations or more accurately get roped into investigations, but this was really it. Yes or no. I couldn't afford to be wishy-washy any longer.

That evening, I drove back to Martin's. I'd been staying with him while my window and back door were being replaced, but mainly, I was there because I feared Steele might have determined who he was and sent someone to seek revenge. That was called a paranoid delusion, but that knowledge didn't stop my worrying.

Martin had barely spoken to me since that night in my apartment. We could sit in the same room or share the same bed, but there were plenty of unresolved issues simmering just below the surface. And I could tell he couldn't take the silence much longer.

"Alexis, look at me." I glanced in his general direction before dropping my gaze back to the table. "You seriously can't be that repulsed by what I did. That man planned to kill you. So don't expect me to apologize for beating him senseless." He licked his lips. "What should I have done instead?"

"It's not that. I'd be dead without you. You know that. You've known that for a long time."

"Then why won't you look at me? You've avoided eye contact ever since that night."

"It's because I can't stand the look in your eyes." I willed myself to remain focused on his face. "I went back to work and didn't tell you. Yes, I was undercover as a heroin-addicted stripper, and there are a lot of things I want to forget. But those damn, soulful green eyes of yours won't let me. You just keep staring, like I betrayed you. I didn't betray you."

"I never said you did."

"Bullshit. The moment I gave 911 dispatch my information things changed."

"Why didn't you tell me sooner? Why did I have to find out like that?" And there it was. The question he'd been harboring.

"I couldn't tell anybody."

"I'm not just anybody. I'm somebody. At least, you should think I'm somebody. Nick knew. Derek knew. Mark fucking knew because you were working for him. Hell, even Jenny probably knew. I'm the only person in your life who didn't know."

"That's not fair."

"But it's true." He circled the room. "You don't trust me."

"Yes, I do." I blinked, resisting the urge to storm out and slam the door. Avoidance was easier than dealing with one of Martin's tirades, but we needed to hash this out. "It wasn't entirely my decision to keep you in the dark."

"Yeah, right."

"It's true. At first, I didn't want to tell you because it wasn't safe for either of us."

"Right, because not knowing some psycho gangbanger might bust into your apartment makes way more sense than allowing me to consider that possibility."

I ignored that comment, intent on taking the high road. "And then once I decided you ought to know, your international business ties and friendships delayed your background check. It's not my fault you know someone in every country on this planet."

"Oh, so it's my fault."

I put my face in my hands. No explanation would ever satisfy him. "I should go. Fighting with you won't change what happened. It's done. You can either accept it or not."

"Dammit, Alexis, do you remember what you said to me when we first started dating?"

"That I better not find you in a stash house with stripper Barbie? Yeah, it's ironic how that description fits me now."

"No, not that. The other thing you said, how you had to choose between the job or me because you couldn't have both." He let the magnitude of his words hang in the air. "Is this your way of telling me you came to a decision?"

The reason for that declaration was because I almost

lost him to a bullet, and after that, I promised myself never to risk his safety again. And the night Steele broke into my apartment I had unknowingly put Martin back into the line of fire. But Martin proved once again he was willing to save me and completely disregard his own safety.

"That's ancient history. Not too long ago, you agreed to stand by me, even if I pursued reinstatement. So have you changed your mind now that you fully comprehend what that entails?"

"Sweetheart, I love you," he fidgeted, rubbing his eyes and face while he sought the proper words that would inevitably break my heart, "but I can't do this. I can't wait around for months at a time while you lie to me about working at some insignificant security firm. You became a different person. Hell, you still aren't completely back to normal. And I understand that's necessary to maintain your well-being, but you can't continue to be so distant. If this is going to work, you have to let me in. You have to tell me what you're doing." An ugly laugh escaped his lips. "Who am I kidding? You've always been distant. You aren't capable of letting anyone in, especially me."

Without waiting for a response, he turned and left the room. As the door slammed behind him, I jumped. It was just a fight. We'd figure it out and get past it. At least, that's what I kept telling myself. But this felt different, and it would take more than a half-assed 'I'm sorry' to fix things.

Returning to the office, contemplative and a bit shaken, I finished reading the reports. The KXDs were behind bars, and Francisco's attempt to take over the Lords had failed. This was one merger that would never come about. If anything, it helped the DA's office rack up additional charges against the two largest gangs in the city. Maybe we really did kill two birds with one stone.

Veronica was the key, and currently, she had been moved into witness protection until after the trial. Sure, her life was on hold for a year or two, but from the outside looking in, it seemed like a positive thing. She had the opportunity to reinvent herself, get away from the negative influences, and solidify her sobriety on a stronger foothold.

Francisco was still hoping to cut a better deal, and there

was some talk that he'd get additional incentives for turning on the gang's drug connections and for testifying against the Lords. But the one person he wouldn't turn on was DeAngelo Bard. Even if Bard was a ruthless killer, he took care of Francisco, and that loyalty was something that wouldn't waver even in the face of decades' worth of prison time.

"I thought you left hours ago," Jablonsky said, sidling up to my desk.

"I did. Now I'm back."

"Uh-huh." He shook his head, unable to make sense of my presence. "The case is closed. You've filed your reports. The only thing left is to give Director Kendall an answer."

"I don't know yet."

"Okay," he rolled my chair backward, "get up." We went into his office, and he shut the door. "Pros and cons, go."

"People die. Martin's pissed. I still don't know if being here is the right decision." I paced in front of his desk. "But we helped cut off a branch of one of the biggest cartels, and in the process, two gangs are on the outs." I chuckled. "You know, you probably could have done those things without me."

"Are you sure?"

"Yes." I'd like to think they needed me, but someone else could have done it. And that someone probably wouldn't have risked Heathcliff's life or endangered their boyfriend in the process.

"It sounds like you've made a decision," Mark said, scrutinizing my expression. "Except for the simple fact that you don't have a hard and fast reason to leave this time."

"Martin threw down the gauntlet." The highlights reel from our fight played behind my eyes. "It might already be too late for us."

"So this job is the only thing you have left?" Mark was playing devil's advocate, and I scrunched my nose at him, making a face.

"I won't do a long-term undercover assignment again."

"There's no reason why you'd have to. You never did before. SACs aren't normally field operatives, and if you come back, everything will be back to the way it was." He saw the pain and protest in my eyes. "Well, as close as it can be." His smile was bittersweet. "After a bust like this, Carver would be proud."

After spending far too much time thinking, I returned to Martin's compound. He was sitting on the couch, surrounded by paperwork, and the phone was glued to his ear. I took a seat on the edge, not disturbing any of the things he was working on.

Mark made a valid point; if something were to happen between us, work would be all I had. Even now, work was still my main priority, mostly. But if I planned to commit to the OIO again, I'd also have to make a commitment in my personal life. This was about balance.

"I'm sorry," I whispered when there was a break in his conversation, and he smiled, mouthing back 'me too'.

He scooted a few of the papers over, and I curled up on the sofa next to him. When I opened my eyes hours later, my head was on his stomach, and his hand was tangled in my hair while the other tapped away at a tablet. I snuggled my cheek into the soft material of his shirt, feeling his washboard abs underneath. It was decision time.

"Martin, is it too late for us?"

He dropped the tablet onto the end table and focused on me. "I hope not. I was just warming to the idea of sleeping with a special agent."

"Some things will have to change. You can't come over anymore."

"Alex," the annoyance was already in his voice, "this is getting ridiculous."

"My apartment is off limits. It's strictly for work because I want to move in with you."

"Ha ha. Very funny. That's not the way you end a fight."

"I'm serious, assuming the offer still stands."

He studied my expression, stared into my eyes, and then lifted me off his lap so he could kiss me. "Yes. My god, yes." He held me tight. "We'll convert the downstairs office into your workspace, and you can change the bedroom if you want." Already, he was planning to hire interior decorators or something equally moronic.

"Stop. This is overwhelming enough. Let's ease into this,

okay?"

He nodded. "So you're staying at the OIO, and you're staying here?"

"It looks that way."

*   *   *

Monday, I reported to the office as usual. Well, the new usual. It felt eerily normal. Almost as normal as staying at Martin's. Maybe the fact that most of my stuff was still in my apartment and I still had an apartment might have had something to do with it. We agreed if I had to work undercover or investigate something particularly dangerous, I would stay at my place, or rather my old place, and I promised to prepare him ahead of time by telling him as much as I could about my assignments.

Agent Cooper put the final touches on the FBI's original investigation that the OIO concluded, welcomed me back to the building, and said a few kind words about the two of us working together in the future. Lucca didn't seem quite as pleased, but he was still a boy scout and knew better than to mouth off. I gave Kendall the news. And he nodded, giving me the task of convincing my contacts in the police department to turn the evidence collected over to us. Civil forfeiture meant a lot of property was now up for grabs to whichever agency made the bust, and of course, the OIO wanted the biggest piece of the pie. I offered to do what I could, which realistically was absolutely nothing, and returned to my desk.

"So you're back for good?" Mark asked, watching as I lined up the stapler, hole punch, and inbox tray on top of my desk.

"I'm back for now."

Mark snorted, shaking his head and continuing to his office. All bets were off when it came to how long I'd stay this time. Even I didn't know if it would last, but it felt like it would.

The next exciting novel in the Alexis Parker series is now available.

Look for *Intended Target* in paperback or as an e-book.

ABOUT THE AUTHOR

G.K. Parks is the author of the Alexis Parker series. The first novel, *Likely Suspects,* tells the story of Alexis' first foray into the private sector.

G.K. Parks received a Bachelor of Arts in Political Science and History. After spending some time in law school, G.K. changed paths and earned a Master of Arts in Criminology/Criminal Justice. Now all that education is being put to use creating a fictional world based upon years of study and research.

You can find additional information on G.K. Parks and the Alexis Parker series by visiting our website at
www.alexisparkerseries.com

www.ingramcontent.com/pod-product-compliance
Lightning Source LLC
Chambersburg PA
CBHW021303250626
47155CB00002B/360